The Speckled Monster

J.R. SMITH

THE
SPECKLED
MONSTER

smallpox in England, 1670-1970,
with particular reference to Essex

ESSEX RECORD OFFICE
CHELMSFORD
1987

Essex Record Office, County Hall, Chelmsford, Essex, CM1 1LX

First published 1987 as an Essex Record Office hardback
Essex Record Office Publication No. 95
© Essex County Council

ISBN 0 900360 68 2

Printed in Great Britain by Witley Press, Hunstanton, Norfolk.

Contents

Illustrations

Tables

Preface

Increasing attention has been given by urban, social and economic historians during the past decade to the study of diseases and public health and the Essex Record Office contributed to this movement in a minor way in 1982 with the publication in portfolio form of Rosalin Barker's *The Plague in Essex*. This was so well received that a decision was taken to issue a second portfolio dealing with smallpox in Essex. As the initial research on this progressed it became clear that the source material was both rich and comprehensive, meriting fuller treatment than that possible in a portfolio. Other factors taken into consideration in deciding to expand the work into a volume were the somewhat limited amount of published literature dealing with the history of smallpox in England and a tendency for recent publications to cover relatively short periods, concentrating instead on examinations of specialised subjects such as inoculation and the nature of cowpox virus. With this in mind it seemed that the most helpful contribution would be a volume less detailed in its approach to some individual topics, taking instead a broader look at the problem of smallpox over a period of 300 years, and approaching the pathogenesis of the disease, its effects on communities and individuals, and the methods employed to contain, prevent and finally to eradicate it, as interlocking parts of a longer process.

In setting out a framework over a period of three centuries this volume makes no claim to being definitive and rich fields of study await the attention of other researchers. For the greater part of the 300 years Essex was a predominantly rural county with no large towns, distinguished from all other rural counties except Kent by proximity to London, a long coastline with numerous small ports and a main trading route (to Colchester, Harwich and East Anglia) running north-eastwards through its centre, factors which have given added interest to the work and which contributed to a high level of exposure to the disease. Despite these peculiar features much of what happened in Essex appears to have been fairly typical of the experience in rural southern England. But such representativeness ends there and further studies of contrasting regions such as Cheshire, towns like Norwich and Bristol and the new industrial centres would be of particular interest and value.

The present organisation of public archives in England, that is, in county or borough record offices primarily geared and required to serve the interests and demands of their local government areas, has been a decisive factor in shaping the editorial policy of those offices with publishing programmes. Although it has long been accepted that a record office should exploit its own source material in its publications, this approach has a number of pitfalls, among them a tendency to encourage a parochial and archive-led perception of events divorced from the national context. The Essex Record Office first demonstrated an awareness of the limitations of purely county interpretation as long ago as 1952 with the publication of A.C. Edwards' *English History from Essex Sources, 1550-1750* and A.F.J. Brown's *English History from Essex Sources, 1750-1900*, and this volume follows in that part of the Office tradition so ably pioneered by those authors. In addition, however, where suitable or adequate Essex material has not been available, or sometimes for the purposes of comparison or where important events took place wholly outside the county, considerable use has been made of non-Essex evidence.

Many people have given generous help during the preparation and those not mentioned individually will, it is hoped, know that their contributions are neither forgotten nor undervalued. Within the Essex Record Office thanks are due to Jennifer Butler and Claire Harrington for hours of tedious proof reading and numerous helpful suggestions, and to Jill Henderson for her patience and perseverance in typing and re-typing the text. Nancy Briggs, Jennifer Butler, Jane Bedford and Wendy Walker all pointed out helpful references. Outside the confines of the Office tribute must be paid to the excellent research facilities and helpful staff at the Wellcome Institute for the History of Medicine, while others who afforded special help in differing ways include David Bartrum, J. Andrew Campbell, Hilda Grieve, Wendy Haysman, Malcolm Jefferies and Mr and Mrs Julian Royle. Finally, particular thanks are due to Penelope Corfield, Victor Gray and John Hodgkins for valued criticism and suggestions in the final stages of preparation and to Penelope Corfield for writing the foreword.

Southend-on-Sea   J.R. Smith
1987

Editorial Notes

Places and sources

Unless otherwise noted and with obvious exceptions, towns, villages and parishes mentioned in the text are in Essex and manuscript sources cited in footnotes are in the custody of the Essex Record Office.

Dating

All dates before 1 January 1752 are rendered in New Style.

Introduction
by P.J. Corfield

'Disease was very human indeed. For to be man, was to be ailing'. So spoke sombrely one of the patients on Mann's *Magic Mountain* (1924). On the contrary, argued the hero, 'Illness ... was detrimental to human dignity. It dragged man down to the level of his body. Thus it might be said that disease was unhuman'. It was a pithy exchange, the dispute fundamental.

Historically there was much to be said for the sombre view. Diseases have attended constantly upon humankind. Mortality rates were traditionally very high, and those who did not die young were often unwell. Yet modern medicalised societies have increasingly tended to endorse the 'new' heroic viewpoint: rejecting fatalism, chafing at pain and expecting (if not always getting) health as the social norm.

To that epic shift in attitudes, many factors have contributed. Not least among them has been the optimism engendered by successful campaigns of preventive medicine. Noxious diseases, however endemic and however venomous, could be circumvented, counter-attacked or even eradicated entirely. It was a heady dream — and rendered even more so when translated into actuality. The initiative began to pass from assorted pestilences to the now less aptly-named patients and their medical attendants.

Smallpox was the first major infectious disease to be eliminated by interventionist immunology on a world-wide basis. The repellent and terrifying 'speckled monster', in Jenner's vivid phrase, has been entirely routed. Its history therefore takes on a particular importance, in modern culture as well as epidemiology. With hindsight the eventual outcome of the campaign perhaps seems unsurprising. Looked at closely, however, as this account so clearly shows, it appears as a remarkable saga of optimism backed up by organisation, technical know-how and endless vigilance. It was, additionally and concurrently, not without misadventures, malpractices and heated controversies.

Some form of the 'pocky' disease had been known in Western Europe, it seems, at least since medieval times. Many accounts, however, converge in suggesting that a particularly virulent strain (or strains) began to afflict people of all ages and social backgrounds in the middle and later decades of the seventeenth century. Indeed, it is possible that smallpox may have contributed significantly to the 'pause' in population growth in those years. Not only did it kill the living, it also tended to depress the birth rate (the disease being notably inimical to pregnant women and associated with above-average incidence of uterine haemorrhage and early miscarriage).

Furthermore, smallpox was loathsome to experience and could be continuingly unpleasant in its after-effects for survivors, in the form of pitting, scarring or impaired vision. It was not the most dreaded disease of all: nothing quite matched the ferocious reputation of the plague. But smallpox was second only to that in generating fear and aversion, while severe pock-marks, particularly on the face,

11

could cause great anguish to individuals. When Laclos wished to portray the visible expression of moral infamy he inflicted upon the villainess of *Les Liaisons Dangéreuses* (1782) an attack of the contagion. The smallpox left her looking hideous: 'her soul now visible on her face'. Little wonder that much attention was devoted to the search for treatment or cure of a disease that was no respecter of status, whether social or moral.

It was notable that laymen and women, as well as the emergent medical profession, shared in the initial quest and endless public debates. A cure for the disease always proved elusive. Increasingly, therefore, attention focussed upon the possibilities of minimising or preventing smallpox by prior immunisation. In the course of the eighteenth century inoculation, a traditional practice in the Near East, was gradually introduced into Western Europe. Always controversial, it nonetheless had some undoubted successes in halting epidemics, particularly outside the great cities (which long remained reservoirs of the smallpox contagion).

The ramifications of this were extensive. Patterns of mortality were altered, popular attitudes changed, scientific research encouraged and optimism engendered. Simultaneously, the status and claims of the medical profession were greatly enhanced. As one practitioner observed in 1767, successful inoculation showed that doctors could 'triumph over a cruel and merciless distemper, which has committed greater ravages among the human species than the famine, the sword, or even, perhaps, the pestilence (plague) itself'. Already, in the 1760s and '70s, a few visionaries were calling for the total eradication of smallpox and it was a country doctor, Jenner from Gloucestershire, who pioneered vaccination, which eventually — with yet more controversy — was adopted as the technique of immunisation that turned hopeful dreams into reality around the world.

The study that follows illuminates the entire saga from the earliest attempts at cure and control to the last recorded fatality. It takes the experience of Essex as a case-history, skilfully interweaving the broad context and the local diversity. A wealth of important new documentation stands revealed, from a record office with excellent sources and an enlightened policy of publication to match.

One English county, of course, is not the universe. Yet the history of smallpox and its opponents in Essex over three centuries has a universal significance. It forms part of the optimistic modern quest to prove humanity healthful, not ailing. John Smith's deftly-patterned analysis makes manifest the importance of the 'case of the speckled monster'.

Penelope J. Corfield is a senior lecturer in history at Royal Holloway and Bedford New College, University of London, and author of The Impact of English Towns, 1700-1800 *(Oxford University Press, 1982).*

Chronology of Main Events

1666	'Great Plague' ends. Smallpox supersedes bubonic plague as chief killer disease
1694	Smallpox kills Queen Mary
1716	Inoculation of first two Britons performed in Turkey
1718	Edward Wortley Montagu inoculated in Turkey
1721	Inoculation of Anne Wortley Montagu, the first to be performed in England
1721-1723	469 inoculations performed in England
c.1727-c.1740	Incidence of inoculation very low
c.1741-c.1750	Modest revival of inoculation
1751-1753	Great nationwide epidemic. General inoculations performed in several provincial towns
1761	Robert Sutton perfects new method of inoculation
1763	Daniel Sutton leaves father's and sets up own inoculation practice
1766	General inoculations performed to halt epidemics in several provincial towns, including Maldon
1767	Essential features and secrets of highly successful 'Suttonian method' revealed in Thomas Dimsdale's *The Present Method of Inoculating*
1767-1800	Widespread confidence in inoculation established. Substantial proportion of poor immunised in general inoculations
1798	Results of vaccination experiments published by Edward Jenner
1798-1840	Controversial transitional period during which both inoculation and vaccination were performed
1803	Royal Jennerian Society founded
1807	London Vaccine Institution founded
1808	National Vaccine Establishment founded
1834	Parish pest houses replaced by union workhouse infirmaries under provisions of Poor Law Amendment Act
1837-1840	Epidemic smallpox kills more than 42,000 in England and Wales
1840	First Vaccination Act makes vaccination freely available to all and inoculation an imprisonable offence
1848	First Public Health Act creates General Board of Health for whole country except London, with power to create local boards
1853	Vaccination Act makes infant vaccination compulsory and non-compliance or neglect by parents punishable by fine
1858	Local Government Act abolishes General Board of Health, transferring its medical duties to the Medical Department of the Privy Council
1861	Vaccination Act permits boards of guardians to appoint vaccination officers to institute and conduct legal proceedings under 1853 Act
1867	Metropolitan Asylums Board established, embracing all parishes and unions in London

13

1867	Vaccination Act consolidates and strengthens provisions of earlier Vaccination Acts. Neglect to have children vaccinated becomes punishable by repeatable fines. Boards of guardians now required to take proceedings against defaulters.
1867	Anti-Compulsory Vaccination League founded
1868	Poor Law Amendment Act empowers provincial boards of guardians to provide separate infirmaries for infectious diseases
1870-1872	Epidemic smallpox kills almost 45,000 in England and Wales
1871	Local Government Board established under Local Government Board Act. Takes over all duties of Poor Law Board and those of the Privy Council and Home Office relating to public health and sanitation
1871	Vaccination Act strengthens 1867 Act. Penalties for defaulters now include imprisonment. Effective from 1 January 1872
1872	England and Wales divided into urban and rural sanitary authorities under Public Health Act
1874	National Anti-Compulsory Vaccination League founded
1880	London Society for the Abolition of Compulsory Vaccination founded
1889	County councils formed, with provision for appointment of county medical officers, under powers of Local Government Act, 1888
1889	Infectious Diseases (Notification) Act
1889-1895	Royal Commission on Vaccination
1893	Isolation Hospitals Act empowers county councils to provide hospitals for infectious diseases
1896	National Anti-Vaccination League founded
1898	Vaccination Act, effective from 1 January 1899, exempts parents and guardians from penalties under 1867 and 1871 Acts if a certificate of conscientious objection obtained from a magistrate
1901	Isolation Hospitals Act strengthens powers of county councils in provision of isolation hospitals
1901-1902	Last nation-wide epidemic
1907	Vaccination Act. Parents exempted from penalties under 1867 and 1871 Acts by making a statutory declaration of conscientious objection
1908	Smallpox ceases to be endemic in Britain
1930	Powers of Metropolitan Asylums Board transferred to London County Council
1948	Compulsory vaccination of infants replaced by free and voluntary vaccination under provisions of National Health Service Act, 1946
1971	Routine vaccination of infants discontinued in Britain
1977	World-wide eradication of smallpox accomplished

1

The Cost of Smallpox

Before the appearance of syphilis in Europe at the end of the fifteenth century the febrile disease of smallpox was known simply as 'pockes' or 'pox', derived from the Anglo-Saxon 'poc' or 'pocca', a bag or pouch, but thereafter the prefix 'small' was used in order to distinguish it from the great pox or syphilis. The most infectious human disease ever known (its world-wide eradication not being achieved until 1977) smallpox was greatly feared, in England particularly so from the cessation of the final great visitation of bubonic plague in 1665-1666 until the early twentieth century, when it ceased to be endemic.

Medical research in the present century has demonstrated that the virus existed in two variants, *variola major* and *minor* which, as the names suggest, differed in the spectrum of severity. It was not always possible to distinguish the variants by the symptoms exhibited nor until the 1950s were laboratories able to differentiate between the two viruses with any degree of certainty. The first cases of *variola minor* in Britain appear to have occurred in 1919 and between then and 1935 there were some 81,844 reported cases in England and Wales, mostly north of a line from Bristol to the Wash. The mortality rate was exceedingly low, less than one per cent., there being only 209 fatalities. For the purpose of this work *variola minor* is therefore of relatively little interest or significance and, unless otherwise stated, all examples and statistics relate to *variola major*.

The chief sources of virus infection were from a sufferer's respiratory tract, from the corpses of smallpox victims, from handling a sufferer's clothing or bedding and by aerial spread, sometimes over distances of hundreds of yards. In the great majority of cases of naturally acquired smallpox the virus entered the body through either nose or mouth, or both. From an epidemiological viewpoint the proportion of cases resulting from the other means of infection, that is through a break in the surface of the skin due to abrasions or cuts, constituted an insignificant minority. Once the virus had entered the body the non-immune human host was infected and the incubation period had begun. This initial phase ranged from 10 to 14 days but was usually 12 days, during which the victim remained a passive (non-infectious) carrier. Thereafter he was highly infectious, in the event of survival remaining so until the removal of the final scab or in the event of death until the decomposition or destruction of the corpse.

The first signs of illness were a high temperature accompanied by headache, general malaise and sometimes vomiting. A rash began a few days later starting with the face and spreading to the rest of the body. This in turn developed into pustules which as they suppurated gave off an offensive odour. Eating and drinking could become difficult or even impossible if pustules formed on the mucous membranes of the mouth and throat. The duration of the illness from the onset of high temperature until the last scab peeled off was about three weeks. Convalescence could be lengthy and facial disfigurement and scarring often severe, accompanied in

15

a minority of cases by blindness in one or both eyes. Patients surviving a very severe attack were left so weak and vulnerable that they often succumbed to secondary infection shortly afterwards. Death from smallpox could be either peaceful, resulting from increasing toxaemia, or traumatic, accompanied, for example, by massive vomiting of blood from the stomach or lungs. These descriptions of the disease are, of course, greatly simplified. In reality its effects varied greatly from patient to patient according to the strain of virus. A classification of ten types of smallpox with much fuller descriptions of their effects is given in Appendix 1.

In the first half of the eighteenth century almost everyone suffered the disease at some stage and smallpox was generally thought to be directly responsible for one death in every five to six cases. In fact this is probably a slight underestimate for fulminating smallpox with 100 per cent. mortality was not recognised as a form of smallpox until the nineteenth century while a minority of deaths occurred as a result of secondary infection following a smallpox attack, so that the disease was either directly or indirectly responsible for about one death in every five. After about 1750, however, the first of the prophylactic measures against smallpox, inoculation or variolation which had been introduced into England in 1721 and which used the smallpox virus itself to give subsequent immunity through a mild attack of the disease, began to be widely practised and to have a marked effect in reducing the incidence of the natural disease. The second measure, vaccination, which began to be used at the close of the eighteenth century, employed the virus of cowpox, a disease of the udder of the cow, to give gradually waning protection. Both these forms of treatment are discussed in subsequent chapters.

Although death from smallpox was commonplace in the seventeenth and eighteenth centuries the effect on the family unit remained, at the very least, traumatic. In 1685 John Evelyn recorded his own and his wife's grief at the deaths of their daughters Mary and Elizabeth. On 7 March 'Newes coming to me that my Daughter Mary was fallen ill of the Small Pox, I hasten'd home full of apprehensions'. She died aged 19 years on 14 March

> to our unspeakable sorrow and Affliction, and this not to ours (her parents) only, but all who knew her ... O deare, sweete and desireable Child, how shall I part with all this goodness, all this Vertue without the bitterness of sorrow, and reluctancy of a tender Parent ... how desolate hast Thou left us, Sweete, obliging happy Creature! To the grave shall we both carry thy memory.[1]

In August Evelyn's other daughter Elizabeth caught the disease and

> to our unspeakable affliction, loosing another Child in the flower of her age ... departed this life on (Saturday) 29: Aug: at 8 in the Morning: fell sick [and died] on the same day of the weeke, that my other most deare and dutifull daughter did, and as also one of my servants (a very pious youth) had don the yeare before.[2]

Evelyn expressed in these entries the desolation felt by countless parents at the loss of children. For other families less affluent than the Evelyns smallpox could in addition result in severe financial hardship. In October 1701 Michael Holmsted, a Chelmsford yeoman, explained to Essex Quarter Sessions how

Your poor Pet[itione]r Hath by Gods Providence beene of late visited with the small Pox, whereof his Wife dyed, and after that his Landlord did seize all ye Petitioners Goods, not leaving him a Bed to lye on, so that he is reduced by it to great penury and want. Your Pet[itione]r humbly supplicates this Hon[oura]ble Court, to Com[m]iserate his indigent and deplored Condition, and Contribute some Charitable Benevolence towards his present reliefe against this Winter season[3]

At Little Horkesley in the early summer of 1732 smallpox struck George Patterson's family. By 9 June five of the children had the disease and the parish paid for a woman nurse to move in to assist the family. On 12 June it was reported that

the son ab[ou]t 13 years of age who fell down on Thursday last is ... full of purple spots, so that He is not likely to live many days at all appearance ... 3 of the children have risen ever since Thursday and one of four rose yesterday the first time. The wife is now likely to fall down, having the usual Symptoms ... they begin to be craving for victuals ... there must be provision made of that kind, they have no firing nor any thing necessary but what is bought by the penny from hand to mouth ... the woman saies she must get another woman to help her, now the mother is likely to fall down, and if the son dye there will be charges to bury him; The distress the family is in is undoubtedly great, considering they must at this time wholly rely upon a parish for Relief[4]

For those directly involved the memory of smallpox often remained vivid. Some fifty years after the event Reginald Ward recalled how his family had suffered in the epidemic of 1870-1872. In 1871 Ward, then a young boy, had moved with his poverty-stricken family from Suffolk to Wickford, where his father obtained work as a blacksmith. Shortly afterwards

my father was stricken with the most dreaded of all diseases at that time — smallpox ... Amongst strangers, no club and a disease that no-one would go near unless compelled, and at that time no artisan would think of going to the Parish for relief, nor would he get much of a reception if he did. Well how my parents managed is known only to themselves but one thing I shall never forget is one Saturday night when my father was at the worst. My mother cut up the last bread that was in the house and gave us for supper and as she had nothing to give us with it she went to a drawer and found an apple and cut that up with the bread, and then she cried and we cried ... she did not know where more was to come from for she had but one penny in the house and none to come.[5]

Even for those whose families escaped the disease the horror of smallpox was neither easily nor quickly forgotten. A serious outbreak at Belchamp St Paul in the 1880s was witnessed by the vicar's young son Gerald Tindal-Atkinson. Writing to his sister some 70 years later he recalled how

> my most vivid memory of the Belchamp years is the small-pox time. There was a *complete panic* — only Father and Doctor Barnes kept their heads and did anything. Mother must have had a dreadfully anxious time — we were vaccinated — I'm not sure if all the children were but we older ones were. Father had a very bad arm but carried on ... The whole time was an absolute nightmare which only faded when vaccination got to work. Father's pluck was never forgotten there.[6]

The terror of smallpox did not end with the death of a victim and fear of contagion continued until the corpse was covered with earth and sometimes even after burial. It was often difficult to find bearers prepared to take the dead to the graveyard and frequently necessary for those involved in burial to be drunk.[7] At Belchamp St Paul in the 1880s

> Funerals took place at night. Sometimes, no hearse being available, farm carts had to be used. I remember Father saying how old Whiffen, the Clerk, had buoyed himself up with beer to ring the bell, and, as the dutch courage evaporated, the ringing grew feebler and feebler, the coffin was finally got into the grave with the help of two passing Salvationists who were themselves well "Primed". What an eerie scene ... the dark deserted Church — the spasmodic toll of the bell sounding over the darkened countryside.[8]

Such nocturnal burials were commonplace and stemmed from dread of the disease and a desire to get corpses into the ground the same day as death while using darkness to cloak the awful reality of smallpox fatalities. At Great Clacton on 16 February 1851 the body of Zebulum Rowling aged five years was buried 'by moonlight' and on 10 March John Emmany Barnes aged 40 'died of Small Pox and buried at 10 p.m. the same day'.[9]

These fears, coupled with concern about trade and the spread of infection, led some market towns to carry the dead out of town rather than to the churchyard for burial. Thomas Dimsdale, writing in 1778, observed that 'due care is taken to bury the dead privately',[10] while during a severe epidemic in 1760 at Maidstone 102 children were 'buried out of town'.[11] Pest-house corpses were sometimes buried in the grounds, as at Pinchgut Hall, Maldon's pest house for most of the eighteenth century, where human bones were discovered during building work in 1984. Similar considerations about contagion were probably responsible for people occasionally being buried in their own gardens as at South Shoebury where George Isaac's son was 'buried in his father's garden' during a smallpox outbreak in 1749.[12] Nocturnal and non-churchyard burials were probably rather more commonplace than evidence in parish burial registers suggests, for many were not registered. For example, at least nine out-of-town burials were not registered during an epidemic at Salisbury in 1760.[13] Only very occasionally were such omissions rectified at a later date, as in the Sible Hedingham register where the burial 'at night' of Alfred Elsdon aged 24 years on 24 May 1863 was recorded about three weeks later with an acknowledgement of the original omission.[14]

Although most people survived the smallpox itself many had to endure after-effects such as severe scarring, impaired sight or blindness. Writing in 1819 the physician Sir Gilbert Blane quoted a statement in a report of the Hospital for the Indigent Blind that 'two-thirds of those who apply for relief have lost their sight by the small pox'.[15] For young women in particular facial scarring was an emotionally distressing experience. Until an attack of smallpox in London in December 1715 left her disfigured at the age of 26, Lady Mary Wortley Montagu had been greatly admired for her beauty.[16] Shortly afterwards she gave expression to her anguish in verse.

> The wretched Flavia, on her couch reclin'd,
> Thus breath'd the anguish of a wounded mind,
> A glass revers'd in her right hand she bore,
> For now she shunn'd the face she sought before.
>   "How am I chang'd! alas! how am I grown
> A frightful spectre to myself unknown!
> Where's my complexion? where my radiant bloom,
> That promis'd happiness for years to come? ...
> Fir'd by one wish, all did alike adore;
> Now beauty's fled, and lovers are no more! ...
>   "Ye meaner beauties, I permit ye shine;
> Go, triumph in the hearts that once were mine:
> But 'midst your triumphs with confusion know,
> 'Tis to my ruin all your charms ye owe ...
>   "Ye cruel chemists, what withheld your aid?
> Could no pomatum save a trembling maid?
> How false and trifling is that art ye boast!
> No art can give me back my beauty lost.
> In tears, surrounded by my friends, I lay
> Mask'd o'er, and trembled at the sight of day; ...
>   "Cease, hapless maid, no more thy tale pursue,
> Forsake mankind, and bid the world adieu!"[17]

In severe cases the destruction of skin tissue sometimes led to localised secondary infection. One of the victims of an epidemic at the Staffordshire pottery town of Burslem in 1742 was Josiah Wedgwood, then aged 11 years. The attack left his face severely scarred but much more serious was the secondary infection in his right knee which gradually developed into the so-called 'Brodie's abcess' and which eventually disabled the joint causing great pain and making surgery inevitable. The amputation of the leg was carried out in May 1768 when Wedgwood was in his 38th year.[18]

19

For criminals, absconding employees, apprentices, servants and run-away husbands to have had a recent attack of smallpox was a hazard for they could be identified by the marks on their faces. The risk of identification tended to become greater in the later eighteenth century when the widespread practice of inoculation greatly reduced the incidence of natural smallpox and of severe scarring. In February 1735 Dick Turpin was described in an advertisement for his capture as

> a tall fresh-coloured man ... very much marked with the smallpox,
> about 26 years of age, about five feet nine inches high, wears a
> blue grey coat and a light natural wig.[19]

This disfiguration, however, would probably not have attracted undue attention. Thirty years later in 1763 the run-away servant Samuel Barnard of Langenhoe had rather more to fear from this notice in the *Ipswich Journal*

> Whereas Samuel Barnard ... Servant of Mr. Daniel Page of
> LANGENHOE, near Colchester ... Farmer, lately run away and
> deserted his service ... This is to give Notice, that if ... Samuel
> Barnard will return immediately ... he may be forgiven; but if he
> refuses he will be prosecuted as the law directs: and whoever gives
> information where ... Samuel Barnard is, and brings him to his
> said Master, shall receive Two Guineas ... Samuel Barnard is
> about 21 years of age, has black curled hair, brown eyes, very
> much pitted with Small-Pox, and when hot his Face appears very
> red, he having lately had that Distemper: and is about five feet six
> inches high or thereabouts.[20]

On 25 September of the same year Samuel Smyth, apprentice to Roger Hines of Harwich, fisherman, 'did abscond from his said Master'. Hines advertised for his return, offering to pay reasonable expenses to anyone bringing Smyth to Harwich, describing him as 'a low Lad, just got up from the Small-Pox, and hath an Impediment in his Speech'.[21] At the end of 1769 John Wilson of Billericay deserted his family, leaving it 'a Charge to the Parish'. In an advertisement in the *Chelmsford Chronicle* seeking his apprehension and return the parish officers described him as wearing

> a dark coloured Coat with Black Horn Buttons, Waistcoat striped
> with red and white, Leather or dark Fustian Breeches, his own
> Hair, a cast with his Eye, much pitted with the Small Pox, about
> five Feet four Inches high, a round Hat with a Buckle in it[22]

For others, notably journeymen, apprentices and domestic servants seeking places, evidence of a smallpox attack was an advantage. The position was made clear by a correspondent to the *Gentleman's Magazine* who wrote in December 1750 that for the 'lower ranks ... not having had the small-pox often occasions their losing a good place, that generally being the first question asked of a servant offering himself'.[23] In June 1762 Eleanor Onyon, a Colchester currier, wanted 'a Stout Lad as an APPRENTICE', but 'If he has not had the Small Pox he need not apply'.[24] In February 1780 a 'Gentleman's Family' advertised for

A MAID SERVANT who understands dressing plain victuals; she must have had the small-pox, and bring a character from her last place of her honesty, sobriety, and neatness.

In the same family is wanted a smart lad about 16 years of age, that has been used to horses, to be under a coachman, to go errands, and do any work that may be required of him. He must have had the small-pox.[25]

Those advertising for employment often made a point of stating that they had had the disease. For example, this advertisement appeared in the *Chelmsford Chronicle* in July 1766

A sober girl, who has had the small-pox, and who can be well recommended for her honesty, wants either a place to be a dairy-maid, or house maid, or to do all work, where there is a good mistress, and not a great family.[26]

Conversely it was extremely rare for those seeking a place to state that they had not had smallpox. This advertisement, appearing in the *Chelmsford Chronicle* in the summer of 1766 when smallpox was at a serious level in Chelmsford and other Essex towns, further illustrates the fear of such places felt by those who had neither had the natural disease nor been inoculated.

A lad between thirteen and fourteen years of age, to be postillion or an assistant under an older servant. He has not had the smallpox, so would rather chuse a place detached from any town.[27]

In the later eighteenth century, when the practice of inoculation was widely accepted, some employers were prepared to engage servants who had not had smallpox and to have them inoculated, as in March 1791 when Thomas Sewell, a Colne Engaine attorney, paid Dr Thomas Raynbird to inoculate his servants William Siggers and Hannah Berring.[28]

If the cost of the disease to individuals and families was grievous and tragic the impact of smallpox, especially epidemic smallpox, on whole communities in towns and villages could be socially, economically and occasionally demographically disastrous, particularly before mass or general inoculation of the poor was employed to halt the contagion. But the saving of lives among the poor and labouring classes which resulted from free general inoculations tended to be a fortunate by-product rather than a principal objective among town authorities and parish vestries for most of whom the protection of trade and a desire to minimise the poor rate were the main considerations.

Once smallpox had broken out in a town or village the news spread quickly in the surrounding countryside causing people to stay away from markets and fairs. At Great Oakley and Earls Colne in 1773, Dedham in 1773 and 1785, and Boxted in 1798, for example, annual fairs were cancelled due to the presence of the disease.[29] Much more serious, however, was the closure of weekly markets which in extreme cases could be ruined for more than a year. At Dartford, Kent, in 1741 'the country people became so alarmed that the market was nearly deserted, and did not recover for some years',[30] while at Bury St Edmunds, Suffolk, between 1738 and 1743

the small-pox was so severe ... that the town had been deprived of a sixth part of its inhabitants: there were no markets, and the town was avoided as the seat of death and terror.

This was no more than a common calamity at that time[31]

When the disease cleared towns were quick to make the fact widely known in order to revive their trade. In a serious outbreak in central Essex in 1711-1712 country people had refused to go to Chelmsford, as a result of which the town's market and inns were empty and its trade and economy devastated. With the outbreak almost ended no less than 67 inhabitants including the rector, four doctors and several innkeepers signed a notice addressed to the sheriff and county magistrates certifying

That the Small Pox wherewith the Town of Chelmsford Hath been afflicted is Not only Abated But the Towne is so very well in Health That the Markett is as full as Formerly And of Above a Thousand Familyes but Six Persons Sick therein And Those in Private Retirements: Not in any Great Inn or Publick House.[32]

The development of provincial newspapers enabled towns and villages to give press notices. For places in Essex, Norfolk and Suffolk this became possible with the establishment of the *Ipswich Journal* in 1720. For example, on 3 January 1750 six leading inhabitants of the small cloth and market town of Dedham, including the master of the grammar school and an apothecary, gave notice that

The SMALL-POX is not in Dedham-Street, and is only in Two Families at Prince's-Green, and no where else in the Town, excepting the Pest House (where only one or two have it) as far as we know, and as we believe.[33]

On 15 September 1756 four ministers, a physician and five surgeons and apothecaries at Colchester gave notice of the virtual end of an outbreak announcing that

Upon a strict Enquiry made by the Clerks thro' their respective Parishes, delivered to us, and attested by them, there is but SIX Persons now afflicted with the SMALL-POX in this Town.[34]

In the next week's issue it was stated that there were only two cases in the town and on 14 October notice was given that 'As the Number is now only ONE, in so large a Town, its thought unnecessary to advertise any longer'.[35] At Braintree in December 1757 the curate, churchwardens, overseers, four surgeons and apothecaries and 13 inhabitants certified that there was not one person 'now ill with the said Distemper in the said Parish, either in the Town or at the Pest House'.[36] Following an outbreak with several fatalities at Rayleigh in April 1763[37] this notice signed by, among others, the minister and 16 'Leading Inhabitants' appeared in the *Ipswich Journal* on 21 and 28 May

RALEIGH, Essex, May 16, 1763
Upon a strict Enquiry in this Town, NOT ONE Person is
afflicted with the SMALL POX; nor is it in but one House in the
Parish, and that a Mile from the Town ...
N.B. On MONDAY the 30th Day of May, being the Fair-Day,
will be a large Shew of Horses and Colts.

Several Essex towns were badly afflicted in the 1790s when the disease was
widespread for sustained periods. Chelmsford appears to have been especially
affected and notices were placed in the *Chelmsford Chronicle* in September 1791 and
again in July 1794 when it was stated that

Upon enquiry into the State of the Small-Pox at every house, we
do not find one person infected with that disorder in this town,
and only three children in the Hamlet of Moulsham.[38]

Maldon was also ravaged by the disease in that decade. It was so bad in the winter of
1796-1797 that on 30 January the vestries authorised a general inoculation of the
poor by the local doctors, but it was not until August 1797 that the vicar of All
Saints, three surgeons, a churchwarden and three overseers announced 'that the
Town ... and its Environs, are entirely free from the Small Pox, and have been so
for some time past'.[39]

Notices like those cited above of the cessation of smallpox outbreaks in market
towns were commonplace in provincial newspapers in the second half of the eighteenth century and further Essex examples have been noted for Dedham, 1759,[40]
Colchester, 1763,[41] Maldon, 1766,[42] Witham, 1779,[43] Chelmsford, 1783[44] and
Halstead, 1790.[45]

Sometimes trade was disrupted by a rumour or false report. At Romford in
August 1761 the curate, vestry-clerk and two doctors were among the signatories to
a notice denying a rumour spread in Essex by 'some evil-minded People ... that
SMALL-POX still rages in the Town of Romford, to the great Detriment of the Inhabitants there', and certifying that 'Small-Pox is intirely ceased in the said
Town'.[46] Smallpox was also 'falsely reported' at Castle Hedingham in the early
months of 1765 and on 23 April the minister, churchwarden, two overseers, two
surgeons and eight inhabitants put their signatures to a notice declaring that 'there
is not, nor has been for some Time, any Person that has it either in the natural Way,
or by Inoculation'.[47]

Closure of markets and dislocation of trade over sustained periods had far-
reaching consequences. In 1697 an epidemic in London soon spread to the rest of
the country. Essex suffered badly and nowhere more than the cloth and market
town of Coggeshall which by April 1698 was in serious difficulties

by a great and violent Contagion of the Smallpox which hath ut-
terly (for want of Trade) Impoverished many familyes, the ... Inhabitants of Great Coggeshall are not able amongst themselves to
levy Sufficient Summs of money for the necessary releife and
Support of their poore nor to provide work for the Children of

such Poor as cannot provide for them[48]

The inhabitants applied to the Lexden divisional justices for help and on 18 April six neighbouring parishes (Aldham, Colne Engaine, Earls Colne, Wakes Colne, Copford and Markshall) were ordered to raise a total of £133 by 28 April 'for necessary releife of the poor of Great Coggeshall'.[49]

The enormous and sometimes crippling expense of payments to the sick poor coupled with the inability of a substantial proportion of inhabitants to pay rates during outbreaks of this severity affected the legal obligation of parishes to maintain the fabric of roads and bridges. In 1712 the old timber Winkford Bridge in Little Waltham which carried the main road from Chelmsford to Braintree over the River Chelmer was reported as being 'very much Decayed'. The three parishes responsible for its upkeep, Broomfield and Great and Little Waltham, explained in a petition to Quarter Sessions

> the charges now ... being very great for amending the highways
> and maintaining the poor in the said parishes especially in this
> very sickly season by reason of the smallpox, that they are
> rendered almost unable by any parish Rates to Repaire the said
> Bridge[50]

In addition to damage to trade and its associated effects, such as loss of rates, smallpox disrupted many aspects of everyday life including education and church services as well as county administrative and legal proceedings. At Bury St Edmunds between 1738 and 1743 for example 'the smallpox was so severe ... that the assizes were twice, if not three times, held at Ipswich'.[51] If the assizes or quarter sessions were not moved to an uninfected town people often refused to attend, as in July 1766 when William Dore, a Chipping Ongar attorney, wrote explaining that although he and Henry Mullucks, surveyor of the highways for Norton Mandeville, were due to appear at the Midsummer sessions 'the Small pox being so bad in Chelmsford that neither the Surveyor or myself dare attend'.[52] On 5 October 1779 Joseph King of Colne Engaine addressed this letter to the Clerk at Chelmsford

> I am warn'd to appear this day at the Sessions to be one of the
> Petty Jury, and I should have readily attended but am inform'd
> that the Small Pox is very much about Chelmsford and its
> neighbourhood and neither my Self Wife nor any of my Children
> have had it, it strikes such a Dread and Horror upon me that I
> dare not venture to attend so I humbly beg of your Worship for
> this time to excuse me, I have never omitted attending before this
> time, whenever I have been warn'd, and desire to attend at any
> time when it is not so dangerous.[53]

The education of Charles Barrington was interrupted in April 1683 when his father, Sir John Barrington of Hatfield Broad Oak, ordered him to be brought home from Felsted School 'feareing the small pox to be in the house whare he boarders'.[54] Closure of schools could result in severe financial problems for the proprietors. In the winter of 1712-1713 smallpox caused Widow Margaret Epes, the proprietress of a school in Essex, 'to disperse her schollers and they not as yet come againe ... is reduced to great Extremitys'.[55] Closure periods were sometimes lengthy. Rivenhall Church of England School was closed on 24 April 1871 'to prevent smallpox spreading in the village' and was not reopened until 26 June 'having been closed nine weeks'.[56] Disruption of religious life occurred in May 1790 when

> On account of the small-pox being at Brentwood, we hear the
> Bishop of London will not hold his visitation and confirmation
> there, but at South Weald, on Friday, the 21st instant.[57]

It was common for parishioners to avoid their church and churchyard during outbreaks, some even fearing contagion from newly-buried corpses. At Sandon in February 1799, for example, William and Frances Hunter refused to have their baby son William baptised in church, the child 'being ill and apprehended in danger of catching the small pox if brought to the church'.[58]

Communities were burdened not only with the economic cost of damage to trade during smallpox outbreaks but also with that of caring for the sick poor and such expenditure, which varied greatly from parish to parish, was always a source of concern to overseers and vestries. The cost of an individual case in the late seventeenth and eighteenth centuries ranged from a few shillings to about £5 and the following examples are typical of entries to be found in almost every overseers' account book of that time. At the bottom end of the scale E.G. Thomas cites the case of Widow Smith of Braintree who in 1685 received 1s. 6d. relief, nursing which cost 7s. and 'watchers' for four nights at 1s. a night, a total of 12s. 6d.[59] In the late 1690s the most usual cost of nursing a victim seems to have been in the region of £2 to £3 as, for example, in 1699 when the overseers of Great Coggeshall spent £2 7s. on the 'maintenance' of Thomas Westwood, a 'poor person of Stisted who lay sick in Great Coggeshall of small-pox'.[60] Costs *per capita* appear to have risen only slightly as the eighteenth century progressed. In 1735 the overseers of Aveley spent £3 16s. 7d. on 'ye man with the Smallpox'[61] and when William Drache of Stapleford Tawney had the disease in 1749 nursing him cost the parish £4 2s.[62] In November 1793 the nursing and other expenses incurred by the Aveley overseers in looking after John Forman and Mrs Stickling, both 'with the Small pox', was £4 3s. 8d. and £2 7s. respectively.[63] Only very rarely did the cost of caring for an individual smallpox patient during the term of illness and recuperation exceed £5 and one of the most expensive eighteenth-century cases must have been that of William Cook of Kirby-le-Soken whose illness in 1796 required nursing and maintenance for five weeks at a final cost to the parish of £5 15s.[64]

The examples looked at so far show that expenses varied not only from parish to parish but also from individual to individual, according to the severity and length of illness and of the particular circumstances and needs. When whole families of the poor contracted smallpox the expenses were inevitably greater. At Thaxted from July to September 1717 John Lindsell and his family had the disease, from which two of the children died, and expenditure by the overseers for the doctor's and nurses' fees, for food, drink, other necessities and burial costs amounted to £10 10s. 1d.[65] The greatest cost, however, occurred when a breadwinner died leaving a family unable to support itself. This happened at Hadstock in December 1782 when the Onion family contracted the disease. Nathaniel Onion and two daughters, Sarah aged 11 months and Elizabeth aged eight years, all died and the expenses for nursing, food, beer, other necessities and the three burials amounted to £6 13s. Nathaniel's widow Sarah was left with two young children, Nathaniel aged six and Susannah aged four years, and thereafter received a weekly allowance of 1s. 9d. from the parish.[66]

The possibility of avoiding recurring expenditure on families like the Onions was one of the arguments used in the later eighteenth century by a growing number of doctors, clergymen and philanthropists when advocating the benefits of mass or general inoculations of the poor. The argument was admirably stated in March 1788 by the Revd William Stuart, vicar of Luton, Bedfordshire, and grandson of Lady Mary Wortley Montagu,[67] in a letter to the physician Sir William Fordyce in which he proposed annual inoculations at parish expense.

> For nine years that I have held the living of Luton, the average number of small-pox patients is 25. These at the lowest computation, stand the parish at two guineas each, exclusive of medical assistance. The disease is so apprehended in the country, that the nurses require double pay; and both they and the patients are confined to an airing-house several weeks after recovery. Should my plan of annual inoculations take place, the expence would not amount to the fifty guineas which are now paid for those who have small pox naturally. But, alas! these fifty guineas are but a small part of the real charge and inconvenience produced by this dreadful malady. Its almost constant effect is a permanent augmentation of the parish expenditure. If a labourer dies, his family must be supported. If a mother is lost, the children must be removed to the workhouse, as their father cannot spare time for employments that are merely domestic. In a workhouse they lose innocence, reputation, and that sense of independence which is the surest principle of industry.[68]

Stuart's proposals came to nothing and although inoculation had greatly curbed the disease by the end of the eighteenth century smallpox nevertheless remained in Macaulay's words

> the most terrible of all the ministers of death ... tormenting with constant fears all whom it had not yet stricken, leaving on those whose lives it spared the hideous traces of its power, turning the babe into a changeling at which the mother shuddered, and making the eyes and cheeks of the betrothed maiden objects of horror to the lover.[69]

Smallpox was endemic only in London and the very large provincial towns.

Elsewhere it was commonly absent for sustained periods, often as much as five or ten years and among particularly remote communities sometimes very much longer, sporadic outbreaks being always the result of infection introduced from an outside source. Market towns and villages on main trading routes were especially susceptible to random infection by travellers with the disease. In Essex the places most at risk appear to have been those on the road from London to Colchester and East Anglia (the present-day A12), places such as Romford, Chelmsford, Witham and Colchester. In addition to the costs of disruption of trade and of caring for their own sick these places were also faced with the expense of isolating and nursing (and sometimes burying) travellers with smallpox. For example when John Lord, a sailor from H.M.S. *Dunwich*, was on his way through Essex to Great Yarmouth in July 1698 he

> was taken with small pox and goeing through the towne of Colchester the Guardians of the pore seing he was not fit to travill tooke pity of him and put him into a house and provided him a nurs and all thing nesesary for the distemper — and the Guardians ... of St James in Colchester have laid out for Releife and succer of ... John Lord the sum of forty two shillings : 6d and he being now recovered and ready to goe his Jurny to North Yarmouth and from thence to returne to his ship againe[70]

One mile north-east of Brentwood the same road passed through the tiny village of Shenfield where on 16 August 1794 an unnamed traveller was buried at parish expense having 'died of the Small Pox'.[71]

In order to avoid the economic costs which were an inevitable result of the presence of smallpox town authorities, parish vestries and occasionally individuals took steps to prevent its introduction. It has already been shown that travellers with the disease constituted a risk of infection and to their ranks were added in the second half of the eighteenth century a growing number of people undergoing inoculation. Many towns banned them absolutely until their treatment was completed and they were no longer infectious, as in May 1774 when the 'Gentlemen' of Maldon gave notice that people 'under the Course of Inoculation ... with the Small-Pox upon them' were not to come to the town and they were 'determined to prosecute all such who shall offend'.[72] Prosecution was also threatened by the townsmen of Halstead who believed that smallpox had been introduced in the winter of 1789-1790 by vagrants, beggars and 'idle Persons'. In future such people 'found lurking about the parish' would be apprehended and taken before a magistrate and no lenity would be shown any parishioner harbouring or lodging them.[73] Although often threatened, prosecution was rarely carried out, one of the very few instances in Essex occurring in December 1698 when William Allen of Halstead, yeoman, was prosecuted at Quarter Sessions by the overseers of Tilbury-juxta-Clare 'for sending Wm Barnard into Tilbury-juxta-Clare being very sick and full of the smallpox'.[74]

Some places took action to protect their ratepayers from the expenses of smallpox among residents whose place of legal settlement was elsewhere. At the small market and port town of Rochford in the late eighteenth century there was a high level of in-migration[75] and in 1787 concern was expressed at 'great inconveniancies and expenses' which were 'likely to Arise from Persons having, and taking Lodgers into their Houses that have not had the small Pox', the churchwardens, overseers and two substantial inhabitants giving notice on 3 May

to all Persons that shall take any Lodgers ... and such Lodgers shall be taken with the small pox that they the said Officers will not be at any expense on Account of the Parish.

But ... the expense shall fall upon the Person so taking them into their Houses.[76]

Inns were always regarded with suspicion as being likely places of infection and because of the public nature of his business the innkeeper's livelihood was particularly susceptible to damage by the presence or rumour of smallpox. In common with those in other eighteenth-century market towns, Chelmsford's inns performed a vital rôle in the town's trading functions so that when the epidemic of 1711-1712 subsided the principal inhabitants, among them several innkeepers, were anxious to make it widely known that the disease was 'Not in any Great Inn or Publick house'.[77] Half a century later in March 1765 Mary Lukely, who kept a public house at the busy Creeksea Ferry, the lowest crossing point on the River Crouch, placed this notice in the *Chelmsford Chronicle* in order to restore her trade following the presence of smallpox there

THIS is to acquaint the Public ... that my House is intirely free from the SMALL-POX and the House well aired; so that no Person ... need be the least apprehensive of any Danger from the said Pest.[78]

Another Essex innkeeper, Thomas Read of Rayleigh, had the disease on his premises and his action in keeping it secret to avoid loss of trade on the annual fair day in June 1640 was to have serious consequences, for it was shortly afterwards reported that he had

a child newly dead of the Small Pox and knowing his house to be infected did conceale the same entertaining a multitude of guests whereby many were infected one of our Town is dead, many other in severall places sicke, and the contagion carryed to other places.[79]

The angry inhabitants of Rayleigh sent a petition to Quarter Sessions requesting that 'your Honours and Worships wilbe pleased to suppresse ... Read from Keeping of victualling in his house'.[80]

The examples cited in this chapter have served to illustrate some aspects of the cost of smallpox, including the often grievous and tragic effects on individuals and families, the damaging and sometimes devastating effects on the trade and economy of towns and villages and the disruptive effects upon the everyday life of communities. Some examples of steps taken by town authorities and parish vestries to prevent the introduction of the disease have also been given. But such steps at best had short-term success and while it is not possible wholly to agree with E.G. Thomas' conclusion, based on a study of Essex overseers' accounts, that smallpox 'was the severest drain on the poor rate',[81] payments associated with the disease nevertheless often comprised a significant part of parish overseers' expenditure and probably the major part during epidemic years in the later seventeenth and most of the eighteenth centuries. Subsequent chapters will show that the only effective means of reducing the terrible cost inflicted by smallpox was immunisation on a large scale.

2

Inoculation: the Early Years, 1721-1752

Before about 1660 smallpox in England was treated by the so-called 'hot' method originally devised by Arabian physicians who believed that heat helped to expel the innate material cause of smallpox from the body. This method involved putting the patient to bed wrapped in warm bedclothes which were not changed for the duration of the illness. Windows were closed and a fire often lit. The sweating patient then steamed out the illness or died. In the early 1660s its efficacy was questioned by the physician Thomas Sydenham who devised a cold method, the principal features of which were to allow the patient as much fresh air as possible with light bed coverings regularly changed and cool beverages.[1] Thereafter medical opinion was divided over the use of these two methods, neither of which was a cure for the disease in its fatal forms. Indeed, no cure was ever to be discovered. As a result people became increasingly concerned about preventing the spread of the disease by isolating the sick in their homes or in pest houses. This was the situation in England in 1720, on the eve of the introduction of the practice, known as inoculation, of inserting smallpox bacteria into the human body to give a mild form of the disease in order to produce immunity.[2]

Inoculation was already being practised in Greece, Turkey, China, India and parts of Arabia in the seventeenth century. It was first reported in England in February 1701 when Dr Clopton Havers presented an account of the Chinese method to the Royal Society and in 1706 Dr Edward Tarry claimed to have seen over 4,000 people inoculated in Turkey. In 1713 the children of the French consul in Aleppo were successfully inoculated and in 1713 and 1714 it was discussed by the Royal Society, much of the information coming from merchants who had lived in Turkey. But there was no statistical information to support the view that inoculation gave lifelong immunity and the practice in Turkey appears to have been a folk tradition based wholly on commonplace observation.

The first Britons to be inoculated were the two sons of Mr Hefferman, Secretary to the British Ambassador in Turkey, who underwent the operation early in 1716 and who were examined by London doctors when they returned to England in March. But far more important was the publicity given by Lady Mary Wortley Montagu whose great beauty had been destroyed by an attack of smallpox in December 1715 and whose younger brother, Lord Kingston, had died from the disease in July 1713.[3] In August 1716 she went to Turkey with her husband Edward, the new Ambassador,[4] and witnessed inoculation for the first time. In a letter to Miss Mary Chiswell, April 1717, she described what she had seen.

> *A propos* of distempers, I am going to tell you a thing that I am sure will make you wish yourself here. The small-pox, so fatal, and so general amongst us, is here entirely harmless by the invention of *ingrafting*, which is the term they give it. There is a set of

old women who make it their business to perform the operation, in the month of September, when the great heat is abated. People send to one another to know if any of their family has a mind to have the small-pox: they make parties for this purpose, and when they are met (commonly fifteen or sixteen together), the old woman comes with a nut-shell full of the matter of the best sort of smallpox, and asks what veins you please to have opened. She immediately rips open that you offer to her with a large needle (which gives you no more pain than a common scratch), and puts into the vein as much venom as can lie upon the head of her needle, and after binds up the little wound with a hollow bit of shell; and in this manner opens up four or five veins. The Grecians have commonly the superstition of opening one in the middle of the forehead, in each arm, and on the breast, to mark the sign of the cross; but this has a very ill effect, all these wounds leaving little scars, and is not done by those that are not superstitious, who choose to have them in the legs, or that part of the arm that is concealed. The children or young patients play together all the rest of the day, and are in perfect health to the eighth. Then the fever begins to seize them, and they keep their beds two days, very seldom three. They have very rarely above twenty or thirty in their faces, which never mark; and in eight days' time they are as well as before their illness. Where they are wounded, there remain running sores during the distemper, which I don't doubt is a great relief to it. Every year thousands undergo this operation; and the French embassador says pleasantly, that they will take the small-pox here by way of diversion, as they take the waters in other countries. There is no example of any one that has died in it; and you may believe I am very well satisfied of the safety of the experiment, since I intend to try it on my dear little son.

I am patriot enough to take pains to bring this useful invention into fashion in England; and I should not fail to write to some of our doctors very particularly about it, if I knew any of them that I thought had virtue enough to destroy such a considerable branch of their revenue for the good of mankind. But that distemper is too beneficial to them not to expose to all their resentment the hardy wight that should undertake to put an end to it. Perhaps, if I live to return, I may, however, have courage to war with them[5]

Apart from describing the Turkish method of inoculation, this letter reveals that Lady Mary had decided to have her son Edward inoculated and that her contempt for the English medical profession was already firmly rooted.

Six-year-old Edward Wortley Montagu was inoculated at Pera, near Constantinople, on 18 March 1718 and five days later Lady Mary wrote to her husband

> The boy was engrafted last Tuesday, and is at this time singing and playing, and very impatient for his supper. I pray God my next may give as good an account of him

She continued by explaining that she could not have their three-month-old daughter Anne inoculated because 'her nurse has not had the small-pox'.[6] This is an important point, showing it to have been understood already that inoculees undergoing treatment were contagious. One English doctor for whom Lady Mary appears always to have had a warm regard was Charles Maitland, surgeon to the British Embassy while the Wortley Montagus were in Turkey. He assisted with the inoculation of young Edward and his own account of the event was published in 1723.

> About this Time, the Ambassador's ingenious Lady, who had been at some Pains to satisfy her Curiosity in this Matter, and had made some useful Observations on the Practice, was so thoroughly convinced of the Safety of it, that *She* resolv'd to submit *her* only Son to it, a very hopeful Boy of about Six Years of Age: She first of all order'd me to find out a fit Subject to take the Matter from; and then sent for an old *Greek* Woman, who had practis'd this Way a great many Years: After a good deal of Trouble and Pains, I found a proper Subject, and then the good Woman went to work; but so awkwardly by the shaking of her Hand, and put the Child to so much Torture with her blunt and rusty Needle, that I pitied his Cries, who had ever been of such Spirit and Courage, that hardly any Thing of Pain could make him cry before; and therefore Inoculated the other Arm with my own Instrument, and with so little Pain to him, that he did not in the least complain of it. The Operation took in both Arms, and succeeded perfectly well. After the third Day, bright red Spots appear'd in his Face, then disappear'd; and thus interchangeably (as it commonly happens) till in the Night betwixt the Seventh and Eighth Day, he was observed to be a little hot and thirsty, yet remain'd so but a few Hours; and then the *Small Pox* came out fair: They became round and yellow, like those of the more gentle distinct kind; and the Red Spots which appeared first, were the fullest and largest of all: They began to crust a few Days after, and then gently died away; so that the young Gentleman was quickly in a Condition to go Abroad with Safety. He had above an hundred in all upon his Body; but without any the least Disorder but what I have mentioned: And they all fell off, without leaving any one Mark or Impression behind them.[7]

Although Lady Mary was already back in England by 1719, in which year there were 3,229 smallpox deaths in London alone, it was not until April 1721, when smallpox in London was thought especially fatal to children, that she called on Maitland to inoculate her infant daughter. This was the first inoculation to be carried out in England. When the pustules appeared the child was examined by three members of the College of Physicians, including Sir Hans Sloane, who had attended Lady Mary in December 1715. Although the evidence surrounding this inoculation is conflicting and confused it seems clear that Lady Mary once again displayed her dislike for the medical profession, believing the doctors to be unwilling to have the treatment succeed, and 'never cared to leave the child alone with them one second, lest it should, in some way suffer from their interference'.[8] Nevertheless another of the physicians present, Dr James Keith, who 'had formerly lost some Children in a very malignant kind of the Small Pox', was so impressed that he had Maitland inoculate his six-year-old son Peter. This took place on 11 May and was completely successful.[9]

There were no further inoculations in England until the autumn when Maitland carried out successful experimental inoculations on six condemned prisoners in Newgate in the presence of Sloane, Dr George Steigherthal and 25 other eminent physicians, surgeons and apothecaries. Although Maitland's own account of the Newgate inoculations, published in 1723, does not contain details of his technique we may be fairly certain that he made deep incisions with a lancet, for the eye-witness account by Dr William Wagstaffe, one of the physicians at St Bartholomew's Hospital, describes the incisions, which were made in both arms and right leg of all six, as 'long and large'.[10] This inexplicable break by Maitland with the method he had seen in Turkey marks the beginning of a severe form of inoculation that was to be used in Britain until the 1750s. As will be shown, the abandonment of the Graeco-Turkish method of superficial scarification was to have far-reaching effects, for it was to be one of the key factors responsible for retarding the progress of inoculation in Britain.

Following the successful outcome of the Montagu and Keith inoculations and the Newgate experiments, the royal family and several aristocratic families and political figures took the decision to have their children inoculated. These included the two-year-old son of the Earl of Sunderland, inoculated by Maitland at the beginning of April 1722, and the Princesses Amelia, eleven, and Caroline, nine, daughters of the Prince of Wales, inoculated by Maitland and Claude Amyand, the King's surgeon, on 17 April. Much publicity was given to these cases. At the same time, Lady Mary was continuing her own campaign to further the new treatment and in the spring of 1722 wrote with evident satisfaction of 'the growth and spreading of the inoculation of the small-pox which is become almost a general practice, attended with great success'.[11]

Just as it seemed that inoculation was beginning to be accepted by the very rich a series of events occurred which was to prove highly damaging to the progress of the new treatment. On 21 April the infant son of the Duke of Sutherland died, reputedly from the effects of inoculation,[12] and on 30 April a strong and healthy 19-year-old footman in the service of Lord Bathurst was inoculated but died from smallpox on 16 May 'following exposure to the Bathurst children', all six of whom had been inoculated by Amyand on 19 April.[13] Although the full impact of these mishaps was not immediately felt opposition was continuing to mount with professional dissent beginning in May 1722 when the surgeon Legard Sparham presented a report to the Royal Society, published shortly afterwards under the title *Reasons against the Practice of Inoculating the Small-Pox, As Also a Brief Account of the Operation.* This was followed in June by Wagstaffe's *Letter to Dr Freind Shewing the Danger and Uncertainty of Inoculating the Smallpox* in which the author suggested that

> 'till we have fuller Evidence of the Success of it ... Physicians at least, who of all Men ought to be guided in their Judgements chiefly by Experience should not be over hasty in encouraging a Practice, which does not seem as yet sufficiently supported either by Reason, or by Fact.[14]

In an anonymous pamphlet published about the same time the author pleaded for parliamentary regulation of 'that dangerous experiment', declaring inoculation to be founded on atheism, quackery and avarice which 'push men to all the hellish practices imaginable; men murther fathers, mothers, relations, and innocent children, and any that stand in the way of their wicked desires'.[15] Religious opposition began on 8 July when the Revd Edmund Massey delivered a sermon on 'The Dangerous and Sinful Practice of Inoculation' in the church of St Andrew, Holborn. The advice and supervision of Lady Mary was much in demand about this time by families undergoing inoculation and she 'constantly carried her little daughter along with her to the house, and into the sick-room, to prove her security from infection'.[16] But distrust and opposition were frequently encountered and in later life Lady Mary's daughter remembered how she

> could see the significant shrugs of the nurses and servants, and observe the looks of dislike they cast at her mother. She also overheard anxious parents repeating to Lady Mary the arguments that had been used to deter them from venturing upon the trial; and aunts and grandmothers, in the warmth of their zeal against it, quoting the opinion of this doctor or that apothecary.[17]

Outside London inoculation was performed in a few provincial towns in 1722, notably Halifax, Yorkshire, where Dr Thomas Nettleton inoculated 'upwards of forty persons' in December 1721 and January and February 1722.[18] The main opposition in the provinces was from the churches, both Anglican and dissenting. At Ipswich the inoculation of three people by Dr William Beeston in 1724 provoked a violent reaction.[19] As Beeston commented later in the year

> The practice of Inoculation in this Town, has so inflamed the angry passions, and stirred up the bitter Zeale of the bigotted high Churchmen, and Dissenters to such a Degree that they Sentence to Damnation, all that are any way Concerned in it. They say the practice is Heathenish, and Diabolical, it is distrusting Pro-

vidence, and taking the Power out of God's hand, it will draw down Divine Judgements ... but reason they do not, upon the subject.[20]

Together the organised opposition of a substantial part of the medical profession and clergy now began to ensure that deaths from smallpox following inoculation were publicised in the press in a manner calculated to deter all but the most adventurous. This opposition even caused Lady Mary Wortley Montagu to regret having introduced inoculation into England, her granddaughter Lady Louisa Stuart recalling in 1837 how she

> seldom passed a day without repenting of her patriotic undertaking; and she vowed that she never would have attempted it if she had foreseen the vexation, the persecution, and even the obloquy it brought upon her. The clamours raised against the practice, and of course against her, were beyond belief. The faculty all rose in arms to a man, foretelling failure and the most disastrous consequences; the clergy descanted from their pulpits on the impiety of thus seeking to take events out of the hand of Providence; the common people were taught to hoot at her as an unnatural mother, who had risked the lives of her own children. And notwithstanding that she soon gained many supporters amongst the higher and more enlightened classes, headed by the Princess of Wales ... who stood by her firmly, some even of her acquaintance were weak enough to join in the outcry.[21]

The statistics for inoculations performed in England in the 1720s compiled by James Jurin, Physician to Guy's Hospital and Secretary of the Royal Society and by the physician John Gasper Scheuchzer show that growing criticism and opposition had a marked effect.[22] In the first three years, 1721-1723, 469 people were inoculated but in 1724 the number slumped to 49. This slump may be attributed in part to criticism and opposition and in part to a decline in the fatality of smallpox compared with the three previous years, Jurin commenting 'so much more are we influenced by our fears of present danger, than by the apprehension of a remote one'. An extensive epidemic in 1725 resulted in inoculations rising to 149 but failed to provide the stimulus to make the practice widely accepted. Thereafter the mounting opposition and absence of a major outbreak had a much more pronounced effect, the number of inoculations declining to 139 in 1726, 76 in 1727 and 37 in 1728. Most of the inoculees were children, between one third and one quarter of the total being under five years of age. In addition to these inoculations in England, ten were performed in Scotland and seven in Wales so that the total for Britain was about 936.[24] Of these 17 were alleged to have resulted in death. According to Scheuchzer there were also 280 inoculations performed in New England (in 1721 and 1722), 25 at Dublin (in 1723-1726), ten at Hanover (nine by Maitland) and one at Pyrmont, but his total of 329 inoculations 'in foreign parts' does not tally with his earlier breakdown.[25] By the late 1720s inoculations in England were so unusual that they were newsworthy items for provincial newspapers such as the *Ipswich Journal* which reported a single inoculation carried out by Beeston at Woodbridge, Suffolk, in the autumn of 1729.[26]

Table 1   Inoculation in England, 1721-1728

Years	In and around London	Provinces	Total
1721-23	164 (inc. 85 by Maitland and 62 by Amyand)	305 (inc. 99 at Salisbury and 80 by Nettleton in Yorks. and Durham)	469
1724	20	29 (inc. 3 by Beeston at Ipswich)	49
1725	94 (inc. 35 by Maitland and 31 by Amyand)	55 (inc. 28 by Nettleton at Halifax)	149
1726	90 (inc. 35 by Amyand and 'above Forty' by Thorold at Uxbridge)[23]	49 (inc. 15 by Nettleton at Halifax)	139
1727	35 (inc. 23 by Amyand)	41 (inc. 11 by Nettleton in and around Halifax)	76
1728	27 (inc. 21 by Amyand)	10	37
	430	489	919[23]

Some of the reasons for the decline after 1723, in particular the opposition from a section of the medical profession and from the churches, have already been discussed. In addition there was genuine fear of the possible fatal outcome of the treatment and while the incidence of the natural disease remained at a relatively low level most people preferred the risk of contracting natural smallpox to the risk of dying from inoculation. Particular concern was felt by parents over the inoculation of young children, among which one in 30 was fatal in 1721-1728. In 1724 the apothecary Francis Howgrave claimed in his *Reasons Against the Inoculation of the Small-Pox* to have proved the risks associated with inoculation to be greater than those associated with the natural disease and pleaded for inoculation to be abandoned. Fourteen years later in February 1738 John Hough, Bishop of Worcester, an advocate of inoculation, wrote

> the method loses ground ... for parents are tender and fearful, not without hope their children may escape this disease, or have it favourably; whereas, in the way of art, should it prove fatal, they could never forgive themselves: for this reason, nobody dares to advise in the case.[27]

The contagiousness of inoculees was another problem. As early as 1722 it had been suggested by Dr John Crawford that inoculation should be done in isolated houses beyond town limits[28] and in 1723 it was banned in Salisbury on the grounds that it would revive and spread the disease following the epidemic there.[29] In 1726 Dr Beard of Worcester stated that he wished to establish an infirmary for inoculation near the city but it is doubtful whether his plans were carried out.[30] Three years later, in March 1729, he reported to Scheuchzer that 'Since that time I have had no opportunity of extending the Practice ...' because of 'the difficulty of bringing a Distemper anew to a Place after it had once quitted it'.[31]

There was one more very important factor which prevented the general acceptance of the practice — the high cost of treatment. In January 1744, for example, Mr Goldwyer, a surgeon at Blandford, Dorset, charged 20 guineas to inoculate two people.[32] The high price was to continue to be a major deterrent until the 1760s.

Inoculation remained at an insignificant level in the 1730s, being generally confined to a few wealthy and educated people in the provinces who, realising that it alleviated the crisis of epidemic smallpox and gave protection to those who underwent the operation, had themselves and their children treated. Writing of the epidemic at Haverfordwest, Pembrokeshire, in the winter of 1731-1732 a local physician observed

> that most of those who have of late been visited with it, have died
> thereof. This probably will incline some to use Inoculation again,
> and to make that Practice, under Providence, their Refuge.[33]

At Bury St Edmunds the physician and philosopher David Hartley had tried to introduce inoculation in 1733 but could only lament the prejudice of the townsmen against it.[34] In contrast to the situation in England inoculation was becoming widely used in New England, Dr William Hillary of Bath remarking in 1735 'its credit at present seems to be sunk at home; though in some of our American colonies, it is now practised with considerable success'.[35] In 1738 it was described in detail in Chambers' *Cyclopaedia*, while the *Gentleman's Magazine* reported its progress in other parts of the world, such as during the epidemics which swept the colonial towns of Philadelphia in 1736-1737 and Charleston, South Carolina, in 1738, when large numbers were inoculated.[36] In July 1738 it was reported that in the Barbadoes inoculation 'is practised with great Success'.[37]

By the early 1740s an increasing number of competent medical practitioners and public-spirited individuals were becoming convinced of its utility. According to Dr Langrish of Winchester, when smallpox 'raged furiously' in the region around Portsmouth, Chichester, Guildford, Petersfield and Winchester in about 1742 nearly 2,000 people were inoculated,[38] again showing that the most potent stimulus to the practice was a major outbreak.

The arrival in London in 1743 of the American James Kilpatrick, who had established a reputation in Charleston for successful inoculation, marked a further step forward. Shortly after arriving he changed his name to Kirkpatrick, published an *Essay on Inoculation* (1743) and with the help of considerable self-publicity quickly became the leading inoculator. His *Essay*, his rôle in the founding of the Smallpox and Inoculation Hospital in London in 1746 and other activities have been credited with reviving the practice in England, an opinion which Kirkpatrick himself expressed in his influential *Analysis of Inoculation*, 1754. Although this myth has been discredited by Genevieve Miller he clearly made an important contribution towards the widespread acceptance of inoculation in England.

The decision in January 1744 of the Governing Committee of the Foundling Hospital to inoculate the children in the Hospital is further evidence of a widening appreciation of its efficacy.[39] In April the *Gentleman's Magazine* reported that 14 children were treated, 'all with good Success', after which the Governors made inoculation compulsory for all children who had reached the age of three.[40] The *Magazine* indexer clearly thought these inoculations particularly significant for he indexed them as 'Inoculation for the small pox revived'.[41]

The year 1746 was marked by a severe epidemic in London where the bills of mortality listed 3,236 deaths, the highest number since they were first published in 1629. Many of the upper classes were now being inoculated quietly and with little publicity, the London doctor, traveller and medical writer Charles Perry remarking in 1747 that 'this Salutary Practice ... is indeed generally approved by all reasonable considerate People'.[42] In the opinion of Woodville another of 'the causes which at this period tended to promote the practice' was the publication in 1747 of the physician Richard Mead's *Treatise on Small Pox and Measles* containing a chapter showing the advantages of inoculation.[43] In London attention began to be focused on the protection and relief of poor sufferers. The first important step in this direction was taken when the Middlesex County Hospital for the Small-Pox was set up in September 1746 largely through the efforts of Isaac Maddox, Bishop of Worcester.[44] The Hospital was specifically 'for the relief of poor distress'd housekeepers, labourers, servants, and strangers, seiz'd with this unhappy distemper, who will here be immediately relieved in the best manner without expence'.[45] Inoculation was already being conducted at the Hospital by 1750 when it had three buildings in separate parts of the capital and in 1752 a new building with 130 beds was opened in Cold Bath Fields on the site of the present-day Kings Cross railway station. A house in Islington was provided for inoculation and inoculated patients were removed to Cold Bath Fields for nursing as soon as the pustules began to appear. In its early years there was considerable local opposition to the siting of the Smallpox and Inoculation Hospital, as it had become known by 1752, on the grounds that it spread infection in the neighbourhood by being a focus of contagion and by allowing inoculees to leave too soon.

Following the establishment of the London Smallpox Hospital private inoculation houses began appearing in the provinces. Owned or rented by local doctors, they were used by wealthy patients for a few weeks whilst undergoing the treatment. These doctors included the prominent Sussex surgeon Thomas Frewen of Rye, who had been studying the disease for a number of years and who was possibly the first in England to operate a private hospital for inoculated patients.[46] Although the number of these houses increased steadily from the late 1740s those in towns in particular were objects of concern, criticism and attack. As Miller has pointed out, the complaint was heard repeatedly that such a house introduced smallpox into a town which otherwise would have been free from the disease. It was claimed that as a result smallpox tended to spread in the locality, tradesmen avoided the region, provisions became expensive, and thousands suffered for the benefit of the favoured few who were obtaining protective immunity by inoculation ... What was resented particularly was that people came from other regions to be inoculated in their town

Inoculating houses situated outside towns were also frequently subject to local opposition. Frewen's house was on a main highway and travellers began to cut across adjoining fields in order to avoid passing close to a source of contagion. He was sued by the landowners and forced to cease inoculating in the house.[47]

At the same time as inoculation began to revive in the 1740s increasing emphasis was placed on the preparation of well-to-do patients, Perry remarking in 1747 that successful inoculation depended on 'the previous Management, or Preparation of the Person's Body who is to be inoculated, with Regard to Diet as well as Medicine'.[48] Frewen was another advocate of thorough preparation and his influential book *The Practice and Theory of Inoculation*, published in 1749, was based on careful observation and experience. It was the first to formulate current practice and became a handbook for other inoculators. Frewen's thesis was that choice of variolous matter for inoculation was immaterial but that the inoculee's bodily condition was of the greatest importance. Preparation began at least two weeks before inoculation and included a strictly regulated diet with only the lightest animal foods. Patients with florid complexions were bled, given emetics and purged, those with weak constitutions were given a light infusion of bark after a vomit or purge while those of 'gross habit' received Aethiops mineral or cinnabar with a milk diet for four to six weeks. Moderate exercise and adequate rest were also considered essential.

By the late 1740s public confidence in inoculation was rising and the treatment becoming firmly accepted among educated and well-to-do people. It was, however, still conducted on a very limited scale and although some doctors and commentators advocated its more general application, including Perry who pointed to the 'Benefit to the State ... if it was universally practised throughout the King's Dominions',[49] further stimulus was required to make the practice widespread. Moreover it remained very much an act of faith and trust, for sufficient time had yet to elapse before it could be shown that infant inoculees were immune from natural smallpox for a full life-span. The necessary stimulus came in 1752 when the most extensive and fatal epidemic so far experienced spread throughout England and marked the beginning of what may conveniently be termed the age of inoculation.

3

The Age of Inoculation, 1752-1798

The great epidemic of 1751-1753 began in London in December 1751 and in 1752 was attributed with 3,538 deaths in the capital alone.[1] In the spring of 1752 it started to attack the suburbs and neighbouring villages and thence spread throughout the country. Inoculation among the well-to-do was employed on a widespread scale as soon as the epidemic got under way, Dr John Fothergill remarking early in 1752 that 'The practice of inoculation seems to gain ground considerably'.[2] The age of inoculation had now begun.

The upsurge in London witnessed by Fothergill was repeated in provincial towns throughout England, as at Stroud, Somerset, where a local physician noted its 'rapid Progress and Fortune'.[3] At Woodbridge, Suffolk, by 26 May 1752 a prominent local doctor, Mr Lynn, had 'had great Success in the Matter of Inoculation for the Small-Pox, with his own Family and several other Persons',[4] while inoculation on an increased scale was carried out at Chelmsford and Colchester. An enlightened Chelmsford surgeon, Benjamin Pugh, who had been practising inoculation 'upwards of seven years' noted in a letter to the *Gentleman's Magazine* in April 1753 how opposition evaporated when confronted by the disease which 'has been almost universal in *England* this last year and still continues much, and in many places very fatal'.[5] Expressing particular surprise that there should still be opposition among 'people of better learning' he continued

> This universal good is *inoculation*, and notwithstanding envy has laid such batteries against it, yet happy for this kingdom it gains ground daily; the lower class of people coming into it very fast in these parts ... As to religious objections they are almost given up as 'tis high time they should (except amongst a few bigots indeed). For as the allwise creator has subjected mankind to so fatal, so terrible a disease, and at the same time has shew'd him a method how to reduce it in such a manner, that in general it can scarce be call'd a disease at all, I say, in refusing the method, surely we most affront, rather than offend in using it. But the learned bishop of *Worcester's* sermons one wou'd think sufficient to remove all kind of objections, religious as well as other, with all reasonable people.[6]

The Bishop of Worcester referred to in Pugh's letter was Isaac Maddox, who had been a champion of inoculation within the established church since the 1730s and who had succeeded John Hough as Bishop in 1743. His leadership became even more conspicuous when he preached in favour of inoculation at the annual meeting of the Governors of the London Smallpox Hospital, 5 March 1752, in St Andrew, Holborn, from the pulpit formerly occupied by its arch-enemy, the Revd Edmund Massey. Maddox's *Sermon* provided a powerful stimulus for the acceptance of in-

40

oculation and, as Genevieve Miller has pointed out, was 'one of the most influential pamphlets on the subject in the entire literature'.[7] The voices of remaining clerical opponents such as Theodore Delafaye, a Canterbury rector who preached in June 1753 on the wickedness of inoculation, claiming it to be self-destructive, inhuman, impious, hazardous, unnecessary, 'inconsistent with ... Duty to the Creator' and a practice condemned by religion, were drowned by the advocacy of Maddox and a growing number of churchmen.[8]

In December 1755 inoculation received the public approval of the College of Physicians which issued a statement to the effect

> That the arguments which at the commencement of this practice were urged against it had been refuted by experience; that it is now held by the English in greater esteem, and practised among them more extensively than ever it was before; and that the College thinks it to be highly salutary to the human race.[9]

The next major step forward, marking the beginning of a great increase in the popularity of inoculation, occurred as the result of a new method of treatment developed and refined between 1755 and 1761 by Robert Sutton, a surgeon at the Suffolk village of Kenton. Earlier English inoculators considered it necessary to make deep cuts with the lancet and to insert large amounts of material from mature pustules to produce large, freely suppurating, primary lesions in the belief that protection was not obtainable unless the patient suffered a pronounced smallpox attack. As a later inoculator pointed out 'patients (exclusive of many that died) had the disease so extremely heavy, that little difference was perceived between the natural Smallpox, and that conveyed by inoculation'.[10] All this was rejected by Sutton who reverted to the original Graeco-Turkish technique of superficial scarification using small amounts of lymph. Even more important was his use of 'unripe, crude or watery matter',[11] that is, lymph taken from a smallpox pustule in its early (vesicular) stage of development, usually about the fourth day, rather than from a mature pustule which was likely to be contaminated with a variety of organisms. As a result the severity of symptoms in inoculees was greatly reduced, as was the number of pustules, and the risk of a healthy patient dying from inoculation almost eliminated. In brief, the Suttonian method comprised treatment which was almost painless, relatively mild in its effects and which resulted in a greatly decreased number of pustules, thereby lessening subsequent disfigurement.

Although this new method was pioneered by Robert Sutton it was his second son Daniel[12] who was chiefly responsible for making it widely known. In the autumn of 1763, having learnt his father's method, Daniel set up his own practice at Ingatestone, an Essex village between Brentwood and Chelmsford. He continued to use his father's operational technique of superficial scarification with very small amounts of fresh lymph and a doctor who observed him at work in 1769 wrote

> Mr. *Sutton*, with his almost invisible quantity of matter on the point of a lancet, just raises the cuticle as little as possible, and his operation is finished, without plaister, or roller, or any sort of dressing at all[13]

The residential period for fee-paying patients was reduced from a month to a fortnight. The main feature of the stay was abstention from animal food, spices and fermented liquor, which were replaced by a diet of milk and fruit with the addition of mercury powder and purging salt. Open-air exercise was advocated and excess of any kind discouraged. All this, of course, followed on from the Suttons' belief that the cold method was an important part of successful treatment. In fact the residential régime for preparation and recovery was relatively unimportant in the success of the treatment but was a means whereby the Suttons and other inoculators could enhance their profits and they therefore encouraged popular belief in its importance. Nevertheless, it is probable that the Suttons actually believed it to be necessary until the highly successful results of a series of general inoculations in 1766 (when most of the patients were unprepared poor who returned to their own homes immediately after the operation) demonstrated otherwise. It did, however, serve the useful purpose of isolating infectious inoculees.

In the early 1760s there was a marked increase in the number of provincial doctors seeking a share in the lucrative business of inoculation. This gave rise to competition for custom and a reduction in fees. In the small port and summer resort of Wivenhoe the enterprising local doctor Thomas Tumner was inoculating by May 1762 and a year later had acquired 'a proper House for the purpose'. In order to encourage custom both for his sea-water bath and for inoculation, Tumner pointed out that Wivenhoe enjoyed a 'pleasant and healthful situation ... free from those unwholesome Fogs that attend most Sea Ports, and entirely free from the Small Pox'.[14] By November 1763 Baptist Spinluff, a surgeon in the populous village of Sible Hedingham had already had 'great Success ... in the Practice of Inoculation' having 'fitted up a House in the neatest Manner for that Purpose'. Patients stayed for a month and his fees were five guineas for ladies and gentlemen and four guineas for servants.[15] A year later he had reduced his charge for servants to three guineas.[16] Daniel Sutton began inoculating at Ingatestone in December 1763 and by 1764 the Chipping Ongar apothecary Mr Lenham had 'A Very convenient House, at a proper Distance' from the town 'for the Reception of such Persons as are willing to be inoculated', promising 'Just Care and Attendance, with all Necessaries (Tea and Sugar excepted)' at four guineas a head.[17] Spinluff's practice was well-established by the spring of 1765. His success

> has been so great, that he has never lost a Patient, notwithstanding the Variety of Subjects of all Ages and Constitutions which have been committed to his Care: The favourable Manner in which he conveys the Disease, and the Care taken to render every Accommodation agreeable will, he flatters himself, continue the great Encouragement he has received from the Publick.[18]

In the spring of 1765 Jonas Malden, a Maldon surgeon, apothecary and senior alderman of the borough, took up inoculation, having 'hired a convenient House ... about a Mile distant from the Town'. As a demonstration to the suspicious townsmen of Maldon his first eight patients included six members of his own family.[19] Five miles north of Chelmsford in the village of Great Waltham Mr Griffiths began inoculating at the end of 1765 or beginning of 1766. His 'first Sett of Patients', 26 in all, was so pleased with the treatment that Griffiths was able to include a testimonial from them when he advertised in the *Chelmsford Chronicle* in February 1766.[20]

In May 1766 the *Chelmsford Chronicle* carried advertisements for inoculation by six Essex doctors including Mr Menish of Chelmsford, Mr Wood of Danbury and Daniel Sutton. Halfway between Maldon and Chelmsford, at the village of Danbury, Mr Wood was already well-established and was practising 'with the greatest Care, Assiduity and Success, and on the most reasonable Terms'.[21] To readers of the *Chelmsford Chronicle* he announced on 16 May that

PERSONS are taken in for INOCULATION, on very reasonable Terms, at the Houses of DANIEL DANIELS, Farmer, at SANDON, and THOMAS WILSH at LITTLE BADDOW.

Mr. WOOD, Surgeon and Apothecary, at DANBURY, is engaged to inoculate at the abovesaid Houses; who has also handsome and commodious Apartments for Ladies and Gentlemen.

He takes this Opportunity of thanking his Friends for the great Encouragement they have given him, he having, at this Time, more than seventy Patients under his Care, from four Months old to the Age of Sixty and upwards

These newspaper advertisements probably represent only a small proportion of doctors carrying out inoculation by the mid 1760s, for it was stated that at Chelmsford in the summer of 1766 '*every Apothecary in the town was an Inoculator,* and had long practised round the neighbourhood'.[22]

All these inoculators had one thing in common, a desire to keep inoculation and the profits from it within the medical profession. Although as early as 1750 the *Gentleman's Magazine* carried a lengthy letter from a correspondent at Sherborne who 'Without any skill in physick or surgery' successfully inoculated five members of his family,[23] inoculations by laymen remained very uncommon in the pre-Suttonian era. As the treatment became increasingly commonplace from the early 1760s, however, the beginnings of an erosion of the exclusive rôle of doctors can be observed. In Essex in May 1766 the lucrative practices of inoculators like Sutton, Lenham and others were seriously threatened when *A Treatise on Inoculation*, price 2s. 6d., appeared, purporting to be 'a full and true Discovery of the method, as practised in ... Essex'. Its purpose was to enable anyone to inoculate 'themselves and others with the greatest Ease and Safety' and it included 'a true Recipe to make the Preparative Powder, Repellent Pills and Physic used in Inoculation'. Sufficient medicine for the treatment of one person went free with every copy, which the author claimed 'will in a great Measure ease the Contagion in those who do not chuse to be inoculated; or if they should catch it, will cause the prospects to be much more favourable'.[24] Not surprisingly established inoculators, and Sutton in particular, were horrified. Lenham was associated with the authorship but made a public denial and Sutton called it an 'absurd Pamphlet'.[25] On 23 May Sutton launched a vehement attack on the *Treatise* and addressing himself to the anonymous author described his medicines as being

> in many Respects, very dangerous ... As the Author ... is well
> known not to be of the Faculty, Mr Sutton advises him to confine
> himself within the limits of his humble Business, and not expose
> himself farther, as a Writer, or Pretender to Physic. But above all
> does he advise him not to acknowledge himself the Author of so
> base an Imposition, if he has any Regard for his reputation, and
> would avoid the Ridicule and Odium of the Public

The matter rumbled on for a few more weeks, with replies by the author to the attacks. At first the *Treatise* apparently enjoyed successful sales. In June it was announced that a second edition was available, but nothing was heard of it thereafter.[26] Three years later Essex doctors must have been especially annoyed when one of their own colleagues, the eccentric Dr John Cook of Leigh, expressed the opinion in the August 1769 issue of *The Town and Country Magazine* 'that any mother or nurse' might perform inoculation and gave advice as to 'The best and easiest way to perform the operation'.[27]

Although the complaints and warnings of professional inoculators were undermined by the generally successful results being achieved by old women and other amateur inoculators, the fears of professionals that a lucrative branch of their practice would be severely eroded by laymen or by families performing the operation themselves were much exaggerated and subsequently proved to be largely unfounded. The publicity given to the fortunes being made by inoculators like Daniel Sutton and Thomas Dimsdale in the 1760s undoubtedly attracted enterprising amateurs like the livery-servant 'belonging to a friend' of Dr William Watson, who 'left his master's service ... to practise inoculation'[28] so that in the last three decades of the century a good many lay people were carrying out inoculation. The easy availability of handbooks on inoculation, notably Thomas Dimsdale's *The Present Method of Inoculating for the Smallpox*, must also be held partly responsible for the proliferation of amateur inoculators. Their activities, however, were generally both small-scale and local and their patients confined to the labouring and poor classes.[29] Most were probably like John Dearsley, a Thorpe-le-Soken farmer, who in 1791 was warned by the parish officers to cease operating because he allowed his patients to leave while they were still infectious,[30] and it was the increasing tendency to regulate inoculation in towns and villages (a topic which will be discussed later in this chapter) that was largely responsible for controlling and restricting the activities of such amateurs. Professional inoculators worried by operators like Dearsley sometimes forestalled their activities by inoculating the very poor free of charge. For example, in October 1763 one of Robert Sutton's sons announced that he or his father was prepared to inoculate 'very poor People' in the neighbourhood of the Suffolk village of Ashfield without charge 'to prevent their putting themselves under illiterate and unskilful Persons, such as Farriers, &c. to the

Disgrace and Injury of the Practice'.[31]

In the second half of the eighteenth century the knowledge that infection could spread from patients undergoing inoculation to the non-immune population was almost universal. Although some inoculators, like Daniel Sutton, denied the possibility others, including some of the doctors who adopted the Suttonian system, notably Thomas Dimsdale of Hertford, continually issued warnings of the danger and advocated isolation.[32] Voices like Sutton's were increasingly in the minority so that when in March 1779 Benjamin Pugh stated that 'small-pox, in whatever manner produced, is infectious beyond a doubt, and should and ought therefore to be kept from the public as much as possible' it is unlikely that many would have disagreed with him. Pugh claimed to be 'among the first inoculators in England' and wrote with very considerable experience and authority, citing the case of Reginald Branwood of Writtle, carpenter, who died 4 May 1759 of confluent smallpox 'having taken the infection from persons inoculated in the same village'.[33] But far more worrying than the possibility of isolated deaths was the danger of an epidemic being caused by infection from inoculees. Indeed, Daniel Sutton was put on trial at Chelmsford Assizes in July 1766 on the charge of bringing infected patients to the county town on market days and thereby being responsible for starting a major outbreak earlier in the year.[34] Outside the medical profession nearly everyone knew or believed that patients undergoing inoculation were infectious and the knowledge was not confined to well-to-do or educated people. When Mary Tabor of Tollesbury 'an Idle and disorderly person, and of bad behaviour' stood trial at Essex Quarter Sessions in 1768 the charge was one of threatening to inoculate her children 'in order to spread the Distemper'.[35]

The widespread employment of inoculation during the epidemic of 1751-1753 brought the problem into sharp focus. Particular resentment and concern was expressed over country people coming into market towns where, as Kirkpatrick complained, 'without any medical Advice, and very little Consideration, they procure Inoculation from some Operator, too often as crude and thoughtless as themselves; congratulating each other after it over strong Liquor, and returning immediately to their ordinary Labour and Way of Living'.[36] As a result town authorities began taking steps to control and regulate inoculation while in some places the ordinary inhabitants 'threatened to demolish the houses where inoculation is performed'.[37] In the autumn of 1753 the editor of the *Gentleman's Magazine* commented that inoculation was now 'a matter of great dispute, whether it should be continued or not'.[38] At Chelmsford, where from the beginning of July 1752 to the beginning of the following April 290 people caught the disease out of which 95 died,[39] there is little doubt that inoculation was thought responsible for prolonging the outbreak. On 17 May notice was given that

All the Surgeons and Apothecaries in this Town have unanimously agreed not to Inoculate any Persons from this Time 'till October next; and that convenient Houses are already hired above a Mile from Chelmsford, for that Purpose; and that they

45

will inoculate no Person or Persons for the future, unless they
consent to be removed to such House or Houses.[40]

The reaction at Colchester, where the Corporation was suspended from 1741 to
1764, was stronger, notice being given on 28 March 1753 that 'If any one, after the
Date hereof shall take in any Person to be inoculated, they will be prosecuted'.[41]

The further increase in the popularity of inoculations in the 1760s was matched
by the growth of controls and regulations. At Colchester a number of the principal
inhabitants and traders announced in May 1762 that

> The practice of bringing People out of the Country into this
> Town to be inoculated for the SMALL-POX being very pre-
> judicial to the Town in many Respects, but especially to the
> Trade thereof, and as by this Practice the Distemper may be con-
> tinued much longer in the Town than it otherwise, in all pro-
> bability would, it is thought proper that this publick Notice
> should be given, that they are determined to prosecute any Person
> or Persons whomsoever, that shall hereafter bring into this Town,
> or who shall receive into their Houses in the Town, as Lodgers,
> any Person for that Purpose, with the utmost Severity that the
> Law will permit

They continued by stating that they had no wish to discourage 'a Practice so salutary
and beneficial to Mankind as Inoculation' and did not object to surgeons doing it so
long as it was confined to 'Houses properly situated for the Purpose'.[42] At
Debenham, two miles south-west of Robert Sutton's village of Kenton, in June
1763 the parishioners threatened to prosecute anyone performing inoculation
there.[43] Early in 1765 Jonas Malden had begun inoculating in an isolated house a
mile from the town of Maldon but had given it up by May because, as he explained,
'many of the Inhabitants ... disapprove of it, lest it may spread the Infection, and
hurt the Trade'.[44] A doctor in a small town well supplied with doctors could not
afford to risk his livelihood by alienating fellow townsmen and Malden had no
choice but to stop operating. As will be shown later in this chapter the townsmen of
Maldon never ceased to regard inoculation with great caution.

Towards the end of the eighteenth century rural parishes and villages were also
regulating inoculation. As in towns the chief consideration was to prevent the
spread of infection. When in 1795 Woodford vestry learned that William Carpenter
wished to have one of his children inoculated he was informed that 'if you persist in
such a Measure, the Small Pox not being in this Parish, we will immediately take
steps against you as the Law warrants'.[45] At Thorpe-le-Soken in 1791 John Dearsley
ignored a warning by the parish officers and was prosecuted at Essex Quarter
Sessions for keeping an inoculating house in the parish 'and inoculating Sundry
Persons therein and permitting them afterwards to go at large, with the Infection
upon them', having already 'been duly warned to the contrary'.[46]

Closely associated with the growing regulation of inoculation in towns and
villages was the development of mass or general inoculations of the poor paid for

out of the poor rates. Although the epidemic of 1751-1753 led to an upsurge in the popularity of inoculation private treatment was still an expensive process and beyond the means of most families. As a result it was chiefly the artisan, labouring and poor classes who were now at risk of the disease. An anonymous correspondent observed in the *Gentleman's Magazine* in November 1752

before it can come into general use, it must be done in a less expensive way. The charge of it, as it is now managed, must necessarily exclude a great part, nay I may say the greatest part of mankind, from the benefit of it. The poor in general are absolutely cut off from all share in it, except only those few, who can be so happy as to be admitted into ... the inoculating hospital, and the children of the Foundling hospital; which are the only places in the kingdom, so far as I know, where inoculation is performed upon the foot of charity ... And not only the very poor people, but multitudes of others, many farmers and tradesmen, cannot be at the expence of so much a head for their whole family, as is at present demanded, merely for the operation of inoculating, besides the other additional charges, which must necessarily accrue.[47]

The desirability of general inoculation was first expressed as early as 1737 when smallpox was 'raging in several large Towns'. In an essay in the *Gentleman's Magazine* the anonymous author set out the advantages and then commented

had a general Inoculation been in Use heretofore, none, at this Time, but the young ones, would have wanted it, and *Tamworth, Chipping Norton, Reading,* and other Towns that have had it almost a Year ... [would have] been free from it long ago.[48]

He continued by recommending that a general inoculation of infants should be carried out as soon as the disease made its appearance in a town. But the essay was too far ahead of its time and apart from an isolated general inoculation at Guildford, Surrey, in the 1740s,[49] its recommendations were not acted upon until the great epidemic of 1751-1753 when general inoculations were performed at Salisbury, Wiltshire (1751-1752), Bradford-on-Avon, Wiltshire (1752-1753)[50] and Blandford, Dorset (1753), where 309 people were inoculated.[51] These were followed in 1756 by the inoculation of the First Regiment of Foot Guards,[52] of 336 poor inhabitants of the small Gloucestershire market town of Wotton-under-Edge during an epidemic there[53] and in 1758 by a general inoculation at Beaminster, Dorset.[54]

Another eight years then passed before any further general inoculations were carried out. The next, in April 1766, took place at Blandford where an epidemic of a very malignant type had broken out in the first week of the month. A resolution was passed on 13 April for a general inoculation and a total of 384 people were treated, of whom '150 were poor people, for whom the parish paid the Operators'.[55] This was followed in May by the general inoculation of 487 inhabitants of the small market and port town of Maldon, of 249 people at Ewell, Surrey and of several hundred at Maidstone, Kent in July and August, all by Daniel Sutton.[56] In addition

Thomas Dimsdale performed a successful general inoculation of the poor in 1766 at his own town of Hertford which, like the Blandford and Maldon inoculations, effectively halted an epidemic,[57] while a Sussex doctor was conducting general inoculations in the Lewes area by March 1767.[58] The impact of these events was enormous. Any lingering doubts about the protective power of inoculation were dispelled and people realised that even epidemic smallpox could be brought under control. As the words of William Lipscomb's Oxford University prize poem for 1772, 'On the Beneficial Effects of Inoculation', proclaimed, the nymph of inoculation who 'Had oft on Turkey's plains the fiend subdued' now also protected 'The sacred beauties of Britannia's isle'.[59]

At this point it is appropriate to pause for a closer examination of events at Maldon in the years 1765-1806, when the townsmen refused to permit individual inoculations in the fear that infection could spread but used general inoculations to halt a series of epidemics. This highly cautious attitude first became apparent in the early part of 1765 when, as has been shown, the apothecary Jonas Malden had no choice but to abandon his plan to establish an inoculation practice.[60] But the townsmen were powerless to prevent the spread of the natural disease and less than a year later in the spring of 1766 smallpox, after being absent for many years, 'broke out violently' in the unprotected town, in the face of which opposition to inoculation crumbled. Although several people were dying daily the leading townsmen were more concerned that 'their market would be ruined, if the disease continued any time'.[61] An emergency general inoculation was agreed upon, a public subscription set up to defray the cost of treating the poor and in a single day late in May Daniel Sutton inoculated everyone there who had not already had smallpox, a total of 487 inhabitants representing between a quarter and a third of Maldon's population.[62] The patients were aged between one month and 80 years, 417 being classed as poor, the remaining 70 as tradespeople and gentry.[63] No-one died as a result of inoculation and three weeks later fewer than ten inhabitants still had the natural disease.[64] On 11 July a notice in the *Chelmsford Chronicle* by the bailiffs, vicars, churchwardens, overseers, surgeons and seven inhabitants announced that 'this Town is now entirely free from the Small-pox'.

The controversy broke out again in April 1774 when a child contracted smallpox and the local doctors proposed 'a general Inoculation through the Town'. But a meeting of the townsmen on 9 May 'divided more than three to one *against* a general Inoculation', those in opposition claiming it was unnecessary because 'no person had received the Infection: Therefore it is hoped that People will no longer be alarmed on that Account'. At the same time steps were taken to deter patients undergoing inoculation from entering the town, notice being given that

> As many unthinking People, under the Course of Inoculation, have very imprudently come to Maldon with Small-Pox upon them, the Gentlemen are *determined* to prosecute all such who shall offend for the future in that Manner. There will be persons appointed to look out especially on *Tuesday next*, which is the

Visitation Day at Maldon.[65]

Five years later, in the winter of 1778-1779, smallpox once again attained serious proportions in Essex and a second general inoculation, about which very little is known, took place at Maldon. In response to a request for information from Benjamin Pugh, now retired and living at the village of Great Baddow, eight miles west of Maldon, Dr Tomlinson of Maldon wrote on 19 May 1779

> I CANNOT give you a just account of the number inoculated and those who had the small-pox in the natural way, having never numbered them; but think I may safely pronounce them a thousand in and about Maldon. I don't know of but one who died by inoculation only[66]

The next mass inoculation took place early in 1788. The total number treated is not known but in All Saints, the smallest of the three Maldon parishes, 23 poor inhabitants were inoculated by three Maldon doctors (Jonas Malden, Richard Paxton and James Tomlinson) for which the parish paid 4s. a head.[67] Inoculating ceased on 28 March, a notice in the *Chelmsford Chronicle* signed by five Maldon doctors announcing that

> We the Surgeons employed to inoculate the Poor, and others, in this town ... for the Small-Pox, Give Notice, That we will not inoculate any person within the several parishes of All Saints, St Peter, or St Mary, in Maldon, after this day.[68]

Three infants from All Saints buried between 25 March and 6 April were stated to have died from 'a General Inoculation Smallpox', indicating that the inoculations were considered responsible for the deaths. Whether this was actually so must remain open to question but it does help to explain continuing local suspicion of the treatment.[69]

Following the outbreak of war with France in 1793 Maldon became a garrison town and suffered from a number of smallpox outbreaks which struck down both inhabitants and soldiers. Yet as late as April 1795 the three vestries jointly resolved 'Not to inoculate the Poor of this Town at this Time'.[70] The disease caused many deaths in the summer of that year but it was the epidemic which began in the summer of 1796 and continued throughout the autumn and the winter which finally forced a change in policy. On 30 January 1797 All Saint's and St Peter's vestries judged that

> it appeared absolutely necessary, that the Poor Inhabitants ... should be immediately Inoculated ... the Churchwardens and Overseers should authorise each Poor Inhabitant ... to apply to such of the resident Apothecaries ... as they best approve, it having been agreed by and with the ... Apothecaries, that they shall Inoculate and attend, such Poor persons at the rate of four shillings per head ... The whole expense ... shall be defrayed by an equal pound rate, on the inhabitants[71]

Once again inoculation was held responsible for deaths, this time in All Saints and

St Peter's parishes where three of the four fatalities between mid-February and early March attributed to this cause were infants.[72] Nevertheless the epidemic, which in common with most others by this date was especially severe among infants and young children, was ended by the summer and on 9 August notice was given 'that the Town of Maldon and its Environs, are entirely free from the Small-Pox, and have been so for some time past'.[73] A fifth general inoculation took place in the town in February 1806.[74]

By the early 1770s general inoculations like those at Newport in north-west Essex, 1772,[75] and Mistley, 1773,[76] were becoming commonplace in country towns and populous villages. That at Newport, however, was somewhat unusual for it was not the result of an outbreak of natural smallpox. Instead early in 1772 nearly half the labouring and poor families were inoculated on a haphazard basis by two old women in the parish. Not surprisingly, concern was expressed by the parish officers and complaints voiced by farmers and principal inhabitants at this 'imprudent example'.[77] With the support and encouragement of Percy Wyndham O'Brien, Earl of Thomond, owner of the Shortgrove estate and chief ratepayer, a systematic general inoculation was agreed at the beginning of March. The bailiff of the estate, William Smith, together with one of the parish officers, Mr Livings, then made a survey of the families of labourers and poor 'to enquire who was already innoculated and how many remained that was willing to be done'.[78] This revealed that about 130 inhabitants had already been inoculated and that about a further 140 were willing to undergo the treatment. Only four families refused the offer 'so they must take their Chance'.[79] Although the inoculations performed by the two old women had apparently been completely successful it was not thought prudent to employ either of them 'as in case of any accident it might occasion great reflections to be cast upon the Parish'.[80] Instead it was agreed that Mr Welch of Stansted Mountfitchet should undertake the work for 20 guineas and the inoculations were carried out in the second week of March. On 15 March Smith reported to his employer that the inoculees were progressing 'as well as can be expected'. Wood had been distributed and three sheep from the Shortgrove flock slaughtered so that each poor family could have 'a little piece of Mutton to make Broth and firing'.[81] A fortnight later Smith reported that all the inoculees had come through the treatment 'except a sucking Child belong[in]g to y[ou]r Lordships Shepard who has dyed'.[82] This Newport evidence is particularly important for it reveals an overwhelming vote of confidence in inoculation by the labouring and poor classes, so that within the space of a few weeks all but a very small minority of the inhabitants had been immunised.

Most general inoculations, however, were used to curb isolated epidemics such as those at Hertford in 1770 and 1774. Thomas Dimsdale's accounts of these and other general inoculations conducted by him were published in 1776 in his *Thoughts on General and Partial Inoculations*,[83] in which he also set out what he considered to be the ideal method and suggested

> That every parish (with the exception of such large places as
> should be thought too populous to be included) should be enjoin-

ed to offer Inoculation to all their poor who should be willing to admit of it; that the patients and their families should be maintained during their illness; that the person employed to inoculate should have had some education in medicine as physician, surgeon, or apothecary; and that once in five years the same offer should be renewed, leaving the time of year and other circumstances to the option of the parish.[84]

This provided a further stimulus so that in 1778 Dimsdale was able to observe that general inoculation had been widely practised

within the last two years in the counties of Bedford, Bucks, Herts, and Cambridge, and others contiguous to London ... To such extent has this practice been carried, that I imagine the number must amount to many thousands.[85]

Later in the same year a correspondent to the *Gentleman's Magazine* remarked that

The success of general inoculations in country villages or towns is not new ...

The great advantage of these inoculations is, that they are general; for the few who decline the operation may easily secure themselves by proper precautions ...

In a general inoculation it is obvious, the infection cannot be "spread", because there are no objects to receive it; and where all have had the disease, it must certainly be "eradicated".[86]

The knowledge that inoculation could provide last-minute protection and immunity when an epidemic threatened also had the effect of reducing people's fear of catching the natural disease. At the small Northamptonshire town of Oundle smallpox broke out at the beginning of 1778 and by 24 January, in the words of the local diarist John Clifton, 'almost half the people are preparing for inoculation which is intended to go forward Directly'.[87] By 31 January

Nothing is talked of here now but the Small Pox and instead of people being afraid of the Dreadful Affliction as they used to be some while ago, they seem to make nothing of it now but a piece of Fun and a Holiday.

The lack of concern, even lighthearted attitude, of the inhabitants was similar to that observed by Lady Mary Wortley Montagu in Turkey in 1717 and was given vivid expression in this rhyme

Poll Muckason Joins us to Night,
She'll tip us a Jorum or Diddle,
Small Poxy is all our Delight,
And we'll foot it away to ye Fiddle.
Fol lol de rol lor vol lol lol—
And when the Small pox we have got
Not one shall appear on our Faces
Forty five S[rs] we thinks a good lot

And they all shall come out in our A...s
Fol lol.

By 23 May only one inhabitant had the disease and Clifton recorded that 'we are now clear again and nobody hardly ever mentions the Small Pox'.[88]

The reappearance of smallpox in Essex about this time prompted Benjamin Pugh to join the discussion. Now in retirement, he nevertheless maintained a keen interest in medical advances and wrote to the *Gentleman's Magazine* on 20 March 1779

> When the practice of inoculation was first introduced, it had many and great difficulties to encounter; and even now, though its great success has sufficiently appeared and proved its utility, it is wonderful how it has been neglected by the common people for the last 7 or 8 years. It seems as much forgot in many parts of this kingdom as though it has never been known, until the natural small-pox comes ... and awakens them out of their lethargy. The Faculty, then, are hurried into inoculation, perhaps, with too much precipitancy, and are under the necessity oftentimes of complying with the impatience of the people ...

> In the partial manner inoculation has been, and still continues to be practiced, many suffer who will not submit to it, or who cannot have time and opportunity to avail themselves of its advantages. The full benefit of it cannot be properly reaped from it till it is made general, as a few years produce such a number of fresh subjects. — It is surely, then a national concern, and one of the first magnitude.

> The royal family, nobility, and people of fortune, have now their children inoculated at proper ages; the people too in middle life inoculate pretty generally; and the poor (seeing so many instances of the happy success of it) are every where desirous of being inoculated as soon as the natural small-pox begins to rage near them. Would it not, then, be highly expedient that a law should pass to oblige church-wardens to cause the children of the poor to be inoculated about a certain age? Would not this be a means of diffusing the blessings of this discovery to its full extent? ... Many advantages would attend such a salutary law ... besides relieving the people from one of the most dreadful diseases that human nature knows: the industrious farmer would go to market with peace and safety; the soldier and sailor do service to their country without fear of being cut off in prime of life ... and nations abroad would trade with Englishmen with more freedom when the fear of being surprised by this destructive disease was removed. In short, should this scheme of general inoculation take place, seamed faces, blind eyes, and such disfigurements, would rarely be seen[89]

Although Pugh's scheme for the compulsory free inoculation of poor children was never realised there was a marked increase in general inoculations in the years which followed, while in his own county of Essex the widespread reappearance of smallpox in the winter of 1778-1779 led to a revival of the practice. In the market towns, however, decisions to inoculate the poor had the economic incentive of the protection of trade, which the presence of smallpox could ruin. One such market town was Witham, five miles north of Maldon, where smallpox broke out at Easter 1778. Many of the better-off inhabitants were privately inoculated in their own houses but it was not until December, by which time the disease had 'spread throughout the parish',[90] that the 'gentlemen of the parish' determined 'to cause the poor in general to be inoculated'.[91] On 14 December their decision was ratified in vestry when it was agreed 'that it is absolutely necessary, that the Poor ... should be forthwith inoculated; at the common Charge of the ... Parish'.[92] The inoculations began immediately and within a week more than a thousand people had been treated 'without any previous preparation whatever'.[93] The whole process was completed by the end of January with only three fatalities directly attributed to inoculation. In a letter to Pugh giving details of the general inoculation the Witham surgeon John Heatherly concluded with the remark that 'so salutary a measure as a general inoculation (from the great success it has met with) must appear very plain to every unprejudiced person'.[94] Later in the eighteenth century there is evidence to suggest that Witham made inoculation a condition of residence for non-immune immigrants. For example, when James Lester, yeoman, moved with his family from Rayleigh early in 1795 all four children were inoculated and were reported by the Witham overseers on 5 March to be 'doing very well'.[95] Other places in Essex which inoculated their poor in the smallpox outbreak of 1778-1779 included Maldon and the rural parish of Great Chishall in the extreme north-west of the county.[96]

Further general inoculations took place in Essex towns and villages in 1785, including the rural parish of Great Warley, near Brentwood, where on 2 October the vestry 'a Greed that the Overseer Should have all Such Poor as Chose to be Enoculated to be dun at the Parish Exspence'.[97]

General inoculations were now commonplace in villages and market towns throughout the country, the eminent Dr John Haygarth of Chester observing in 1785 that 'whole villages in this neighbourhood, and many other parts of Britain, have been inoculated with one consent'.[98] Rural parishes, many with small scattered populations, were also adopting the practice to protect their poor inhabitants. The inoculations at Great Chishall in 1778-1779 and Great Warley in 1785 were followed in November 1787 by Rawreth vestry which resolved

> that Edmd Taylor the present Overseer, shall have all the poor that are living in Rayleigh and in the poor house at Rawreth, Inoculated, and further agree that Mr. Wm. Dobson of Rayleigh shall Inoculate them, and for so doing and giving them all proper attendances and finding them all with suitable mediciens we agree to allow him five shillings pr head.[99]

53

In the late 1790s smallpox was once again widespread in Essex, as a result of which there was a further increase in general inoculations. Dr Tomlinson of Maldon inoculated 20 Woodham Ferrers paupers for 2s. 6d. a head in 1797[100] and when the disease reached serious proportions at Canewdon in the winter of 1798-1799 the vestry resolved on 11 February 1799 'that Mr Swain shall inoculate the Poor of Canewdon who undertakes it at 5 shillings per head'.[101] The poor of the small fishing village and port of South Benfleet were inoculated in June 1799,[102] while in the populous parish of East Ham in the same year Robert Cook was employed to inoculate 70 poor inhabitants at 5s. a head.[103]

At the beginning of the eighteenth century it was becoming common for parishes to enter into annual contracts with local doctors to treat the sick poor and by the end of the century all but the very smallest and poorest parishes had made such arrangements. The increasing popularity of inoculation which gradually changed the doctors' rôle from treaters to preventors of smallpox is reflected in the growing number of contracts which specifically excluded inoculation. Instead, vestries preferred to pay for occasional individual or general inoculations as circumstances demanded, thereby retaining control of inoculation policy in so far as it related to the poor. For doctors additional payments for inoculation could be very lucrative and a welcome enhancement to their salaries. Examples of the exclusion of inoculation are commonplace and have been found for many Essex parishes including Colne Engaine, 1747-1778,[104] High Laver, 1753-1755,[105] Great Coggeshall from 1774,[106] Thundersley, 1787-1796[107] and Canewdon, 1788-1798.[108] Examples of overseers' payments to doctors for inoculation are similarly commonplace and provide evidence not only of general but also of occasional inoculations of individuals or families. Payments for such occasional inoculations have been noted for the parishes of Theydon Mount, 1772-1793,[109] Roydon from 1779,[110] Little Parndon from 1787[111] and Thundersley, 1795, when the overseers paid 10s. 6d. for the inoculation of Mrs Williams' children.[112] *Per capita* payments to doctors ranged from about 1s. received by Dr Tweed of Bocking when he inoculated 500 of the poor there in November 1790,[113] to the quite exceptional half guinea at Barking in 1788.[114] Most fees, however, were in the range of 2s. 6d. to 5s. with something around 4s. as an average.

The logical continuation of reduced smallpox mortality by inoculation would have been the eradication of the disease. Indeed, this proposition was advanced as early as 1767 by Dr Matthew Maty, physician and Principal Librarian to the British Museum. In a paper 'The Advantages of Early Inoculation' he recommended the inoculation of babies as soon as possible after birth at a time when half the infants in London died before the end of their third year. By making infant inoculation universal he thought smallpox could be extinguished, for

> When once all the adults susceptible of the infection should either have received it or be dead without suffering from it, the very want of the variolous matter would put a stop to both the natural and artificial smallpox. Inoculation then would cease to be

necessary, and therefore be laid aside.[115]

The proposition of eradication by inoculation was taken up in 1774 by two German physicians, Dr Krause of Leipzig and Dr Frederick Casimir of Mannheim. In September 1775 the *Gentleman's Magazine* reported that

> While the opposers of inoculation have had the mortification to see almost all the able physicians of *Europe* declaring themselves more and more in favour of this practice, new subjects of grief and offence are preparing for them. At least, two *German* physicians have undertaken to prove, that the extirpation of the small pox ... is very possible. Dr. Krause, an eminent physician at *Leipsick* ... has ventured to maintain, that the smallpox ... which almost all men must undergo once in their lives, might very easily be prevented ... Dr. Casimir ... encouraged by the example of Dr. Krause ... undertakes to prove ... it is possible to extirpate the small-pox[116]

English doctors who followed Maty in appreciating the full potential of inoculation included Benjamin Pugh, John Haygarth and the Leeds surgeon James Lucas, the first named adopting a forceful stance as early as 1779 by advocating legislation for the compulsory inoculation of children with provisions for the censure of 'those who should, through obstinacy, singularity, or, as they might pretend, scruples of conscience, oppose its injunctions'.[117] This proposal was then adopted and modified by Haygarth, who had founded the Chester Small-Pox Society in 1778 and been instrumental in establishing separate fever wards at Chester Infirmary in 1783, the first in a provincial English infirmary. Having experienced considerable success in curtailing the disease at Chester he remarked in 1785

> there might be safely and successfully founded a general law to promote inoculation, or, what would be incomparably more easy ... to establish regulations that would *exterminate the Small-pox from Great Britain*. To attain so important a blessing would require the general, united and persevering exertions of our legislators and magistrates, as well as the medical faculty. It would employ much time and labour, executed with assiduous zeal, care and attention. No service could deserve to be more amply rewarded, if we estimate its value by the multitude of lives it would preserve, and the infinite variety of human misery it would prevent.[118]

Haygarth's opinions were endorsed by Lucas who wrote in 1789

> There is no febrile contagion so well understood as that of the small-pox, nor any country where the means of preventing its fatality have been more successfully employed than in this island. However sanguine it may appear, I have, with my worthy and intelligent friend Dr. Haygarth, little doubt that the disorder might be so far eradicated as never to prevail[119]

Four years later in 1793 Haygarth drew on his vast experience of inoculation and the Chester Small-Pox Society's rules for quarantine for his more detailed recommendations in *A Sketch of a Plan to Exterminate the Casual Small-Pox from Great Britain and to introduce General Inoculation.* The hypothesis that inoculation could have eradicated smallpox was, in the event, prevented from being put to the test by the introduction of vaccination at the close of the eighteenth century. Instead the next forty years were to be marked by controversy over the merits of the two methods of immunisation which ended with the banning of inoculation in 1840.

It has been shown that as the second half of the eighteenth century progressed a rising proportion of the population was given immunity from smallpox by inoculation and that this process was dramatically accelerated as mass or general inoculations became commonplace. The non-immune proportion of the population was both declining and increasingly made up of children and the potential breeding ground for smallpox was steadily contracting. In the remainder of this chapter it will be demonstrated that although smallpox remained unconquered at the end of the century both its incidence and mortality were very substantially reduced.

Eighteenth-century observers all agreed that very few people who were not inoculated escaped the disease, although a small minority did not have it until old age. An essay in the *Gentleman's Magazine* in 1737 expressed the opinion that 'All Mankind (very few excepted)' was 'once in Life liable to the Small-Pox',[120] while an editorial comment in 1747 claimed that 'the small-pox is a more general distemper than any other ... few escape being affected thereby one time or other'.[121] A correspondent to the *Magazine* estimated in 1752 that only 'five in a hundred all their lives escape it'.[122] Dr Angelo Gatti, whose vast knowledge of smallpox and inoculation was based on nearly half a century of observation on the European mainland, wrote in the 1760s

> It is certain, there are some who never have it; whole families are
> free from it for many generations; and it has been observed, that
> upon a hundred persons dying of old age, five or six had escaped
> it, though equally exposed to their contemporaries. Inoculators
> have met with much the same proportion of fruitless attempts.[123]

Gatti's estimate was confirmed in 1778 by Haygarth who calculated that one person in 20 was incapable of being infected.[124] Benjamin Pugh, writing in 1779 with the benefit of a lifetime's experience of dealing with smallpox in central Essex, believed there was 'scarcely an instance to be produced, in town or village, where any escaped the infection before inoculation was in use'.[125] It is clear from these contemporary observations that smallpox was almost universal among the uninoculated and it is postulated that most of the very small minority who escaped it enjoyed biological immunity.

Before moving on to assess the fatality rate of the natural disease in England some figures derived from Essex examples will be examined. In an epidemic at Dedham in 1724, 339 people caught the disease, of whom 106 died, giving a fatality rate of 31.3 per cent.[126] The population at the time was unlikely to have been much in excess of 1,000 and may well have been slightly less.[127] In round figures, therefore, the disease attacked about one third and killed about one tenth of the population within a year. In the same year smallpox was responsible for the vast majority of the 114 burials recorded at Witham, where the population in 1723 was 'about 270 families' or about 1,200 people.[128] At Wivenhoe, which had a population of about 700 at the beginning of the eighteenth century, 49 inhabitants died from the disease in 1726[129] and subsequent epidemics resulted in 38 smallpox burials in 1762-1763 and 23 in 1766-1767.[130] The coastal parish of St Osyth suffered a serious epidemic in 1737-1738. The population at the time was probably in the order of 700[131] and the average number of burials for the four years 1733-1736 was 31. The epidemic began in June 1737, the first smallpox death occurring on the 28th. Between then and the end of April 1738, when the epidemic ceased, there were 86 burials.[132] Although the number who died from smallpox is not given a figure of 70 is postulated, in other words about 10 per cent. of the population. At Chelmsford between July 1752 and April 1753 there were 290 cases of which 95 resulted in death, giving a fatality rate of 33 per cent. Chelmsford's population at this date was about 2,300, so smallpox attacked about 13 per cent. and killed just over four per cent. of the inhabitants within nine months.[133] In contrast, the parish of Stisted with a population of 588 in 1752 escaped lightly, having only 21 cases with one fatality.[134] At Rayleigh there were 29 burials recorded between January and August 1753 of which 25 were smallpox victims.[135] Finally, at Witham, 51 cases with 15 deaths in 1778-1779 represent a fatality rate of 29 per cent.[136]

The statistics for Dedham, Chelmsford, Stisted and Witham taken together suggest an Essex fatality rate of about 31 per cent. during the years 1724-1779, but the sample is small and a more comprehensive assessment is obtainable from the epidemic statistics for 32 towns and villages in the years 1721-1731 compiled by Dr Thomas Short. These show that of 13,192 cases 2,264 ended in death, giving a fatality rate of 17.2 per cent.

Table 2   Censuses of Smallpox Epidemics in England, 1721-1731[137]

Place	Date	Cases	Fatalities	Fatalities expressed as percentages of cases
Halifax	1721-22	276	43	15.9
Rochdale	,,	177	38	21.4
Leeds	,,	792	189	23.8
Halifax parish towards Bradford	1722	297	59	19.9
Halifax parish another part	,,	268	28	10.4
Bradford	,,	129	36	27.9

57

Wakefield	,,	418	57	13.6
Ashton-under-Lyne and two neighbouring villages	,,	279	56	20.0
Macclesfield	,,	302	37	12.2
Stockport	,,	287	73	25.4
Hatherfield	,,	180	20	11.1
Chichester	,,	994	168	16.9
Haverfordwest	,,	227	52	22.9
Barstand, Ripponden, Sorby and part of Halifax parish 4 miles from the town	,,	230	38	16.5
Bolton	1723	406	89	21.6
Ware	,,	612	72	11.7
Salisbury	,,	1244	165	13.2
Romsey, Hants.	,,	913	143	15.6
Havant	1723	264	61	23.1
Bedford	,,	786	147	18.4
Aynho, near Banbury	1723-24	133	25	18.8
Shaftesbury	1724	660	100	15.1
Dedham	,,	339	106	31.3
Plymouth	,,	188	32	17.2
Stratford-on-Avon	,,	562	89	15.8
Bolton-le-Moor	,,	341	64	18.8
Cobham	,,	105	20	19.0
Dover	1725-26	503	61	12.1
Deal	,,	362	33	9.1
Kempsey, near Worcester	1726	73	15	20.5
Uxbridge	1727	140	51	36.4
Hastings	1730-31	705	97	13.7
Totals		13,192	2,264	17.2

For the later period the statistics of eight epidemics in the years 1740-1783 involving some 5,610 cases with 968 deaths give a fatality rate of 17.3 per cent.

Table 3   Censuses of Smallpox Epidemics in England, 1740-1783

Place	Date	Cases	Fatalities	Fatalities expressed as percentages of cases
Northampton[138]	1740	899	132	14.7
Northampton[139]	1747	821	126	15.3
Chelmsford[140]	1752-53	290	95	32.8

Salisbury[141]	1753	1,244	165	13.3
Chester[142]	1774	1,385	202	14.6
Witham[143]	1778	51	15	29.4
Leeds[144]	1781	462	130	28.1
Huddersfield[145] and neighbourhood	1783	458	103	22.5
Totals		5,610	968	17.3

The mean fatality rate of 17.2 per cent. derived from the examples in Tables 2 and 3 shows that in English epidemics during the years 1721-1783 slightly more than one case in six was fatal. This conforms fairly well to the findings of contemporary observers. James Jurin calculated in the 1720s that 18 per cent. of all cases were fatal,[146] and in 1747 Charles Perry stated that 'at an Average ... at least one sixth Part die of it, of such as take the Disease in the natural Way'.[147] A correspondent to the *Gentleman's Magazine* in 1752 claimed 'It appears, from the moderate computation of the experienced and impartial, that a fifth part of those die who have the small-pox in a natural way',[148] while Daniel Sutton, writing at the end of the century, concluded that 'in the natural way of receiving the smallpox, one patient at least dies out of five or six'.[149]

In fact the fatality rate was likely to have been even higher, for fulminating smallpox which was always fatal remained unrecognised as smallpox until the next century.[150] Other forms of smallpox were commonly misdiagnosed, often as chickenpox or measles, and examples of probable or suspected incorrect diagnosis are frequently to be found in parish burial registers. In December 1753, at the end of the nationwide epidemic of 1751-1753, the vicar of Finchingfield commented that 'An Endemical Fever raged this year',[151] while two deaths at Thundersley early in the nineteenth century attributed to 'mortification' at a time when smallpox was prevalent in the parish may in reality have been cases of malignant confluent smallpox.[152] In addition, a small minority of lives was claimed by secondary infection following recovery from the smallpox attack.

After 1750 the level of smallpox mortality began to decline as the practice of inoculation became more popular but it was the adoption of mass or general inoculation in a growing number of towns and villages which was to have the main impact. The first person to write at any length on the relationship between inoculation, smallpox mortality and population was the clergyman, statistician and political economist, the Revd John Howlett. Born in 1731, he graduated from St John's College, Oxford, in 1755 and was vicar of Great Dunmow and Great Baddow from 1771 until his death in 1804.[153] Howlett also spent much time at Maidstone and therefore had personal experience of the situation in Kent as well as Essex, while at Baddow his parishioners included the advocate of inoculation, Benjamin Pugh. In his first published work, *An Examination of Dr. Price's Essay on the Population of England and Wales*, which appeared in 1781, Howlett expressed the opinion that the diminished mortality in country towns and villages appears to be chiefly owing to the salutary practice of inoculation ... as soon as this disorder makes its appearance, inoculation takes place amongst all ranks of people, the rich and poor, from either choice or necessity, almost instantly have recourse to it; and where two or three hundred used to be carried to their graves in the course of a few months, there are now perhaps not above 20 or 30.[154]

The *Examination* includes information about the Kent parish of Great Chart, two miles west of Ashford, where 'almost 100' of the 192 burials in the 20 years 1688-1707 'were occasioned by the smallpox; whereas in 20 years beginning with 1760, there appears to have been only 4 or 5 who died of that disorder'.[155]

Following the publication of his *Examination* Howlett began a nationwide demographic inquiry and in September 1782 described how

during the last twelve months I have sent out between 3 and 4000 written letters and printed papers to the clergy in different parts of the kingdom, in which I have ventured to solicit not only register extracts for different periods in their respective parishes, but likewise, wherever conveniently attainable, actual surveys of the people[156]

He also sought other 'curious, perhaps important information', including references to inoculation.[157] Using some of this information in a pamphlet *Observations on the Increased Population ... of Maidstone,* which he published anonymously in 1782, Howlett asserted his belief that inoculation was responsible for the decline in smallpox mortality there and attached particular significance to the general inoculation conducted by Daniel Sutton in 1766.[158]

In the 30 years before that date smallpox deprived the town of between five and six hundred of its inhabitants; whereas in the 15 or 16 years that have elapsed since that general inoculation it has occasioned the deaths of only about 60. Ample and satisfactory evidence of the vast benefit the town has received from the salutary invention[159]

Similar patterns were to be found 'in the kingdom at large' and 'may ... be ascribed ... principally and chiefly to that distinguished blessing of providence, inoculation'.[160] Howlett wrote this in 1782. Twenty years later the decline in smallpox mortality was even more marked, as the Maidstone figures in Table 4 demonstrate.

Table 4   **Smallpox Mortality at Maidstone, 1740-1799**[161]

Date	Total number of deaths	Smallpox deaths	Smallpox deaths as percentages of all deaths
1740-51	1,594	260	16.3
1752-63	1,616	202	12.5
1764-75	1,798	76	4.2
1776-87	1,992	122	6.1
1788-99	2,308	31	1.3

In the remaining years of the century other writers not only confirmed Howlett's conclusion that inoculation had reduced smallpox mortality dramatically but additionally regarded it as the main reason for the great increase in the population of England and Wales after 1750. Arthur Young commenting in 1781 on the rising population and especially the 'rapid state of progression' since 1770 'could find nothing to which it can be owing, unless the general prevalence of inoculation, which certainly has been attended with a very great effect'.[162] By 1788 Dr John Heysham had reached the conclusion that inoculation had

> greatly contributed to the increase of population, not only in Carlisle, but likewise in the county of Cumberland. In the year 1779, when the lower class of inhabitants were extremely averse to this salutary discovery, no fewer than 90 persons died of natural smallpox; whereas only 151 have died during the eight succeeding years; which is, upon an average, not quite 19 in each year[163]

Heysham also pointed out that since the opening of the Carlisle Dispensary, 1 July 1782, 'the poor have enjoyed the privilege of having their children inoculated; an advantage which they have in general with great readiness embraced'.[164] Eight years later, in January 1796, a correspondent to the *Gentleman's Magazine* wrote

> The increase of people within the last 25 years is visible to every observer; and is to be accounted for on a principle irrefragably true ...
> Inoculation is the mystic spell that has produced this wonder ...
> It is now 30 years since the Suttons, and others under their instruction had practiced their skill in inoculation upon half the kingdom, and had reduced the risk of death to the chance of one in 2000. Hence the great increase in people[165]

Another correspondent writing in March 1803 was equally certain that inoculation had produced the rise in population, for the reduction in smallpox deaths 'alone would account for our increasing numbers, without perplexing ourselves for any other cause'.[166]

In attempting to test the validity of these statements it is necessary to give consideration to several factors as yet undiscussed, including the regional and town-size variations in the application of general inoculations, the age-specific distribution of smallpox fatality, the age-specific distribution of smallpox before and after the introduction of general inoculations and the completeness of general inoculations.

It has been shown that general inoculation was pioneered in small and medium-sized market towns in south and south-east England. The practice then spread to villages and rural parishes and, with time lags, to other regions of the country. However, because it took an epidemic to persuade most vestries or town authorities to pay for the protection of the poor the dates of first general inoculation, even in south and south-east England, exhibit considerable variation between places of comparable size. In large towns the situation was very different, for here inoculation generally did not achieve the same degree of popularity nor have much impact. At Chester epidemics in 1774 (when the population was 14,713) and 1777 failed to persuade the common people of its benefits, and in 1793 John Haygarth wrote that the same prejudice against inoculation and fatalistic attitude towards smallpox

> probably prevails in other towns especially in those which are so
> large as perpetually to nourish the distemper, by a quick succes-
> sion of infants as constantly to supply fresh subjects for
> infection.[167]

In small towns and villages on the other hand Haygarth thought 'the young generation grow up to have consciousness of the danger before they are attacked by the dreadful disease'.[168] At Newcastle as late as 1792 there was still 'a great and general prejudice against ... inoculation' among the lower classes, some of the objections here rather surprisingly being on religious grounds.[169]

Using nineteenth and twentieth-century evidence earlier writers have already established the 'U' curve principle to illustrate the higher levels of smallpox fatality among the very young and the aged. The only eighteenth-century statistics known to give fatalities as a proportion of cases in separate age groups are those relating to the epidemic in the Northamptonshire village of Aynho in 1723-1724 where the overall fatality rate was 19 per cent.

Table 5   Smallpox Fatality at Aynho, 1723-1724[170]

Age in years	Number of cases	Number of fatalities	Fatalities expressed as percentages of cases
0-5	13	3	23
6-10	15	1	7
11-15	33	3	9
16-20	14	1	7
21-30	25	6	24
31-40	12	3	25
41-50	10	4	40
over 50	10	4	40

These figures of age-specific fatality conform fairly well to patterns established from nineteenth-century sources, demonstrating the high vulnerability of children in their first five years and the much reduced fatality between the ages of six and twenty which Creighton thought was 'according to the experience of all times'.[171] The same marked drop in fatality after the age of five was experienced in unvaccinated cases in the Metropolitan Asylums Board's hospitals between 1867 and 1872 where the overall fatality was also 19 per cent.

Table 6   **Age-Specific Fatality of Smallpox in London, 1867-1872[172]**

Age	Fatalities expressed as percentages of cases
Under 5	52
5-10	26
10-20	9
20-30	17
30-40	24
40-50	29
50-60	28
over 60	20

The age-group distribution of smallpox varied from place to place, depending to a large degree on the frequency of outbreaks. In places where it was endemic it was almost wholly a children's disease. Nearly all native inhabitants of London had it by the age of seven, while at Chester, where it remained endemic until the 1780s, 180 out of a total of 202 fatalities in the epidemic of 1774 were in children under the age of five and the remaining 22 in children aged between five and ten years.[173] Three years later at Chester all 136 fatalities were in children under the age of eight, 129 being six years and under.[174] At the Ayrshire weaving town of Kilmarnock 563 out of a total of 613 fatalities in the years 1728-1762 were among the under fives, the mean age of smallpox death being 2.62 years,[175] while at the expanding Lancashire industrial town of Warrington in 1773 smallpox killed 209, of which 197 were in the 0 to 5 years age group, the remainder being aged 6 to 10 years.[176] It is unclear whether smallpox was endemic at Kilmarnock and Warrington. If it was not then the visitations must have been very frequent. For places where smallpox was not endemic there are no known satisfactory statistics for the period before general inoculations began to alter the pattern. Existing evidence, however, supports the logical assumption that both the proportion of non-immune inhabitants and the age-range of potential sufferers should increase as the intervals between visitations lengthened. The best evidence known is from Aynho where 132 inhabitants out of a total population of about 350 caught the disease in the epidemic of 1723-1724. That such a high proportion should have been susceptible points to an interval of several years at least since the previous visitation and this was

63

reflected in the age-group distribution of sufferers.

Table 7   Age-Group Distribution of Smallpox Cases at Aynho, 1723-1724[177]

Age	Number of cases	Cases expressed as percentages of total number of cases
0-5	13	9.9
6-10	15	11.4
11-15	33	25.0
16-20	14	10.6
21-25	16	12.1
26-30	9	6.8
31-40	12	9.1
41-50	10	7.6
51-60	4	3.0
61-70	4	3.0
over 70	2	1.5
Total	132	

The high number of sufferers in the 11-15 group is somewhat puzzling, but the pattern is otherwise very much as would be expected in a village community. At Wivenhoe where, like Aynho, smallpox was not endemic 35 epidemic-smallpox burials were recorded between 27 April 1762 and 16 February 1763. The population at this time was likely to have been in the region of 800.

Table 8   Ages of Fatalities in Wivenhoe Epidemic, 1762-1763[178]

Age	Number of fatalities
'infants'	10
under 10	6
10-15	2
16-20	2
21-30	7
31-40	3
40-56	3
unknown	2

These figures, unsatisfactory because the number of cases is unknown therefore making the calculation of fatality rates impossible, nevertheless show the greatest number of deaths to have been among the very young.

General inoculations made radical changes to these patterns of vulnerability, incidence and fatality. Before considering such changes it is necessary to assess the level of immunity achieved by general inoculations. At Maldon in May 1766 everyone in the town who had not already had smallpox was inoculated, while at Newport in 1772 only four families declined the offer of free treatment. This picture of completeness or very near completeness is confirmed by evidence from other English towns and villages.

Table 9   Completeness of General Inoculations

Place	Date	Numbers inoculated	Total population	Numbers inoculated expressed as percentages of non-immune inhabitants
Maldon[179]	1766	487	about 1,610	100
Newport[180]	1772	270	about 500 (663 in 1801)	about 96
Irthlingborough,[181] Northants.	1778	'upwards of Five Hundred'	811 in 1801	unknown
Brighton[182]	1786	1,887	3,620	100
Lewes[183]	1794	2,890	4,909 in 1801	unknown
Dursley,[184] Gloucs.	1797	1,475	2,379 in 1801	unknown

Although the exact extent to which the non-immune were inoculated at Irthlingborough, Lewes and Dursley is unknown the proportion, if not complete, was clearly very high. Even if they were not in agreement most poor inhabitants of a town or village probably preferred participation in a general inoculation to refusal whereby they ran a high risk of contracting smallpox from the inoculees. As William Smith remarked in March 1772 of the Newport families who refused the treatment, 'they must take their Chance as there wont be two Houses together which wont be infected'.[185] On the whole therefore general inoculations seem to have been well organised and comprehensive. A notable exception was an incomplete general inoculation at Bedford in 1778 when 1,100 people were treated in one week. 250 non-immune inhabitants then contracted the disease and 'at least' 59 died.[186] But experiences such as this appear to have been unusual and Dimsdale, discussing the subject in 1778, concluded that 'the extensive practice of general Inoculations ... for the most part has been conducted properly, that is to say, every one has been inoculated, or retired from the scene of infection'.[187]

The first general inoculation in a town or village gave protection to the non-immune sector of the population, the age-range of which depended on factors already discussed but which was likely to have included a substantial proportion of adults. Thereafter the chief future risk lay with children born subsequently and with non-immune immigrants. Second and subsequent general inoculations were therefore almost wholly restricted to these two categories of inhabitant. When a second general inoculation at Calne, Wiltshire, was performed in September 1793, eleven years after the first, a local surgeon remarked that those treated 'were mostly children'[188] while at Rawreth a second general inoculation in 1792, five years after the first, was specifically for 'the poor Childrin of the parish' born in the intervening years.[189] In 1797 Leyton vestry paid for 83 inoculations by Mr Hobbs, 81 of which were of children aged between two weeks and 10 years and 'All did well'.[190] More Leyton children were inoculated in 1798 by Mr Heaton, apothecary, for five guineas.[191] At Maldon, where high in and out-migration coupled with regular changes in regiments garrisoned there probably resulted in the town having a higher continuing susceptibility to damaging epidemics than most other places, there were five general inoculations between 1766 and 1806.[192] One town, Witham, appears to have responded to the problem of non-immune immigrants by making inoculation a condition of residence.[193] In villages and parishes with very small populations a second general inoculation often appears to have been unnecessary and the level of immunity was instead maintained by the *ad hoc* inoculation of families and individuals.

The complex and variable nature of the factors surrounding general inoculations and the inadequate state of existing information makes assessment of the rôle of inoculation in relation to population growth very difficult. The immediate effect was a reduction in the death rate by preserving lives of all ages, but the long-term effect of increasing the stock of potential parents was far more significant. This point was understood by Howlett's correspondent at Great Chart who in 1780 commented

> no register can, as yet, properly inform us of the thousands that
> have been preserved by this salutary practice for these 20 years
> past all over the kingdom. As they have been chiefly infants and
> *young people* they are *ordinarily* too young to die, and scarce yet
> old enough to marry; but they are latent in society, and will great-
> ly swell *both* registers in due time.[194]

In order to establish in round figures the likely extent of this increase a model has been constructed of events in an imaginary small town. Here before the introduction of inoculation half the inhabitants died before reaching adulthood and smallpox killed one in five of the population in the proportions of one-third adults and two-thirds children. Of every 100 children about 14 died of smallpox, another 36 of other causes. Of the 50 who survived beyond the age of parenthood smallpox killed about six. Following a complete general inoculation this pattern changed roughly as follows. In a group of 100 children 14 smallpox deaths were prevented but seven of the 14 succumbed to other childhood diseases so that 57 per cent. now reached adulthood, representing an increase of 14 per cent.[195]

During the half-century 1751-1800 the population of England and Wales rose from just over six million to nearly nine million. Contemporary observers may have been correct in stating that inoculation had reduced smallpox mortality greatly but it is clear from these crude calculations that it was not wholly nor even mainly responsible for that population rise. In the post-war population debate a number of other causes have been put forward by demographic historians and in a review published in 1981 of the existing state of knowledge Michael Flinn identified as the main factor the greater degree of mortality control established by the middle of the century.[196] Improvements in diet and the nutritional standard of food stemming from advances in agriculture after about 1740, the introduction of new crops and improved famine relief were, in Flinn's view, important subsidiary components. More important, however, was the publication in the same year of Wrigley and Schofield's monumental work *The Population History of England, 1541-1871*, the result of 15 years' research by the S.S.R.C. Cambridge Group for the History of Population and Social Structure. Using a wealth of new evidence from over 400 selected parish registers the authors concluded that changes in population growth rates, including the stagnation of much of the seventeenth century and spectacular growth of the later eighteenth, were chiefly derived from responses of marriage and reproduction customs to changing economic conditions.[197] More recently, in an essay in *Past and Present*, Wrigley emphasised that while mortality improved in the eighteenth century the rise in life expectancy 'was not dramatic'. Instead 'fertility accounted for the lion's share of the acceleration in population growth' and 'in seeking to understand the remarkable pace at which English population grew in the eighteenth century, we should look to changes in nuptiality as the principal reason'.[198]

The evidence presented in this chapter of greatly reduced smallpox mortality in market towns, villages and rural parishes in the last third of the eighteenth century and, more importantly, that inoculation improved in the order of ten to 20 per cent. the chance of a child reaching adulthood thereby increasing to the same degree the number of potential marriage partners and parents, underpins the findings of Wrigley and Schofield in relation to nuptiality. It also points to the desirability of a reassessment of the importance of inoculation and highlights the need for much more case and statistical evidence, particularly in relation to general inoculations, such as could possibly be achieved by a nationwide town and parish survey. What may be said with some certainty is that Peter Razzell's claims in 1977 that inoculation was responsible for preventing a demographic catastrophe of the kind experienced in fourteenth-century Europe and that without inoculation there would instead of the Industrial Revolution have been 'a very prolonged period of decline and stagnation' should be treated with caution.[199]

4

The Impact of Daniel Sutton

The increasingly widespread acceptance and incidence of inoculation from the mid-1760s owed much to the system of milder and safer treatment developed by Robert Sutton and modified by his son Daniel. So significant was the impact of this treatment that the rôle of the Sutton family, in particular the career and work of Daniel Sutton whose ambition and energy led to the system becoming widely known and used, demands closer attention.

The family's involvement with medicine and surgery began with Robert (c.1708-1788)[1] who was apprenticed in September 1726 to John Turner, an apothecary at Debenham, Suffolk.[2] In October 1731, shortly after the completion of his apprenticeship, he married Sarah Barker of Debenham[3] and had probably already returned to his native village of Kenton by 1732 to start his own practice as a surgeon and apothecary for in that year Robert, the first of his eight sons, was baptised in the parish church there.[4] He then worked for 'many years' as a country doctor without performing inoculation during which time he had his eldest son inoculated by 'a surgeon of his acquaintance' from which he was severely ill 'and it was with the utmost difficulty that his life was saved'.[5] As a result of this experience Robert determined 'to dedicate his thoughts solely to the Small-pox; to endeavour to investigate a means whereby the force of that distemper might be lessened and danger, if possible, prevented by inoculation'.[6] Following a lengthy period of study he evolved a plan for inoculation. After a further delay and 'many wavering resolutions' he finally tested his plan on a single patient in 1755, having 'previously taken the greatest precaution, and saw that the patient observed the strictest preparation and regimen'. The results were successful and there began a series of trials which 'convinced him that he had made some valuable discoveries'.[7] In April 1757 he began advertising in the *Ipswich Journal* announcing that he had

> hired a large commodious House for the Reception of Persons who are disposed to be INOCULATED by him for the SMALL-POX, on the following Terms, viz. Gentlemen and Ladies will be prepared, inoculated, boarded and nursed, and allowed Tea, Wine, Fish and Fowl, at Seven Guineas each, for one Month; Farmers at Five Pounds, to be allowed Tea, Veal, Mutton, Lamb, &c.: And for the Benefit of the meaner Sort, he will take them at Three Guineas for a Month, if they are not fit to be discharged sooner; and those that can board and nurse themselves, he will inoculate them for Half a Guinea each.
>
> N.B. He has for one of his constant Nurses, the well-known Mrs. ELIZ. ALEXANDER, Widow, of Framlingham; he likewise has met with remarkable Success hitherto.[8]

The new venture quickly proved to be a 'remarkable success' and by late September Robert had 'two commodious Houses for the Reception of Persons disposed to be Inoculated'.[9] In the summer of 1758 he 'erected a new House, to carry on the Business of Inoculation' and by the autumn was visiting Framlingham and Halesworth (Suffolk), Diss and Harleston (Norfolk) on market days in search of new customers.[10] In February 1759 he stated that not one of his inoculation patients had died or suffered blindness as a result of the treatment.[11] The business continued to expand. By September 1759 he had three large houses, 'one for the Reception of his Patients to be inoculated in, one to be nursed in, and one to be aired in'.[12] In October 1760 he claimed to have inoculated more than 200 people within the last twelve months. He now had agents in 16 towns and villages in Suffolk, south Norfolk and north-east Essex, including Mr Lynn of Woodbridge, Suffolk, surgeon, Mr Sturgeon of Birch, Mr Goslin of Horkesley and Mr Barton of Bradfield, from whom those contemplating inoculation could obtain further information about the treatment offered.[13] In 1761, probably as the result of advertisements in the *Ipswich Journal* by a rival inoculator, Sutton reduced his top fee to five guineas with easier terms 'for the Benefit of the lower Class of People' for whom there was now a separate house. At the same time he admitted that 'of the many Hundreds he has had under his Care' one had died.[14]

By December 1761 the observations and modifications of several years' practical experience led Sutton to believe that he had achieved a perfect technique and method. Four months later he reported that since December his 'new method'

has succeeded so well, that upwards of Two hundred Patients have not had, upon an Average, a hundred Pustules each, and ten or twelve of whom were from forty to fifty-two Years of Age, and had drunk very hard for fifteen or twenty years[15]

Further information about his 'new method' appeared in an advertisement in September 1762. This

being done without Incision, the most curious Eye cannot discern where the Operation is performed for the first forty-eight Hours; and with this Advantage, that he is always certain of determining whether the Patient receives the Infection or not. He has inoculated since December last, three hundred and sixty-five; several of whom were hard Drinkers for many years, and not one has been confined in Bed two Days ... He verily believes he has found out Medicines within these last nine Months, that will very much reduce the Fomes of this dreadful Distemper, and which he has experienced on several lately in the natural Way, as well as on the Inoculated, with great Success.[16]

Two 'commodious Houses' had lately been hired 'for the Reception of Gentlemen and Ladies by themselves' and he offered his own or his son's attendance 'within thirty or forty Miles, if desired' on anyone who had been exposed to the infection and believed they had caught the disease.[17] This is the first indication that a son, probably Robert, the first, was playing a major rôle in the practice, although the three eldest sons had received instruction from their father in 'the principles of his method of inoculation'.[18] It was also about this time that one of the sons, probably the third, was killed in a shooting accident.[19]

By about the middle of November 453 people had been inoculated by the new method. For ladies and gentlemen within 50 miles who preferred to be inoculated in their own houses Sutton now offered to 'reside with them till the Distemper is past its Crisis, having a Son well qualified to attend his Patients at Home'. This son may have been his second, Daniel, for Robert junior had recently hired two houses at the Suffolk village of Barrow, six miles west of Bury St Edmunds, where he was establishing a branch of the practice.[20] Again Robert senior placed particular emphasis on the efficacy of his medicine which

> renders the Distemper very benign ... it answers in all Ages and Constitutions ... does not in the least injure the Constitutions ... Infants take it with the greatest Safety ... He hopes he may, without Vanity, say, he has brought Inoculation to its greatest Perfection, since so large a Number has had it so favourably, to the Amazement of every Spectator. If his Regimen is strictly adher'd to, and his Medicines regularly taken, previous to and after the Operation, he is (with the Concurrence of Providence) morally certain of Success.[21]

Expansion continued in 1763. In May Robert senior announced that he had hired 'a large and commodious House at Toftmonks in Norfolk, near Beccles, for the Reception of such Persons as are disposed to be inoculated by him for the Small-Pox'. Patients were to be taken every fortnight on Mondays beginning on 20 June. Meanwhile 'his Son', probably Robert, had inoculated between five and six hundred since 1 January.[22] By October Robert senior had begun inoculating at Yelverton Hall near Norwich while another of his sons had hired a house in Ashfield, six miles north of Stowmarket, where inoculation would be carried out 'under the Direction and Inspection of his Father' at a guinea a week. Those 'in very low Circumstances' would be inoculated 'on Terms something less', while 'very poor People' would be prepared, inoculated and attended free by him or his father.[23]

For the first few years the Suttons' inoculating business under the control of Robert senior had operated at a modest level despite regular advertising and the appointment of agents, but expansion had been rapid following the introduction of the new method in December 1761. Thus by the autumn of 1763 it was a well-established and profitable concern which had spread beyond the Suffolk borders.[24] It was at this point that Daniel, then aged 28 years, left his father's practice to set up his own at Ingatestone, a parish and large village astride the main road between Brentwood and Chelmsford.

Much of Daniel's early history is unclear. Born 4 May and baptised 23 May 1735 in Kenton parish church[25] he trained under his father and after being inoculated in 1757 spent the next three years working for his father 'attending to the small-pox'.[26] He then 'acted as an Assistant to an eminent Surgeon and Apothecary' in Essex before returning to work for his father late in 1762 or early 1763,[27] possibly as a result of the death of one of his brothers. He stayed at Kenton only a few months, during which he learned his father's new method, and was at Ingatestone by October 1763. An account written five years after the move to Ingatestone stated that he was encouraged by the success of his elder brother Robert[28] but William Woodville, writing in the 1790s, claimed he was informed by Daniel that the move was the result of a disagreement with his father over the preparation period which Daniel proposed to reduce from a month to eight or ten days 'to obviate the objections that many persons had made to inoculation, from the great length of time it required'.[29] Daniel also suggested that instead of being confined indoors inoculees should be obliged 'to be in the open air as much as possible during the whole progress of the distemper'.[30] But his father

> could not be persuaded to adopt any innovation ... and would not
> hear the whole of his son's new scheme, which he condemned as
> not only rash and absurd, but as extremely dangerous.[31]

Against his father's wishes Daniel then experimented with his modifications and their advantages 'were soon perceived by the patients, who now began to manifest a desire of being solely under the direction of Mr. D. Sutton'.[32] This not surprisingly led to 'a dispute' between father and son with the result that Daniel 'determined to practice inoculation uncontrolled by parental authority'.[33] As will be shown later in this chapter, the disagreement did not prevent subsequent co-operation between Daniel and his father.

Shortly after arriving at Ingatestone Daniel began distributing hand-bills[34] and on 5 November his first newspaper advertisement appeared in the *Ipswich Journal* stating that he had hired two houses in Ingatestone which would be ready for the reception of patients at the beginning of December. He also stated that he would be using his father's method, mentioning that he had practised with him in Suffolk 'for some Years past'.[35] Those who wished to be inoculated at their own homes would be 'attended upon on very moderate Terms'.[36] The two houses lay within the parish of Ingatestone between one and two miles from the village and close to 'a much frequented Road'.[37] Their exact locations are unclear but they were probably in the Mill Green area. The choice of Ingatestone as the centre of his practice was doubtless the result of careful consideration, for the village was on the main road from London to East Anglia and was an established stopping-place for travellers and for changing teams of stage-coach horses. Furthermore it was sufficiently near London to tap a wealthy clientèle from the metropolis while, as Abraham and Dixon have pointed out, being outside the areas of jurisdiction of the Corporation of Surgeons and College of Physicians, for Sutton was an unqualified practitioner with no medical degree.[38]

Local reaction was immediate and angry. Sutton, by not informing the lessors of his profession nor that he intended to use the houses for inoculation had, in the opinion of the principal inhabitants of Ingatestone, acted deceitfully.[39] Alarmed at the prospect of 'having a perpetual Pest fixed among them',[40] they pointed out that the neighbourhood was then free of smallpox but because of the position of the houses 'the Infection must be spread in time' and if Sutton proceeded with his project

> the principal Inhabitants of this and the neighbouring Parishes ...
> are determined to give all the Opposition thereto that the Law
> will enable them to do; as infecting a Town of so much Traffick
> will be a Detriment to the Public, and may be easily proved a
> Nuisance[41]

As to the houses, Sutton described them as 'commodious ... fitted up in a very neat and elegant Manner',[42] the smaller having been rebuilt about two years previously, but the inhabitants claimed it to be a semi-detached cottage worth 50s. a year at most and suggested that he could not tell the difference between rebuilding and repairing.[43]

This local opposition and criticism nearly spelt disaster as no-one came to be inoculated. After three months, 'dispirited and almost on the point of quiting', Daniel persuaded a few poor people to be inoculated without charge, overcoming their very considerable apprehension and prejudice. The success of these inoculations resulted in two or three poor families coming to him voluntarily and again the outcome was entirely successful. Word was spreading in the neighbourhood and some families 'above the level of poverty and distress' now came forward. It was thus by gradual steps that Daniel Sutton began to establish himself in the spring of 1764.[44]

By the autumn the situation had changed completely. He was now meeting with 'extraordinary Encouragement' from the public and at the end of his first year of independent practice had earned 2,000 guineas.[45] His first advertisement in the newly-established *Chelmsford Chronicle* in October 1764 provides much information about the expanding practice. All his patients had been successfully treated and had

> been able to quit their Bed or Room, and take the Air at any one
> Stage of the Distemper, except a few Hours, whilst they are
> breeding it; having upon an Average, not more than twenty
> Pustules each; a Practice essentially interesting and worthy the
> Attention of the Public, particularly the Fair Sex; as by this
> Method the Face is effectually prevented from being disfigured.
> By communicating the Small-pox thus favourably, the Patients in
> general are enabled to return in fresh Company in three Weeks,
> or less; a Circumstance which particularly affects the Working
> Hand, etc.
> The general Terms are Four Guineas on the Day of Inocula-
> tion, without Exception; and all Necessaries found Tea and Sugar
> excepted.
> Persons that are desirous of being inoculated by him, at their
> own Houses, will be attended on very reasonable Terms.[46]

The majority of Ingatestone inhabitants viewed these events with alarm, regarding Sutton's presence as an evil which they were powerless to remove. The coaching trade suffered a decline as travellers became reluctant to stop there and in the spring of 1765, in an effort to prevent further damage, the innkeepers and doctors of Ingatestone and the adjoining parish of Fryerning placed this notice in the *Chelmsford Chronicle*.[47] Their former threatening attitude was now replaced by one of resignation.

> The great Success with which Mr. SUTTON has carried on Inoculation for the Small-Pox in the Neighbourhood of Ingatestone, and the great Number of Patients he has had and discharged, has in Consequence, occasioned many of their Friends, and even some of those who designed to be inoculated, previous to the Operation to lodge in the public Inns of the Town. From these Circumstances many Reports came to be spread about the Country, that are prejudicial to the Interest of the Inhabitants, by deterring Travellers from stopping there. And whereas it has been said in particular that Mr. Coverdale at the Swan had lett Part of his House for this Purpose of Inoculation; This is to certify the Public that no part of the said House has been lett for that Purpose and that none of Mr. Sutton's Patients have at any Time, to our Knowledge, laid in any of the Inns of the said Town during their State of Infection. We do further assure the Public, that we have great Reason to think, that no Person in the Town has catched the Small-Pox from Mr. Sutton's Patients coming into the Town, because many single Persons and some whole Families, who have never had the Small-Pox, still continue free from it, though they have such frequent Intercourse with Mr. Sutton, and his Patients, as must have communicated the Infection, were the Contagion in any Degree equal to what is from the same Distemper in the Natural Way. We do further assure the Public, that every possible Precaution is and shall be taken by us the Innkeepers in the said Town to guard against any Danger to Travellers who may have Occasion either to stop or to lodge in the Town. We hope therefore, as it is not in our Power, either through Defect in the Laws or Remissness in the Magistrates to execute them to remove the Evil to a greater Distance, the Public will accept our best Endeavours to accommodate them with Safety.

Sutton meanwhile continued to prosper, inoculating 923 people in the 20 weeks leading up to the middle of May 1765.[48] During the summer of that year he improved and modified the accommodation in readiness for the forthcoming winter season by having three houses for three different classes of patients, announcing at the end of September that

> MR. SUTTON being on a new Plan this Season, is determined to remove every Objection that can possibly be alleged against the

Accommodation of his Patients, as far as it is consistent with his singular Method of treating the Small-Pox; which has hitherto given universal Satisfaction, having inoculated near Four Thousand Persons, many of whom were upwards of Seventy Years old, others not more than three Months, and of various bad Constitutions, without the Loss of *a single Patient*. Agreeable to his present Scheme he has fitted up three very convenient Houses, classed out for Six, Four, and Three Guineas Patients; by which Method one Class of Patients will not be subject to the Interruption of another, nor will they now be liable to the Inconvenience of being removed daily from House to House; and for the greater Regularity in each of the Houses, he has established Rules extremely familiar to every individual.[49]

In this advertisement he tacitly admitted that there had been criticism of his accommodation and arrangements. One of the critics was the Quaker Joseph Cockfield of Upton House, West Ham, who wrote that 'The terms are so moderate that men in mean circumstances, men of low education and dissolute life, repair to his house', which was 'confused and disorderly'.[50] Such criticism, however, does not seem to have caused serious damage to his practice, the income of which increased to £6,300 in 1765.

Late in 1765 Sutton extended his business into London, taking a house, which he called Sutton House, in Kensington Gore and another five miles to the west in rural Brentford to accommodate patients. In conjunction with his father and brothers he then began setting up a series of partnerships throughout the country. Aided by his considerable flair for publicity the practice was now expanding rapidly. 'Every paper throughout the kingdom echoed with its success' and 'Eminent physicians and surgeons were daily applying to the family to be appointed partners for particular counties, or for foreign parts'.[51] At the same time he was employing a number of personal assistants.

Early in 1766 Sutton took action both to protect and further to publicise the business by hiring the services of Robert Houlton, a Somerset clergyman and chaplain to the Earl of Ilchester, to act as publicist and 'officiating clergyman' at the Ingatestone houses. By this astute move Sutton also put himself on the right side of the churches. Houlton's appointment was announced in the *Chelmsford Chronicle* in May 1766 with an emphasis intended to win the approbation of the clergy.

Mr. Sutton, who has inoculated many thousands without losing a single Patient, having it frequently hinted to him by the gentry his patients how agreeable it would be to have the duty of the church performed on Wednesdays and Sundays with a Sermon, has determined to oblige them in their request, and speedily to build a spacious Chapel-Room. The Rev. Robert Houlton, Master of Arts ..., is the Gentleman chosen to officiate. For which he will have the genteel Salary of 200 guineas per Annum. To commence at Michaelmas next, and made certain to him for a term of years.[52]

On 21 May Sutton inoculated the three young sons of the lawyer and politician Bamber Gascoyne who gave a graphic account of their treatment and Sutton's methods of dealing with well-to-do non-residential customers in a remarkable series of letters to his friend the farmer and landowner John Strutt of Terling.[53] The decision to have his sons Bamber, Isaac and Benjamin inoculated was taken by Gascoyne in March 1766 when smallpox was widespread in Essex. At the end of the month Sutton called at Bifrons, the family's country house in Barking,

> having been to London to attend a patient in the natural way, by which he thought himself so infectious that he would neither tarry nor come in; the children were set at 20 yds. distance; he said they were proper subjects, but May he lik'd the best month in the Year and by that time Bamber might have gained strength after his ague, and then he would prepare them on the first of May.[54]

Moor, Gascoyne's servant, was so frightened of catching the disease from Sutton that he 'was afraid to see him through a door out of the other yard' but nevertheless decided to be inoculated with Gascoyne's sons. It was agreed that the inoculations would take place at a tenant's house near Romford which Sutton 'much approv'd of'.[55] This was probably either Brittains Farm in Dagenham or Maylards Farm in Hornchurch.[56] At this stage Gascoyne viewed Sutton with some scepticism and disdain, referring to him on 8 April as 'the pocky doctor'.[57]

Gascoyne observed the preparations closely and with great interest. The diet consisted of 'Asparagus spinnage cucumbers and puddings with plumbs pruens or gooseberries ... cold water and cyder ... and sometimes milk and water'.[58] With regard to the purging, Gascoyne noted

> his powders are taken overnight and worked off with Glauber salts; the powders I am sure by their effects are mercurial as upon being wet shod, cold, or not working off, the patient is affected with white and sore gums, his teeth loose and his breath tainted all which are removed upon repitition of the salts; these from observation I know to be the effects of mercury. I am of opinion it is the golden preparation of antimony and mixed with coral or some of the testaceous powders; I really am physician enough to be thus far certain.[59]

By 20 May the three boys and Moor were almost ready for inoculation, and Gascoyne reported 'My children were pretty well considering they are starved. Moor looks as if he had slip'd the chains from a gibbet ... My fears I need not express'.[60] The inoculations took place the following day. Accompanying Sutton to the farmhouse was

> Mrs. Wallis wife to Joe Wallis ... of Messing and with her the daughter to the parson of Faulkbourne ... they were three in the

75

chaise and the two ladies look'd as well and were as cheerfull as if they were come upon a visit. He applied to my wife and self to point out which had the disease, but this by looks was impossible, he might as well shewn us two young fellows and ask'd which was clap'd. However Mrs. Wallis was the infected person, she had about seven pustles with large white heads on them. The doctr. thrust a lancet in one of them which he immediately applied to the arm of Bamber and put so small a part of the point under his skin that he was not sensible of the point's touching him. Then put on his cloaths without plaister rag or any covering whatever; and so practised upon the others[61]

Two days later, on Friday, the patients' arms

appear'd red as if they had been prick'd with a thistle. And on Saturday they were increased and rather of an higher colour; on that day he gave the children half a pill each and Moor three; these pills stunk confoundedly but he would not permit me to handle them; these purged much. On Sunday evening Moor at times was flush'd in the face and sickish; on Monday he was very sick, chilly, eyes painfull and headache in the evening. Bamber was affected in the same manner, vomited much but was always better for going out; Moor was too much cast down to stir and declared he was so feeble he could not support himself; on Tuesday he continued the same, or rather worse and had a fever both nights as had Bamber and there appeared a few more red spots upon the neck and arms, Isaac fell next into the same way on Tuesday morning and Benny perfectly cheerfull and merry; Moors Bambers and Isaac spots appeared with matter on the edges of the red in the middle; but these were sunken with a black dot in the middle. This day Moor and Bamber were free from sickness etc. but had great pains in their arms. Moor's arm was much putrified between the pustles and very much inflamed; Isaac cheerful and down fell Benny, pale cold sick and nose bleeding and so lethargic that he could not keep his head up or eyes open, Sutton came over ordered him to take the air in the fields, cold and a N. east wind; however he recovered spirrits upon this ... Moor and Bamber may eat butter and eggs to their pudding; Sutton declares them all out of danger and says they will not have 15 pustles a peice; he is to revisit on Saturday and intends bringing physic for them. If this is the small pox I would sooner have it than an ague. Moor is a fine figure his breeches wrap round his thighs and his coat may be fastened to the button on his hip. Bamber looks like a gun barrel, the other two are but little decreased.[62]

Gascoyne's opinion of Sutton had now changed. He had been 'very punctual in his attendance, and ... is a most surprising fellow, and hath a most amazing secret in giving and abating the venom of the small pox'.[63] On 6 June Gascoyne was able to write

> My children Moor etc are all perfectly well and Dr. Sutton has left them, the pock is quite gone down and scaling off, he gave them one dose of physic each and on Tuesday next home they come[64]

About a week after inoculating the Gascoyne boys Sutton carried out a general inoculation of 487 inhabitants of Maldon in a single day, thereby putting an end to a major outbreak in the town.[65] The market revived 'and the public were left in equal surprise and admiration of the safety of the practice, and skill of the operator'.[66] This was a major boost for Sutton's already successful career. In the middle of June he was visited by the surgeon to the King of Poland, an event which he ensured received publicity in the *Chelmsford Chronicle*.

> Mr Ristch, first surgeon to the king of Poland, paid a visit last week from London to Mr. Sutton at Ingatestone; having heard much of that Gentleman's very singular and successful method of inoculation. Mr. Sutton inoculated a patient in his presence, at which he expressed surprise, and was greatly pleased with the slightness of the operation. Fresh patients arriving Mr. Sutton desired Mr. Ristch to inoculate them himself, according to the method he had seen. This he did; and leaving Mr. Sutton his address, begged him to inform him if his operation succeeded.[67]

The very considerable sums now being earned by Sutton enabled him to emulate many other well-to-do professional men of the time and in May he completed the purchase of a country house called Maisonette and 39 acres of land three-quarters of a mile north of Ingatestone village.[68]

A few weeks later Sutton's spectacular run of success, uninterrupted since the spring of 1764, was temporarily halted and replaced by the threat of ruin. It was widely believed in Chelmsford that he was responsible for starting the epidemic which broke out there at the beginning of summer and, charged with causing a public nuisance, he appeared before Lord Justice Mansfield at the Summer Assizes.[69] Although acquitted on the grounds that it was impossible to prove him responsible for spreading the disease since all the apothecaries in the town also practised inoculation, he was publicly admonished for bringing patients under inoculation to the market. For his part Sutton believed the prosecution to be founded on the envy and malice of his enemies in the medical profession who represented him 'as the lowest of mankind; one that had just jumped into the profession, without sense, art, or a single degree of merit'.[70] A few months later Robert Houlton gave this account of the circumstances surrounding the trial:

> ABOUT the beginning of last summer the Small-pox broke out in a most violent manner at Chelmsford ... sweeping off every

week many of the inhabitants. This was a fine opportunity for Mr. *Sutton's* enemies (many of whom live in that quarter) to surmise, invent and propagate what calumnies they pleased; especially as he sometimes comes on market-days to treat with people, who were inclined to be inoculated. If any person chanced to accompany him in his carriage, it was always industriously reported, that such person was a patient brought to inoculate from. Others could see small pocks out in full bloom (as they expressed it) notwithstanding the companion was frequently an acquaintance;— and as it is diametrically contrary to Mr. *Sutton's* practice to inoculate from such kind of patients. But we shall prove presently, by the greatest evidence, that such were no more nor less than *gross lies*. Mr. *Sutton*, however, was declared to be the man that infected Chelmsford with the Small-pox, notwithstanding *every Apothecary in the town was an Inoculator*, and had long practised round the neighbourhood: nay some of them had absolutely inoculated persons of the town at their own houses, and this before the Small-pox raged with any violence. Mr. *Sutton* too must be the man, notwithstanding Chelmsford lies in the great road from London to Colchester, Ipswich, Norwich, Harwich, &c. where many stagecoaches stop, and which it is reasonable to suppose, frequently bring passengers just come from infected houses, and many doubtless that are just recovered from the Small-pox, with their infectious bundles of linen, &c. — Scandalous accusation! base partiality! In short, the unjust insinuation was industriously and artfully kept up, and influenced a general belief. On this, a set of men, whose *justice, honour* and *integrity* I want words to express, waited on a distinguished personage to head their *benevolent* design. This Gentleman who has, in fact, an heart ever ready to do good, a heart that is naturally an enemy to oppression, was borne down with repeated asseverations, and forced as it were by the cries of the people, to appear in a prosecution, which, had not calumny and prejudice strongly barricaded the voice of truth from his ears, he would never have countenanced. — In consequence of these groundless insinuations and misrepresentations, an inditement was prefered last summer assize at Chelmsford, against Mr. *Daniel Sutton*, Surgeon, for a nuisance; when the Grand Jury not only not found the bill against him, but observed publicly in Court to Lord MANSFIELD, *"that not one single article alledged against him in the inditement was proved; and that moreover they thought it partial to prosecute* Mr. Sutton *in particular, since they did not find but that the Apothecaries of the town inoculated likewise."*

Such was the cause and issue of the Chelmsford indictment. A prosecution founded on sinister and malicious prejudice, supported by lying clamour, carried on with vindictive rage, but opposed by TRUTH, and frustrated by JUSTICE.[71]

There is little doubt that Sutton was extremely worried by the prospects of the trial. As a result he took action which was later admitted to be designed 'to weaken the Chelmsford Indictment ... an innocent means to influence an unjust prosecution. It had its effect'.[72] The circumstances, briefly, were as follows. After the undoubted success of his general inoculation at Maldon in May Sutton began approaching other towns with a smallpox problem, offering to conduct general inoculations. On 13 July his offer was taken up by Maidstone vestry which asked him to visit the town to discuss the matter, having preferred Sutton's offer to that made by a well-established local doctor, Mr Pine. Sutton grasped with both hands this opportunity to reply to his critics and to influence the outcome of the trial. The *Chelmsford Chronicle* of 18 July carried this notice:

Mr. SUTTON to the PUBLIC

THE following Letter shews the Greatness of Mr. Sutton's Character, and his Interest; and is no small Reflection on those who are maliciously and with the most partial Prejudice endeavouring to cramp him in his Practice, and obstruct that Blessing and Advantage to Mankind, which, under Providence, he daily dispenses with the most happy Success, but a proper Lesson, for the Junto who are combined against him.

The letter from Maidstone which followed claimed, among other things, that 'a great Majority' of those present at the Maidstone vestry meeting voted in Sutton's favour and that the number to be inoculated was 'about Seven Thousand in the Town and Neighbourhood'. Pine wrote to the newspaper pointing out alterations and substituted falsehoods in the letter but his complaint was suppressed by the proprietor.[73] To the intense annoyance of Pine several hundred Maidstone people were inoculated by Sutton shortly afterwards.[74] In the autumn Sutton placed his Kent business in the hands of a partner, Mr Peale, surgeon, who by 8 October had 'above Six Hundred Patients under his Care, amongst whom are several of the Nobility and other principal People'.[75]

The bad publicity caused by the Chelmsford trial was probably more than offset by the Maidstone and Kentish inoculations and by a detailed account of 249 inoculations performed at Ewell, Surrey, in July and August which appeared in the influential *Gentleman's Magazine* in September. A first group of 156 people was inoculated on 8 July and on 3 August most of the patients

came to church, to return thanks for their recovery; all ... in good health. Many others, animated with their success, began, at different periods, to prepare themselves; insomuch that the whole number of persons under inoculation, from the 8th *July* to the 12th of *August* amounts to 249 persons, and Mr *Sutton* pro-

nounces them all entirely out of danger from the small-pox[76]
In 1766 as a whole Sutton personally inoculated 7,816 people.[77] The total number
inoculated by him, his assistants and Peale in the three years 1764-1766 amounted
to almost 20,000 without, it was claimed, a single death directly attributable to the
treatment.[78] By February 1767 Peale had performed more than 2,000 inoculations
in Kent.[79]

Early in 1767 Sutton extended his interest into Suffolk and his inoculating
house, the picturesque sixteenth-century Freston Tower overlooking the River
Orwell four miles south of Ipswich, was ready to receive patients by mid February.
Mr Bucke junior, an Ipswich surgeon, was engaged as 'an Assistant in his singular
and *most* successful Method' and placed in charge of the business there. He would
use '*none* but Mr. Sutton's Medicines, as Mr. Peale has always done'. The day-to-
day running of the house was placed in the hands of two of Sutton's 'principal Servants'. Fees were six, four and three guineas according to class 'and due Regard will
be paid to Objects of *real* Charity'.[80] Bucke was still inoculating there in 1779.[81]

Events continued to move rapidly for Sutton. His work was now becoming
known on the mainland of Europe where the method was recommended by the
eminent physician Sir John Pringle, whose own work in the field of military
medicine and sanitation had earned him a European reputation.[82] Having already
acquired a London house and a small country estate, Sutton sought to further his
position in society by applying to the College of Heralds for a coat of arms. This
was granted on 20 August 1767 with the motto 'Safely, quickly and pleasantly' as an
'allusion to and ... memorial of his great skill and unparalelled success in Inoculation'.[83] Four days later at Westminster he married Rachel Westley, a young widow
from Antigua.[84] By the time of his marriage Sutton no longer lived at Ingatestone
and in June 1767 Maisonette was let to John Ratcliffe on a 21-year lease.[85] His
wealth was now such that he began lending on mortgages, his advances including
£150 on copyhold property in Leigh in 1767 and £250 on copyhold property in
South Shoebury in 1772.[86]

The year 1767 was also marked by the publication of Robert Houlton's *A Sermon ... in Defence of Inoculation*. The first section comprises a sermon preached at
Ingatestone on 12 October 1766 in which Houlton dealt with the ethics of and
religious objections to inoculation in general, without mentioning Sutton. Having
found that there could be no reasonable grounds for conscientious or religious
objection he then moved on to the emotional subject of parental responsibility,
concluding that

> If you neglect to have your children inoculated, and they are
> infected, as they grow up, with the natural Small-pox and die,
> have you not *real cause* to be uneasy, and to accuse yourselves of
> carelessness and want of natural affection, as the means to have
> saved their lives, at least from this kind of death, were so
> manifestly efficacious, and so indisputably safe? — The chance
> that children are naturally infected with this distemper, before

they come to years of discretion, amounts to a *great probability*; and that they may die under it, there is too much reason to fear;— but that Inoculation will secure them from all danger, is not to be doubted, much less questioned.[87]

Houlton also recommended that inoculation 'be encouraged ... as much as possible, by the government'. Such encouragement he thought to be particularly relevant

at this time, when the nation is so thin of men, that it is well known, and severely felt, thousands are wanted among the lower class, to perform the common works of husbandry and labour. But how would this scarcity of people be felt, if we were to be engaged soon again in another war! In short, every kingdom is the more powerful the more it increases in population. If then every child's life is of great value to [the] community, of how much more consequence are the lives of lusty youths and robust men! All, all are saved by Inoculation; but thousands, thro' neglect of it, are every year cut off in the prime of youth and manhood. Let any man seriously reflect what an immense loss, in many respects, this must naturally be to the nation.[88]

The sermon was followed by two prayers used in the services at Sutton's inoculating houses, but of much more interest is the 20-page appendix dealing with Daniel Sutton's methods and practice. Here the author claimed his statements to be 'facts as I have long been conversant with his method, frequented his houses and an eye witness to all I assert'. Of the progress of inoculation in relation to the Sutton family, for example, he thought that

NOTWITHSTANDING the art of Inoculation, since it was first discovered, has been in general slow in its progress, and very gradually, and in many respects very injudiciously practised, it has rapidly advanced, within these last ten years, towards the point and summit of perfection ... The merit of this perfection, I readily attribute, without the least apprehension of being contradicted, to the skill, the indefatigable labours and experiments of the Sutton family, who now practice Inoculation with unparalleled and astonishing success, in different parts of the kingdom. Particularly is the public indebted to Mr. *Daniel Sutton* ... whose singular method of Inoculation, and the many great improvements, and lights he has made and thrown on the Practice, have excited the attention, surprize and admiration of the whole kingdom, especially of the faculty.[89]

As well as defending Sutton's method and answering his critics Houlton encouraged more people to undergo the operation, giving this description of the treatment at the Ingatestone houses.

AND first, the slightness of his operation in communicating the infection, may well demand our admiration. It is easier than we can possibly conceive. With respect to pain, it is not equal to the thousandth part which the prick of a pin gives. The operation is performed on most without their feeling or knowing it: and in a minute afterwards, the puncture is scarce visible. I mention this, because many are apt to dread the operation; being apprehensive that a large incision is to be made. — The whole that follows, is perfectly in character with the operation. The patients in general have little or no sickness: their indisposition is so trifling that they are ashamed to complain; and in a few days they are perfectly well. Here is no confinement, no keeping of bed. All is mirth, and all seem happy. In fact this fortnight-visit to Mr. Sutton's, abounds with real pleasure and satisfaction. The pleasing conversation of the company, added to their various amusements, makes the time glide away imperceptibly. — If Mr. Sutton perceives a symptom in patients of a great fever, or a probability of their having more pustules than they would chuse, he quickly prevents both by virtue of his medicines. In short, if any patient in the house has twenty or thirty pustules, he is said to have the Small-pox very heavy. — 'Tis impossible to make the reader conceive, with what ease, with what trifling sickness and extreme safety this Gentleman, his family, and assistants, conduct patients through Inoculation. If there were not thousands that could attest it, I should be backward to risk being believed by the public, though I have the strongest demonstration of it myself.[90]

Houlton also devoted several pages to the problems encountered by Sutton during his early years in Essex, especially the opposition of doctors long established there, prefacing this section with the following remarks:

At the latter end of the year 1763, Mr. *Sutton* came into Essex, and settled in his present habitation, near the town of Ingatestone, under the great disadvantage of being unknown to any in the neighbourhood. Success and merit had scarce owned him for their child, when the sluices of envy, calumny and unprovoked malice were opened against him. Notwithstanding he had long practised Inoculation under his father, he was represented as the lowest of mankind; one that had just jumped into the profession, without sense, art, or a single degree of merit. How much he deserved this character, time has evinced; and I hope long shewn his first enemies the true complexion, the real *blackness* of their hearts. — The limits of this work will not admit of my mentioning a thousandth part of the scandalous means that have been used to obstruct him in the course of his practice.[91]

Sutton was now at the peak of his career but already many others were copying his method successfully and establishing large practices. These rivals shortened and simplified the preparations and reduced the fees so that Sutton's charges, which David Cockfield had complained were 'so moderate' in 1765, were now considered by some to be excessive. At Glynde, a small village four miles east of Lewes, Sussex, on 17 March 1767 the local doctor, Mr Watson, was awarded the contract to inoculate the poor in preference to Sutton, not only because he was quicker and cheaper but also because there seems to have been local resentment at the huge profits being made in the locality by Sutton. According to Thomas Davies, bailiff of the Glynde estate, in the winter of 1766-1767 Watson and Co. had

> inoculated above 2,000 people ... about Rye, Winchelsea, Romney and the East of Sussex, with equal success but less Physicking and more expedition than Sutton or his people. His method is, to inoculate without previous preparation; and physick afterwards as occasion requires ... The Terms he offered to inoculate us I think is reasonable enough, as he was very desirous of making an Attack on Sutton who inoculated at the Park House and environ, *i.e.* about the Broyle, little Horstead etc. He undertook as many as would be innoculated of Glynd people for 20 Guineas and if there were not 40 people in all he would not insist on so much[92]

An offer two days later by Watson to inoculate 300 people in the parish of Southover (between Glynde and Lewes) 'all for £100' clearly pleased Davies, who regarded Sutton as unnecessarily slow, expensive and greedy. Watson's growing patronage and expanding practice would, thought Davies, damage Sutton's business at Plashett House, five miles north-east of Lewes where he

> takes in none under 6 Guineas and 4 Guineas where the lowest price people are crowded 2 in a Bed and 8 Beds in a room. They clear there at present at the rate of 100 Guineas a Week besides other parties, so that it is high time to pull down their prices; or else they would run away with all the Cash of the Country[93]

In April Davies observed that there were at least 20 doctors advertising as inoculators every week in the *Lewes Journal*

> all in the newest Fashion, and I believe as far as I can hear, all with the same Success. For if but one should happen to die, all the County would soon hear of it.[94]

Daniel Sutton's enormous success as an unqualified practitioner made him doubly unpopular with eminent and fashionable physicians and surgeons. When in December 1767 the six Royal Physicians and Surgeons were required to give their joint opinion on the subject of inoculation they seized the opportunity to belittle the Suttons' achievements. Their report, made public in February 1768, concluded that

> no report whatsoever, in respect to the *general* success of Inoculation in this country, can greatly exceed the truth; that for many years past, scarce one in a thousand has failed under the

inoculated Small-pox, even before the time of the Suttons, where the patients have been properly prepared before and rightly treated during the eruption, with respect to external heat, diet, cooling and opening medicines.

That by a steady observance of these rules, and by a much freer use of the open and even cold air, than was formerly known in this country, Messrs Suttons and others have communicated the small pox with very great success, and have thrown some new lights upon the subject of inoculation, particularly with respect to the exposing of patients to the open air; that the inoculators in England in general have adopted this method, and experience the success of it daily.

That they are of opinion, that the great success of Messrs Suttons is to be attributed to the advantages arising from the exposition to colder air, from a judicious treatment, and the due observance of some other rules, which have usually been followed in this country before, and not to any *peculiar nostrum or specific remedy.*

The Suttons are undoubtedly in some respects improvers in the art of inoculation, but by applying their rules too generally, and by their not making a proper allowance for the difference of the constitutions, have frequently done harm. All their improvements have been adopted by other inoculators, and in the hands of these, the art seems to be carried to a very great perfection.[95]

Others were more generous in acknowledging the Suttons' achievements. A correspondent to the *Gentleman's Magazine* remarked in January 1768 'Tis well known what terrible ravages the small-pox has formerly made in this island', but the Suttonian method of inoculation had 'corrected, and as it were *exorcized* the malignity of this frightful disorder'.[96] William Watson, an experienced inoculator and one of the physicians of the Foundling Hospital thought

They have deserved well, not only on account of some real improvements they have made ... but also for the confidence they have excited in the public, from which vast numbers have been inoculated, who otherwise would not.[97]

The inoculating business operated by the Sutton family as a whole had now reached its zenith and there were 47 'authorised' partnerships in England, Ireland, Wales, Holland (The Hague), France (Paris), Jamaica and Virginia by 1768. Eight partners were members of the Sutton family, including Daniel himself and his father. In Dublin they included Robert Houlton, son of Daniel Sutton's 'officiating clergyman', while at Ingatestone a Mr Steed was the authorised partner.[98] partner.[98]

Growth of competition from other inoculators and the damaging report by the

King's Physicians and Surgeons were not the only problems Daniel Sutton had to face for by about 1768 it was probably becoming clear to him that the London enterprise was unlikely to fulfil his intentions. William Woodville, writing in the 1790s, certainly thought he had failed to establish a fashionable and profitable London practice, claiming that by his move to the capital Daniel had

> hoped to profit by his profession still more than he had done in the country; but his practice fell far short of his expectations; and the two houses, one at Kensington Gore, the other at Brentford, which were procured for his inoculated patients, were soon abandoned.[99]

Too much reliance, however, should not be placed on Woodville's account of Sutton's career, for Daniel was still living at Sutton House, Kensington, in June 1772.[100]

The problems posed by the emergence of other successful inoculators who greatly simplified the preparatory treatment and reduced costs, by the failure of the London practice to become a fashionable moneyspinner and by the rise to prominence of Dr Thomas Dimsdale, whose career will shortly be examined, forced Sutton to make changes. In London he began to concentrate his attention on 'the industrious poor' and his new plan 'of universal Inoculation at the Patient's own Habitations' was advertised in January 1770.

> Convenient houses, in different parts of the Town (each being inhabited by a reputable Surgeon or Apothecary, instructed by him) are engaged;— that to these houses he proposes such patients as have tickets of recommendation from subscribers, are to repair on the day and hour appointed in the said tickets, in order to receive preparatory medicines and instructions, they will then be informed, when to return to be inoculated ... when they will finally receive such medicines and ample directions for their conduct, during the progress of their disease, at their own habitations, as will render any further attendance unnecessary ... This plan is principally intended for the benefit of the industrious poor; such as the families of artificers, handicraftsmen, servants, labourers, etc.[101]

Children under the age of three were excluded 'as they require more attendance than is consistent with the nature of this undertaking'.[102] Aware that he was likely to be criticised on the ground that inoculated patients could spread the disease he assured the public that such a belief was

> totally grounded on apprehension; the disorder being reduced to such a benign state, that it scarcely can be communicated at the most infectious time; but from the period of the preparation till the eruption, it is totally incommunicable, at which time the patient is to return to his own habitation, and there remain[103]

The advertisement concluded with Sutton's exaggerated claim and prophecy that his plan

> besides immediately preserving the most useful part of his
> Majesty's subjects, the industrious poor, will be the means of
> eradicating the natural Small-Pox, so far among the present race,
> that, in a little time, it will be more an act of recollection, than
> present knowledge.[104]

Outside London the partners continued to operate from permanent inoculating houses such as Freston Tower and Daniel began to devote an increasing proportion of his time to what amounted to a travelling inoculating service. This had already commenced by the summer of 1769 when he visited Plymouth where smallpox was then 'very epidemic ... and, among the children particularly, very malignant and mortal'.[105] Soon after arriving he distributed hand-bills advertising his services and 'several were inoculated by him'.[106] A Plymouth surgeon who observed his methods concluded that inoculation had now reached a state of perfection and that Sutton by his successes had

> rendered himself very conspicuous. By a peculiar method he has
> been found to excel, and thereby gained a peculiar eminence ...
> and an ... almost incredible fortune. By these circumstances he
> had gained ... and it must be confessed very deservedly, the
> greatest of reputations, and, in consequence, assumed a sort of
> superiority ... over the generality of our practitioners.[107]

In an advertisement in the *Chelmsford Chronicle*, 3 March 1775, Daniel announced a forthcoming visit to Ingatestone

> to practice Inoculation ... in the Neighbourhood ... where proper
> Houses are provided for the reception of Patients in different
> Classes. Those who are desirous of being inoculated, may be sup-
> plied with Medicines, and proper Directions, by applying to Mr.
> *Sutton*, and at Mr. Robert Caton's, Ingatestone; and every Friday
> at Mr. French's, at the King's-Head, in Chelmsford.

A page-by-page scrutiny of the *Chelmsford Chronicle* and *Ipswich Journal* would pro-bably permit of a fairly complete reconstruction of his travelling service in the 1770s and 1780s. In the winter of 1778-1779, for example, he rented a house at Totham, four miles north of Maldon, which was intended for customers from the Maldon-Witham area but especially from Maldon where, as we have seen, inocula-tion was not permitted except during epidemics. On 1 January 1779 this advertise-ment appeared in the *Chelmsford Chronicle*.

> Messrs Suttons inform the Public, That they continue to take
> in patients for the inoculated SMALL-POX, at their house at
> Totham ... their terms, as usual, For inoculation and board for a
> fortnight two guineas, tea, sugar and wine excepted; one guinea
> for inoculation and the use of the house for a fortnight, the patient
> finding every other necessary; people inoculated at their own
> house for ten shillings and sixpence each.

> Messrs Suttons may be treated with at the Angel in Witham;
> at the Bull and White-Horse, at Maldon; every market-day; and at
> their house at Totham any one day in the week.

By March 1779 he had moved on to Prittlewell.[108] Sutton had purchased a house in neighbouring Eastwood in 1773 and this was probably used for residential patients.[109] In June 1780 he visited Dedham, having previously placed this notice in the *Chelmsford Chronicle*.

> MR. DANIEL SUTTON, having received Invitations to in-
> oculate a few families near Dedham, the beginning of the ensuing
> month: those who may wish to embrace that opportunity of being
> inoculated by him, are respectfully informed that his residence
> will be at Mr THOMAS BROWN'S, surgeon, at Dedham
> aforesaid   London, May 23, 1780[110]

Sutton's career was now long past its peak and it is appropriate at this point to look briefly at the career of Dr Thomas Dimsdale who adopted the Suttonian system of inoculation and became Sutton's greatest rival. Born at Theydon Garnon, near Epping, in May 1712, Thomas was the fourth son of John Dimsdale, surgeon, and his wife Susan, daughter of Thomas Bowyer of Albury Hall near Hertford.[111] His family had been property owners in Essex for centuries and were members of the Society of Friends.[112] Dimsdale's Quaker acquaintances and friends were subsequently to play rôles crucial to his success. After studying medicine under his father and at St Thomas' Hospital he set up a practice at Hertford about 1734[113] and in July 1739 married Mary, daughter of the Quaker banker Nathaniel Brassey of Roxford, near Hertford, M.P. for Hertford 1734-1761.[114] Mary died in 1744 without issue and in order to 'relieve his mind under this loss' Dimsdale served as an army surgeon under the Duke of Cumberland in the 1745 rebellion.[115] He was probably already inoculating by this time and thereafter it formed an important part of his practice. As he wrote in November 1766, 'A considerable share of employment in this branch of my profession has for upwards of twenty years occurred to me'.[116] In June 1746 he married Anne, daughter of John Iles and 'a relation of his first wife',[117] by whom he came into a considerable fortune. About the same time Dimsdale succeeded to the Hertfordshire estates of his cousin Sir John Dimsdale following the death of his widow.[118] He was now able to retire from practice for a while but having a number of children by Anne he was obliged to return to it by 1752[119] and in 1761 obtained a degree of doctor of medicine from King's College, Aberdeen.[120] Already well-established in Hertford as a successful inoculator, he adopted the Suttonian method in January 1765[121] having received reports of the Suttons' successes which he first thought 'too extravagant ... to deserve credit'[122] but which

> upon the strictest enquiry, I found ... were for the most part true,
> and that such who were treated in this way, passed through the dis-
> temper in a more favourable manner, than my own patients, or those
> of the most able practitioners in the old method of inoculation[123]

Thereafter he attracted a wealthy clientèle from a wide area. In 1766 this included Joseph Cockfield of Upton House, West Ham and his friend the poet John Scott of Amwell, both Quakers.[124] Like Daniel Sutton he began undertaking general inoculations in 1766, his first, at Hertford, halting an epidemic. The publication early in 1767 of his popular book *The Present Method of Inoculating for the Small-Pox*, which was soon circulated throughout Europe, including Russia, further enhanced his reputation.[125] As with other doctors who adopted the Suttonian system he first questioned and then, as circumstances demanded, greatly reduced or altogether abandoned the preparation of patients, commenting that

> as I have often been obliged to inoculate without any, and have always had the same success, it has inclined me to think, that much, if not the whole of this process may be dispensed with, except in very full habits, or where other particular circumstances may require it.[126]

The Present Method, embodying as it did the essence of the Suttonian system, now became the standard handbook for inoculators and thus made an important contribution towards increasing both the popularity and success of inoculation.

Dimsdale was now in serious competition with Sutton for the custom of wealthy patients and was able to command high fees for private treatment. For example, in May 1768 he charged £50 to inoculate the Quaker merchant and philanthropist Osgood Hanbury of London and Holfield Grange, Great Coggeshall.[127] But Dimsdale's greatest moment came at the beginning of July when, on the recommendation of his Quaker friend Dr John Fothergill, he was approached by the Russian Ambassador to inoculate Empress Catherine II and the Grand Duke. At first he declined but following a second approach from the Ambassador set out for St Petersburg on 28 July[128] accompanied by his son Nathanael who was 'then studying physic in the University of Edinburgh, and was well instructed in my method',[129] inoculating the Empress on 12 October and the Grand Duke on 30 October, both with complete success. News of the inoculations reached England late in November, the *Gentleman's Magazine* reporting that 'The Empress of Russia who has lately been inoculated for the small pox by Mr. Dimsdale, is perfectly recovered, without one day's confinement'.[130] In reward for his services the Empress made him a baron of the Russian Empire 'with an annuity ... of 500l. to be paid ... in England, besides 10,000l. sterling, which he immediately received, together with the miniature pictures of the Empress and Grand Duke' and £1,000 expenses. Nathanael was 'likewise honoured with the same title of baron'.[131] Dimsdale then spent some time, including two months in Moscow, inoculating the families of the Russian nobility. He returned to England in triumph in 1769 and became the talk of London.[132] When he visited the Fothergill family at Harpur Street, Bloomsbury, on 7 December Betty Fothergill recorded in her diary that

> Baron Dimsdale, and Samuel Galton from Birmingham, breakfasted with us. I was much pleased, and perhaps my ambition was a little flattered, to be in the company of a man who a few months

ago made such a noise in the world, from his receiving so many marks of the favour and friendship of one of the greatest sovereigns in Europe. It was a new thing for me to hear talk of Princes, Counts and Barons in so familiar a style.[133]

Dimsdale then returned to Hertford where he opened an 'Isolation House' to accommodate his numerous patients. He began to overshadow Sutton and was rapidly becoming the first-choice inoculator for the wealthy. For example, although Daniel Sutton inoculated the banker Richard Hoare of Boreham for £20 in 1769, it was Dimsdale whom Hoare employed in 1775 to inoculate his children for a fee of £25.[134] As a member of the gentry Dimsdale was more acceptable to the upper classes than Sutton and, as Abraham has pointed out, 'unlike Sutton he was a polished man of the world, his methods of acquiring practice were orthodox'.[135] People wanted to be inoculated by Sutton's technique but they 'shied at his rough manners and the rowdy way he permitted his patients to behave whilst under his care'[136] and Joseph Cockfield's critical remarks about Sutton's arrangements for the accommodation of patients have already been noted.[137] There may also have been an element of resentment that Sutton had amassed his fortune with indecent speed. Further recognition came for Dimsdale in 1774 when, at the request of George III, he inoculated the celebrated Tahitian chief Omiah whom Captain Tobias Furneaux had brought back to England on board H.M.S. *Adventure* in July.[138] In 1776-1779 he received considerable publicity as a result of his pamphlet battle with John Coakley Lettsom, the London doctor, Quaker and philanthropist. Lettsom supported domiciliary free inoculation of the poor but was vigorously opposed by Dimsdale on the grounds that the practice was dangerous and responsible for spreading the infection.[139] He showed that inoculation 'has been upon the whole rather hurtful than advantageous to the city of London, and that the mortality from Small Pox has lately increased to an alarming degree' and thought 'the loss has fallen principally among those who are not the least useful members of the community, viz — on young persons, the offspring of inferior trades-people, and the labouring poor'.[140] This, of course, was also a criticism of Daniel Sutton's activities in the capital.

In 1780, with his fortune made and reputation firmly established, Dimsdale stood as Parliamentary candidate for Hertford and his own popularity together with the Dimsdale-Brassey interest and the Quaker vote enabled him to top the poll by defeating two other strong local candidates.[141] Shortly afterwards the *English Chronicle* wrote of him

He is very much distinguished in his profession by the industrious and honest exercise of which he has acquired an independent fortune ... He owes his seat entirely to the good opinion entertained of him by his electors, amongst whom he is an old and favourite resident.[142]

In 1781 he made a second visit to Russia where he inoculated the Emperor and his brother Prince Constantine.[143] He was re-elected as M.P. for Hertford after a contest in April 1784[144] and in 1787 became a founder-member and first Treasurer of the Benevolent Medical Society for the United Counties of Essex and Herts.[145] He did not seek re-election to Parliament in 1790 and his son Nathanael succeeded to the seat.[146] Thomas now retired to Bath but finally returned to Hertford where he died aged 89 years on 30 December 1800.[147] At his express wish he was buried in the Friends' Cemetery at Bishops Stortford.[148]

Meanwhile Daniel Sutton had continued to run his inoculating business and when his father died in April 1788 he and his brothers were described as being 'very eminent in the practice'. Two, including Daniel, were in London, one, probably Robert, was at Bury St Edmunds, another was in Oxfordshire and two were in France.[149] By 1792 he was spending summer and winter at Maisonette and the other months at his London house, 5 Great Newport Street, near Leicester Square. He was still advertising for customers and was prepared to travel to any part of the kingdom. He inoculated in the capital while resident there and at other times 'he occassionally accommodates Patients' at Maisonette.[150] Daniel's great period of pre-eminence was long since over and the slow but inexorable decline of his business must have been difficult to endure. When he published *The Inoculator* in 1796, some 30 years after it was first promised, no acknowledgement was made of his father's pioneering role. On the title page he described himself as 'Daniel Sutton, Surgeon, Who introduced the New Method of Inoculation into this Kingdom in the Year 1763', while the preface contains this somewhat pathetic and bitter statement:

> I find it has been circulated, That I am not the person who in-
> troduced the New System of Inoculation:— That I am not the
> person, who some years since resided and practised Inoculation at
> Kensington-Gore ... that for many years I had quitted my profes-
> sion, and was long since dead.[151]

After setting out and explaining his method clearly and in considerable detail he then displayed his contempt for the medical establishment by remarking 'What opinion the Faculty at large may entertain of my theory, or speculative reasoning, I know not; nor am I very solicitous about it'.[152]

It has been shown in this chapter how the Sutton family and Daniel in par-ticular made the most important contribution to smallpox control and elimination in Britain since the introduction of inoculation in 1721. While there is a temptation to think of Daniel Sutton as not so much a medical practicioner as a very ambitious, energetic and publicity-conscious businessman intent on amassing a fortune, the fact remains that his three years of unrivalled success and supremacy in the mid-1760s marked the beginning of the widespread acceptance and popularity of in-oculation in the later eighteenth century. Although many doctors quickly adopted the Suttonian system, notably Thomas Dimsdale who achieved popular fame, ac-quired considerable wealth and even overshadowed Sutton, there was no doubt in the mind of William Woodville as to the magnitude of the contribution made by Daniel Sutton when in 1796 he wrote

A new era in the history of inoculation had now taken place, by the introduction of the Suttonian practice, which in the year 1765 had extended so rapidly in the counties of Essex and Kent as to much interest the public, who were not less surprised by the novel manner in which it was conducted, than by the uninterrupted success with which it was attended upon a prodigious number of persons ... Though ... accounts of Mr. [Daniel] Sutton's practice magnified it beyond its real merit, yet not a doubt was entertained but that the Suttonian plan of inoculation was incomparably more successful than that of any other practitioner.[153]

James Moore's summary in 1815 confirmed Woodville's assessment.

Daniel Sutton, with his secret nostrums, propagated inoculation more in half a dozen years, than both the faculties of Medicine and Surgery, with the aid of the Church, and the example of the Court, had been able to do in half a century.[154]

The recognition by Woodville and Moore of Daniel Sutton's rôle was, however, tempered by criticism of his 'unworthy devices' and in particular his attempt to keep secret his method 'until no farther benefit could accrue from concealment'.[155]

In his final years Sutton witnessed the introduction of vaccination (1798) and the rejection of inoculation by the majority of doctors. He died in semi-obscurity aged 83 years at his London residence in Hart Street, Bloomsbury Square, in February 1819. In a short obituary in the March issue of the *Gentleman's Magazine* he was credited with having carried out inoculation

to an immense extent, and with extraordinary success at Ingatestone, and subsequently in the Metropolis, and various parts of the kingdom. The benefits which the world has derived from Mr. Sutton's practice have been duly appreciated, and will cause his name and memory ever to be recollected with respect and honourable distinction.[156]

But the continuing support for vaccination and consequent campaign to discredit inoculation, particularly among doctors and by successive governments, was to culminate in 1840 with legislation banning inoculation, thus ensuring that the name Daniel Sutton was not remembered.

5

Inoculation and Vaccination:
the Transition, 1798-1840

In the history of smallpox immunisation the years *c.*1750-1798 may be viewed as the age of inoculation, when the medical innovation of causing mild illness to prevent a major attack had overcome the considerable opposition of its early years to become a widely accepted practice. The new method of giving immunity, introduced in 1798 and later termed vaccination, also met with suspicion and hostility and inoculation continued to be widely performed until it was made a criminal offence in 1840. The purpose of vaccination was the same as that of inoculation but the virus used was cowpox, a disease of the udder of the cow. Like inoculation, the cowpox virus used in vaccination was introduced into the human body through the skin, usually on the arm. Vaccination was therefore simply inoculation with cowpox and it continued to be thought of as such for many years after January 1803 when the term vaccination, derived from the Latin *variolae vaccinae*, was first used.[1]

The tradition of milkmaids' fine healthy complexions in poems and folk-songs of the sixteenth to nineteenth centuries doubtless derived from the smallpox immunity obtained through contracting cowpox by handling infected udders, but it was not until the eighteenth century that the link was made, in Gloucestershire, between smallpox immunity and the cowpox sores on milkmaids' hands.[2] In 1765 the Medical Society of London received a paper from a Dr Fewster entitled 'Cow Pox and its Ability to prevent Smallpox'.[3] Fewster was also an inoculator 'who in his early days was associated with Sutton' and 'had repeatedly heard the tradition that Cow Pox afforded security against Small Pox, and had met with cases in his own practice which seemed to support the tradition'.[4] Nine years later a Dorset farmer, Benjamin Jesty, who had had cowpox as a young man and was aware of its traditional powers, vaccinated his wife and two sons with cowpox virus direct from an infected udder, using a large needle. Although no account of Jesty's action was published at the time it seems probable that knowledge of the preventive power of cowpox was spreading from isolated dairying areas. This was followed in 1781 with the proposal by a Mr Nash that cowpox should be used in preference to smallpox virus as it was not infectious, but he died in 1785 and his work remained unpublished.[5]

The first scientific experiment with cowpox was carried out in 1796 by Edward Jenner, a successful Gloucestershire doctor and experienced inoculator, who had been interested in the subject since about 1775. Writing in 1801 he recalled how

> My inquiry into the nature of Cow Pox commenced upwards of twenty-five years ago. My attention to this singular disease was first excited by observing, that among those whom in the country I was frequently called upon to inoculate, many resisted every effort to give them the Small Pox. These patients I found had undergone a disease they called the Cow Pox, contracted by milk-

ing cows affected with a peculiar eruption on their teats. On inquiry, it appeared that it had been known among the dairies time immemorial, and that a vague opinion prevailed that it was a preventive of the Small Pox.

This opinion I found was, comparatively, new among them: for all the older farmers declared that they had no such idea in their early days — a circumstance that seemed easily to be accounted for, from my knowing that the common people were very rarely inoculated for the Small Pox, till that practice was rendered general by the improved method introduced by the Suttons. So that the working people in the dairies were seldom put to the test of the preventive powers of the Cow Pox.[6]

On 14 May 1796 Jenner vaccinated an eight-year-old boy, James Phipps, with material from a cowpox sore on the hand of Sarah Nelmes, the daughter of a local farmer, and on 1 July inoculated him with matter from a smallpox pustule, several incisions being made on both arms. No smallpox symptoms resulted and Jenner then submitted a paper to the Royal Society. Further experiments and observations followed; in 1798 he vaccinated John Baker, aged five years, with material from an infected cow and he recorded 17 other cases of people who appeared to have obtained immunity from smallpox by contracting cowpox directly from cows. Later in 1798 Jenner published his *Inquiry into ... Variolae Vaccinae ... known by the name of cowpox.*[7] The idea of calling cowpox smallpox of the cow and giving it a Latin name was Jenner's. His argument was based on the propositions that those who had suffered from naturally acquired cowpox were immune from smallpox, that cowpox could be carried from arm to arm and that all who had been vaccinated would be protected from smallpox. The advantages of cowpox over smallpox lymph were that it was safer to use, generally caused a much less severe illness and the treatment was cheaper to carry out. Moreover, unlike smallpox, cowpox was not transmitted aerially and the use of cowpox virus therefore did not entail the risk of spreading disease among unprotected members of the population. Jenner also believed (incorrectly) that cowpox gave lifelong immunity from smallpox.

Among the leading London doctors from whom Jenner received encouragement was George Pearson, Physician to St George's Hospital, who late in 1798 published *An Inquiry Concerning the History of Cow Pox.* While calling for further experiments and observations Pearson nevertheless strongly supported Jenner. Events now began to move quickly. By March 1799 Pearson was convinced of the utility of cowpox as a preventive for smallpox and began offering to supply cowpox lymph to other doctors. The publication of Jenner's *Further Observations on the Variolae Vaccinae* followed in April and in October Pearson published in *The Medical and Physical Journal* reports from doctors to whom he had sent cowpox lymph,[8] concluding that 'If the vaccine inoculation proceeds with equal mildness as it has done the last four months, doubtless the variolous incision must in no remote period be superseded'.[9]

In 1800 Jenner, who had shown no inclination to embark on large programmes of treatment, accepted an invitation from the Duke of York, Commander-in-Chief, to vaccinate the soldiers of the 85th Regiment and their families at Colchester. The *Chelmsford Chronicle* carried the following report of the treatment, performed in June.

> Dr. Jenner, by desire of his Royal Highness the Duke of York, has been down to Colchester, and with the assistance of his nephew, Mr. G. Jenner, has inoculated the 85th regiment with cowpox. In so mild a manner did the disease shew itself, that scarcely a man was off his duty during the whole progress; and yet so effectually that, on exposing many of those men to the smallpox by inoculation and otherwise, on whom the cowpox had produced no constitutional symptoms, not the least effect was produced. The soldiers wives and the children were at the same time inoculated and experienced the same consequences.[10]

Shortly after the Colchester demonstration the new treatment became general practice in the army and navy

> so that it is now actually practised with success in the naval and military hospitals, and in the regiments and ships of war upon service; when it has this particular advantage over the smallpox [inoculation], that it does not prevent those who are under it from doing their duty.[11]

Later in 1800 Jenner published his *A continuation of Facts and Observations relative to the Variolae Vaccinae or Cowpox* and William Woodville his *Observations on the Cow-Pox*, the latter containing reports of some 2,000 vaccination experiments carried out by him at the London Smallpox and Inoculation Hospital since January 1799.

The new practice soon spread from London to provincial towns and villages. In the winter of 1799-1800 Dr J. Hastings treated 200 poor inhabitants of a Sussex parish 'and surrounding respectable families were so well pleased with its result, that they came with their children and servants, to the number of 150 more'.[12] Another doctor, D. Taylor of Wotton-under-Edge, Gloucestershire, announced in April 1800 that he was

> so fully convinced, by mature investigation, from experiments of my own, and from a critical examination of the practice of others, that this new substitute disease possesses every security, every advantage its discoverer (Dr. Jenner) first inculcated, that I am at this time engaging in a very extensive gratuitous Cow-pox inoculation, from the conviction that the practice demands the support of every professional man, and of every friend to humanity.[13]

It was being widely practised in Essex by 1800 and the Fingringhoe farmer Joseph Page recorded in his diary on 5 November 'Doctor Smyth came and inoculated my wife and 2 children, Sarah Brig, maidservant and Sarah Everit, nursegirl, for the cowpox as a substitute and preventive to the smallpox'.[14] By the end of the year it was also well established and recommended by doctors in Chester, Durham, Leeds and Manchester.[15] The Nottingham General Hospital had abandoned inoculation in favour of the new treatment by the end of 1800[16] and other hospitals, including the Whitehaven Dispensary, followed suit in 1801.[17] In June 1801 the General Court of the Essex and Herts Benevolent Medical Society passed this unanimous resolution:

> That the thanks of this court be given to Dr Jenner, for his invaluable Treatise on the Variola Vaccinae, wherein he has clearly and satisfactorily demonstrated, that the inoculated Cow pox is a certain preventive of the Small pox.
>
> That as men of humanity, associated for the purposes of benevolence, we should be wanting to the character we assume, did we neglect the present opportunity of bearing our testimony to the value of this providential discovery, which, if generally practised, we are of opinion, would effectually eradicate the Small pox, one of the severest scourges of the human race.
>
> That this court, in thus requesting Dr Jenner to accept their unanimous thanks for his inestimable publication, entertain no doubt but posterity will do honour to his memory, and record his name amongst the real friends of man.[18]

In June 1802 Jenner was voted a reward of £10,000 by the House of Commons and in January 1803 a number of his friends and admirers, including the Duke of Bedford, Admiral Berkeley, John Coakley Lettsom and William Wilberforce, formed the Royal Jennerian Society to promote the aims of universal vaccination. On 3 February Jenner became first President with the Queen as patron.[19] Thirteen vaccination stations were opened in London by the Society and over 12,000 vaccinations were carried out in the first year.

In the meantime opposition had already begun, the *British Critic* concluding as early as 1799 'that the Cow-pox is sometimes a severe and even dangerous disease'.[20] Doubts were fuelled by reports of failures, including an incident at Maldon where a child inoculated with cowpox early in 1801 died of smallpox a few weeks later. The *Morning Herald* commented

> The inoculation for the Cow pox, is now clearly ascertained to be no preventative of the small pox — a child at Maldon in Essex, on whom the Eruption of the former was fully produced, took the latter disorder a few weeks afterwards, and died of it; this with many similar, and well attested instances, will, it is hoped, lead to the abolition of this novel and beastly practice of transmixing animal humours, into the human blood.[21]

The *Chelmsford Chronicle*, however, refrained from any criticism, merely reporting that 'The Cow Pox inoculation, we understand ... has not proved efficacious in one or two instances at Maldon'.[22]

Such failures were indeed common and even Jenner had had problems. He lost his original cowpox strain following his return from London in July 1798 and had a series of failures in December 1798 with a strain obtained from an infected cow at Stonehouse, Gloucestershire, eight miles from his own village of Berkeley, his patients suffering severe inflammation and ulceration of the arm.[23] As Peter Razzell has pointed out,

> Jenner's experience with inoculating cowpox up to the end of 1798 was typical of what was to be found by later workers: frequent failures of the injection to take, and in those inoculations which were successful, occasional severe ulceration and inflammation of the arm.[24]

Some members of the medical profession saw cowpox inoculation as a great gift to mankind and a means of exterminating smallpox, but opposition came from others who questioned Jenner's sweeping assertions as well as from those with practices in smallpox inoculation and treatment whose incomes were threatened by the new discovery. In 1800 one of the earliest medical critics, Dr Benjamin Moseley, Physician to the Royal Hospital, Chelsea, put 'some very formidable objections' to cowpox inoculation and the transfer of an animal disease to man in the second edition of his *Treatise on Sugar*.[25] This line of argument, which had a strong popular appeal, was also employed by others like the correspondent to the *Gentleman's Magazine* who wrote in April 1800

> The inoculation of the Cow-pock being in fact the introduction of a bestial disease into the human body, it must be admitted that some other very different diseases, may arise in consequence[26]

A month later Charles Brown, a Hatton Garden surgeon, wrote to the editor of the *Magazine*

> to acquaint your numerous readers with three incontrovertible and most important facts, which, I think, will make families more cautious than they have hitherto been, in suffering practitioners, infected with the Cow-pox mania, to deceive their patients with regard to the advantages to be derived from the introduction of such an unnatural, such a hideous disease: 1. That the Cow-pox, contrary to the assertions of Messrs. Jenner, Woodville, and Pearson, is to be taken by infection; 2. That those who have had the Cow-pox have several of them since had the Small pox; and, 3. That nasty, ugly and inveterate ulcers, have remained in the arm where the matter was inserted long after the disease in the system had subsided. Proofs of these propositions are ready to be adduced, and personal reference given, if required.[27]

Shortly afterwards, in July 1800, another correspondent claimed it to be 'unnatural to transfer to the human species the diseases of any quadruped or other animal' and asked 'Why is it needful to inoculate from the cow? From an human subject it is easy, cheaply done, and perfectly free from danger'.[28] At Nottingham General

Portrait of Daniel Sutton by an unknown artist, *c.*1767 (*reproduced by courtesy of Mr J.A. Campbell*).

Above. Maisonette, Ingatestone, purchased by Daniel Sutton in May 1766 (*photograph by N. Hammond, 1984*). *Below left*. Freston Tower near Ipswich in 1810. It was here that Daniel Sutton's partner Mr Bucke performed inoculation from 1767 to 1779 (*reproduced by courtesy of S.R.O.*). *Below right*. Daniel Sutton's inoculation house in Eastwood. Photograph *c.*1920 (*D/DS 232/27*).

Pinchgut Hall, Maldon's pest house for most of the eighteenth century (*photograph by N. Hammond, 1984*).

Great Coggeshall Pest House, built 1759 (*photograph by N. Hammond, 1984*).

VACCINATION.
Pub.d by J. L. Bugle Plaist Court 70 at Flit St.

June 1802

'Vaccination'. In this cartoon dated June 1802 a monster symbolizes the new treatment. Its body, horns, hind-legs and tail are cow-like but its gaping jaws resemble
those of a crocodile while its fore-feet are feline and its ears serrated. The running-
sores on its body are inscribed 'Pestilence', 'Plague', 'Feotid Ulcers', 'Leprosy' and
'Pandoras Box'. On the left three doctors with horns and cows' tails are throwing
tiny naked infants into the monster's mouth. From the pocket of the most prominent projects a document labelled '£10,000', showing him to be Jenner, to whom a
parliamentary grant of £10,000 was made in June 1802. On the right other infants,
with horns and tails, are being excreted. These a fourth horned doctor, one foot
resting on a volume of 'Lectures on Botany', shovels into a dungcart. This is probably a representation of Jenner's supporter William Woodville who was also a
botanist. The anti-vaccination forces, five men with shields and swords, advance
from the middle-distance having descended from a mountain surmounted by the
'Temple of Fame'. On an adjacent obelisk are inscribed the names 'Moseley',
'Squirrill', 'Rowley', 'Birch' and 'Lipscomb' (*British Museum, Department of Prints
and Drawings, political and personal satire no. 9,925, reproduced by courtesy of the
Trustees*).

The Cow Pock _ or _ the Wonderful Effects of the New Inoculation! _ Vide _ the Publications of ye Anti Vaccine Society

'The Cow-Pock — or — the Wonderful Effects of the New Inoculation!' Cartoon by Gillray caricaturing vaccination at the London Smallpox and Inoculation Hospital where William Woodville was Physician. The vaccinator in the cartoon, however, is Jenner and the date of publication, 12 June 1802, coincides with his first parliamentary grant. The scene combines fantasy and realism. Poor patients crowd in through a doorway on the left while in the room are those whose treatment has had dire consequences. In the centre a comely and frightened young woman sits in an armchair, Jenner holds her right arm and gashes it with his knife while a pauper schoolboy holds up a bucket of 'Vaccine Pock hot from ye Cow'. A medicine-chest and a close-stool stand on the left. On the chest are bottles, a syringe and a tub of 'Opening Mixture'. This a haughty assistant ladles into the mouths of waiting patients. On the wall is a picture in which kneeling worshippers pay homage to the statue of the golden calf (*reproduced by permission of the Wellcome Institute Library, London*).

'Vaccination against Small Pox, or mercenary and merciless Spreaders of Death and Devastation driven out of Society'. This cartoon by Cruikshank was published on 20 June 1808, a few days after the founding, with Government support, of the National Vaccine Establishment. On the right Jenner stands between two colleagues holding a vaccination knife on the blade of which is inscribed 'Milk of human Kindness'. Above a cherub is about to crown him with a laurel wreath, saying 'The preserver of the Human Race'. On the left three inoculators are retreating. The blades of their huge inoculating knives are dripping blood and inscribed with the words 'The curse of human kind'. Addressing the inoculators Jenner says 'Oh Brothers, Brothers, suffer the love of Gain to be Overcome by Compassion for your fellow creatures, and do not delight to plunge whole Famileis in the deepest distress, by the untimely loss of their nearest and Dearest relatives'. The nearest inoculator is saying 'Curse on these Vaccinators we shall all be starved, why Brother I have matter enough here to Kill 50', to which the next adds 'Aye-Aye. I always order them to be constantly out in the air, in order to spread the contagion', the third commenting 'And those would communicate it to 500 more'. The ground is covered by heavily-spotted dead or dying infants. In the centre background a mother clasps a spotted child while her infected husband leans against her. On the extreme right stands a woman saying 'Surley the disorder of the Cow is preferable to that of the Ass' (*British Museum, Department of Prints and Drawings, political and personal satire no. 11,093, reproduced by courtesy of the Trustees*).

Watercolour painting by Lance Calkin depicting a public vaccinator at work, published in *The Graphic*, 1 February 1902 (*reproduced by permission of the Wellcome Institute Library, London*).

County of Essex   *Division of Rochford*

We the undersigned two of His Majesty's Justices of the Peace acting for the said County this 22ⁿᵈ day of January 1903 at the Court House Southend, Rochford in the said County hereby certify that Ebenezer Henry Thompson of Leigh — in the said County fisherman — the parent of a child named Doris Bertha — born on the 25ᵗʰ day of September 1902 has satisfied us that he conscientiously believes that Vacination would be prejudicial to the health of such child

Given under our hands the day and year first above written

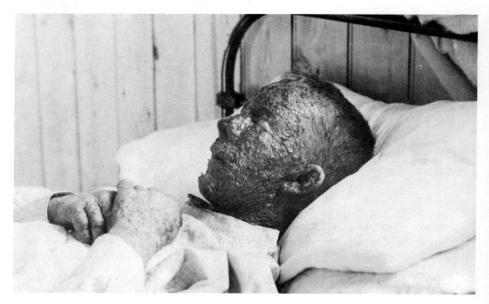

Above. Certificate of consciencious objection exempting Ebenezer Thompson, a Leigh fisherman, from having his infant daughter Doris Bertha vaccinated, 22 January 1903 (*D/DS 321/1*). *Below.* Malignant confluent smallpox ('black smallpox') in its final stage. The patient, Ephraim Beard, a Gloucester baker, was admitted to hospital 5 April 1896 and died eight days later (*reproduced by permission of the Wellcome Institute Library, London*).

Hospital where inoculation was abandoned in favour of vaccination in 1800 the surgeon, Dr John Attenburrow, had 'to contend against the prejudices of old women in men's clothing, among whom were some of the faculty', while 'the prejudice of all classes against the newly adopted practice, was at first very general and violent'.[29]

This early criticism, prejudice and suspicion was answered by the Revd George Jenner, Edward Jenner's nephew. Addressing himself in particular to those who objected to the use of an animal disease he pointed out in May 1800,

> there is not a finer race of people in the island than the farmers and farmers' wives in our Western dairy counties, many of whom had the Cow-pox when they were boys and girls. In short ... it is a well-known fact that it does not injure the constitution in the least; and in this part of the country, we have known the fact for many years past of its being a preventative of the Small-pox, when it has been communicated in its *perfect state* casually from the cow to the milkers. We now look at one another with astonishment, to think that the idea of inoculating this mild disease as a substitute for the Small-pox, and making the experiment of transferring it from one person to another, should not have entered into the human mind till taken up by Dr. Jenner, to whose original labours in this new and unparalleled improvement in science, the world is under great obligations.[30]

The argument was, however, far from being one-sided and other doctors attacked, either directly or by implication, the practice of smallpox inoculation. In June 1800 William Blair, Surgeon of the Lock Hospital, London, refuted 'vague and delusive reports' that a few patients had died of cowpox, that others had suffered from 'obstinate and disgusting ulcers upon the inoculated arm', while 'Mr. Bagster's child, who was said to have died of Cow-pox' he found, on enquiry, 'had fallen a victim of the inoculated Small-pox under the care of Mr. Sutton'.[31] A month later 36 physicians and surgeons, including Blair and Lettsom, pointed out that 'unfounded reports' had been circulated which had 'a tendency to prejudice the mind of the publick against inoculation of the Cow-pox' and declared 'that the inoculated Cow-pox is a much milder and safer disease than the inoculated small-pox'.[32] The contagiousness of patients undergoing inoculation was also emphasized, a regular correspondent to the *Gentleman's Magazine* pointing out in April 1801

> To those who may urge that we already have an antidote to the smallpox in its own inoculation, let it be remembered, that, however salutary this practice may be to those who actually undergo it, it is not so to the community at large.[33]

Another group of doctors preferred to reserve judgement until vaccination had received a longer trial and in the meantime to continue with inoculation. Their attitude was summed up by a 'long experienced' Cambridge physician who wrote in

March 1802,

> The regular mode of Inoculation for the Small-pox is now so easy, so familiar, and general, and so safe and secure, not one in one hundred reputed to be unsuccessful, that it is abandoning a safe established practice for a practice novel, and cannot be ascertained, as to its safety, from future infection of the Small-pox, under twenty years trial and experience.[34]

In London reports of mishaps like the Maldon death and the criticism and doubts of doctors like Moseley and Brown resulted in widespread prejudice against the new treatment and led to an upsurge in the popularity of inoculation. Speaking about this in January 1803 William Wilberforce observed

> that, out of every 100 who had been vaccinated at the Small-pox hospital, not five would have submitted, had they not supposed it to have been the old-fashioned mode of Inoculation.[35]

This suggests that preference for the tried and trusted practice of inoculation was overwhelming in London by about 1802 and that William Woodville, Physician to the London Smallpox Hospital, was forced to employ deceit on a massive scale in order to perform vaccination.

Suspicion and criticism of vaccination mounted as more mishaps were reported and in 1805 Moseley published the second edition of *A Treatise on the Lues Bovilla or Cowpox*, in which he expanded his objections first put forward in 1800. He also believed that cowpox would not prove to be a certain and permanent preventive against smallpox and defended inoculation, condemning the rôle of the Established Church in promoting the new treatment. Among the many examples of alleged failure of cowpox were Mr Green's child and Mr Mitchell's child, both of Maldon, vaccinated in 1801,[36] while Dr Smyth Stuart's child at Billericay, vaccinated on 14 April 1802, suffered 'hard painful tumours, and blotches, that terminated in obstinate phagadenic ulcers' and eventually died on 1 October 'in the most distressing pain'.[37] In calling for the abandonment of vaccination Moseley expressed the opinion that the 'number of valuable beings, exposed to the ravages of the Small Pox, by reliance on the Cow Pox, has increased to an alarming degree, within the last six years'. If inoculation was not immediately restored and adopted 'dreadful havoc must ensue whenever the Small Pox shall rage epidemically, as it did before the practice of Inoculation!'.[38] Moseley's *Treatise* was followed by William Rowley's *Cow-Pox Inoculation no Security Against Small-Pox Infection* in which this prominent doctor, who held the post of Physician to St Marylebone Infirmary, praised Moseley's work in exposing cowpox failures, defended inoculation and pointed out that 'small-pox inoculation was a well-known, proved and absolute prevention from receiving the *natural Small-pox* infection, as millions of people now living can testify'.[39] Was it not, asked Rowley, 'despotic, inhuman tyranny' to force mankind and 'innocent infants' in particular to receive a 'filthy disease of beasts'?[40] In December 1805 George Lipscomb, House Surgeon of St Bartholomew's Hospital, published *A Dissertation on the Failure and the Mischiefs of the Disease called Cow-*

Pox in which he concluded

> it must appear very evident that the judgement which has been
> pronounced in favour of Vaccination *was premature*, and *is in-*
> *defensible* : that the inoculated Cow-pox is sometimes a severe and
> dangerous disease, and sometimes even fatal : that it is productive
> of many horrid and loathsome symptoms, tedious, distressing,
> and destructive; unknown to the human constitution until the un-
> fortunate and incautious introduction of the *Jennerian* practice:—
> I therefore conclude, that the safe, excellent, and well-understood
> practice of Small-pox Inoculation, which always affords a perma-
> nent security against future contagion, is degraded even by a
> *comparison* with the Cow-pox, and that VACCINATION ought
> to be immediately, and *for ever*, ABANDONED.[41]

The flow of anti-vaccination and pro-inoculation literature continued in 1806 with
the publication of John Birch's *Serious Reasons for Uniformly Objecting to the Prac-*
tice of Vaccination. Birch, Surgeon to St Thomas' Hospital and Surgeon Extraordinary to the Prince Regent thought it had been easy to foresee that the initial enthusiasm for vaccination should have subsided and that 'the Public should express
regret that what ought to have been admitted as an experiment only, had been
adopted as practice'.[42] He thought the use by pro-vaccinationists of statistics il-
lustrating the high smallpox mortality amongst the poor in London to be
misleading and asked why it was not remembered

> that in the populous parts of the Metropolis, where the abun-
> dance of children exceed the means of providing food, and rai-
> ment for them, this pestilential disease is considered as a merciful
> provision on the part of Providence, to lessen the burthen of a
> poor man's family?[43]

Convinced that inoculation could reduce smallpox mortality 'to its old standard' he
pleaded for the abolition of vaccination for seven years. If at the end of that time he
was proved wrong he would revise his views 'and become as devout a worshipper of
the Cow, as any idolator'.[44]

Meanwhile another pressure group, with Lettsom, Wilberforce and Edward
Jenner himself amongst its members, had emerged by 1802 and was seeking legislation to promote vaccination and ban inoculation. Jenner was privately urging the
statutory prohibition of inoculation and Wilberforce, among others, took up the
matter publicly. Enthusiastic as ever, Lettsom declared in November 1802 that
with Government support 'Inoculation by the Cow-pock ... will ... ultimately
eradicate the greatest scourge of human existence that ever desolated the
Universe'[45] and in January 1803 Wilberforce proposed that the Executive Committee of the Royal Jennerian Society should press Parliament for an 'act for the extension of Vaccination'.[46] A regular Bath correspondent to the *Gentleman's Magazine*
deplored the continuing practice of inoculation 'in the opulent and crowded city of
Bath', for which he blamed the greed of some doctors who

are paid better for inoculating with Small Pox matter than they are when they inoculate with Cow Pock matter, because they look upon the Small Pox [as] more dangerous. In short, I fear that avarice will greatly prevent the total extermination of the Small Pox.[47]

He entreated doctors to join the Royal Jennerian Society 'to bring in a bill to prevent any from inoculating any more with *contagious* matter'. If this could not be achieved he wanted 'an act to oblige all, who inoculate with contagious matter, to do it at a lone house, at least two miles from any town or village'.[48]

Nothing came of this campaign and when in 1806 Jenner, now partly on the defensive as a result of publicity given to vaccination failures and casualties, replied to the critics of vaccination with the publication of his work *On the Varieties and Modifications of the Vaccine Pustule, occasioned by an Herpetic State of the Skin* he was still pressing for the abolition of inoculation. In the meantime the Royal College of Physicians was carrying out an inquiry on vaccination at the request of Parliament and its report in April 1807 in favour of the new treatment concluded that

Till vaccination becomes general, it will be impossible to prevent the constant recurrence of the natural smallpox by means of those who are inoculated, except it should appear proper to the legislature to adopt, in its wisdom, some measure by which those who still, from terror or prejudice, prefer the smallpox to the vaccine disease, may in thus consulting the gratification of their own feelings, be prevented from doing mischief to their neighbours.[49]

The College's report was credited shortly afterwards with having 'greatly tended to remove the mistaken apprehensions of the doubtful, and established confidence in the public mind'.[50] If this was the case such confidence was to be very short-lived.

Jenner now asked Spencer Perceval, the Chancellor of the Exchequer, whether it was the Government's intention to ban inoculation, and upon being told that nothing could be done poured out his disappointment to Lettsom.

You will be sorry to hear the result of my interview with the Minister, Mr. Perceval. I solicited this honour with the sole view of inquiring whether it was the intention of government to give a check to the licentious manner in which small-pox inoculation is at this time conducted in the metropolis. I instanced the mortality it occasioned in language as forcible as I could utter, and showed him clearly that it was the great source from which this pest was disseminated through the country as well as through the town. But, alas! all I said availed nothing; and the speckled monster is still to have liberty that the Smallpox Hospital, the delusions of Moseley, and the caprices and prejudices of the misguided poor, can possibly give him. I cannot express to you the chagrin and disappointment I felt at this interview.[51]

Although Parliament rewarded Jenner with a further £20,000 at the end of July 'for promulgating his discovery of Vaccine Inoculation' and set up the National Vaccine Establishment in June 1808, his efforts to secure the abolition of inoculation remained unsuccessful. The Parliamentary debate on the question of the reward, however, revealed considerable support for abolition, William Sturges-Bourne, for example, remarking

> I think that the legislature would be as much justified in taking a measure to prevent this evil by restraint, as a man would be in snatching a firebrand out of the hands of a maniac just as he was going to set fire to a city.[52]

One further important event took place in 1807, the founding of the London Vaccine Institution at 6 Bond Street, Walbrook, by Dr John Walker following a quarrel with Jenner which had led to Walker's dismissal from the post of Resident Vaccinator of the Royal Jennerian Society. By the end of 1807 the Society, torn by dissention, was already in decline but the Institution had, within the space of a few months, appointed 1,554 doctors as vaccinators 'in various parts of the British Empire'. In the county of Essex, for example, no less than 45 places had a resident Institution vaccinator. By January 1808 the Institution, which described itself as 'an association of zealous friends of the new practice, who had succeeded in extending the benefits of vaccination throughout the empire', claimed to have vaccinated more than 52,000 people free of charge, commenting that

> If it has justly been considered by the Legislature, an object worthy of the national munificence, to reward the Physician who first introduced the valuable discovery of Vaccination, to the public attention; it is still more important that the benefits should be carried into *full effect*. The LONDON VACCINE INSTITU-TION, from the extensive system it has adopted, is calculated to accomplish this great end. The managers are animated with the expectation that the persevering exertions of this society, aided by the wonted liberality of the public, will greatly contribute, at no distant period, to the annihilation of one of the greatest evils incident to the condition of man:— and that the Small Pox, the desolating calamity of twelve centuries, will be remembered only by the name.[53]

Further attempts in the next few years to obtain legislation to restrict or ban inoculation, including a bill promoted by the Vaccine Board in 1813, all failed and a bill to make vaccination compulsory for the poor introduced in 1813 by Lord Boringdon and supported by many doctors 'was discouraged, as injurious to personal freedom'.[54] Discussion in Parliament about the merits and disadvantages of the two methods of smallpox immunisation now ceased and was not revived until the epidemic of 1837-1840.

The progress of vaccination received another set-back in the epidemic years

1816-1819, the worst since the introduction of the new treatment, for the imper-
manence of the immunity it afforded was now being widely revealed. At Ulverston,
Cumberland, 14 previously vaccinated children were inoculated in 1816 as an additional precaution and all of them took the infection.[55] Enquiries made in Norfolk
and Suffolk by Dr John Cross of Norwich showed that 30 out of the 91 doctors who
replied had carried out inoculation in 1819.[56] There was clearly considerable
pressure to inoculate rather than vaccinate from a substantial proportion of the
ordinary population and poor as well as from some vestries, but doctors, appalled
by 3,000 cases with 500 fatalities at Norwich in 1819, increased their demands for
compulsory vaccination. A similar pattern emerged in a smallpox outbreak in the
Chichester area in 1821 when out of 130-140 cases of the disease 80 were in
previously vaccinated people.[57] Although the Chichester doctors advocated vaccination they nevertheless inoculated about 50 children in the city whose parents refused vaccination.[58] In November the disease was carried from Chichester to the
village of Bosham, four miles to the west, and thence spread throughout the surrounding countryside. Bowing to the wishes of the poor inhabitants the Bosham
overseers agreed to a general inoculation, employing the local farmer and amateur
inoculator, Mr Pearce.[59] This led to a great demand for inoculation by Pearce and
other empirics which ultimately overcame 'the conscientious forbearance' of
doctors in the worst-affected area. The floodgates were now opened, for inoculation

> once acceded to by a single Practitioner ... was immediately
> followed by his brethren, as a matter of course, and almost of
> necessity. Accordingly, variolous inoculation was at length
> adopted by all the Surgeons of Emsworth, Havant and the vicini-
> ty, and was carried on, in that part of the country, with great
> vigour, for a space of six or eight weeks.[60]

With these events in mind the writer of this account, John Forbes, Senior Physician
to the Chichester Dispensary, observed in August 1822

> it is ... not only unfair, but decidedly injurious to the cause of vac-
> cination, for medical men to attempt to maintain the same high
> ground, which they were accustomed to assume in defending vac-
> cination some years since. The numerous failures, in all parts of
> the kingdom, of late years, must have convinced every medical
> man, that the cow-pox is not, what its discoverer and every friend
> of humanity had fondly deemed it, — an almost infallible preven-
> tive of small-pox; but only a preventive in a great majority of cases
> and an almost invariable mitigator of the symptoms in the small
> proportion of individuals whom it fails to secure from the
> disease.[61]

Two years later Forbes' comments were echoed by the pro-vaccinationist Dr H.W.
Carter, Senior Physician to the Kent and Canterbury Hospital, following a serious
smallpox outbreak at Canterbury which caused the number of free vaccinations at
the Canterbury Hospital to rise from 50 in 1823 to 588 in the first six months of

1824, but which also stimulated demand for inoculation. When the epidemic had passed Carter reported that

> The cases which came to light of small-pox after vaccination were unfortunately numerous; some, it must be confessed, were exceedingly severe; others were exaggerated. These instances of failure naturally fortified the prejudices of many parents against vaccination, and furnished the female inoculators with a fine opportunity of recommending their pernicious practice.[62]

At the Humberside port of Grimsby in 1816 vaccination was stubbornly resisted by 'the lower orders of the community'. Smallpox had reached the town by October and local doctors were faced with a continuing preference for inoculation coupled with a fatalistic attitude toward the disease. One angry and frustrated doctor wrote at the end of the month that

> The delusion under which the lower orders ... labour cannot be more strikingly evinced than by the prevalence of that fatal disorder, the smallpox ... Fourteen children had already fallen victims, seven of whom have suffered within the last sixteen days. The infatuated parents, with minds steeled against conviction, still continue to comfort themselves with this futile argument. *If it pleases God to afflict them and they die, all is well.* Natural affection seems to be absorbed in this deadly fanaticism, which depopulates the place and causes rational people to suspect that there is something more in this species of obduracy than a pretended resignation to the will of heaven.[63]

The arguments of pro-vaccinationists and the advance of the new treatment were further undermined by the carelessness or faulty technique of some vaccinators. A general vaccination at the Buckinghamshire parish of Great Missenden some years previous to 1824 had 'contaminated the people with decomposed virus' which resulted in ulcerated arms 'and left them all liable to smallpox'. Not surprisingly 'Great prejudice prevailed against vaccination' and when smallpox broke out a few years later there was a general inoculation of 800 inhabitants.[64]

Confidence in vaccination was again shaken in the general epidemic of 1825-1826. Most doctors continued to retain faith in vaccination but in many parishes the faith of ordinary people had been destroyed while in large towns the number of vaccinations was dropping. At Manchester, for example, where vaccination was freely available to the poor, Dr John Robertson reported in 1827 that it had already been on the decline for a number of years.[65] In rural areas preference for inoculation was commonplace. Inoculation had been offered to the poor on a significant scale only towards the end of the eighteenth century and there was probably now reluctance to abandon a treatment so recently embraced and which had proved so effective. Moreover as most doctors had now given up inoculation the old treatment was frequently performed by amateurs, mostly from the poor classes, with whom the bulk of the rural population was closely identified. These comments about the transitional period are necessarily broad generalisations and the short Essex case study which follows seeks to give a clearer understanding of the policies of rural vestries and attitudes of country people.

In attempting to establish the extent to which inoculation and vaccination were practised or preferred in the transitional period at a local level, the contemporary terminology has presented a serious obstacle for although the term vaccination was used as early as January 1803 the new treatment continued for many years to be thought of as inoculation with cowpox, which of course it was. In the absence of supporting information on the nature of the virus employed, the use of the term inoculation between about 1800 and about 1815 cannot therefore be admitted as evidence that the process was variolation. This problem renders of little value the information from many parishes including Leyton in 1801 where 62 inhabitants, chiefly children, were 'Inoculated' by Mr Hobbs.[66] Other places where the treatment offered or given after 1800 was described by the unqualified term inoculation include Ashdon in 1802 (where Joseph Rouse 'died of inoculation aged 78'),[67] Chipping Ongar in 1809,[68] Kirby-le-Soken in 1800,[69] Upminster in 1803,[70] and Woodford in 1801 and 1803.[71]

Even allowing for such defects in contemporary evidence, it is clear that a substantial proportion of Essex vestries were fairly quick to adopt the new treatment and abandon inoculation. At Castle Hedingham on 19 April 1802

it was agreed that such Poor ... as might be willing, should receive
the Vaccine Inoculation under the direction of Mr. Seymour, who
is desired to make a list ... for the information of the Parish for his
remuneration.

Seymour's work was obviously successful and in 1808 he vaccinated nearly 200 poor inhabitants, a very substantial proportion of Castle Hedingham's population (1,052 in 1811), for a fee of 12 guineas. The vestry continued to encourage vaccination. In 1813, for example, it was again agreed that 'such poor ... as may be willing should be vaccinated under the direction of Mr Seymour'.[72] At Great Braxted in 1804 the vestry resolved 'to enoucalate all the poore of the parish with cow pock that chues to be enoculated' for which the doctor appears to have received 5s. a patient.[73] Rayne was another parish making an early decision to use vaccination. In July 1806 84 inhabitants received 'Vaccine Inoculation' and in February 1809 a further 35 were treated, including a boy who was 'cut 8 Times'.[74] At Lambourne the annual contract made in April 1810 between the vestry and Mr Copeland, the parish doctor, included for the first time provision to 'Inocullate the poor for the Cow pock Gratis'.[75]

Vestries which offered free inoculation in preference to vaccination probably formed a decreasing minority after 1800. To do so after about 1820 was very unusual yet this may have been the situation at Aveley where the poor were inoculated in 1809[76] and where the vestry was still allowing the parish doctor an additional 7s. 6d. 'for innoculation' in 1816.[77] It was not until 1824 that free vaccination was offered to 'such of the families as belong to the Parish who choose to be innoculated with Vaccine matter'.[78]

A large group of vestries sidestepped the problem of deciding which treatment to use by leaving the choice to individual families. When smallpox broke out at Messing in 1806 the vestry agreed

> That a general Inoculation ... should immediately take place + that Mr. John Frost should attend thereto — leaving it to the respective Families themselves to determine whether to have the Cow Pox or Small Pox — + that a Compliment of Twenty five Guineas be given to Mr Frost for his attendance[79]

Other examples are commonplace. At Barking in April 1808 the vestry ordered notice to be given in church that as many parishioners as possible would be given the opportunity 'to be inoculated for small-pox, either by the vaccine mode or by the former process, free of expence'. The two doctors employed received 5s. 3d. per patient and it was reported in July that 492 people had been treated at a total cost to the parish of £129 3s.[80] Wickford was another place to offer its poor inhabitants the choice, a policy which continued at least until 1827.[81] Canewdon vestry adopted the same policy, resolving on 11 December 1820 'that the Children ... shall be innoculated ... or Vaccinated free of Expence — The parents to have their choice'. The treatment was to be carried out by the two medical gentlemen 'who usually attend the Parish' and they were to share the fee of £10.[82] At South Benfleet both methods were available to the poor during the years 1811-1826 and perhaps later,[83] while at Thundersley in November 1833 the parish doctor, Thomas Byass, agreed with the vestry to vaccinate or inoculate 'all the poor of the parish that require such treatment' as well as 'to attend in all cases of smallpox occuring in the ... Parish up to Michaelmas Day 1834' for a salary of £5.[84] In the adjoining parish and market town of Rayleigh in April 1834 the vestry resolved

> That in consequence of the small pox making its appearance in this Town and neighbourhood It was resolved ... That such poor families belonging to this Parish and receiving parochial relief and not able to pay for either vaccinating or Inoculating their children should receive a ticket for that purpose[85]

Although some vestries like Thundersley and Rayleigh continued to offer both forms of treatment as late as the 1830s they were few in number, most others having abandoned inoculation in the intervening years. This trend is well illustrated by events at Great Coggeshall. In 1808 the inhabitants appear to have been given the choice of treatment, for Messrs Godfrey and Eagle were paid £10 'for inoculating and Vaccinating the Parish' in that year,[86] but by October 1815 the vestry's attitude had changed and it was 'order'd ... that Mr Eagle and Messrs Godfreys be requested to use their best endeavours to Vaccinate (free of charge to the parties) all the Poor inhabitants'. In November the doctors reported 'a great disinclination to the Cow Pox' whereupon the vestry reaffirmed its conviction that 'it is the mildest and a safe prevention to the Small Pox. We request the ... Gentlemen to use every endeavour to vaccinate'.[87] Witham vestry was even stronger in its opposition to inoculation but its views were not shared by Mr Mackey, the parish doctor. Instructions had been given to him to vaccinate the poor and when it was discovered in May 1818 that he had 'deviated from the resolutions ... by recommending inoculation' he was dismissed. Smallpox was then 'general in this Parish' and it was advocated that all pauper women in labour should have their children vaccinated free of charge 'and that vaccination should be recommended to all paupers at the same period every succeeding year'. At the same meeting in May the vestry also heard that William Allaston, a watchmaker, had inoculated several paupers 'in a part of the Parish where the disease at that time had not been' and clearly suspected that he may have been responsible for spreading the disease. Instructions were given for taking 'the best legal means to punish William Allaston for practising as a Surgeon contrary to the statute'. Shortly afterwards the vestry learnt that Mackey had also inoculated several paupers, which action had 'endangered the lives of the Poor', and on 1 June ordered a 'minute enquiry' into his conduct.[88] At Woodford both forms of treatment were available to the poor at parish expense until 1828 when

> Mr. Morgan having communicated to this Vestry the contents of two letters he had received from Mr. Brown and Mr. Davies (two of the parish doctors) by which it appeared that the pestilent disease of the smallpox had been propagated among the Poor of this Parish by Inoculation at the Hands of a Mr. Brown of Walthamstow. Resolved that this Vestry feel obliged by Mr. Morgan's communication and that the overseers be instructed to take notice of this circumstance in order to its being stopped.

In the following year 67 inhabitants were vaccinated at parish expense.[89] References to general vaccinations elsewhere in Essex after about 1830 are commonplace. For example, in the tiny rural parish of Little Horkesley, five miles north of Colchester, 20 families were vaccinated about 1830[90] while at Great Bardfield 123 poor inhabitants received the treatment in 1833.[91]

A vaccination mishap within a community could result in the vestry abandoning the new treatment. At Maldon, a town where inoculation had always been regarded with much caution on the grounds that it could spread the disease, vaccination was employed at an early date but was abandoned following the death from smallpox in 1801 of a child a few weeks after being vaccinated, so that when smallpox appeared in the town early in 1806 it was a general inoculation that the vestries authorised to combat the outbreak. Further fuel must have been added to the controversy when one of the infant inoculees, Hannah Powell of All Saints, died, allegedly as a result of inoculation.[92]

The Essex evidence looked at so far illustrates in the main the evolving policies of vestries rather than the preferences of the ordinary inhabitants and poor. It was shown earlier in the chapter how vaccination mishaps and the campaign of anti-vaccinationists resulted in growing suspicion and even active opposition to the new treatment and how the poor in particular were reluctant to abandon inoculation. This was certainly the situation in early nineteenth-century Essex. The 'great disinclination to the Cow Pox' among the poor of Great Coggeshall in 1815 has already been noted,[93] while at Wickford the poor retained a preference for inoculation as late as 1827. Since contemporary accounts giving a breakdown of the number of poor accepting either inoculation or vaccination are unusual, the Wickford figures are worth citing in some detail. They begin in 1811 when, during a smallpox outbreak, poor parents were allowed to exercise their preference for the treatment of their children and 34 were inoculated and seven vaccinated by Dr D'Aranda.[94] In 1818 a total of 111 inhabitants were treated, including 73 at 5s. a head at parish expense, of whom 51 were children. Of these 51 children 48 were inoculated and only three vaccinated.[95] Wickford parents continued to have the choice of treatment in the 1820s. In 1827, for example, when the disease was once again prevalent, the parish paid £7 17s. 6d. for 45 children to be treated, of whom 36 were inoculated and only nine vaccinated or 'cut with cow pox'.[96] Quite clearly the preference of the great majority of ordinary people at Wickford was for inoculation. It would be a mistake, however, to assume too much from so small a sample, for attitudes varied from parish to parish. Indeed, taken on its own, evidence from neighbouring Rayleigh would suggest a marked change in preference by the poor in the early 1830s for during a smallpox outbreak there in April 1834 only seven families chose inoculation whereas 29 chose vaccination.[97]

There was another factor at work which affected the level of acceptance of both methods of treatment. The knowledge that last-minute inoculation or vaccination could afford immunity when the disease appeared had bred a somewhat casual attitude toward the threat of smallpox, although not toward the disease itself. This in turn reinforced the widespread reluctance to obtain immunity unless faced with the disease, a problem noted by Benjamin Pugh as early as 1779. Another medical observer commented in 1807

> Unless, therefore, from the immediate dread of epidemic Small-
> pox, neither Vaccination nor Inoculation appear at any time to
> have been general, and when the cause of the terror has passed by,
> the Public have relapsed into a state of indifference and apathy,
> and the salutary practice has come to a stand[98]

In the tiny rural parish of Willingale Doe, eight miles west of Chelmsford, three inhabitants 'died of the natural Small-Pox' in the late summer of 1809, as a result of which 'many others in the parish were then Vaccined'.[99] At Chelmsford the indifference and reluctance noted by Pugh was undiminished 40 years later. In 1821 during a period of apathy following the epidemic years of 1816-1819 the vestry embarked on a vaccination campaign, distributing this notice in the town

> Whereas it appears that the prevention of that dangerous disease,
> the smallpox, by means of vaccination has been lamentably
> neglected in very many families resident in this parish — the
> Select Vestry, fully convinced of the great utility of vaccination in
> preventing altogether in *most* cases, and universally in mitigating
> the contagion of small pox do most earnestly recommend to the

inhabitants (and to the poor in particular) to vaccinate without
delay such of their Children as are still exposed to that loathsome
and fatal disease.[100]

A further outbreak in 1829 led to a second campaign and the poor were once again encouraged to protect their children.[101]

This Essex evidence shows that in the 40 years following the introduction of vaccination the new treatment encountered a mixed and changing response. Although quickly preferred by the majority of doctors and the wealthy, its adoption by parish vestries was rather slower and more uneven, some still paying for their poor inhabitants to be inoculated as late as 1830. Among the bulk of the population (the labouring classes and the poor) there was a mixture of caution, indifference, suspicion and even hostility. This was due partly to vaccination failures and partly to the propaganda of anti-vaccinationists but there was also a continuing confidence in inoculation, which gave lifelong protection, whereas it was widely known by about 1820 that full protection by vaccination was impermanent.

The terrible epidemic of 1837-1840 in which more than 42,000 victims, chiefly babies and young children, died in England and Wales began in the west and south-west in the summer of 1837, spread throughout Wales in the following winter and was widespread in the eastern counties by the end of 1838. By 1840, having largely ceased in rural areas of the country, it was concentrated in the Lancashire manufacturing towns.[102]

The epidemic had the effect of highlighting the destructive capacity of epidemic smallpox and of reviving discussion about the methods of preventing the disease. Under the influence of Dr John Baron, executor and biographer of Edward Jenner, the Provincial Medical and Surgical Association began agitating for the abolition of inoculation and in 1840 a petition to that effect was presented to Parliament by the Medical Society of London. The transitional period was about to end.

6

The Age of Vaccination, 1840-1907

Discussion in Parliament about smallpox, inoculation and vaccination began again in 1840 when a Bill was introduced to enable the poor to have their children vaccinated free of charge and to prohibit inoculation by amateurs or empirics. Among the evidence used to support the Bill were statistics showing that following the introduction of compulsory vaccination in Bavaria (1807), Denmark (1810), Prussia (1818) and other German states, mortality from smallpox had fallen dramatically, but the debates which followed revealed the full extent of the unpopularity of vaccination with the majority of the poor in England. The medical reformer Thomas Wakley, Member for Finsbury, who had founded *The Lancet* in 1823, declared in the Commons that 'no one could be ignorant that the working classes entertained great prejudices against vaccination', but it was his opinion that the recent epidemic was caused by the contagiousness of the smallpox lymph used in inoculation. The House took his statements seriously and he succeeded in carrying an amendment to ban inoculation both by amateurs and by doctors.[1] In the Lords' debate Charles Blomfield, Bishop of London, pointed out that many of the ignorant poor in agricultural districts were strongly prejudiced against vaccination and paid much greater attention to empirics than to the advice of the clergy.[2]

Parliament was therefore well aware of the widespread unpopularity of vaccination when on 23 July 1840 it passed 'An Act to extend the Practice of Vaccination'.[3] The legislation came into immediate effect, ordering the Poor Law guardians in England, Wales and Ireland to contract with their medical officers or other qualified medical practitioners for the vaccination at public expense of anyone in their union not previously vaccinated who asked for the treatment. Inoculation (variolation) was made illegal and offenders were liable to one month's imprisonment. The medical profession had opposed the linking of vaccination with the Poor Law, predicting that it would provoke more resistance and make vaccination an object of terror for those whom it was principally intended to benefit, the poor. Parliament's failure to heed this advice was to have far-reaching consequences.

The Poor Law Commissioners were conscious that problems would be encountered in encouraging people to embrace vaccination. For example, they had received early in 1840 a detailed report from the Manchester physician Richard Baron Howard lamenting what he thought to be 'indifference to vaccination' among the labouring classes and fearing it to be 'an increasing evil'. There had been 'a very considerable' diminution in the numbers of children vaccinated by the various Manchester medical charities in the previous five years, which Howard attributed 'to a positive prejudice against the practice, or to a doubt of its efficacy as a protection against the small-pox; but ... more generally ... to indifference, procrastination, or thoughtless negligence'.[4]

The desire to overcome or circumvent these problems was much in evidence in a lengthy printed letter, 20 August 1840, sent by Edwin Chadwick, Secretary to the Commissioners, to every board of guardians explaining the Act and detailing the steps to be taken. It began by setting out the 'benevolent object of the statute ... to prevent as far as possible the mortality and sufferings occasioned by small-pox'. Although by the 1830s the incidence of smallpox had already declined to the extent that there were four other diseases which killed more people annually, the number of smallpox deaths nevertheless remained unnecessarily high. The average fatality rate of smallpox cases was still subject to dispute, some claiming it to be one in six, others one in four. On the basis of the latter figure the Commissioners calculated that

> the number of persons attacked in England and Wales must amount, on an average, to nearly 50,000 ... or about 12,000 persons killed and 36,000 persons who recover subjected to the sufferings of disease

These conclusions were, however, based on the statistics of the recent epidemic, a point not mentioned in the letter. With regard to inoculation the familiar and biased arguments of the pro-vaccinationists were repeated.

> It appears that the practice of inoculating with the small-pox has long been abandoned by the whole of the respectable part of the medical profession, on the grounds, first, as respects the individual inoculated, that it is much more dangerous than the cow-pox; secondly, as respects others, that it makes the person inoculated a source of contagion, thus multiplying the chances of its spreading; and, without absolutely protecting the life of the one person inoculated, exposes to imminent risk the lives of others ... The practice of inoculation ... is mostly pursued by ignorant and unqualified persons, old women, and itinerant quacks. Excessive mortality is frequently traceable to the proceedings of such persons ... it ought not to be allowed to any one to act against the experience of the medical profession, and of the best-informed persons in the country, and to do that which may spread disease, death, or the causes of disfigurement and loss of sight amongst the community

In order to help stamp out inoculation the Commissioners were issuing instructions to medical officers to enquire

> in each case of small-pox which comes before them ... whether the party had been inoculated, and by whom; or whether the infection was taken from a person inoculated; and, on ascertaining by whom the offence had been committed, that they will inform the magistrates.

Not unexpectedly, the practice of vaccination was defended and the benefits included 'an enduring influence, and will protect the constitution as much as if the person had had small-pox'. The Commissioners had to point out, however, that the poor had not taken full advantage of the facilities for free vaccination already available. In London the people who had attended the vaccination stations with their children were 'chiefly of the well-dressed, cleanly, and respectable classes of mechanics', whereas the 'more pauperized classes had not brought their children to be vaccinated in proportionate numbers'. This the Commissioners attributed to 'ignorance, indolence, and their habits of procrastination, and carelessness about their offspring, and sometimes from the influence of quacks'. In asserting that re-vaccination was unnecessary the Commissioners quoted from a report prepared in 1839 by the pro-vaccinationist Dr John Baron, biographer of Edward Jenner, for the Provincial Medical and Surgical Association, which concluded that the majority of doctors 'are of opinion that re-vaccination can only be required where doubts are entertained of the correctness of the first vaccination ... Systematic re-vaccinations appear to us uncalled for'. Finally, the Commissioners emphasized that free vaccination was now available to everyone regardless of whether or not they were in receipt of poor relief, and expressed the hope that in addition to their official duties under the Act, the guardians would 'as private individuals ... voluntarily and extra-officially exert their influence to remove prejudice, and promote the general adoption ... of vaccination'.[5]

This guidance was followed by more detailed instructions relating to the contracts to be drawn up between boards of guardians and 'legally qualified' medical practitioners undertaking the duties of public vaccinators, as well as to places to be used as vaccination stations, the frequency of attendance thereat by public vaccinators, and remuneration. On the last point the Commissioners considered that 'a payment of 1s. 6d. for every successful vaccination will, under ordinary circumstances, be adequate'.[6]

In order to help make the public aware of the provisions of the Act and to persuade people to take advantage of free vaccination the Commissioners encouraged boards of guardians to mount a poster campaign. Standard wording was given in an annex to their letter of 20 August, individual boards being left to insert details of the public vaccinators appointed by them and the times and dates when they would attend the various vaccination stations.[7] In Witham Union the guardians proclaimed that 'By Vaccination being made universal, Small Pox would be entirely banished from the country' and announced that three medical practitioners had been appointed as vaccinators. Villages in the Union were to be visited at least once a month; at Faulkbourne 'Mr Groves will ... attend on every Saturday from 12 to 1 at James Claydon's Cottage, Chipping Hill', at Inworth 'Mr. Varenne will attend the third Thursday every Month, from 1 to 2, at George Simpson's Shop', while at the town of Witham Mr Groves 'will attend ... on every Tuesday from 11 to 1 o'clock, at the Union House'. It was recommended that 'Every Child should be taken to be vaccinated when it is Six WEEKS old' and anyone not already vaccinated, or who had not had smallpox or cowpox, should in the event of 'the PREVALENCE OF CASES OF SMALL POX IN ANY NEIGHBOURHOOD ... BE VACCINATED WITHOUT DELAY, even INFANTS a few days after birth'. The public was

119

warned of the danger and illegality of inoculation which, it was claimed, had 'generally been done by IGNORANT Persons' and had resulted in a 'great number of Deaths, and ... Blindness'. Vaccination with cowpox on the other hand

> IS PERFECTLY FREE FROM DANGER and will protect the
> Child from Small Pox as effectually as the Small-Pox itself. In
> nearly all the instances in which Small-Pox had attacked persons
> who had been Vaccinated, the Vaccination has been Imperfectly
> performed, or the attack of Small Pox has been in a very mitigated
> Form and quite free from Danger.[8]

By the end of April 1841, when the Act had been in operation for nine months, 533 of the 583 boards of guardians in England and Wales had entered into vaccination contracts. Some of the remainder had refused because of apprehensions that acceptance of free vaccination would, so far as electoral franchise was concerned, amount to receipt of relief or alms with the effect of disfranchising those accepting free vaccination either for themselves or for their children.[9] This question had been raised within a month of the passing of the Act but, despite reassurances from the Commissioners to the contrary, it was necessary to pass an amending Act in June 1841 which made the position absolutely clear by stating that while expenses incurred in executing the provisions of the 1840 Act were to be paid out of the poor rates, no person being vaccinated free as provided for under that Act was to be considered as having received parochial relief or alms.[10] There was also trouble in some unions as a result of early cost-cutting exercises by the guardians in relation to the doctors' fees for vaccination. Where this took place relations between doctors and local authorities were embittered for a generation and in a few places into the twentieth century.

It soon became apparent that the 1840 Act was failing to achieve its main objective. For the poor, who constituted the reservoirs of the disease, the unceasing and exhausting daily routine of procuring a bare subsistence took precedence over everything else and, unless faced with the immediate threat of smallpox, vaccination remained a low priority. Furthermore the offer of free vaccination was seen as another function of the hated new Poor Law while suspicion of the treatment itself remained undiminished. The legislators, administrators and doctors for the most part failed to understand the attitudes, problems and priorities of the poor and attributed the lack of enthusiasm for free vaccination to supineness of character, apathy, indifference, ignorance, insensibility and fatalism.

Realising that free vaccination would not be embraced voluntarily by the poor the Epidemiological Society of London pressed for stronger measures and in August 1853 a private member's Bill was passed as 'An Act to extend and make compulsory the Practice of Vaccination'.[11] By this Act, which applied to England and Wales only and which was designed to stamp out the disease, it became obligatory for parents to have every child born after 1 August 1853 vaccinated within three months of birth[12] and, on the eighth day after vaccination, for the child to be taken to the practitioner by whom the operation had been performed for the result to be inspected. In order to afford better facilities for vaccination Poor Law unions were to be divided into convenient districts and a place in each district appointed for the performance of vaccination. Notice was to be given of the times at which vaccinations and post-vaccination inspections would take place there. Certificates of successful vaccination were to be given to the parents or guardians. If the vaccinator considered a child not in a fit state of health for vaccination he was to issue a certificate to that effect, valid for two months. A register of successful vaccinations was to be kept by the registrar of births and deaths in every sub-district. He was also to notify the parents or guardians of every child, within seven days of its birth being registered, of the requirements of the Act and those failing to have a child vaccinated or inspected after vaccination were liable to a fine not exceeding 20s. At a local level the provisions were quickly put into operation. In Rochford Union, for example, the Board of Guardians met on 4 October to consider the Act and among other things appointed 21 vaccination stations to be attended by six medical officers.[13]

The Acts of 1840, 1841 and 1853 thus made inoculation (variolation) illegal, placed vaccination under the auspices of the Poor Law authorities and made it successively universal and free, non-pauperising and, finally, compulsory. The 1853 Act also marked the beginning of active anti-vaccinationist dissent and resistance among the poor and artisan classes. For them, as well as for some middle-class families also suspicious of authority, compulsory infant vaccination performed by a Poor Law doctor represented a new and sometimes first intrusion of state authority into the family unit.

The absence of adequate powers of enforcement encouraged resistance to the 1853 Act and soon became a source of concern to pro-vaccinationists like Dr John Simon, Chadwick's greatest disciple, who had justified the Act by remarking that 'the man who indulges in a preference for smallpox does so to the detriment and danger of his neighbour'.[14] Simon's hand was strengthened in 1858 when he was placed in charge of the new Medical Department of the Privy Council[15] and two years later, in 1860, the Department extended its control by taking over the work of the National Vaccine Establishment and began supervising and standardising the distribution of lymph.[16] In 1861 Parliament took steps to remedy the defect in the 1853 Act and by the Vaccination Acts Amendment Act, passed in August,[17] Poor Law unions were enabled to 'appoint some Person to institute and conduct' legal proceedings for the purpose of enforcing obedience. Proceedings could be taken 'at any time during which the Parent or Guardian is in default' and the resulting expenses were to be paid from parish poor rates. Although the Act made important new provisions, in particular that the fine for non-compliance could be repeated if parents or guardians persistently refused to have their children vaccinated, it was nevertheless only a permissive Act and Poor Law authorities were not obliged to carry out its provisions. As a result individual unions adopted differing policies. In Rochford Union no action seems to have been taken but in Lexden and Winstree Union the public was warned that 'in every case of failure to comply ... proceedings under the Vaccination Act 1861, will be taken'.[18] In England as a whole at this time active resistance to the Vaccination Acts was still at a fairly low level and in July 1867 Dr Willing, Medical Officer for the Great Wakering District of Rochford Union, was able to report that 'there were no Children unvaccinated ... within his district'.[19] But in places with large working-class and artisan populations there was growing evasion and neglect, notably at Leicester where vaccinations declined from 66 per cent. of births in 1861 to 40 per cent. in 1866.[20] As will be shown later in this chapter, in 1885 Leicester was to become the centre of the anti-vaccinationist movement in England but even as early as 1866 the percentage of babies vaccinated there was probably lower than anywhere else. The figure for St Marylebone Union in London seems to be more typical. Here in the first three months of 1867 the number of inhabitants who contracted smallpox 'amounted to 378, of whom 300 were children under 5. Fatalities were 46'. The prevalence was attributed to 'unsuccessful or non-vaccination' and it was asserted that in the Christchurch District 'from 15 to 20% of young children ... have never been vaccinated at all'.[21]

Urged on by John Simon, Parliament responded to the growing neglect and resistance by introducing stronger legislation in August 1867 in the form of 'An Act to consolidate and amend the Laws relating to Vaccination',[22] which incorporated most of the provisions of the earlier Acts as well as making a number of important new stipulations. Among these were the requirements that district registrars of births and deaths should make half-yearly lists of all cases in which certificates of vaccination had not been received and that boards of guardians should inquire into such cases and take proceedings against anyone in default. Sections 29 and 31 made neglect of vaccination and post-vaccination inspection punishable by repeatable fines until the child was 14 years old. Because of the importance of section 31 in relation to the subsequent growth of opposition to compulsory vaccination it is worthwhile to quote it in full.

> 31. If any Registrar, or any Officer appointed by the Guardians to enforce the Provisions of this Act, shall give Information, in Writing to a Justice of the Peace that he has Reason to believe that any Child under the Age of Fourteen Years, being within the Union or Parish for which the Informant acts, has not been successfully vaccinated, and that he has given Notice to the Parent or Person having the Custody of such Child to procure its being vaccinated, and that this Notice has been disregarded, the Justice may summon such Parent or Person to appear with the Child before him at a certain Time and Place, and upon the Appearance, if the Justice shall find, after such Examinations as he shall deem necessary, that the Child has not been vaccinated, nor has already had the Smallpox, he may, if he see fit, make an Order under his Hand and Seal directing such Child to be vaccinated within a certain Time; and if at the Expiration of such Time the Child shall not have been so vaccinated, or shall not be shown to be then un-

fit to be vaccinated, or to be insusceptible of Vaccination, the Person upon whom such Order shall have been made shall be proceeded against summarily, and, unless he can show some reasonable Ground for his Omission to carry the Order into effect, shall be liable to a Penalty not exceeding Twenty Shillings:

Provided that if the Justice shall be of opinion that the Person is improperly brought before him, and shall refuse to make any Order for the Vaccination of the Child, he may order the Informant to pay such Person such Sum of Money as he shall consider to be a fair Compensation for his Expenses and Loss of Time in attending before the Justice.

The age limit of 14 years was intended to secure the vaccination of all children not already vaccinated who had been born since the passing of the 1853 Act. The 1867 Act was therefore partially retrospective in so far as it sought to remedy the cases of neglect since vaccination had been made compulsory. In addition the Act stipulated that those without the qualifications required by the Privy Council should not be public vaccinators. Parents were now required to have a child vaccinated within three months of its birth and any other person having custody of a child was to have it vaccinated within three months of taking custody. Post-vaccination inspections were to take place on the same day in the week following vaccination and public vaccinators were empowered to take lymph from children for the performance of other vaccinations.

There was little opposition in the House of Commons debate on the 1867 Bill but Sir Thomas Chambers, Liberal M.P. for Marylebone, predicted that 'when this Bill is passed, an agitation will commence that will never cease until the Act is repealed'.[23] Within a few weeks of the passing of the Act organised opposition began in London with the establishment of the Anti-Compulsory Vaccination League and scattered elements appeared in the provinces shortly afterwards.[24] A series of public lectures against compulsory vaccination was organised in Nottingham by Dr Charles Pearce and at Bradford a district league was set up by the Quaker tailor and temperance leader William White. Organised opposition at Leicester, which was to embrace thousands of parents in the 1880s, began with a public meeting in 1869 attended by fewer than 20 people. Stuart Fraser has described them as 'a small number of mainly working-class parents who for some personal or religious conviction believed vaccination to be useless, harmful, or even evil'.[25]

The responsibility for carrying out the non-medical aspects of the legislation, including the prosecution of parents or guardians for non-compliance, was in the hands of the local boards of guardians. In Rochford Union, where compulsion under the 1853 Act had not been enforced, the Board was quick to use its powers against defaulters under the mandatory 1867 legislation and on 14 April 1868 ordered the clerk to 'take proceedings for enforcing the penalty incurred by Nathaniel Lancaster of Hawkwell for refusing and neglecting to have his Child Vaccinated'.[26] In August the registrar of Prittlewell District reported cases of neglect to the Board and the clerk was instructed to 'write to the parties'.[27] When Mr Williams, one of the relieving officers, reported on 5 December 1871 that three children of Mr W.A. Potter of South Fambridge had not been vaccinated the clerk was directed 'to take usual proceedings to procure the Vaccination of the children'.[28]

Meanwhile opposition was continuing to grow in England as a whole. In August 1869 the Manchester temperance leader Henry Pitman began a weekly penny-periodical, *The Anti-Vaccinator*, which in 1870 combined with another Manchester journal, *The Co-operator*, to become *The Co-operator and Anti-Vaccinator*.[29] At Leicester in 1869 three parents were imprisoned[30] but it was the case of the Revd H.J. Allen of St Neots, a poor Primitive Methodist preacher who refused to have any of his five children vaccinated, which received considerable publicity in the latter part of the year. He was twice brought to court where the magistrates refused to honour certificates of medical unfitness signed by Dr William Collins, an anti-compulsory-vaccinator, and was fined 20s. plus costs for each child. In November 1869 Allen appealed against the second conviction in the Court of Queen's Bench, but Lord Chief Justice Cockburn held that under the 1867 Act a parent could be convicted and fined repeatedly for as long as he remained in default. Motivated by this case John Candlish M.P. introduced an amending Bill in July 1870 which proposed some relief from successive penalties and Candlish's motion coupled with the mounting opposition led the Home Secretary, Henry Bruce, to set up a Select Committee of the House under the chairmanship of the Vice-President of the Council, William Forster, Liberal M.P. for Bradford.[31] At the same time the greatest smallpox epidemic in British history, which had begun by the fourth quarter of 1870, added greater urgency to the matter. Although the Committee was to 'inquire into the operation of the Vaccination Act (1867) and to report whether such an Act should be amended', the Government felt confident that the inquiry would dispel all doubts about the value of compulsory vaccination.[32] In May 1871 the Committee reported overwhelmingly in favour of compulsory vaccination but recommended the modification of penalties for non-compliance in order to conciliate opposition. Shortly afterwards Forster introduced a new Bill which, at the insistence of John Simon, made obligatory the appointment of vaccination officers by boards of guardians. The Bill also contained a clause to limit penalties as recommended by the Committee but it was deleted in the Lords and the Government sacrificed it so as not to delay the legislation.[33] The Bill was passed in August as 'An Act to amend the Vaccination Act, 1867'[34] and came into operation on 1 January 1872. The main provision was contained in section 5 which enacted that boards of guardians 'shall appoint and pay' one or more vaccination officers to prosecute offenders. By section 4 the term 'parent' was taken to include any person having custody of a child, which in practice meant that the law now required all children to be vaccinated within three months of birth unless certified as being unfit for or unreceptive to vaccination. In order to assist the new vaccination officers district registrars of births and deaths were required by section 8 to provide a monthly return of all births and deaths of infants under twelve months old. Penalties were extended by section 10 to include anyone preventing a public vaccinator from taking lymph from any successfully vaccinated child, for which offence a fine not exceeding 20s. was payable. The Act's most important aspect was that it compelled and strengthened enforcement by making the appointment of vaccination officers mandatory and by confirming section 31 of the 1867 Act whereby parents could be fined repeatedly until a child was vaccinated, or imprisoned for non-payment.

As already noted, responsibility for the non-medical aspects of vaccination remained vested in the local boards of guardians. In Rochford Union in January 1872 a committee of four guardians was appointed 'to consider what fresh arrangements are necessary'. Its report, read to the Board on 27 February, included recommendations that the two relieving officers 'should be appointed Vaccination Officers for their respective districts in lieu of the present appointment of the Clerk as Vaccination Officer' and that the remuneration should be 6d. for every successful vaccination registered. The Board adopted these recommendations but increased the remuneration to 8d. for every vaccination registered for Foulness, Wallasea and the other islands in the Union, presumably because of the difficulties of access. The total amount received as remuneration was not to be less than £10 per annum.[35]

Instead of quelling opposition the 1871 Act had the immediate effect of widening the argument and increasing the protests. Early in 1872 the Society for the Suppression of Compulsory Vaccination was founded and in the summer of that year the Liberal M.P. Joseph Pease, a supporter of the anti-compulsory-vaccination cause, introduced a Bill to amend the Vaccination Acts. But the smallpox epidemic was still raging and there was insufficient support for the Bill which was withdrawn in July after its second reading. It was during this reading that the scientist and Liberal M.P. Lyon Playfair asserted that 'individual disbelief in a remedy which science and experience had confirmed beyond all reasonable doubt is no justification for relieving the conscience of that individual at the expense of society'.[36]

As the new vaccination officers received their monthly lists and began their rounds of inspection the number of prosecutions mounted. At Northampton in the first six months of 1872 the magistrates dealt with 120 offenders, less than half of whom could be persuaded under threat of penalty to have their children vaccinated.[37] In Rochford Union where, as already shown, the two vaccination officers had a direct financial inducement to obtain successful vaccinations, inspections were conducted in an energetic fashion. In late September 1872 proceedings were commenced against 'several persons' in the Rayleigh District[38] and on 5 November the Board was informed of the conviction obtained against W. Burrell of Foulness 'for neglecting to take his child for inspection after Vaccination'.[39] In July 1873 a summons was issued against George Potter of South Fambridge, farmer, 'for neglecting to procure the Vaccination of his child Ethel Grace Potter born 4 August 1872'.[40] At the small north-Essex town of Coggeshall the working-class leader John Castle, Secretary of the Coggeshall Co-operative Society and local sponsor of Joseph Arch, Organising Secretary of the newly-founded National Agricultural Labourers' Union, refused to have his children vaccinated on grounds of conscience and because a relative's child had died as a result of vaccination. The Coggeshall magistrates, mostly wealthy landowners and farmers, took the opportunity to persecute Castle, dragging him into court 18 times in the years 1873-1875. The case came to the notice of the Anti-Compulsory Vaccination League which helped Castle in his stubborn resistance by paying some of his fines.[41]

Elsewhere anti-vaccinationists were aided in their fight by the casual attitude or sheer inefficiency of boards of guardians and public vaccinators in carrying out their duties. In August 1871 it was necessary for Mr Byass, one of the public vaccinators appointed by the Rochford Board, to be reminded 'of the great importance of making provision for public vaccination' following a report that he had not been vaccinating lately 'from not having a supply of Vaccine'.[42] In June 1872 prosecutions against two Brightlingsea people were dismissed when the magistrates learned that compulsory vaccination was only performed there one day in every three months and that on the day prescribed the vaccinator had told one of the defendants to wait until 'another time' as he 'hadn't any stuff'.[43] Even more disquieting to magistrates and doctors was evidence of a lingering respect among the very poor for old superstitions and home-spun remedies. When at the beginning of June 1872 the Colchester magistrates heard the case of a baby who died after it had been taken by its mother to Mrs Croker, a poor smallpox sufferer, in order that it should catch the disease, it was stated that this was 'standard practice' among the very poor. The case only came before the court because Mrs Croker was blamed for the baby's death and assaulted by her neighbours. It is impossible to ascertain with any degree of accuracy to what extent the ancient practice of 'buying the smallpox' was still observed, although Andrew Phillips has noted 'it seems probable that such crude and backstreet remedies continued to operate for many years' in Colchester.[44]

Other anti-vaccinationists continued to portray vaccination as disgusting, unnatural and contrary to Christian teaching. The rector of Helmingham, Suffolk, the Revd George Cardew, described it in April 1873 as

> the cutting with a sharp instrument of holes in your dear little healthy babe's arm, a few weeks after it is born, and putting into the holes some filthy matter from a cow — which matter has generally in addition passed through the arm of another child. So that your ... babe, just after God has given it to you, is made to be ill with a mixture of the corruption of both man and beast[45]

Cardew's neighbour, the Revd Mundeford Allen, vicar of Winston, claimed shortly afterwards

> our natural instinct and common sense tell us that such an unnatural proceeding as deliberately cutting through the skin, and implanting in our system an evil disease of a beast, cannot possibly be effected without danger[46]

Compulsory vaccination also began to be portrayed as alien to individual liberty and parental rights. George Cardew thought the law was 'a national sin ... a disgrace to free England',[47] while at a meeting of the Society for the Suppression of Compulsory Vaccination in May 1873 it was denounced as 'one of the grossest en-croachments upon the liberties of Englishmen that has ever been known'.[48] At the same time the opposition was beginning to be perceived by some along class lines as a working-class movement with middle-class leaders. The penalties for non-compliance caused no hardship for the well-to-do, for they could afford to pay the fines, but for the poor they could result in severe financial hardship or imprison-ment. Cardew regarded this as a 'cruel injustice' and emphasised the differing im-pact of the law on rich and poor objectors.

> If he be *a rich man*, he pays a few shillings, which are literally nothing to him ... scorns the wicked Law ... and goes his way. He does not Vaccinate his child, and suffers nothing at all for not doing it. If he be *a poor man*, he is fined too; but the fine is a serious thing to him, for he has to pay the costs as well, which [are] often more than double the fine. Sometimes he is able to pay the money himself, or some kind friends ... pay it for him. But when he cannot find the money anyhow he is sent to prison and his family to the Union.[49]

Compulsory vaccination was now becoming an electoral issue, Cardew, for example, writing on the eve of the 1874 general election

> Let those who are opposed to *Compulsory* Vaccination — whether they regard Vaccination as a good or an evil — support no can-didate who will not pledge himself to vote for the Repeal of the Compulsory Vaccination Act.[50]

The next legislation, the 1874 Vaccination Act,[51] was the result of the discovery by the legal advisor to the Local Government Board that because of an oversight in the drafting of the 1871 Act there existed no statutory provision requiring boards of guardians to prosecute vaccination offenders.[52] The preamble to the 1874 Act stated that 'doubts are entertained ... with respect to the proceedings to be taken by the guardians or their officers for the enforcement of the provisions of the Vaccination Acts, 1867 and 1871' while section 1 made it clear that the Local Government Board had control over the guardians 'in relation to the institution and conduct of the proceedings to be taken for enforcing the provisions of the ... Acts'. Partly in response to the 1874 Act the National Anti-Compulsory Vaccination League was set up late in 1874 by the Revd William Hume-Rothery of Cheltenham whose feminist wife, a daughter of the radical Joseph Hume, protested that an Englishman's house was no longer his own, for

> Under favour of the odious Vaccination Acts a poor man's house may be entered by emissaries of the Medical Star Chamber to ascertain whether his children have been blood-poisoned accor-ding to law.[53]

Although during the next six years the League enjoyed a good deal of success it fail-ed to win the sustained support of a sufficient number of members of Parliament and failed to identify its interests sufficiently closely with the urban artisan class, particularly in the industrial north of the country.[53]

Instead, opposition in those years was centred on the north-Oxfordshire market town of Banbury which by 1880 had gained the reputation of being 'the home and headquarters of the anti-vaccination agitation'.[54] Events there in the 1870s have been vividly portrayed in a recent study by Barrie Trinder.[55] Resistance began in 1871 and in 1872 several Banburians refused to pay fines. In November 1873 the Board of Guardians decided not to prosecute objectors but were reminded of their duty by the Local Government Board in 1874. A Banbury branch of the Anti-Compulsory Vaccination League was formally constituted about this time and by 1875 had a membership of more than 200. In June 1875 the release of a labourer from the neighbouring parish of Middleton Cheney, who had been imprisoned for not having his child vaccinated, was greeted by bands, flags and a purse of sovereigns. The release in February 1877 of the first Banburian to be imprisoned was marked by a torchlight procession and the burning of Edward Jenner's effigy.

Although most of the supporters of the Banbury branch of the League were labourers and working men the leadership was middle class and included the Quaker banker Charles Gillett who was reckoned among the national leaders. By 1878 the branch began to seek redress by political means. When Gillett was elected a guardian in April 1878 he pledged himself to oppose prosecutions for refusal to vaccinate and at the Borough election in 1879 three of the four candidates elected were sympathetic to the League's cause. The Banbury branch also organised social functions, such as a fête in June 1878 when blue silk favours were worn by unvaccinated children. A campaign of direct action began in 1879 when an anti-vaccination station supplying borax to wash the vaccine from the arms of vaccinated children was opened near the vaccination station. By 1880, in an effort to calm the situation, the local magistrates were fining objectors a nominal 6d. and the Board of Health had difficulty finding anyone to accept the post of vaccination officer. At the 1880 general election the vaccination controversy was a major issue, both the Conservative and Liberal candidates promising support for the anti-compulsory vaccination movement. The Banbury branch of the League was only one of the intimately connected and increasingly intermixed radical movements centred on the town in the 1870s, the others being the local branches of the National Agricultural Labourers' Union, the Co-operative Society and the Temperance Society. By the end of the 1870s this radicalism 'was increasingly class-orientated, directed against magistrates, publicans, doctors and parson-magistrates, and proud of its moral superiority to the wealthier classes'.[56]

Apart from Banbury and Leicester there was particularly strong opposition in the 1870s in the south-coast towns of Brighton and Hastings, in Northampton, Kettering, Keighley, Oldham, Newcastle and Middlesbrough, and in some of London's East End unions. As F.B. Smith points out, all these places had a strong lower-middle and working class with a powerful voice in local political culture and which was opposed, amongst other things, to the state and anonymous professional authority.[57]

In February 1880 the London Society for the Abolition of Compulsory Vaccination was formed. Its leaders were dissatisfied with the Hume-Rothery leadership of the National Anti-Compulsory Vaccination League and aimed both to cultivate the capital's enormous working-class population and to win the support of established leagues in the north. They also recognised the importance of support from members of Parliament, doctors and administrators in order to achieve a government inquiry into the whole vaccination problem. The Society had little immediate success but just as its hopes appeared to be flagging the greatest demonstration ever held against the Vaccination Acts took place in Leicester on 23 March 1885, in which over 20,000 people took part. The whole movement was now revitalised and from that date Leicester became the centre of the anti-vaccination movement. The town had suffered severely in the epidemic of 1870-1873 when 358 victims died, including a number who had been vaccinated.[58] The local authorities were frightened and enforced the Acts with such severity that the Home Secretary, Richard Cross, accused the Leicester magistrates of being 'guilty of a petty abuse of power'.[59] In 1876 the local league was refounded as a branch of the National Anti-Compulsory Vaccination League and nine parents were imprisoned.[60] In 1880 the Vaccination Acts became an important issue in the municipal elections and by 1882 a majority of the Corporation was anti-vaccinationist.[61] The Board of Guardians, however, remained in favour of compulsory vaccination and 996 cases of default had been prosecuted and 21 fathers imprisoned by October 1884. When the great demonstration took place there were more than 4,000 people in Leicester awaiting summonses.[62]

Whilst all this had been taking place Leicester had evolved an alternative system of smallpox control and prevention. This was formulated in 1877 by Dr William Johnston who had been appointed Assistant Medical Officer of Health in May. The chief elements were notification of all cases of smallpox within 12 hours of discovery, admission of all cases to hospital and the quarantine of all contacts and disinfection of their homes.[63] Johnston was fortunate in having the support of Leicester Corporation which in 1879 was successful in obtaining Parliamentary sanction for compulsory notification by the Leicester Corporation Act.[64]

Although the membership of the anti-vaccination movement embraced many points of view, including those with objections on religious grounds and those who believed in the liberty of parents to accept or decline treatment, one of its major and most effective arguments was that vaccination could lead to complications or other diseases and was therefore dangerous. The post-vaccinal complication of greatest emotional importance was undoubtedly syphilis.[65] In official circles it was claimed that it could not be transferred by arm-to-arm vaccination but in 1880 it was demonstrated that it was possible to contract syphilis at the time of vaccination when the lymph was taken from a donor suffering from the disease.[66] The epidemiologist and pathologist Charles Creighton, a convinced syphilophobe, believed that cowpox had stronger relations with syphilis than with smallpox. In 1887 his theories appeared in print with the publication of his *The Natural History of Cow-pox and Vaccinal Syphilis*,[67] followed in 1888 by an article on vaccination in the last volume of the ninth edition of *Encyclopaedia Britannica*. Creighton was savagely criticised by *The Lancet*, which expressed amazement 'at the inclusion of such teaching in a work which should be authoritative and should serve as a standard of reference for a generation' and which believed his arguments could be 'more fittingly described as pathological transcendentalism'.[68] In the spring of 1889 Creighton replied to his critics and sought to justify his stance with the publication of his *Jenner and Vaccination : a Strange Chapter of Medical History*. Once again he was severely criticised in *The Lancet*.[69] Although Creighton's theories and opinions were at odds with those of the medical establishment they were valuable fuel for the anti-vaccination movement, with some of the more prominent members of which he is known to have had contacts over many years.[70] More recently Dixon has suggested that a number of the nineteenth-century cases of supposed vaccinal syphilis were probably cases of *vaccina gangrenosa*.[71]

Anti-vaccinationists were infuriated by the insistence of official bodies such as the Local Government Board and most members of the medical profession that government-sponsored and enforced vaccination could never be wrong and that severe complications and deaths from vaccination were due either to failure of the individual vaccinator to take sufficient care or, more usually, to negligence on the part of the patient or relatives but were in no way the fault of the procedure itself. For parents the results of post-vaccinal complications in their young offspring could be traumatic and, not surprisingly, often resulted in them refusing to have further children vaccinated. This was the problem which confronted the Essex farmer F.W. Gladwell of Vinesse Farm, Little Horkesley, in 1894. Gladwell had obeyed the law by having his first three children vaccinated but the third, vaccinated in 1891

> suffered very severely from the operation, and came out one mass
> of sores all over her body, and they continued for three years. I
> took her to Doctors and they told me the cause was bad Vacine
> that was used, one used the word Rotten vacine[72]

As a result Gladwell was 'frightened' and refused to have two further children vaccinated for which offence he appeared at Lexden and Winstree Magistrates' Court on 16 June 1894. He was fined a total of £3 8s. or 14 days' hard labour. Gladwell refused to pay the fine and ten days later wrote to his M.P., James Round, seeking help:

> it was my first offence ... The Police came today and leved a
> distress telling my wife that if I dont pay £3. 8. 0. they will sell
> our Furniture in five days ... I have not the money to pay as Farm-
> ing is so very bad with me ... trusting you will do what ever is in
> your power, as I dont want my home sold; nor the disgrace of hav-
> ing to go to prison ...
> PS I am in no way connected with any Anti Vaccination Society[73]

Meanwhile, encouraged and revitalised by events at Leicester in 1885, the London Society had continued its campaign with renewed vigour and its efforts were finally rewarded in 1889 when a Royal Commission was appointed with terms of reference which brought under scrutiny the entire anti-vaccinationist position. The Commission's proceedings took six years, during which 187 witnesses were examined. *The Lancet*, which favoured compulsory vaccination, deplored the anti-vaccinationists and viewed the Commission with scepticism but nevertheless realised that 'we are in many respects only now at the very threshold of some of the most important questions of human liberty in civilised communities'.[74] The first witness was the pro-vaccinationist Sir John Simon, now 73 years of age, who attributed the decrease in smallpox mortality in the past 35 years to the increasing enforcement of compulsory vaccination. But the rest of his evidence was hesitant, confused and vague, doing nothing to vindicate vaccination.[75] In 1890 objections to vaccination and the operation of vaccination laws in other countries was discussed. Objections were based on moral and medical grounds and witnesses linked smallpox epidemics and venereal disease with compulsory vaccination. Although these arguments were refuted it was more difficult to deny the claim that vaccination had not resulted in a significant decline in smallpox. Evidence from continental Europe showed that in general physicians there now tended to be more sceptical of vaccination than were their British colleagues.[76] Later in 1890 the Commission concentrated on Leicester and other Midland cities where opposition was particularly strong and where epidemics had occurred since the introduction of compulsory vaccination. An examination of the Leicester method revealed that infant vaccination there had fallen from 95 per cent. in 1872 to 3.6 per cent. in 1889 when smallpox mortality was nil. James Stansfeld, the Liberal M.P. for Halifax and a former President of the Local Government Board, supported vaccination but urged that objectors should not be penalised.[77] This view was partially endorsed in 1892 when the Commission issued an interim recommendation that repeated penalties for non-compliance should cease and that persons imprisoned under the Vaccination Acts should not be treated as common criminals.[78] The Commission ended its inquiry in 1895 and in the following year published its *Final Report*. It found that vaccination, while not protecting absolutely, nevertheless reduced the chances of contracting or dying of smallpox. The claim that vaccination was responsible for the increased incidence of syphilis and cancer was rejected but the risk of occasional post-vaccinal disease was acknowledged. In order to diminish this risk the use of calf lymph was recommended. The establishment of a domiciliary system was urged, together with the extension of the age for compulsory vaccination from three to six months and revaccination at puberty. Although the retention of compulsory vaccination was felt to be desirable it was suggested that allowance be made for conscientious objection by parents. While the *Final Report* was generally pro-vaccinationist the concessions made, in particular the recommendation that conscientious objection should enjoy legal recognition, were widely thought to destroy the very basis of the Vaccination Acts.

On learning of the Commission's recommendations the London Society amalgamated anti-vaccinationists into a new National Anti-Vaccination League and made an all-out effort to introduce a new Bill, using the Commission's *Final Report* as a manifesto. By now the controversy was highly political and was seen by *The*

Spectator as 'a social question lying on the border-line between parties, and offering opportunities for rival political aspirants to outbid one another'.[79] In March 1898 Henry Chaplin, the new Conservative President of the Local Government Board and a pro-vaccinationist, introduced a Bill to implement the recommendations but with relief for conscientious objectors omitted. There followed a lengthy parliamentary debate during which the National Anti-Vaccination League launched a tremendous campaign to amend the Bill. The arguments of the League were put before Parliament by a number of Liberal members and the issues raised included post-vaccinal complications, the variable and often poor quality of lymph, the bad technique of some vaccinators and the resentment felt by many ratepayers at financing a compulsory service to which they had moral or practical objections. One member, Dr Clark, himself a former public vaccinator, told the House that he had experienced post-vaccinal complications but that his evidence 'was denied on behalf of the L.G.B.'.[80] Sir Walter Foster, a doctor and former Parliamentary Secretary to the Local Government Board, suggested that an honest parent should be permitted to avoid punishment for not having a child vaccinated by making a statutory declaration before a magistrate that vaccination would be injurious to the child's health. When Chaplin refused to amend his Bill the League increased its efforts and in July the by-election resulting from the death of C.T. Murdoch, Conservative member for Reading, gave it the opportunity it needed. The Government candidate, C.E. Keyser, had the personal backing of Balfour and was strongly favoured but refused to support the National Anti-Vaccination League while the Liberal candidate, George William Palmer, initially had little local support but agreed to promote the League's policies in Parliament. Palmer thus secured the votes of anti-vaccinationist Tories and was elected with a comfortable majority.[81] The election defeat had a dramatic effect on the Conservative party and Balfour, who held strong anti-vaccinationist sympathies, promised Government action. When the Bill re-entered the House Foster put forward his proposals again stating

> However small the risk may be, the risk exists all the same, and as
> long as the fear of it exists in the mind of a parent, we have no
> right to punish him, or to compel him to vaccinate his child.[82]

Chaplin's Bill was now criticised by a growing number of members. Henry Broadhurst, the trade unionist member for Leicester, asked Chaplin whether he would imprison the whole population of Leicester if no conscientious clause was passed while William Steadman, the radical member for Tower Hamlets, denounced Chaplin's indifference to the problem of illness and consequent time away from work which the operation of the Vaccination Acts caused working men.[83] Balfour now intervened, proposing a compromise whereby Foster's 'statutory declaration' would be replaced by a rule requiring parents to 'satisfy the court' of their conscientious objection. As MacLeod has pointed out, Balfour in putting forward this resolution 'overthrew the policy of his own Cabinet, the Bill of his own Government and the wishes of his own Minister'.[84] A new Bill was rushed through Parliament and on 12 August 1898 was passed as 'An Act to Amend the Law with respect to Vaccination'.[85] The most important provision was contained in section 2 (1) which specified that

> No parent or other person shall be liable to any penalty under section twenty-nine or section thirty-one of the Vaccination Act of 1867, if within four months from the birth of the child he satisfies two justices, or a stipendiary or metropolitan police magistrate, in petty sessions, that he conscientiously believes that vaccination would be prejudicial to the health of the child, and within seven days thereafter delivers to the vaccination officer for the district a certificate by such justices or magistrates of such conscientious objection.

Other sections provided for domiciliary vaccination and abolished repeated penalties under section 31 of the 1867 Act. The upper age limit for vaccination was raised from three to six months and 'arm to arm' vaccination was superseded by vaccination with calf lymph. Persons committed to prison on account of non-compliance with any order or non-payment of fines were henceforth to be treated in the same way as first-class misdemeanants.

Short of complete repeal the Act conceded everything moderate League members had asked. The victory was due as much to the absence of a major pro-vaccinationist lobby as to the actions of the League. In 1900 Henry Chaplin admitted that 'The Antivaccination League was a strong body and there was nothing like it on the other side'.[86]

Having traced events to the end of 1898 within the national context consideration will now be given to some of the factors at work in Essex in the years leading up to the passing of the 1898 Act. Here, from the 1870s, there was emerging an additional group opposed to vaccination. This was the membership of a religious sect known as the Peculiar People which had its origins in Rochford in 1837. From small beginnings the sect soon began to flourish and congregations and chapels ultimately stretched from Wakes Colne in the north to Upchurch (Kent) in the south, and from Foulness in the east to Camberwell (Surrey) in the west. Its chief centre, however, was always in south-east Essex. It was their belief in divine healing and rejection of doctors and medical aid, even to death, that was to gain the Peculiar People a more than local reputation. The first real trouble came in April 1872 when two children of George Hurry, a leader of the chapel in Woolwich (Kent), died of smallpox. Hurry had refused medical aid and was committed to Newgate Prison for trial at the Old Bailey on a manslaughter charge. Shortly afterwards a third child, who had been removed from the family's house and vaccinated, also died. When it was learnt that the children had been taken to crowded meetings so that hands could be laid on them in an attempt at divine healing, great alarm and indignation resulted in the neighbourhood. Thomas Hines, another of the local congregation's leaders, who had performed the office of laying on of hands, was dismissed from his job of coal carter at the Royal Arsenal when he refused to discontinue the healing rite. Smallpox spread rapidly in the district and the coroner expressed the opinion that the fatal cases were a result of the activities of the Peculiar People. A visitor to the area wrote

> The neighbourhood was literally up in arms against them — a fact on which I found the 'Peculiars' greatly prided themselves, as going to prove them in the coveted minority of the saints as opposed to the world[87]

The prosecution of Hurry failed because the doctors called to give evidence could not state positively that the children's lives would have been saved had medical assistance been sought. Hurry was acquitted, but not before the Grand Jury had issued a strongly worded statement asking for public attention to be drawn to the Peculiar People who 'are in fact practising a doctrine dangerous to the community at large'.[88]

From then on the activities of the Peculiars were regarded with suspicion, disapproval or hostility and they came to be associated with the spread of infectious disease. For example, when scarlet fever became prevalent in the Rayleigh area in 1894 the Medical Officer for the Rochford Rural District Council, Dr George Deeping, stated that in his opinion it 'was no doubt spread by the negligence and carelessness of the "Peculiar People"'.[89]

In the 1890s John Thresh, the County Medical Officer of Health, and the district medical officers were tireless in advocating vaccination. In 1892 there were 33 smallpox cases notified in the administrative county, of which three were fatal and Thresh wrote that as vaccination and revaccination 'alone can prevent the extension of this disease it behoves the Boards of Guardians ... entrusted with the enforcement of the Vaccination Acts to discharge their duties faithfully'.[90] In the following year the number of cases notified rose to 235, which Thresh attributed in part to the increasing proportion of unvaccinated children.

> We have received abundant warning, and if Boards of Guardians continue to be lax in their administration of the Vaccination Acts ... and if people continue to pay attention to the foolish outpourings of anti-vaccinationists, we know what to expect.
> The mild character of the attack in well-vaccinated persons has in many instances caused the nature of the disease to be mistaken until some well-marked case has occurred and revealed its true character.[91]

In 1895 there were 63 notified cases of smallpox in the administrative county, of which 11 were fatal. All the fatalities occurred in places with congregations of Peculiar People and Thresh did not miss the opportunity to attack what he regarded as the erroneous beliefs of the sect.

> In certain parts of the County there are many persons belonging to the sect of "Peculiar People" who having no faith in medicine, never call in a medical attendant. As they are unable to diagnose disease and cannot be proved to know the nature of the illness from which any member of such a family may be suffering,

necessary precautions are not taken, the cases escape notification, and we are powerless, since no penalty attaches to non-notification unless the responsible person can be proved to know from what disease the patient is suffering.

There is no doubt that the Notification of Infectious Diseases Act requires amending in many particulars, and if, in some way, these people with peculiar views could be compelled under penalty to call in a medical man, for diagnostic purposes, if not for medical or surgical aid, such a clause should be inserted in any Bill which may be introduced for amending the above Act.

At present this sect cause Medical Officers of Health great anxiety, often unwittingly disseminate disease, and put the County to considerable expense for Inquests which under other circumstances would be unnecessary.

In justice to these people, I must add that they are in very many respects eminently worthy, and not lacking in affection for their offspring. In no instance have they refused to allow me to see a patient, and if I have found one suffering from anything of an infectious character, they have willingly adopted all precautions which did not clash with their religious beliefs.[92]

At Southend where four of the fatalities had occurred the disease was successfully contained by the revaccination and quarantine of contacts. The Medical Officer, Dr A.C. Waters, wrote shortly afterwards

I wish to emphasize the fact that no smallpox developed in those who had been re-vaccinated, and it is of vital importance to the town for vaccination to be done, and re-vaccination offered free to the public.[93]

Although in 1896 the incidence of smallpox once again declined and there were only 19 cases notified in the administrative county, the laxity of boards of guardians in enforcing the Vaccination Acts remained a source of concern for the medical officers.[94]

Following the passing of the 1898 Act there was an immediate stampede throughout the country for conscientious objection certificates and by the end of the year no less than 203,413 had been issued by magistrates in England and Wales.[95] The 'conscience' clause was greeted with dismay by most of the medical profession and, in particular, by medical officers of health. Dr Waters thought in February 1899 that

as a result of the present Vaccination Act. It is a matter for regret that after years of experience in the value and efficacy of Vaccination that now owing to the 'Conscience Clause' ... a large number of children will not be vaccinated, and thus be subject to the ravages of small pox with its resultant disfigurement if not death.[96]

Dr Robert Young, Medical Officer for Rochford Rural District Council, reported that the large number of conscientious objectors in his district rendered it impossible to reckon upon immunity for any length of time. 'In fact, an outbreak may be looked for at no distant date'.[97] The Medical Officer for Waltham Holy Cross stated

> Vaccination and re-vaccination prevent and control Small-pox, and without Vaccination no sanitary precautions can *prevent* Small-pox, but isolation and segregation of individuals may control it. It is impossible to predict what will be the result of the omission of re-vaccination or what fruit the 'conscience' clause will bear, but the utterly absurd statements made by so-called conscientious objectors to presiding magistrates that have appeared in the weekly press tend rather to strengthen the wavering than add recruits to the anti-vaccinationists.[98]

The number of 'conscientious objection' certificates issued in England and Wales declined following the initial scramble and in 1899 only 39,511 were granted.[99] While a sharp decline was to be expected, it was increased by the unsatisfactory drafting of clause 2 (1) of the 1898 Act (the 'conscience clause') which led magistrates to question what constituted satisfaction of conscientious belief. They were often undecided and such indecision began to result in some benches refusing certificates. In addition the agitation of the newly formed pro-vaccination Imperial Vaccination League and the reports of medical officers of health were beginning to have an effect on public opinion and the magistracy by redressing the propaganda of the National Anti-Vaccination League.

The epidemic of 1901-1902, which in the administrative county of Essex resulted in 1,561 notified cases and 204 deaths, led to a further hardening of attitudes by magistrates. On 27 February 1902 *The Southend-on-Sea Observer and South-East Essex Gazette* reported

> There were four applicants for vaccination exemption certificates at Latchingdon on Saturday. Ordinarily, certificates are granted without much palaver at Latchingdon, but on this occasion the applicants were thoroughly cross-examined.

On 6 March the same newspaper reported that Southend magistrates had refused three applications for exemption certificates on 4 March. It is clear from contemporary newspaper reports that among the Essex benches there were considerable variations in interpreting clause 2 (1) so that exemption certificates were relatively easy to obtain in some areas but difficult in others. At the same time the Local Government Board, under the presidency of the pro-vaccinationist Henry Chaplin, repeatedly encouraged boards of guardians to prosecute anti-vaccinationists so that the number of prosecutions increased as it became harder to obtain certificates. At Stratford Magistrates' Court on 19 July 1902, for example, six Ilford fathers were prosecuted by the Romford Board of Guardians for failing to comply with orders issued by magistrates to have their children vaccinated and all were fined.[100]

Meanwhile the medical officers of health were continuing to emphasise the benefits and efficacy of vaccination and to deplore anti-vaccinationists. Of the 227 notified cases in the administrative county of Essex in 1901, 23 were fatal. The worst hit areas were Orsett Rural District and Grays Urban District with a total of 159 notified cases, of which 18 were fatal. The Medical Officer for Grays pointed out in his report for 1901 that

> no vaccinated person under 19 years was attacked ... It is to be regretted that during recent years the district as a whole has become much prejudiced against vaccination, mainly owing to misleading statements propagated by the leaders of the anti-vaccination movement. Parents have been encouraged to take advantage of the "conscientious clause" of that weak kneed Act of the late Government, with the result that about 60 per cent. of the children attending school were unvaccinated at the beginning of the present outbreak. They are now fortunately becoming disillusioned, and the proportion of unprotected persons is rapidly being reduced.[101]

At Southend, where the Medical Officer had for a number of years been giving public lectures extolling the benefits of vaccination,

> Portions of a lecture ... were printed and distributed widely, pointing out that efficient vaccination confers an immunity which lasts for a considerable time, but which gradually lessens. Therefore to insure absolute immunity in face of an epidemic, recent efficient vaccination is essential.[102]

In the following year, 1902, the epidemic reached its peak and there were 1,334 notified cases in the administrative county of Essex with 181 deaths. The Medical Officer for Billericay Rural District, Dr Carter, held harsh opinions of anti-vaccinationists and the Peculiar People, believing that as the Vaccination Acts were 'administered by different local benches of magistrates they have become little better than a farce'.[103] With regard to the Peculiar People

> The law has at last asserted itself ... and a parent neglecting to provide his child with medical aid has now a fair chance of a few weeks or months in prison. I see no difference in him and the man who neglects to have his child vaccinated, except that the latter exposes his child to a much greater risk, and should have a correspondingly more severe punishment.

He was in favour of compelling anti-vaccinationists to provide hospitals adding

> it is common experience that the conscientious objector is a vanishing quantity as soon as small-pox threatens his livelihood, and as receivers encourage thieves and vagrant wards encourage tramps, so small-pox hospitals encourage the anti-vaccinator.[104]

In a somewhat more logical report Dr Stovin, Medical Officer for Ilford Urban District, pointed out that 'Power to enforce re-vaccination of contacts would be a great help to Sanitary Authorities in dealing with Small-pox'.[105]

When the epidemic passed the necessity for vaccination appeared to many to have lessened but the number of prosecutions remained high as a result of continued pressure from the Local Government Board. At the same time the medical officers of health were assessing the lessons learnt from the epidemic. John Thresh, using figures contained in the report of the Medical Officer of Grays Urban District where a record had been kept of the persons who had been in contact with smallpox victims, concluded that

> amongst those who submitted to vaccination immediately after exposure to infection only about 1 out of 200 was attacked with Small-pox, amongst those who submitted to vaccination some days after exposure about 6 per 200 were attacked, whilst amongst those who refused to be re-vaccinated no less than 41 out of 200 were subsequently attacked ... Could any results be more conclusive as to the effect of vaccination in preventing this loathsome disease?[106]

Dr J.T.C. Nash, Medical Officer for the Borough of Southend-on-Sea where there were five smallpox deaths in 1902, issued a particularly lengthy report. One of the fatalities was a child of four years whose 'parents disbelieved in vaccination, and the unfortunate child lost its life through a severe attack of unmodified confluent small-pox'.[107] With regard to the Leicester method of control

> Our experience ... clearly shows that, though the important measures of notification, isolation, and disinfection enable us to control and limit the spread of infectious diseases, they do not enable us to eradicate them altogether. On the other hand if all susceptible persons who have been in contact with small pox are promptly vaccinated, an outbreak can be *stamped out* very speedily.[108]

The measures adopted in Southend 'while the disease was prevalent from January to June 1902' and which 'proved so eminently serviceable' were as follows:

(1) Antecedent efficient vaccination.
(2) Immediate isolation if a case of smallpox occurs.
(3) Immediate efficient vaccination of all contacts (direct and indirect) as far as practicable.
(4) Efficient disinfection of infected premises, and articles and contacts.
(5) Surveillance of contacts for 15 or 16 days.

> If contacts submit to disinfection and vaccination it is only necessary to keep them under daily observation; irksome quarantine can thus be dispensed with ...
> Hitherto the quarantining of contacts has proved both irksome and expensive. Quarantine was adopted in the first three or four instances of smallpox cases occurring in the Borough, but I subsequently abandoned strict quarantine for mere surveillance

of contacts for 16 days after exposure to infection, provided vaccination and disinfection had been first carried out. Such contacts
were allowed to return to their employments, and the Borough
was thus saved considerable expense. It is gratifying to find that
this method has now received the official approval of the Local
Government Board. In a memorandum dated September 25th,
1902, it is stated "the Board are advised that, under ordinary circumstances, the quarantining at their homes of inmates of such
(infected) dwellings is not necessary in districts in which sanitary
matters are properly administered and vaccination and revaccination are efficiently carried out."[109]

All the Essex medical officers agreed that the community was at risk from unvaccinated persons and several pointed to the problem posed by tramps in relation to
localised sporadic outbreaks such as those which occurred in Essex in 1903. Thresh
found that 54 of the 96 cases in the administrative county 'were definitely traced to
tramps and 'for many of the other cases in which the source of infection was not
ascertained, tramps may have been responsible'. He concluded that

> This is in accordance with the general experience throughout the
> country of recent years, much attention having being directed of
> late to the danger resulting to the community from the facility
> with which, owing to their peculiar habits and mode of life,
> Small-pox is disseminated by members of the tramp fraternity ...
> The desirability of compulsory vaccination and revaccination for
> persons of this class, as advocated by Dr Savage ... and by many
> other Medical Officers ... appears ... to be unquestionable ... It
> must be borne in mind that one beneficial result of the recent
> widespread epidemic is that the population as a whole is now
> much better vaccinated than it was three years ago, but for which
> circumstance it is very possible that some of the numerous
> sporadic outbreaks recorded would have spread much more wide-
> ly than they did.[110]

The Peculiar People continued to be a source of infection. At Southend in 1903
the single outbreak was confined to a family living in one house, all members of the
sect. To the dismay and annoyance of Dr Nash the vaccination of four children
which had been purposely neglected in infancy 'was declined even after the introduction of Small-pox into the household'. Nash concluded his report on the outbreak with a strong condemnation of anti-vaccinationists

> It matters little whether Anti-vaccination is, as in the present
> instance, a religious fanaticism, or otherwise, it is fraught with
> peril to its advocates should Small-pox invade their families. It en-
> tails needless suffering, and needless spread of Small-pox, and is a
> burden on the pockets of the ratepayers. Again, not only does the
> neglect of vaccination or revaccination induce the spread of the

disease, but the average length of detention in a Small-pox Hospital of an unvaccinated case of Small-pox, is two or three weeks longer than that of a once vaccinated person. In this manner again anti-vaccination is an expense to the ratepayers.[111]

Early in 1903 the Government decided to extend the 1898 Act to 31 December 1904, but the National Anti-Vaccination League was already campaigning for a complete repeal of what it now regarded as defective and unsatisfactory legislation. When it became clear that the spirit of the 'conscience clause' was being widely ignored by magistrates and officials the League sprang back to life with a much expanded membership. It gained further support when, following a Government inquiry set up to examine the high cost of domiciliary vaccination and of providing calf lymph during the epidemic of 1901-1902, the fee-scale of public vaccinators was reduced and the fines on negligent parents were increased in 1905,[112] with the effect of antagonising many doctors and alienating many parents. The anti-vaccination issue had been highly political since the 1898 Reading by-election and at the general election in January 1906, in which the Liberal Party swept to victory with a majority of 84 over all other parties combined, more than a hundred signed supporters of the National Anti-Vaccination League went in with the new Parliament. Among these was Arnold Lupton, a friend of Charles Creighton, who replaced Henry Chaplin as M.P. for Sleaford, Lincolnshire. Lupton was opposed not only to compulsion but also to vaccination itself believing, like Creighton, that it was dangerous and useless,

> and the sooner the Government ... dissociates itself absolutely from such a piece of eighteenth century quackery, the better it will be, not only for the health of the nation, but for the progress of true science, and for the honour and dignity of Parliament and the executive authority.[113]

In April Lupton introduced a measure to give greater freedom from the law for anti-vaccinationists. The measure was unopposed but at this point John Burns, the working-class leader who had replaced Chaplin as President of the Local Government Board, promised swift action if Lupton withdrew his Bill. The Bill was withdrawn and Burns introduced a Government measure to facilitate the granting of conscientious objection certificates. There was little opposition and in August 1907 Burns' amending Bill received the Royal Assent.[114] The Act, which came into operation on 1 January 1908, repealed section 2 of the 1898 Act and made it possible for a parent not wishing to have a child vaccinated to obtain exemption from any penalty under sections 29 and 31 of the 1867 Act by making a simple statutory declaration before a magistrate or commissioner of oaths within four months of the child's birth that 'he conscientiously believes that vaccination would be prejudicial to the health of the child'. Thus, after a campaign lasting some 40 years, the anti-vaccinationists had finally achieved the virtual end of compulsory infant vaccination and parents were henceforth free to choose whether or not their children should be vaccinated. The new procedure was essentially that which had been suggested by

Sir Walter Foster in the spring of 1898, which Chaplin had refused to incorporate in his Bill and which Balfour had rejected as too great a compromise.

The coming into effect of the Act coincided with the probable cessation of endemic smallpox in Britain, all isolated outbreaks after 1908 appearing to have been introduced from abroad. In 1909 Arthur Newsholme, Medical Officer of the Local Government Board, reported with regard to England and Wales that

> Small pox occurred in 13 towns during 1908, the largest number of cases occurring in Liverpool and Southampton. In nearly every instance the infection appeared to have been imported from foreign districts in which small-pox prevailed ... in similar outbreaks elsewhere, infection was introduced from abroad.[115]

Two years later he reported that there had been 128 cases of smallpox in England and Wales, excluding London. Although in 'a considerable' number the source of infection remained undiscovered, Newsholme concluded that

> light is thrown on the origin of many of the cases by tne fact that 22 cases of small-pox were notified to port medical officers, and there is definite evidence in other instances, in which patients had recently arrived in England, that the infection was imported from abroad.[116]

7

The Decline of Vaccination, 1908-1971

The effect of the 1907 Act on the vaccination of infants in England and Wales was dramatic. In the years 1907-1912 births fell from 918,341 to 872,799, successful vaccinations decreased from 651,050 to 436,951 while exemptions rose from 76,709 to 280,529. Expressed as percentages successful vaccinations fell from 71 per cent. to 50 per cent. of births while exemptions quadrupled from 8 per cent. to 32 per cent.[1] These figures disguise wide regional variations. In Leicestershire the level of successful infant vaccination, already by far the lowest in the country, fell from 24 per cent. to 10.5 per cent. of births between 1907 and 1912. In Cheshire, by contrast, the fall was from 81.1 per cent. to 62.5 per cent. in the same period. Wales, as a whole, was well-vaccinated; successful infant vaccination was 83.1 per cent. of births in 1907 and had only fallen to 67.5 per cent. five years later. The effect of the Act was felt most dramatically of all in Cambridgeshire where successful infant vaccinations fell from 78 per cent. of births in 1907 to 39.8 per cent. in 1912. In Essex the level fell from 62.9 per cent. to 40.4 per cent. in the same years, while the number of 'conscientious objection' exemptions rose from 6.2 per cent. to 36.7 per cent. of births.[2]

Provincial medical officers viewed with concern the rising proportion of unvaccinated inhabitants but their attempts to persuade parents to have their infants vaccinated were hampered by a growing sense of indifference engendered by the very low incidence of smallpox after the epidemic of 1901-1902. In Essex there were no notified cases in 1906 and 1907, three in 1908, none in 1909 and seven in 1910. In 1911 there were six cases, all in Grays Urban District and Orsett Rural District, the infection being introduced at the end of March by a river tugman, and John Thresh remarked shortly afterwards

> Considering that less than half the population under 12 years is now protected by vaccination, the county is to be congratulated upon the limited number of cases which followed the introduction of the case into Purfleet. To prevent an epidemic, which might easily reach an appalling magnitude, ceaseless attention is now required to prevent a mild case escaping recognition. Fortunately there is rarely any difficulty in persuading "contacts" to be vaccinated or revaccinated as the case may be, and if this is done early enough any marked extension of the disease is very unlikely. There is always the danger however of an unrecognised case infecting a number of persons before the nature of the disease is discovered, in which case very prompt and energetic action might not avail to prevent a serious epidemic.[3]

In the face of the continued pro-vaccination stance by the Ministry of Health and majority of doctors the National Anti-Vaccination League remained active and in 1914 found a new cause to fight as the War Office required all servicemen enlisted into the armed forces for the duration of the war to be vaccinated. A vehement campaign was mounted by the League and by Arnold Lupton, its outspoken champion in Parliament. The Government could ill afford to lose volunteers because of the League's propaganda and in January 1916 the War Office announced that vaccination was no longer compulsory for servicemen.[4]

The incidence of smallpox in England and Wales remained at a generally low level until 1920. In Essex, for example, there were only 29 cases in the years 1908-1919. Medical officers nevertheless continued to regard with apprehension the rising number of unvaccinated children. In 1919 there was a single case in Ilford Urban District and Dr Burton, the Medical Officer, pointed out that 1,167 births there had been registered during the year but only 611 infants had been vaccinated, observing that 'this is an undesirable state of affairs and it is only by extreme vigilance on the part of the Public Health Department that spread of the disease does not occur'.[5] The Medical Officer for Chelmsford Rural District, Dr MacDonald, writing early in 1920, thought that the increase in the number of objectors

> would enormously handicap the control of Smallpox should this disease unfortunately be imported into the district. The phrase 'Conscientious Objector' is a misnomer, and for all practical purposes the word 'conscientious' might have been omitted from the Statute.[6]

An outbreak of smallpox in south-west Essex in the first six months of 1920, in which six of the 31 cases were fatal, greatly alarmed medical officers in the area who thought 'there seemed every prospect of a very severe epidemic'. The outbreak was nevertheless halted by employing what was subsequently to be referred to as the 'English method' of smallpox control. This entailed, in the words of Thresh's successor as County Medical Officer, William Bullough, 'alertness and vigilance' on the part of medical officers, local doctors and sanitary inspectors and included

> the isolation of actual cases, disinfection of infected homes and clothing, tracing and keeping under observation all contacts, vaccination and re-vaccination of a large number of people, and the dissemination of information in regard to the usual precautionary measures.[7]

Their task was made easier by the 'eagerness with which large numbers voluntarily sought re-vaccination', showing that 'large sections of the community who under normal circumstances demand exemption from vaccination recognise the value of such a preventive measure when brought face to face with the actual disease'.[8] However, a small minority, including members of the Peculiar People, which refused to be vaccinated or revaccinated, caused considerable problems. The most difficult case of all was a 37-year-old unvaccinated Grays coal carter, a member of the Peculiar People, who caught the disease from his wife. He was admitted to Orsett Hospital on 29 March but 'disregarded all instructions and was careless and obstinate, making it very difficult for anyone to control his movements'.[9] Of the six fatalities three were unvaccinated but the other three, aged 18, 46 and 56 years,[10] had been vaccinated in infancy and thus gave support to the contention of the anti-vaccinationists that vaccination in infancy did not give protection in adulthood.

The national epidemic of *variola minor* in the 1920s and early 1930s resulted in the efficacy of vaccination once again becoming the subject of inquiry and controversy. In an article in *The Lancet* in 1924 Dr C. Killick Millard, the Medical Officer for Leicester, put forward the view that infant vaccination was disadvantageous not only because the protection waned but also because subsequent attacks of smallpox in vaccinated persons were often modified to the extent that they were unrecognisable as smallpox and therefore easily missed while, of course, being highly contagious. He believed that infant vaccination had no effect in protecting the community against smallpox and advocated instead the vaccination of all contacts during an outbreak and the isolation of all victims.[11] The chief proponent of the opposite viewpoint was Dr J.C. McVail who thought that

> to discourage vaccination in order that the unvaccinated individual may have an easily diagnosable (therefore possibly fatal) attack of smallpox seems to me a proposition contrary alike to the principles of medical ethics and to the interests of the public health.[12]

As the *variola minor* epidemic progressed yet another opinion gained ground, that it was unjustifiable to use vaccination against what was normally a mild disease for it was often more unpleasant and involved more risks than the disease itself.[13]

In 1926 the Ministry of Health and Medical Research Council, alarmed by the unabated spread of the disease and the rise in notified cases in England and Wales from 315 in 1921 to 5,405 in 1925, appointed a committee on vaccination. Its purpose was to inquire into and report on the preparation, testing and standardisation of vaccine lymph, the means by which the element of risk in vaccination could be diminished or removed and 'the methods of vaccination most appropriate to give protection against risk of smallpox infection in epidemic and non-epidemic periods'.[14] The committee's first report was issued in July 1928 and in August 1929 the Ministry of Health issued a *Vaccination Order* which amended existing practice in a number of directions. Cross or multiple scarification was abolished in favour of one insertion with a minimum of trauma and it was recommended that children be revaccinated between five and seven years of age and again after the age of 14 years. Seven months later, on 1 April 1930, the Local Government Act, 1929, came into force and transferred from the boards of guardians to the county and county borough councils duties in respect of vaccination under the Vaccination Acts, a change which William Bullough thought 'should lead to further improvements in the co-ordination of preventive measures against the spread of smallpox'.[15]

For seven years Essex escaped the *variola minor* epidemic which was at its height in England and Wales in 1927 with 14,767 notified cases. The first 17 cases appeared in the administrative county in 1928. In the following year there were 69 cases and the epidemic reached its peak in Essex in 1930 when 602 cases were notified, the vast majority (more than 500) occurring in Barking, Dagenham, Ilford, Leyton, Walthamstow and Tilbury.[16] By the early part of 1931, having had three years' experience of dealing with *variola minor*, Bullough, like other medical officers in England and Wales, now realised that 'the "English method" of notification, isolation, disinfection, vaccination and tracing and supervision of contacts, is competent to control Variola Minor in spite of the failure to secure universal infant vaccination'.[17] On the wider question of the merit of compulsory vaccination he had reached the following important conclusions:

The general public are becoming less afraid of Smallpox owing to their familiarity with Variola Minor, and this makes it more than ever impossible to secure 100 per cent. of compulsory infant vaccination. It is admitted that the present system of compulsory vaccination is a sham, and does not effect its purpose. Moreover, the idea of compulsion, though ineffective, is apt to create opposition in the minds of a lot of people, who might by other methods be disposed to accept vaccination. Furthermore, we cannot ignore the possibility, even though remote, of Encephalitis Lethargica being a sequel to adolescent primary vaccination.

It would appear that the time has arrived when the present method of inefficient compulsory vaccination should be given up, and in its place voluntary vaccination and re-vaccination should be introduced by a steady educational campaign, mainly through the Health Visitors and District Nurses. If this were decided upon, then consideration would have to be given to such matters as, closer co-operation with the general practitioners, provision of vaccine lymph direct to general practitioners, and provision of additional powers for tracing and supervising contacts.

The only times when compulsory powers would be useful would be in connection with the vaccination of all contacts of notified cases of Smallpox.

The most appropriate time for voluntary vaccination would be shortly after reaching the age of one year, and for re-vaccination shortly before leaving school.[18]

Infant vaccination continued to decline in the 1930s and 1940s although isolated outbreaks of *variola major* had the effect of creating a mass, if short-lived, demand for vaccination in the areas affected. One of these isolated outbreaks occurred in Essex in 1946. It began in Grays in January, being introduced by a soldier who had returned from India. His two young nephews caught the infection and the unvaccinated sanitary inspector called in to disinfect the houses died of haemorrhagic smallpox shortly afterwards. It was now obvious that the situation was very dangerous and by 23 February the list of known contacts exceeded 1,000. There were long queues of people standing in the rain and snow outside the public vaccinators' surgeries and within the space of five days, 5 to 9 March, 15,000 vaccinations were performed in the district. By about the middle of March the medical officers thought that the outbreak had been restricted to the Grays area but shortly afterwards it appeared in Southend-on-Sea, having been introduced by a 20-year-old unvaccinated laundry worker, Mercy Petley. She became ill on 16 March but no doctor was called by her immediate family, all of whom were members of the Peculiar People, and she died of confluent smallpox in the family's terraced house in Moseley Street, Southchurch, on 28 March. After the coroner was called in the three other members of the family and a 69-year-old woman who had moved in to help the family were all offered vaccination or revaccination which they stubbornly refused. Each developed the disease and was removed to Colchester Smallpox Hospital where one, Mercy Petley's 24-year-old brother who had not been vaccinated in infancy, died of haemorrhagic smallpox on 11 April. The parents and the old woman, all of whom had been vaccinated in infancy, survived. Fortunately for the local Medical Officer, Dr J. Stevenson Logan, other members of the sect who had had contact with the family were persuaded to accept vaccination in the form of cruciform insertions. Logan publicised vaccination facilities in the immediate neighbourhood of the infected house and within the space of six weeks no fewer than 5,000 vaccinations and revaccinations had been performed in Southend by public vaccinators, private doctors and the staff of the Public Health Department. Logan made his own thoughts on the matter plain.

> The public who lived in the area required little persuasion to accept vaccination and re-vaccination. At the vaccination station we treated many unvaccinated children of tender age and we can be excused some cynical reflections as to the shallowness of the conscientious objections which had led to their being deprived of this protection, and to speculate how rapidly scruples vanished when real danger threatened.

With regard to the Petley family

> There was considerable public alarm and resentment in the neighbourhood ... In many ways they were anxious to behave as good citizens, but when it came to divulging information about any activities which might reflect upon their religious beliefs and sect, they were stubborn and unyielding.[19]

Smallpox outbreaks like that in Essex and Southend in January-April 1946, in which 21 people caught the disease and six died, were now very uncommon and it had been demonstrated beyond doubt that they could be contained by the 'English method' of smallpox control. In England and Wales during the Second World War there were only 21 cases of smallpox with three fatalities but 60 cases of post-vaccinal encephalitis, of which 31 were fatal. It was now widely realised that vaccination was itself more of a hazard to life than the disease it was intended to prevent.[20] Although Parliament at last recognised that infant vaccination should no longer be compulsory, replacing it in 1948 by free and voluntary vaccination under the provisions of the National Health Service Act, 1946, the official attitude remained firmly in favour of the treatment and the Ministry of Health and county councils began a campaign extolling its benefits and pointing out the risks of non-vaccination. Essex County Council, for example, resolved in May 1948

> To take all practicable steps ... to encourage parents and others to take advantage of the arrangements for ... vaccination against smallpox ... and to keep constantly before the public details of the facilities available.[21]

In the first complete year of vaccination becoming voluntary, infant vaccination fell to 27 per cent. of births in England and Wales, having stood at 41.6 per cent. in 1946. Thereafter the level of infant vaccination and post-infant vaccination varied markedly from place to place, with peaks being caused by localised outbreaks of *variola major*. The highest figures were achieved in 1961-1962 when six separate importations of smallpox into England and Wales resulted in 24 fatalities out of 99 cases.[22] In the administrative county of Essex the publicity given to a single case of smallpox at Rainham in January 1962 had a dramatic effect, causing vaccinations to rise from 23,253 (mostly infants) in 1961, to 210,585 in 1962 and revaccinations to rise from 5,818 to 190,010.[23] In all there were more than seven million vaccinations and revaccinations in England and Wales, many being performed on people who were in no immediate danger of catching the disease, and it was later estimated that at least 18 died from post-vaccinal complications.[24] Meanwhile the Ministry of Health continued to advocate vaccination throughout the 1950s and early 1960s, issuing films like 'The Surprise Attack' and 'The Story of Dr. Jenner', to which the National Anti-Vaccination League replied by pointing to 'ridiculous claims ... still being made in regard to the effect of vaccination, on smallpox'.[25] In an influential article in *The Lancet* in July 1971 Professor George Dick found that in Britain between 1951 and 1970 about 100 deaths were attributable to vaccination of which about half were neurological complications but he could only guess at the number of individuals with residual brain damage.[26] Having presented the evidence he concluded that

> there is no place for mass vaccination unless the control of an outbreak gets out of hand. It is the duty of the media to discourage mass vaccination in outbreaks of limited proportions ... The time is overdue to debate the advantages and disadvantages of retaining smallpox immunization as one of our routine procedures.[27]

Official recognition that the risks associated with primary vaccination were 'now out of proportion to the risk from smallpox in Britain' came later in the year.[28] The routine vaccination of infants was discontinued and a great medical controversy came to an end.

Although smallpox had been eradicated from Europe it remained a serious problem elsewhere in the world, particularly in parts of Africa, Asia and South America. In 1967 the World Health Organisation embarked on an intensified global programme of smallpox eradication which it was hoped would be achieved within ten years.[29] This, the first ever world-wide eradication scheme, was brought to a successful conclusion in 1977 with the last case of natural smallpox occurring at the town of Merka in Somalia. While the ultimate fulfilment of Jenner's vision was at the time believed to have been achieved by the use of mass vaccination, the origin of the lymph used was uncertain, nor was it clear whether it was cowpox, a hybrid of cowpox and smallpox, or some other unspecified virus that completed the eradication.[30] It is now very unlikely that the mystery will ever be solved.

8

Pest Houses and Smallpox Hospitals

Some of the steps taken by communities to guard against the risk of infection from both natural and inoculated smallpox have already been traced and this chapter will look at the development of facilities for the isolation and nursing of those suffering from the natural disease, in particular at the parish pest houses and their successors, the smallpox hospitals.

Pest houses were an early and primitive form of isolation hospital, set up and run by the parish vestries with the overseers having day-to-day control. In the first half of the eighteenth century, before inoculation became commonplace among the well-to-do, there is evidence to suggest that although they were financed from the parish poor rates pest houses were not for the sole use of the poor. Indeed, Thaxted vestry in 1715 offered to provide all necessities free of charge to any inhabitant with smallpox who would enter the pest house 'for the good and advantage of the Town'.[1] The situation began to change in the second half of the century when the poor, who could not afford to pay for inoculation, comprised an increasing proportion of those at risk. Furthermore, it was because the poor were unable to pay for nursing and relied on parish relief during the period of illness and recuperation when they would not be earning any wages that vestries, under the control of the local gentry and other substantial ratepayers, were able to insist that they go to the pest house. As a result pest houses became places used almost exclusively for the isolation of the sick poor.

The earliest known Essex pest houses are those which stood at Collier Row near Romford and at the Thames-side fishing port of Barking, both in existence in 1666.[2] In view of the proximity to London of both these places it is postulated that they were used to confine plague as well as smallpox sufferers. Evidence has been found for only one other seventeenth-century Essex pest house, that in use at the market and cloth town of Braintree by 1688.[3] While it is possible that more references remain to be discovered it seems probable that only a very few populous parishes had a pest house before 1700.

In the eighteenth century an increasing number of places began to make provision for the isolation of smallpox cases. Among the first was the small market town of Thaxted where smallpox was rife from 1698 to 1723. At a vestry meeting in December 1715 it was resolved to take a three-year lease of a house at Bardfield End Green, a mile east of the town, at an annual rate of £4 and

> that all persons who received Collections or desires Collection upon being Visited with the Small pox upon Complaint or as Soon as tis known that they are infected ... be immediately removed to the ... house and there be allowed them what is necessary and all persons to have the Same allowance who will remove for the good and advantage of the Town[4]

The wording of the resolution needs careful interpretation, for the term 'Collection' means assistance from the poor rates. The removal of the poor and anyone else accepting parish relief was therefore mandatory. Others, over whom the overseers had no control, were encouraged to remove themselves for the good of the town with the promise of being 'allowed them what is necessary'. In the event of the house at Bardfield End Green proving 'not sufficient to hold the infected and to aire them' provision had been made for another house, in the occupation of John Pledyard, to be used as a pest house 'for aireing or otherwise as occasion requires'.[5] In 1747 a new pest house 'away in the fields' was 'built or restored with old materials taken from Yardleys farm buildings ... It was long in use as an isolation hospital'.[6]

At Maldon the joint workhouse erected in Fullbridge Street about 1713 may have been used to house smallpox patients regardless of status until October 1723 when a more restrictive policy was adopted by the parish vestries of All Saints and St Peter which resolved that henceforth

> No Person whatsoever young or old, Having the Small Pox come
> out on Them or Being Reasonably Judged to be in Danger of The
> Small Pox ... shall be Admitted, Received, or put into The
> Workhouse, other Than the Parish Poor of the Three Parishes.[7]

In 1735 the same two parishes decided to establish a separate infirmary in Fambridge Road, about half a mile south of the town, the third parish, St Mary, being invited to join the scheme. The premises were a timber-framed cottage called Portlands, leased for 14 years from Samuel Pond, senior, a Maldon apothecary and alderman, at an annual rent of £3.[8] At the end of the term the lease was renewed and the cottage was still being rented late in the century by which date it had acquired the nickname Pinchgut Hall.[9]

Other places which leased buildings included the north Essex cloth town of Halstead where a cottage was being rented from the Rt Hon. John Tylney, Earl Tylney, in 1755[10] and the small market town of Harlow where in 1762 the rented pest house stood in Mill Street.[11] Another market town, Witham, had a rented pest house by 1767 and paid Mr John Firman an annual rent of £2 10s. from 1782 to 1785[12] while at the parish of Ardleigh, a few miles north-east of Colchester, the annual rent of the thatched pest house belonging to Mr Bedford was four guineas in the 1790s.[13] At Great Bentley, six miles east of Colchester, the pest-house rent was five guineas in 1780. In the following year a different or additional house called Gunn's was rented by the vestry 'for the purpose of a Pest House ... for twelve years at £4 4s. per year ... commencing Michaelmas Day 1781'.[14]

It was less common to purchase buildings. One of the earliest examples was the house at Wethersfield which the parish bought about 1730 and which was still being used as the parish pest house in 1796.[15] A late example was the purchase by Newport parish of a copyhold cottage at Bury Water, about a quarter of a mile west of the village, in June 1810.[16]

A few places owned purpose-built pest houses. The earliest known Essex example is that at Great Coggeshall where the house erected in 1759 on Perryfield, half a mile north of the town, was brick-built with six rooms. The Quaker merchant and philanthropist Osgood Hanbury of Holfield Grange was closely involved in its construction and held it in trust for the townsmen. It was sold in March 1799 to Robert Greenwood for £99.[17] In June 1778 it was reported that the parish of Colne Engaine had 'lately been at great expence in not having a proper place for the reception of Persons afflicted with the Small Pox' and the vestry resolved

> to Build an House upon ... Townfield otherwise the poors Land,
> on purpose to receive Such Persons as shall be afflicted with the
> Small Pox ... And ... to allow the Overseer a Rate, which shall be
> sufficient to raise a sum of Mony for the Building the same.[18]

Chelmsford was another place which had a purpose-built pest house. By the early 1790s the old pest house in Tainterfield, which the parish had acquired at an unknown date between 1717 and 1767, was inadequate for the town's needs. Plans for a new house were approved by the vestry and the building was erected in 1793 at a cost of £120. It was timber-framed, weather-boarded and tiled, with a chimney at each end, was 25 feet long, 16½ feet wide and had one large room on the ground floor and two chambers above.[19]

In 1778 a pest house was built in the heavily wooded parish of Woodford, about eight miles north-east of the City, where the mansions of wealthy Londoners were a prominent feature. Like other parishes near the capital Woodford used the London Smallpox Hospital for its victims but in the 1770s, when smallpox was a serious problem in the parish, there were difficulties with the Governors over the number of Woodford patients who could be accommodated. In 1778 the decision was taken to build a pest house 'at some convenient spot in the forest' at a cost not exceeding £40. When not required for patients with infectious diseases it was to be used to house the ordinary poor but it was so much in demand for smallpox cases in its first year that it was decided to add an additional room at an approximate cost of £20. A parish pauper, Mrs Shirley, was placed in charge as resident nurse and supervisor. By 1779 it was clear that accommodation at the new pest house was insufficient and another approach was made to the London Smallpox Hospital, but on being informed that the annual subscription of £5 would only secure the admission of one Woodford patient at a time the vestry resolved not to subscribe.[20]

Woodford was not the only parish to exhibit a reluctance to spend a sum of money sufficient to make adequate provision for the isolation of its smallpox cases. In 1792 at the adjoining parish of Chigwell, also distinguished by the fine houses of London merchants and professional men, the author and pamphleteer Joshua Jenour, then one of the overseers, supported by three local doctors, proposed a scheme to build a pest house out of the poor rates. When Jenour's proposal was placed before the vestry, however, it was defeated by a powerful combination of farmers and substantial ratepayers.[21]

A few places made arrangements whereby cottages or houses could be used as pest houses when the need arose. At Great Bardfield the parish had such rights over a copyhold cottage at Tom's Green. When its ownership changed in 1773 the new owner William Pollett, a local gentleman, took possession upon trust

> that the ... Cottage ... may from time to time be used as a pest
> House for the poor of ... Great Bardfield ... or others Or be let or
> otherwise used ... for the benefit of the said parish ... Or ... may
> be sold or ... disposed of as the major part of the Inhabitants ...
> assembled at any publick vestry ... think fit.

The arrangement at Bardfield was still in operation in 1808.[22]

Sometimes parishes without a pest house were forced by the presence of smallpox to make emergency arrangements for the isolation of the sick, usually by renting premises for short periods, like Woodford which hired a house for four weeks in 1770 at 2s. 6d. a week in order to segregate a single victim.[23] Another parish forced to provide such accommodation was Great Tey, a few miles west of Colchester, where an outbreak in 1799 resulted in the vestry authorising the payment of £2 for a year's rent 'For use of an House for Pest House'.[24]

The examples of pest houses looked at so far belonged to populous parishes with nucleated settlements. There were exceptions, like the rural parish of Eastwood, near Southend. Here the scattered population was only 396 in 1801 but the parish had a pest house as early as 1764.[25] Nevertheless, it seems to have been unusual for rural parishes with very small populations to have had pest houses. Instead they either rented temporary accommodation or used facilities available in other more populous parishes when the necessity arose. An example of the latter option is afforded by the tiny Thames-side marshland parish of Wennington which had only 14 houses in the late eighteenth century and where the population was only 91 in 1801. When Widow Staggs and her three children contracted smallpox in 1764 they were sent to Rochford pest house, some 20 miles distant, where two of the children died. The mother and surviving child then went into the 'airing house' to convalesce. The total cost to Wennington parish for moving the family, medical treatment and so on was £18 0s. 2d.[26]

Fear of the spread of infection was the chief factor in the siting of a pest house. Most stood on isolated sites, usually to the north or north-east of the main centre of population so that the prevailing south-westerly winds would carry any escaping infection away from the town or village. Great Dunmow pest house stood about half a mile north-east of the town in St Edmund's Lane, known locally in the nineteenth century as Deadman's Lane,[27] St Osyth's was at Chisbourn Heath about a mile north-east of the village[28] while that belonging to Hatfield Broad Oak was nearly two miles away to the north on the edge of Hatfield Forest.[29] At Epping the pest house stood on the Plain, about half a mile north-east of the town. Here in August 1760 George Hodson was paid 4d. for 'stoping a gap at the pest house', an indication of the concern that infection should not escape its walls. In addition the house was completely surrounded by a carefully maintained hedge.[30] The one notable exception in Essex to these general rules of position and proximity was the first Chelmsford pest house, in use until 1793, which stood on Tainterfield, on the edge of the built-up area within about 100 yards of the parish church and 200 yards of the market place.

Sometimes there was opposition to the presence of a pest house from those who lived near it or from owners of adjoining property. At Wethersfield in 1785 Samuel Perry obstructed the chaseway across his land on which 'the People of the Pest House were always conveyed up and down' declaring that 'he was determined to demolish ... the ... Pest House'. Although Perry did not carry out his threat of demolition the chaseway was still obstructed in 1789 when smallpox broke out in the parish, so that at a vestry meeting on 12 February it was reported that it was 'necessary (to prevent as far as may be the spreading of the disease) To carry the sick poor to ... the Pest House' but that 'some obstacles' had been 'raised that render the Road ... difficult to pass'. In order that 'no time be lost to lessen the danger of the ... distemper spreading through the parish', the overseers and churchwardens were forced to make alternative arrangements for access across fields belonging to another farmer. In August 1792 it was reported that Perry had removed the pest-house doors, that his obstructions, including a gate, were still in place and that he had 'frequently refused the Chaseway'. An exasperated vestry at last resolved that the obstructions should be removed, that 'the Gate shall be broke open' and that 'an Action shall be brought against Mr. Samuel Perry for the depredations committed by him'.[31]

The nurses were generally untrained pauper women employed on an *ad hoc* basis. At Maldon in May 1784 Widow Lydia Crow of All Saints received 7s. 6d. 'for Nurs[g] people with the Small Pox' and died in December 1790 while attending John Salmon's wife.[32] Discipline for nurses and patients was generally lax, with large quantities of alcohol frequently being consumed. At Canewdon in about 1712 Mr Carter's bill of 11s. 2d. for drinks, including four pints of gin, was among the parish expenses incurred for 'the People ... That is down of ye Small Pox' in February and March[33] while at Thaxted the expenses for Widow Norris' family 'haveing ye Small pox' in September 1717 included £1 9s. for nursing and £1 3s. 6½d. for 'beare strong and small'.[34] A rather unusual system of nursing care operated in the 1770s at Rochford where it was the overseers' practice to order workhouse inmates to visit pest-house patients. Such a visit took place on 19 May 1777 when John Warren and William Ridgewell were 'directed to sit by ... a poor man, ill with the Small Pox in the Pest house belonging to Rochford'.[35]

Most pest houses were probably sparsely furnished and ill-adapted and equipped for their purpose. A rare inventory of household furniture, 1804, survives for Ashdon pest house which contained

One	Flock Bed and Bedsted
one	Blanket
one	Coverled
Three	Sheets
Foure	Chairs
one	Warming-Pan
	Fire-Shovel + Tonges

one	Tramel
one	Boiler
one	Tea Kittle
one	Earthen Chamber-Pot
one	Table, + one Padlock[36]

The general standard of hygiene was extremely bad. Many were unclean with windows shut and floors covered with straw or sanded. Beds were often swarming with vermin, for patients were rarely washed and bed linen seldom changed. Sanitary arrangements were primitive and most pest houses were foul-smelling in the extreme. Sometimes the smell became so offensive that it was necessary to use deodorising substances, as at Terling in 1804 when the overseers spent 2s. 6d. on frankincense.[37] But these comments are made in the context of late twentieth-century standards and for many poor patients the pest house with its stuffiness and warmth, regular supply of food and free nursing must have seemed a harbour of refuge.

From these examples it is clear that most pest houses were very small, capable of accommodating only a handful of patients at any one time and unable to cope with large numbers of sick poor in an epidemic. Nevertheless, they fulfilled a useful rôle in isolating individual cases as they occurred, thereby helping to prevent the initial spread of infection, while at the same time being places where smallpox victims could receive rudimentary medical care and nursing free of charge.

Parish pest houses ceased to exist as such when the Poor Law Amendment Act, 1834, came into force. The ancient parishes were combined into unions and care of the able-bodied and sick poor passed to the newly created boards of guardians. In Essex, for example, 409 parishes were combined into 21 unions in 1835. As the new union workhouse infirmaries came into use those pest houses owned by parishes were sold, like that at Epping which was purchased by Samuel Latham for £90 in 1837 shortly after the opening of the Epping Union Workhouse.[38]

Meanwhile and independently, in London and provincial towns, another element in public health care, the hospital and dispensary movement, had been growing in significance. The beginning of the movement was marked by the publication in 1714 of John Beller's *An Essay towards the Improvement of Physick* in which the Quaker philanthropist advocated the foundation of hospitals, the attachment of a doctor to every parish and state aid to medicine.[39] In London 13 new hospitals were founded between 1719 and 1800, so that in 1800 there were six general and six maternity hospitals as well as one for smallpox and inoculation, one for venereal diseases, one for destitute children and a lunatic asylum.[40] In the provinces during the same period 31 hospitals were founded.[41] These began with the Cambridge Hospital (1719) and included Bath General Hospital (1738),[42] Northampton General Hospital (1743),[43] Salop Infirmary (1745), Chester General Infirmary (1755), Leicester Royal Infirmary (1766),[44] Nottingham General Hospital (1781),[45] Hull Infirmary (1782)[46] and Sheffield Infirmary (1797).[47]

By the 1740s and probably earlier smallpox and other infectious diseases were excluded from London hospitals, the Middlesex Hospital for the Small-Pox being founded in 1746 to combat the disease in the capital.[48] Although it was stated in 1747 that all the London general hospitals were excluding infectious diseases,[49] Guy's Hospital may have been an exception for the Dutch traveller Petrus Camper reported that it had a ward for 'infectious diseases, chiefly small-pox' in 1748-49.[50] In addition the Foundling Hospital played an important rôle in experimental studies in inoculation methods from 1744 until that practice was replaced by vaccination.[51] Most provincial hospitals also adopted policies of exclusion. William Watts, founder of the Leicester Royal Infirmary, wrote in 1766 that 'No person affected with any contagious distemper is ever admitted into an Infirmary of the kind proposed' to be established at Leicester,[52] while the governors of Newcastle Infirmary decided to exclude all fever and skin cases in 1774.[53] The exceptions were at Chester, Worcester, Northampton and Manchester. Chester was the first provincial town in England to have wards for the specific reception of fever patients. The driving force was John Haygarth, Physician to Chester Infirmary from 1767 to 1798. In 1778 he founded a Small-Pox Society there which laid down strict rules for the isolation of the sick in their own homes and the prevention of the spread of infection. Inoculation was also strenuously advocated.[54] Haygarth subsequently wrote that the 'success of our ... society in checking variolous contagion ... encouraged me to propose a plan, which ... might prevent the communication of infectious fever from one ward of the infirmary to another'. The plan came to fruition in 1783 when separate fever wards were opened in the Infirmary and 'effectually suppressed the febrile contagion which alarmed Chester, in 1784'.[55] At Manchester it was the influence of the public health reformers Dr Thomas Percival and Dr John Ferriar which led to improvements. Both were leading figures in the Manchester Literary and Philosophical Society and prominent in the formation of the Manchester Board of Health in 1794, the first in the country. In 1789 Ferriar became a physician to the Manchester Institution and in 1792 special rooms were set aside for fever cases which occurred in the hospital, so that it was no longer necessary to dismiss almost all the patients when fever began. A much more ambitious scheme was fulfilled in 1796 when the Board of Health accepted Ferriar's plan for a fever ward in four small houses adapted for the purpose. In order not to spread alarm it was called a House of Recovery but in reality it was the first provincial isolation hospital for infectious diseases.[56] Such provisions, however, were exceptional[57] and in general, as Dr Champney wrote in 1797, 'Public Hospitals ... it is well known, are not favourable to the cure of diseases'.[58]

The number of hospitals continued to grow between 1801 and the passing of the Poor Law Amendment Act. The London Fever Hospital, otherwise known as the London House of Recovery, opened in 1801-1802 and was directly modelled on the Manchester House. Other fever hospitals were founded in Leeds in 1802 and in Stockport about the same time.[59] The Liverpool House of Recovery, opened in 1806, was also built to Ferriar's plans. Although the fever hospitals were intended primarily for typhus fever they also treated smallpox and other infectious diseases.

155

For example, in 1810 scarlet fever, smallpox, measles and whooping cough, as well as typhus fever, were being treated at Liverpool.[60] In addition 11 general hospitals were built in the provinces during the years 1803-1815 but infectious diseases were still excluded by 'almost every County and City Infirmary in the kingdom' in 1819.[61] Even as late as the 1860s most hospitals, in both London and the provinces, were continuing the same policies of exclusion. At St Bartholomew's, St Thomas' and Guy's Hospitals in London admissions remained 'subject to the ... exclusion of smallpox'.[62] Indeed, no advance in provision for smallpox patients in the capital had been made since 1801-1802. At Salop Infirmary in 1859 the rules stated that 'no persons ... suspected to have smallpox or other infectious distemper ... be admitted as inpatients',[63] while in the early 1860s at the Colchester and Essex Hospital in Lexden Road, Colchester (opened in 1820) 'all cases where there is a suspicion of contagiousness are carefully excluded'.[64]

Thus at the time of the passing of the Poor Law Amendment Act, 1834, the facilities in England for the isolation and treatment of smallpox cases consisted of the numerous parish pest houses, two hospitals in London and wards in five provincial hospitals. As poor relief and medical care at parish level was replaced during the years following the Act by the new system of unions the situation deteriorated, most if not all of the new union workhouses making no special provision to deal with infectious diseases. Although the *Poor Law Report*, 1834, had advocated the classification and segregation of paupers and had emphasized the need for separate buildings, the hopes of Bishop Blomfield, Nassau Senior, Edwin Chadwick and others concerned in the preparation of the *Report* were quickly dashed, for the Poor Law Commissioners appointed under the Act were driven within their very first year to depart from the *Report*'s recommendations. Instead of having the recommended separate facilities the new union workhouses (most of which were built in the years 1835-1850) were enlarged versions of the pre-1834 'General Mixed Workhouses' which the Poor Law Inquiry Commissioners had found so unsuitable. This resulted in unsatisfactory treatment of the sick and had the effect of keeping at home many patients who most needed to be admitted and isolated. Furthermore, when outbreaks of infectious diseases occurred among workhouse inmates the sick were rarely isolated, those with the disease instead remaining in the general wards to spread the infection to other inmates. By 1 May 1839, five years after the Poor Law Amendment Act came into force, 583 unions had been formed in England and Wales. Of these 252 had already built and a further 67 were currently building a new workhouse, while 37 had agreed to build new or to alter existing premises. In 175 unions an old workhouse was being used.[65] The situation in Essex was slightly better than in most English counties. Of the 17 unions wholly within the geographical county, nine (Braintree, Chelmsford, Colchester, Epping, Lexden and Winstree, Orsett, Rochford, Saffron Walden and Witham) had already provided new and 'adequate' workhouse accommodation, two (Maldon and Ongar) were using old premises, four (Dunmow, Halstead, Romford and Tendring) were building new workhouses and two (Billericay and West Ham) had agreed to build a new workhouse but had not begun work.[66]

The attempt in 1838 by the Shoreditch Guardians, under pressure from epidemic influenza and typhus, to improve sanitary conditions in their union marks the beginning of the movement for the reform of public health in Victorian England. As a result of objections by their auditor to the extra expenditure Edwin Chadwick, Secretary to the Poor Law Commissioners, who was always interested in preventable disease and believed that disease was the main cause of poverty, obtained authority for an investigation. The subsequent report, forming an appendix to the *Fourth Report of the Poor Law Commissioners*, 1838, revealed that widespread neglect of sanitary precautions was defeating the purpose of the Poor Law Amendment Act. An era of agitation and public inquiry had begun. Two major reports by Chadwick, *The Sanitary Condition of the Labouring Population of Great Britain*, published by the Poor Law Commission, 1842, and *The State of Large Towns and Populous Districts*, published by the Royal Commission on the Health of Towns in two volumes in 1844 and 1845, revealed almost unbelievable conditions of filth and squalor as well as the lack of adequate drainage and wholesome water supplies and paved the way for the passing of the Public Health Act, 1848. By this Act a General Board of Health was set up for the whole country except London, with power to create local boards. In municipal boroughs the town council was constituted the local board while elsewhere a local board could be created by a petition of the inhabitants of an area. The General Board also had power to impose a local board on any area with an annual death rate above 23 per thousand. By the Public Health Act of 1854 the Board was subordinated to the Privy Council and in 1858 it was abolished by the Local Government Act, its medical duties being transferred to the Council where John Simon became Medical Officer. At the same time its administrative duties went to the Home Office where a small department was formed to deal with applications to set up local boards. Although the powers of local boards were sanitary rather than medical and had no direct concern with smallpox, the 1848 Act was the first in a great series of related reforms in the fields of public health, medicine, sanitation, workhouses and infirmaries.

The movement for the reform of workhouses and workhouse infirmaries, culminating in the passing of the Metropolitan Poor Act, 1867, and the Poor Law Amendment Act, 1868, was part of this wider movement. It began in 1853 when Louisa Twining, daughter of the wealthy tea merchant Richard Twining and sister of the physician and author Richard Twining,[67] protested publicly about the state of the workhouses. In the following year the Poor Law Board reversed an earlier decision by allowing parties of ladies organised by Louisa Twining to visit Strand Workhouse for the purpose of 'giving comfort and instruction'. Further revelations by Miss Twining resulted in a debate in the House of Lords in 1857, following which permission for the ladies to visit Strand Workhouse was withdrawn. They responded in 1858 by forming the Workhouse Visiting Society and successfully infiltrated a number of workhouses. By 1860, 140 members were visiting 12 metropolitan workhouses and branches had been established in several parts of the country. In the late 1850s the campaign was joined by another new organisation, the National Association for the Promotion of Social Science, whose influential members were in touch with the more enlightened Poor Law medical officers and ensured that workhouse scandals received wide publicity.

Philanthropic doctors and nurses added their weight to the campaign in the early 1860s. The doctors' professional and social status had been enhanced following the passing of the Medical Protection Act, 1855, which set up a medical register and gave the public and the medical profession their first real protection against quacks. As a result many doctors were unwilling to tolerate exploitation by boards of guardians or domination by workhouse masters (whom they regarded as professional and social inferiors) or to acquiesce in the neglect of the sick poor. The nursing reformers were led by Florence Nightingale who in 1860 published *Notes on Nursing* and set up a nursing school in St Thomas' Hospital. By 1863 she had turned her attention to workhouse infirmaries and in 1865, with the help of the wealthy philanthropist William Rathbone, was able to put her ideas into practice when her best pupil Agnes Jones and 12 trained nurses were sent to Brownlow Hill Workhouse in Liverpool. After severe initial problems the Liverpool scheme proved a spectacular success. Meanwhile agitation by a number of workhouse medical officers and revelations in December 1864 about gross neglect in Holborn and St Giles' Workhouses prompted Thomas Wakley, the new owner and editor of *The Lancet*, to set up a commission of three doctors to inquire into workhouse-infirmary conditions in London. Its damning report appeared early in 1866[68] and was followed by similar reports in the provincial press. The *Lancet* report led to the formation in February of the Association for the Improvement of the London Workhouse Infirmaries, its secretary being the medical journalist and reformer Dr Ernest Hart of St Mary's Hospital, one of the three *Lancet* commissioners, while the membership included Charles Dickens and John Stuart Mill.[69] One of the Association's first acts was to force the Poor Law Board to hold an inquiry into conditions in the Strand and Rotherhithe Workhouses following reports of neglect, intimidation and physical abuse by Mrs Matilda Beeton, Head Nurse at Strand Workhouse. The Medical Officer at Strand, Dr Joseph Rogers, was outspoken in his criticisms of conditions in his workhouse and in the same year, 1866, formed the Association of Poor Law Medical Officers as a pressure group for reform.[70]

The 1864 revelations about Holborn and St Giles' Workhouses also spurred Florence Nightingale into further activity and she persuaded Charles Villiers, President of the Poor Law Board, to undertake an investigation into the treatment of the sick poor with the ultimate aim of major workhouse reform. The investigation was carried out by H.B. Farnall, Poor Law Inspector for the Metropolitan District, and Dr Edward Smith who was appointed first Medical Officer to the Poor Law Board in 1865.[71] Their reports were printed in 1866 and recommended far-reaching reforms and improvements. Meanwhile Florence Nightingale's own plan for reform had been accepted by the Prime Minister, Viscount Palmerston, but his death in October 1865 and the collapse of the Government in June 1866 dashed her hopes for a Bill. However the pressure for reform was now so overwhelming that it was not to be delayed for long. When the new Government was formed Prime Minister Disraeli appointed Gathorne Gathorne-Hardy as President of the Poor Law Board and early in 1867 a committee set up by Sir Thomas Watson, President of the Royal College of Physicians, whose advice Gathorne-Hardy had sought, put forward new recommendations for the reform of workhouses and workhouse infirmaries, including the removal of fever and smallpox cases to separate hospitals. On 8 February Gathorne-Hardy introduced the Metropolitan Poor Bill in which he strongly advocated the need for separate fever and smallpox hospitals. The Bill received the Royal Assent in March and, as Brian Abel-Smith has pointed out, 'was the first explicit acknowledgement that it was the duty of the state to provide hospitals for the poor'.[72] In May the Metropolitan Asylums Board was established by an Order of the Poor Law Board pursuant to the provisions of the Act. It embraced all unions and parishes in London and its first fever hospital, for smallpox and scarlet fever, was erected in 1870.[73] The 7,912 epidemic-smallpox deaths in London in 1871 gave urgency to the Board's programme and by 1930, when its powers were transferred to the London County Council, it had been responsible for building 14 infectious-diseases hospitals and had 'developed into one of the largest and most effective hospital systems in the world'.[74]

The next step forward came in 1871 when the Local Government Board Act[75] established a new government department, the Local Government Board, to which were transferred all the powers and duties of the Poor Law Board together with those of the Privy Council and Home Office relating to public health and sanitary legislation. Public health and care of the poor thus came together again. John Simon, Medical Officer to the Privy Council since 1858 and a critic of the policy of the Poor Law Board particularly in relation to workhouse infirmaries and vaccination, now became Chief Medical Officer to the Local Government Board. This important legislation was followed by the Public Health Act, 1872,[76] which made further transfers of health and local government powers from other government departments to the Local Government Board and which for all sanitary functions divided England and Wales into urban and rural districts. In country districts the guardians were constituted the rural sanitary authority, while in towns the sanitary authority was the town council in a borough, the improvement commissioners in an Improvement Act district, or a local board of health. The Local Government Board was also empowered to create sanitary authorities at ports.[77] The appointment of a medical officer now became mandatory for all local sanitary authorities 30 years after Edwin Chadwick had concluded that for the general promotion of the means necessary to prevent disease 'the appointment of a superior medical officer independent of private practice ... would ... be a measure of sound pecuniary economy'.[78] Three years later the Public Health Act, 1875,[79] consolidated most of the existing legislation and repeated and widened the powers of local sanitary authorities. Section 131 laid down that any local authority might, for the use of its inhabitants, provide hospitals or temporary places for the reception of the sick. Like the powers given under the 1866 Sanitation Act, however, those of the Public Heath Act, 1875, were seldom used and a Local Government Board inquiry in 1879 revealed that only 296 of the 1,510 sanitary authorities in England and Wales had any means of isolating infectious diseases. By 1891 the number had advanced to about 400 but most of these were small and inadequately staffed and equipped.[80]

In London in the 1870s considerable problems were experienced with the siting of isolation and smallpox hospitals. There were loud protests that hospitals dealing with smallpox cases acted as sources of contagion for their neighbourhoods and the appearance of large numbers of malignant smallpox cases early in 1880 provoked an appeal by the Metropolitan Asylums Board to the Local Government Board for authorisation to deal effectively with the disease. The outcome was the establishment in May 1881 of a canvas camp adjoining the Metropolitan Asylums Board's large mental institution at Darenth, near Dartford, Kent, capable of accommodating 640 patients. Those who were thought to be capable of withstanding the journey were assembled at the Board's Deptford Hospital and taken to Darenth by road, a distance of some 18 miles. But the camp was inadequate for the outbreak, which had reached alarming proportions, and in the early summer of 1881 the Board adopted the suggestion of Sir Edmund Hay Currie, Chairman of its Fever Committee, by chartering two old wooden warships from the Admiralty and mooring them off Greenwich.[81] The adaption of the *Atlas*, a former ship-of-the-line, to accommodate acute cases and the frigate *Endymion* for administrative purposes cost £11,000. The Board now pressed for legislation to define and, if appropriate, enlarge its powers

> to enable it to perform in the present and any future epidemics, in
> a successful and satisfactory manner and without molestation, the
> duties which the Act of 1867 contemplated it should perform.[82]

In the autumn of 1881 a number of Fulham residents succeeded in obtaining an injunction restricting the admission of smallpox cases to Fulham Hospital, opened in 1877, to residents from within a mile radius. The Local Government Board instructed its inspector, Dr William Henry Power, to undertake an inquiry and his report revealed that the incidence of smallpox within a mile radius of the Hospital was four times greater than in districts further out. The situation in London was now critical. The work of both the Fulham and Hampstead Hospitals was severely hampered by court injunctions and similar proceedings were likely at Stockwell, Deptford and Homerton. They existed merely on sufferance of the local residents and operated under continual threat of closure. The outcome was the appointment in December 1881 of a Royal Commission on Smallpox and Fever Hospitals. The recommendations in its *Report*, presented to Parliament in August 1882, were based on the conclusions of the Fulham inquiry and its main concern was the alleged dissemination of the disease in their localities by smallpox hospitals. It urged that smallpox be treated in isolated positions on the banks of the Thames or in floating hospitals. Cases which could not be moved so far should be accommodated in specially designed isolation wards in the Board's fever hospitals but no urban institution should treat more than 40 smallpox patients at a time.

The Metropolitan Asylums Board took immediate steps to implement the Commission's recommendations and in 1883 permission was obtained from the Local Government Board to establish floating hospitals on the Thames some distance downriver from London's boundaries for less acute cases. The *Atlas* and *Endymion* were purchased from the Admiralty and in addition a disused cross-Channel steamer, the *Castilia*, was acquired and equipped as a hospital ship. All three vessels, together capable of accommodating 350 patients, were moored in Long Reach, 17 miles below London Bridge, between Dartford and the riverside industrial village of Purfleet, in the Essex parish of West Thurrock. Additional land was purchased at Darenth for the erection of convalescent wards. The siting of the floating hospital at Long Reach was to have serious repercussions for the unprotected inhabitants of central-south Essex.

The problem of infection spreading from smallpox hospitals was next given official consideration by the Local Government Board in 1887-1888 and a memorandum sent to all local authorities in England and Wales in March 1888 included the following advice

> Sites for hospitals designed to receive small-pox require a very much larger space about them than sites for other infectious diseases hospitals. Small-pox hospitals, as we know them, are apt to disseminate small-pox, and their sites should, therefore, be placed outside of towns, and should indeed be sought at places as far distant from any populated neighbourhood as considerations of accessibility permit.[83]

A further memorandum issued by the Board in January 1895 revealed that little progress had been made and that

> great difficulty has arisen in the selection of sites for the reception of patients suffering from small-pox. Small-pox hospitals have again and again served to disseminate that disease to neighbouring communities ... There is, as yet, no evidence available to indicate at what distance from populations, whether aggregated in institutions or living in dwelling-houses, small-pox hospitals may be established without risk to persons who are susceptible of small-pox infection; but that distance is often a very considerable one.

Local authorities were advised that they should not contemplate the erection of a smallpox hospital within a quarter of a mile of another hospital, a workhouse or similar establishment, or a population of 150-200 persons nor within half a mile of a population of 500-600 persons.[84]

Outside London (where the Metropolitan Asylums Board, set up in May 1867, embraced all the unions and parishes) the provincial boards of guardians were empowered by the Poor Law Amendment Act, 1868, to provide separate infirmaries for infectious diseases but there was no common fund and the Act was permissive, not mandatory. Although the Poor Law Board and the Local Government Board (which took over the powers of the Poor Law Board in 1871) pressed the guardians to make adequate provision there was little progress and by 1902 only eight are known to have been built. They were at West Ham and Leeds (both 1871), West Derby (1884), Birmingham (1888), Brentford (1896), Portsmouth (1898), Halifax and Kingston-on-Thames (both 1902). The West Ham hospital, which stood in Western Road, Plaistow, was for smallpox only. The other seven were for infectious diseases in general.[85] Elsewhere by the early 1870s a number of provincial boards of guardians had made improvements to workhouse conditions by building isolation wards on the workhouse site. Towards the end of 1870 Colchester Board erected isolation wards nicknamed the 'Pesthouse' adjacent to the main workhouse premises and close to a row of 18 cottages on Balkerne Hill, despite the protests of Dr Charles Bree, Physician to the Colchester and Essex Hospital, who realised the danger of infection to neighbouring residents.[86] The poor record of the Local Government Board in relation to the Poor Law infirmaries after 1871 has been explained by W.M. Frazer.

> A strong Medical Department at the Local Government Board could have been of great assistance to the Poor Law side of the work, which was developing year by year more responsibility for hospitals and other medical services. But the layman's jealousy of the medical administrator stood in the way and during the years between 1871 and 1876 the Medical Branch at the Local Government Board continued, if anything, to lose ground, becoming more and more subject to the secretarial side. Simon resigned his appointment as Medical Officer to the Board in 1876, being dissatisfied with the scope which he and his Branch were afforded in the determination of Public Health policy ... Lacking medical guidance, the Board had no consistent policy in regard to the development of the Poor Law Infirmaries which, by the end of the century, were undertaking a large proportion of the total hospital treatment not only of the destitute but also of the working classes of this country. Because there was no carefully considered medical policy, workhouse infirmaries were kept poorly equipped and badly staffed ... with the result that their medical work was often inefficiently performed and only in rare cases was it up to the standards of the best voluntary hospitals.[87]

In Essex in the 55 years between the passing of the Poor Law Amendment Act, 1834, and the creation in 1889 of the County Council,[88] there were few improvements in facilities for the isolation of infectious diseases as a result of action by statutory bodies. In West Ham the Guardians, using powers conferred by the 1868 Poor Law Amendment Act, opened a smallpox hospital in the great epidemic year, 1871.[89] Following the passing of the Public Health Act, 1872, Halstead Urban Sanitary Authority converted two old cottages in Mount Pleasant into a fever hospital in 1873[90] and by February 1885 Halstead Rural Sanitary Authority had set up an infectious diseases hospital in Castle Hedingham, 'some distance' from the village, capable of accommodating eight patients.[91] Harwich Corporation had an infectious diseases hospital at Dovercourt by 1882[92] and in 1884 Colchester Corporation opened an isolation hospital in Myland farmhouse, one mile north of the town.[93] Finally, West Ham Local Board of Health leased a row of cottages in Pragell Street, near Western Road, Plaistow, in 1884 for use as a temporary smallpox hospital but which was still in use in 1890.[94]

At the same time most voluntary hospitals, which had increased greatly in number since 1834, still had no facilities for isolation and continued to refuse admission to infectious cases. The situation at Halstead Hospital was typical. Opened in 1884 'for the benefit of the sick poor of Halstead and neighbourhood' there were no provisions for dealing with infectious diseases and the regulations stated that 'Infectious and incurable cases shall not be admitted'.[95] There was one notable exception in Essex. This was the Colchester and Essex Hospital where a small isolation block was opened in 1867.[96] It comprised two wards, each 15 feet by 14 feet, and a nurses' room. In 1879, when the hospital was extensively altered and enlarged, a detached 'iron house' was erected in the grounds which was used both as an isolation ward and a store.[97]

The Local Government Act, 1888, by which the county councils were created, also provided for the appointment of county medical officers of health and empowered county councils both to see that the provisions of the Public Health Act, 1875, were being properly enforced by district sanitary authorities and to report to the Local Government Board if they were not.[98] In the autumn of 1890 Essex County Council appointed Dr John Thresh, Medical Officer of Health for the Maldon and Chelmsford Rural Sanitary Districts, for the task of 'collating the reports of the local Medical Officers of Health and reporting generally thereon to the Council', the first summary report to be submitted in April 1891. Thresh's fee was £100 and the arrangement was evidently renewed annually until 1895.[99] Quickly realising that his powers under the 1890 agreement were too limited to enable him to exert the degree of pressure necessary to bring about a radical improvement of facilities in the sanitary districts Thresh began a campaign to persuade the County Council to appoint a full-time medical officer. Although clearly displeased with what he considered to be the unsatisfactory character of some of the reports submitted by the district medical officers, he remarked in 1893 'I should be exceeding my duty were I to criticise them'.[100] At the same time the county councillors were told quite bluntly that

> full advantage cannot be taken of the Reports until an Officer is appointed by the County, who shall give his whole time to their study and to investigating many of the subjects referred to therein. The services of such an Officer, whom the District Officers and Sanitary Authorities could consult, would probably save the County very much more annually than the County

> Council would have to pay for such services. Still the Statistics and Reports now being furnished will be of the greatest service to a County Medical Officer whenever appointed.[101]

Nothing was done and a year later, in June 1894, Thresh was losing patience with the councillors. His reputation had recently been enhanced and his abilities recognised by his appointment as Lecturer in Public Health at Kings College, London, and he had no hesitation in making his feelings clear

> The desirability of exercising a little more supervision and of rendering Sanitary Authorities and their Officers a little more assistance, I have several times tried to impress upon you, and I hope the time is not far distant when you will act upon advice given in the best interests of the County.[102]

This, combined with the passing of the Isolation Hospitals Act, 1893, which empowered county councils to provide hospitals for infectious diseases out of the county rate,[103] put sufficient pressure on the Essex County Council to force it to create a Sanitary Committee in November 1894[104] and in October 1895 Thresh was appointed County Medical Officer of Health despite opposition from some rural district councils.[105] He now had the authority to exercise control over the districts and he lost no time in seeking changes in those where 'administration is lax or ... definite sanitary improvements are urgently needed'.[106] Although the Council had demonstrated a reluctance to exercise fully the powers in relation to public health provided by the Local Government Act, 1888, it was nevertheless among the least dilatory counties to appoint a Medical Officer of Health, for in 1896 only 15 of the 62 counties in England and Wales had made such an appointment.[107] Much of the credit for this must be attributed to the pressure exerted by the energetic and ambitious Thresh.

Even before his appointment as Medical Officer of Health, Thresh had been paying great attention to infectious diseases, having urged local authorities to adopt the permissive Infectious Diseases (Notification) Act, 1889, which required medical practitioners to notify cases of certain infectious diseases, including smallpox, to their local medical officer of health. By 1892 all but one of the 41 sanitary authorities lying wholly or partly within the administrative county of Essex had adopted the Act[108] and by 1893 the one exception, Linton Rural Sanitary Authority, had also adopted it.[109]

Thresh's detailed *Summary* for 1894 enables an assessment to be made of the progress in relation to the provision of isolation hospital facilities in Essex since he started reporting to the County Council five years earlier. By the Local Government Act, 1894, the county was now divided for local government purposes among 21 urban and 20 rural district councils, plus the three port sanitary authorities and the autonomous County Borough of West Ham. These new district councils inherited the public health functions of their predecessors, the sanitary authorities and local boards of health. Of the 20 rural districts five (Billericay, Epping, Halstead, Orsett and Rochford) now had a permanent hospital while Braintree had purchased two 'Berthon' huts as a temporary hospital, Lexden had a tent hospital and Saffron Walden had a sharing arrangement with Saffron Walden Urban District. Of the 21 urban districts 10 had a permanent hospital and Maldon had erected a wooden temporary hospital 'at considerable expense' to accommodate patients in a smallpox outbreak started by a sailor in 1894. In the same year Waltham Holy Cross, which had previously sent its smallpox cases to Highgate Hospital, was instructed by the Local Government Board to 'make provision for any further case of Small-pox that may arise' and a wooden hut was acquired 'and stored for future use'. In addition to these existing facilities, a 'Model' isolation hospital had been erected in 1894 in Chelmsford Rural District, where Thresh was Medical Officer, but it was not due to open until January 1895. In Romford Rural District plans had been prepared for a hospital 'and its erection decided upon', while in Halstead Urban District an isolation hospital was in the course of erection.[110]

Following his appointment as County Medical Officer Thresh began pressing local district councils to provide permanent isolation hospitals, while at the same time urging that greater use be made of existing facilities, pointing out in 1896 that

> It is a somewhat singular fact that in certain districts where some
> form of Isolation Hospital is provided, very few cases are removed
> and isolated therein. Apparently they are more or less reserved for
> use in epidemic periods, rather than for isolating the first cases,
> which otherwise become foci, from which epidemics spread. In
> other words, they are used for arresting instead of for preventing
> epidemics.[111]

Although by the end of 1898 there had been a considerable improvement the overall situation was still far from good. Only nine districts had hospitals which Thresh considered adequate and satisfactory, another eight had hospitals in need of some enlargement or improvement while the hospitals in a further eight were altogether too small or of a temporary nature. In 20 districts there was still no hospital although hospitals were currently being built in five, one had a 'satisfactory' arrangement to use the hospital belonging to a neighbouring district and a further four had 'unsatisfactory' sharing arrangements.[112]

Progress continued to be made, albeit slowly, over the next two years and by the end of 1900 new and permanent isolation hospitals had opened in Braintree Rural and Urban Districts (joint), Clacton Urban District and Epping Rural District. Rush Green Isolation Hospital was opened by Romford Rural and Urban District Councils in 1900 to serve the expanding populations of Romford, Dagenham and Hornchurch. In the same year Ilford Urban District Council opened a new isolation hospital in Chadwell Heath Lane, while Grays Urban District joined Orsett Rural District Council in the management of the isolation hospital in Long Lane, Little Thurrock. Meanwhile major enlargements had taken place in Barking Urban District, while in Brightlingsea Urban District two hospital marquees each capable of holding six beds had been purchased.[113] The vast majority of isolation hospitals built in Essex in the 1880s and 1890s were, like those elsewhere in England, intend-ed to treat scarlet fever, enteric fever and diphtheria as well as smallpox. The only local authorities in the geographical county to have separate smallpox hospitals by 1900 were Barking Urban District, Southend-on-Sea Borough and the County Borough of West Ham which had opened a new purpose-built hospital in Rainham Road South, Dagenham, in 1899.[114]

Difficulties with the 1893 Isolation Hospitals Act, in particular the requirement that money borrowed by a county council for the purpose of contributing towards the expense of an isolation hospital should be repaid out of the local rate of the district concerned, led to further legislation, the Isolation Hospitals Act, 1901.[115] This enabled local authorities providing isolation hospitals under the provisions of the Public Health Act, 1875, to transfer them to their county council, subject to the Local Government Board being satisfied that accommodation sufficient for the needs of the district was or would be provided. County councils were empowered to contribute to any infectious-diseases hospital provided by a local authority and the money borrowed from the Local Government Board for such purpose was no longer to be repaid out of the local rate. The new Act thus strengthened the rôle of county councils in the provision of isolation hospitals but before it could have any effect existing hospital accommodation was put to a severe test by the epidemic of 1901-1902.

In the late summer of 1901 smallpox in London reached epidemic proportions. It quickly spread to the adjoining counties, the first cases in Essex appearing at Grays in August, at Orsett and Walthamstow in September and at East Ham, Leyton and Romford in October.[116] By 1902 it had covered the whole country. When the epidemic finally ended in Essex in the summer of 1902 there had been 1,561 cases of which 204 were fatal.[117] At the height of the epidemic in London Sir William Henry Power, Principal Medical Officer to the Local Government Board, who had a particular interest in infectious diseases, prepared a memorandum deal-ing with the provision of isolation hospital accommodation by local authorities.[118] Reports submitted to the Board by provincial medical officers in the 1890s con-tinued to demonstrate that hospitals used to treat smallpox frequently disseminated the disease to neighbouring communities, revealed the dangers of cross-infection when treating more than one infectious disease in a hospital and were doubtless a major factor in the shaping of Power's memorandum. Henceforth any smallpox hospital provided by means of a loan sanctioned by the Board was not to have

> within a quarter of a mile of it either a hospital, whether for infec-
> tious diseases or not, or a workhouse, asylum, or any similar
> establishment, or a population of as many as 200 persons ... [nor]
> within half a mile of it a population of as many as 600 persons,
> whether in one or more institutions, or in dwellinghouses.

It was also made clear that such hospitals 'must not be used at one and the same time for the reception of cases of small-pox and of any other class of disease'. Because smallpox hospitals could conveniently serve a larger area than isolation hospitals for other infectious diseases it was pointed out that there was 'often advantage in a combination between districts for the purpose of providing smallpox accommodation'.[119]

Essex evidence that smallpox hospitals were disseminating the disease had first come to light in the mid 1880s when it was reported that the three smallpox hospitals then in West Ham (belonging to the Local Board of Health, West Ham Poor Law Union and Poplar Board of Works) were a health hazard to the rapidly growing suburb. As a result the Borough Council put forward a scheme in 1890 to close all three (those belonging to the Union and Poplar Board to be converted into a hospital for infectious diseases other than smallpox) and build a new hospital on an isolated site outside West Ham. Events were hastened by a report in 1894 by the Medical Officer of East Ham that he suspected West Ham Council's smallpox hospital of spreading the disease into nearby East Ham and it was closed shortly afterwards.[120] But far more significant than this was the controversy surrounding the Metropolitan Asylums Board's floating smallpox hospital moored in the Thames at Long Reach. The hospital ships were suspected of being a source of contagion and an investigation carried out in 1892-1895 led Dr Rea Corbet, Medical Officer for Orsett Rural District, to conclude that the 'sole cause' of the excessive prevalence of smallpox in Orsett Union 'was the proximity of the Small-pox ships of the Metropolitan Asylums Board'.[121] Of the 12 cases of smallpox in the Rural District in 1895 no less than 11 were in the parish of West Thurrock where the distance from the hospital ships to the nearest cottages was 'some 600 yards'.[122] The problem of the ships was highlighted again during the epidemic of 1901-1902. In the six-month period 1 August 1901 to 31 January 1902 there were 454 smallpox cases in the administrative county of Essex, of which 197 were in Orsett Rural District and 93 in Grays Urban District, three miles east of the ships. In February 1902 Corbet reported that

> all the results point to some central continuous focus of infection, corresponding exactly in position with the Small-pox ships ... most careful enquiry fails to show any means whereby this continuous flow of infection can occur except on the hypothesis that it is airborne.[123]

With regard to Grays, Corbet doubted whether the influence of the ships extended that far and attributed the high incidence of smallpox there to men employed in the cement and other industrial works in West Thurrock carrying the disease into the town.[124] Dr John Ward, Medical Officer for Grays Urban District, wrote about the same time that

> a considerable outbreak had arisen at Purfleet and neighbourhood, and was spreading towards Grays through West Thurrock and South Stifford. As the inhabitants of these villages do much of their shopping in Grays it was natural to expect that we should not enjoy exemption for long.[125]

These disturbing reports resulted in a Local Government Board inquiry, conducted in 1902-1903 by Dr George Seaton Buchanan, who concluded that

> When considered along with previous experience of the ability of small-pox hospitals to disseminate infection in their neighbourhood, and with the history of smallpox in the Orsett Union since 1884, the facts of this epidemic give strong grounds for inference that smallpox prevalence in Purfleet was set going and from time to time throughout the epidemic was reinforced by infection aerially conveyed from the Metropolitan Asylums Board small-pox hospital ships[126]

After reading these reports John Thresh, who for ten years had been urging local authorities in Essex to build isolation hospitals, remarked that

> Under ordinary circumstances one would expect to find that the largest proportion of cases had occurred in the thickly populated working class districts adjoining the metropolis, but such was not the case. On the contrary, the districts which suffered most were the comparatively thinly populated rural districts adjacent to the hospital ships and the Dagenham Small-pox hospital.[127]

As the epidemic subsided, county and district councils began turning their attention to implementing the 1901 Isolation Hospitals Act. In Essex by the end of 1902 the Sanitary Committee of the County Council had drawn up a list of 17 isolation hospitals in the administrative county to which it was proposed that grants should be made. With the encouragement of the Local Government Board more attention was now being given to the siting of hospitals and to the provision of separate accommodation for smallpox cases. Indeed, any local authority building a new hospital by means of a loan sanctioned by the Board after May 1902 did so on condition that it was 'not to be used at one and the same time for the reception of cases of small-pox and of any other class of disease'.[128]

In the years leading up to the First World War the rôle and utility of isolation and smallpox hospitals were subject to reappraisal by the Medical Department of the Local Government Board and county medical officers. This was prompted by three factors; the continuing problem of the spread of infection from the hospitals, the declining incidence of the disease and the greatly improved means, afforded by the motorised ambulance, of transporting infectious cases to hospital. A 149-page *Report on Isolation Hospitals*, compiled by Dr H. Franklin Parsons and submitted to the Board in 1912, repeated the need for smallpox to be treated in separate hospitals situated 'at a safe distance from populous areas'[129] and drew attention to 'the recent improvements in means of communication and transport enabling a hospital to serve a considerably larger area than was formerly thought practicable'. Joint hospitals serving a number of districts were already in operation in many places and more districts were recommended to combine in order to have the benefit of 'important advantages, as regards both economy and efficiency ... which are seldom practicable for small separate hospitals'.[130] This was thought to be particularly relevant for hospitals for smallpox, 'a disease in which there is seldom any objection to removal ... and in which patients have often been found to bear a journey of many miles without injury'. Parsons further observed that in many instances it had already been found advantageous to form combined areas for smallpox hospitals 'more extensive and embracing a larger number of districts than the combined areas formed for providing hospitals for other infectious diseases'.[131] Accommodation for smallpox patients was to be of the simplest kind. 'Ornament and luxury are quite out of place, especially in view of the class of people from whom the majority of small-pox patients come'.[132] When not needed for their primary purpose smallpox hospitals could be utilised to treat other diseases provided arrangements were made beforehand for the immediate clearance of patients in the event of a case of smallpox occurring.[133] As smallpox patients were 'often of the vagrant class' it was recommended that smallpox hospitals should be surrounded by a fence six feet six inches high to prevent escape.[134]

In Essex, combination of districts for the purpose of providing joint isolation hospitals began in the 1890s[135] and extended to smallpox hospitals in 1903 when Maldon Joint Hospital Board obtained and fenced a site for a smallpox hospital and Braintree Joint Hospital Board acquired land for the same purpose at Black Notley.[136] The trend accelerated in the first decade of the twentieth century so that by the end of 1910 seven of the 10 permanent smallpox hospitals in Essex were in combinations of two or more districts while the County Borough of West Ham had entered into building agreements with nine neighbouring districts to use its large smallpox hospital at Dagenham.[137] In other districts there were premises which could be quickly put into use to make a further nine smallpox hospitals. In addition a number of districts were currently discussing the possibility of combination. John Thresh, who had experienced two epidemics in Essex, now considered the accommodation and emergency arrangements to be 'fairly satisfactory' and concluded

> that as the large centres of the population are all provided for, the smaller urban and rural districts without accommodation could arrange for the provision of tent hospitals when an epidemic threatens, and that there need be no such delay as would effect the process of stamping out.[138]

In the next decade Thresh began pushing for the logical extension of combination, the creation of regional smallpox hospitals, but his efforts met with little success. The subject was given some urgency in 1918 when the agreement between the County Borough of West Ham and its neighbouring local authorities for the use of the hospital at Dagenham came to an end. Negotiations to reach a new agreement had failed and 'provision for cases of small-pox, now that the Dagenham Hospital ... is not available, requires immediate attention'.[139] Writing at the beginning of 1919, shortly before his retirement, Thresh told the County Council

> Two or three Hospitals could be made to serve for the whole County. The one at Colchester might serve the Northern portion, the one near Grays the South-East portion, and one should be provided for the South-West and extra suburban districts. My

suggestions on this subject ... have been before the Public Health Committee on more than one occasion. It is within the power of the County Council to provide such an Institution for a number of districts and it would be much easier to do this than to get it done by the District Councils themselves combining together for this special purpose.[140]

This strongly worded statement obviously had the desired effect for in 1919 the administrative county was divided for smallpox purposes into five regions.[141] The new scheme had, thought William Bullough, Thresh's successor, resulted 'in adequate and efficient accommodation being provided',[142] but a few authorities still preferred to make their own, sometimes primitive, arrangements and there was a major problem with the metropolitan suburbs. With almost 600,000 people, south-west Essex was by far the most heavily populated region. A smallpox hospital at Stifford with accommodation for 10 patients served Grays and Tilbury Urban Districts and Orsett Rural District which had a combined population of nearly 44,000 but the remainder of the region, comprising the urban districts of Barking, Brentwood, Buckhurst Hill, Chingford, Epping, Ilford, Leyton, Loughton, Romford, Walthamstow, Waltham Cross, Wanstead and Woodford and the rural districts of Billericay, Epping, Ongar and Romford, with a population of almost 550,000 (about 60 per cent. of the population of the administrative county) 'had not ... any definite provision for the segretation and treatment of small-pox patients'.[143] As the County Borough of West Ham was still 'not prepared to accept the terms and conditions offered' for the use of the Dagenham hospital, an adequate central smallpox hospital for the whole region was planned, sanction for which was being sought from the Ministry of Health. In the event of a smallpox outbreak in the interim period accommodation would be made available by the Metropolitan Asylums Board.[144] At the other end of the scale the south-east region, comprising Rochford Rural District and Shoeburyness Urban District, had a population of 24,555 and was served by a smallpox hospital at Nobles Green, Eastwood, capable of accommodating 10 patients.[145] The mid-Essex region had two hospitals, one with six beds at Galleywood serving Chelmsford Borough and Rural District, the other at Little Totham serving the Borough of Maldon and the urban districts of Maldon and Witham. The north-east Essex region comprised the urban districts of Frinton, Walton-on-the-Naze and Wivenhoe, the rural districts of Lexden and Winstree and Tendring, plus the Borough of Colchester and was served by Colchester Smallpox Hospital which had permanent accommodation for 20 patients and emergency tent-accommodation for a further 50. The fifth region, north-west Essex, comprised the urban districts of Braintree and Halstead, the rural districts of Belchamp, Braintree, Dunmow, Halstead and Saffron Walden, and the Borough of Saffron Walden. It was served for sporadic cases by Colchester Smallpox Hospital and in the event of a more widespread outbreak the hospital at Sible Hedingham used by the County Council as a children's sanatorium, would revert to its primary rôle of a smallpox hospital.[146] The local authorities which still preferred to make independent arrangements were the Borough of Harwich, the urban districts of Brightlingsea, Burnham-on-Crouch and Clacton, and the rural districts of Bumpstead and Stansted. Such arrangements generally left much to be desired. Harwich, for example, had the use of a hulk in the dockyard belonging to the Port Sanitary Authority while Burnham-on-Crouch, for years a thorn in the side of the County Medical Officer, had arranged for a tent to be placed in a field on the adjoining marshes, 'but this can hardly be regarded as satisfactory, the County Council are pressing the Local Authority to make better provision'.[147]

Protracted negotiations in 1919 between the County Council, the Ministry of Health, the County Borough of West Ham and the Orsett Joint Hospital Board concerning smallpox hospital accommodation in south-west Essex remained inconclusive when, in January 1920, smallpox broke out in Grays Urban District and Orsett Rural District and from there spread to metropolitan Essex and London to become the biggest outbreak since the epidemic of 1901-1902. The 31 cases in Essex, all of them in Grays, Orsett and the south-west of the County, were sent to Orsett Smallpox Hospital or the Metropolitan Asylums Board's hospitals. By early summer the outbreak, which at one point had looked as though it might develop into a full-scale epidemic, was over, having been contained by prompt isolation of the sick, the vaccination and revaccination of large numbers of people and the tracing and observation of contacts. Negotiations continued after the outbreak but achieved nothing and in May 1921 the County Council decided to leave the responsibility for providing smallpox accommodation to the individual local authorities in south-west Essex.[148] A year later agreement was reached between the County Borough of West Ham and 19 local authorities in south-west Essex whereby the County Borough undertook to provide for the isolation and treatment of cases of smallpox occurring in the whole of that area at its Dagenham hospital.[149]

The incidence of smallpox, mainly *variola minor*, was now increasing in England and Wales once again, rising from 315 notified cases in 1921 to 5,405 in 1925. Although by the end of 1925 no case of *variola minor* had yet been notified in Essex, the threat was sufficient for William Bullough to review the smallpox hospital accommodation in the administrative county. There had been a few minor improvements since 1920 but three local authorities, Leyton and Walthamstow Urban Districts and Bumpstead Rural District, had still made no provision for the isolation and treatment of smallpox cases. In addition, Bullough regarded a number of existing arrangements as unsatisfactory; Burnham Urban District still proposed to erect a tent on the marshes, while Maldon Joint Hospital Board (serving the Borough and Port of Maldon, Maldon Rural District and Witham Urban District) had only a shed and a temporary building at Little Totham. In the knowledge that *variola minor* could reach Essex at any time Bullough concluded that

> It cannot be said that the ... schemes make satisfactory provision
> for the Administrative County as a whole, as they are piecemeal
> in character and tend to overlap one another. The extra-
> metropolitan portion of Essex is so interwoven with the

metropolis that provision for the isolation and treatment of small-pox should be common to all these populous districts. The rest of the Administrative County could be served adequately by the Orsett Small-pox Hospital for South-Essex and Colchester and Sible Hedingham Hospitals for North-Essex. This would liberate the remaining institutions for other purposes.

To bring about this re-arrangement, the County Council would need to obtain the necessary powers and past experience shows that a serious emergency or even catastrophe will be necessary before this can be achieved.[150]

The *variola minor* epidemic finally reached Essex in 1928 and the 17 cases in that year were the first of smallpox in the county since 1921.[151] In 1929 the number of cases increased to 69, ten of which were in Walthamstow where the Urban District Council responded by opening a smallpox hospital at Low Hall Farm.[152]

In the following year a major change took place in the structure of public health in England and Wales with the coming into effect of the Local Government Act, 1929.[153] With regard to hospital accommodation for infectious diseases, section 63 required county councils to make a survey and prepare a scheme for submission to the Ministry of Health for the provision of adequate hospital facilities. In the meantime the number of cases of *variola minor* continued to increase. In Essex, where 602 cases were notified in 1930, the increase was marked, the places worst affected being Leyton and Walthamstow with 136 and 190 cases respectively.[154] The Essex County Council's scheme for isolation hospitals was delayed by other administrative matters, particularly the reorganisation of sanitary districts as required by section 46 of the Act, and was not submitted for approval until late in 1934. The delay also made possible consideration of the problem without the immediate pressure of epidemic smallpox, for the number of cases of *variola minor* in the county declined after 1930, from 195 in 1931 to 13 in 1933.[155] In formulating the scheme the Council took into consideration two factors in particular: firstly that experience had shown a large hospital serving a wide area to be more satisfactory than a number of small hospitals serving smaller areas and secondly that with modern means of transport the removal of patients to a hospital some distance from their homes presented little difficulty. The Council was henceforth to provide accommodation for the treatment of all cases of smallpox occurring in the administrative county except for those in the Borough of Colchester. Under the terms of an agreement between the County Council and Colchester Corporation a hospital to be built by the Corporation was also to be made available for all cases from the administrative county[156] and this arrangement was approved by the Minister of Health in June 1935. The new hospital in Mill Road, Mile End, Colchester, was opened in April 1936 replacing the seven smallpox hospitals which served the administrative county at the time of passing of the 1929 Act.[157] Its ability to cope with a serious outbreak was never put to the test.

9

Smallpox in Retrospect

While set in a national context, most of the eighteenth and nineteenth-century examples of the cost of smallpox in economic, social and demographic terms cited in this study are drawn from a well-populated county in southern England where a number of factors, of which proximity to London was the most important, resulted in a continuous high level of exposure to the disease. Yet the experience of Essex towns and villages (where smallpox, commonly absent for several years at a time, tended to come in the form of damaging but generally short-lived outbreaks or epidemics) was markedly different from that of London and large provincial towns like Norwich where the disease was endemic and which served as reservoirs of contagion. The Essex experience was also different from that of isolated communities where the absence of the disease for very long periods led to few, if any, inhabitants enjoying immunity through a previous attack. In such circumstances the population was highly vulnerable when smallpox appeared and in the most extreme and spectacular British example, on the tiny Shetland island of Foula, less than ten out of about 200 inhabitants survived an epidemic of what must have been a particularly virulent strain in 1720. There were other less marked differences. Under the influences of Daniel Sutton and Thomas Dimsdale general inoculations had achieved popular acceptance in south-east England by the late 1760s but there seems to have been a time-lag of about ten to 20 years before the same degree of confidence was reached in northern counties like Cheshire, Cumberland, Lancashire and Yorkshire. Case studies of such contrasting places and regions would be of considerable interest.

Seen in the light of the admittedly extreme Foula experience the measures taken by market towns and villages to prevent the random introduction of the disease were, while understandable, potentially harmful, especially in the period before outbreaks could be halted by general inoculations. It was therefore fortunate that such measures appear to have had limited and relatively short-term success, most places experiencing an outbreak every few years and thereby maintaining the level of natural immunity at fairly regular intervals. A more logical system was that of deliberate exposure of children to mild cases of the disease in order that they should obtain immunity through what was hoped would be a similarly mild attack, the risk of fatality being tempered by the knowledge that of those who died many would have succumbed to another childhood disease. This practice, known as 'buying' smallpox, was part of the traditional folk-medicine of Pembrokeshire and a number of other isolated areas. With the availability of the safer methods of inoculation and vaccination the practice declined and its survival among the very poor at Colchester as late as 1872 is both striking and unexpected, being the only known Essex example of 'buying' smallpox.

For 30 years following its arrival in England inoculation had little or no demographic significance because of the limited scale on which it was carried out.

This situation began to change during the epidemic of 1751-1753 when the treatment enjoyed a considerable rise in popularity but it was the introduction of the Suttonian method which had the greatest impact. Daniel Sutton's demonstration of the method's mildness and safety in the mid 1760s quickly led other practitioners to adopt it and heralded inoculation's period of great exploitation. From 1766 considerable strides were made in mitigating the effects of epidemic smallpox in market towns, villages and rural parishes by the use of general inoculations in which protection of the poor was paid for out of the poor rates. In large towns, however, smallpox remained endemic and inoculation failed to achieve much popularity amongst the poor. While the present paucity of evidence capable of statistical analysis renders impossible any satisfactory assessment of the significance of infant inoculation in demographic terms it nevertheless seems that those children who were inoculated benefited from an improvement in their chances of surviving into adulthood in the order of ten to 20 per cent. In other words the chief short-term demographic effect of inoculation, that of reducing the level of smallpox mortality, led to the more important longer-term effect of an increase in the number of potential marriage partners and parents. This in turn contributed to the steep rise in the population of England and Wales after 1800 which was specially notable in the years 1811-1821 when the increase from 10,164,256 to 12,000,236 represented a rate of increase for the decade of 18.1 per cent., still the highest recorded since the introduction of the national decennial census in 1801. Tentative and inconclusive as they are, the findings of this study indicate that while the impact of inoculation on population growth should not be overstated it was sufficiently significant to warrant further research and a reappraisal by demographic historians of its utility in country towns, villages and rural parishes where four fifths of England's people still lived in 1800, in order that it might be given its due place in the debate on eighteenth-century population and industrialisation.

This emphasis on the demographic impact of inoculation should not be permitted to obscure its other effects. The immunity it gave lessened the toll of human suffering, contributed to an improvement in the quality of life and to the increasing social mobility of the age while the protection of a growing proportion of the poor from the mid 1760s onwards eased the drain which smallpox imposed on the poor rates. More importantly in the eyes of vestries and town authorities the use of general inoculations to avoid or curb epidemics had the economic benefit of preventing the damage to trade sustained through the closure of markets and disruption of commercial activity. By giving immunity to a significant part of England's labour force, by contributing to the growth of population and to economic stability it may even be argued that general inoculation was one of the many ingredients which came together after 1750 to make England the world's first industrialised country.

The advance of inoculation was halted by the introduction of vaccination in 1798. Although Jenner and his supporters hoped that vaccination would quickly supplant inoculation they were disappointed and in the controversial 40-year transition period arguments reminiscent of those used in the early years of inoculation were employed by advocates of both methods and the suspicions and doubts of ordinary people were revived. The great epidemic of 1837-1840 finally forced Parliament to intervene and the banning of inoculation in favour of vaccination in 1840 ended for all practical purposes the debate over the relative merits of the two methods. In reaching this decision Parliament was heavily influenced by the fact that the disease could be spread by inoculation but not by vaccination, by evidence showing that inoculation was especially dangerous in large, densely populated urban environments like London and by the evidence from European countries where compulsory vaccination had resulted in a dramatic fall in smallpox mortality.

In so far as it was aimed at the reservoirs of endemic smallpox among the urban poor the decision to ban inoculation and promote vaccination was correct. But for country towns and rural parishes where smallpox was not endemic and where the success of general inoculation had been clearly demonstrated it could be argued that it had less validity. Yet to have created a distinction between the urban and rural poor would have been untenable. The evidence from mainland Europe which so influenced Parliament was from countries where vaccination was both compulsory and strictly enforced, but because the Parliamentary debates of 1840 had revealed the widespread dislike and suspicion of vaccination among England's poor and because compulsion such as that rigidly enforced in authoritarian Prussia was quite alien to the English concept of individual liberty, persuasion was preferred. The chances of the Act succeeding in its objectives were further undermined by Parliament's folly, firstly in placing the administration of free vaccination in the hands of the Poor Law authorities and secondly in refusing to acknowledge publicly the waning nature of protection by vaccination, resulting in the absence of provision for revaccination.

The linking of vaccination with the New Poor Law was perhaps not surprising, foreshadowed as it was by the alterations to health care of the poor under the 1834 Poor Law Amendment Act. Such care then ceased to be the concern of parish vestries and overseers and became instead the responsibility of the guardians of the new Poor Law unions. The old parish pest houses were closed and the pauper, sick, aged and infirm were brought together in the unsegregated wards of union workhouse infirmaries which had no separate facilities for infectious diseases. In the eyes of Whitehall administrators and legislators it seemed logical for the guardians to extend their health care functions to embrace vaccination.

The lack of enthusiasm shown by the poor for free and voluntary vaccination resulted in infant vaccination being made compulsory. For many this represented a blow to individual liberty at a deeply emotional level and an unwelcome intrusion of state authority into the family unit. Non-acceptance by parents under the 1840 Act became a criminal offence under the 1853 Act but the lack of adequate means of enforcement encouraged anti-vaccinationists to ignore the new legislation. This in turn led Parliament to strengthen enforcement and increase the penalties for non-compliance by the Acts of 1861, 1867 and 1871. What had begun as a question about the best method of ridding the country of smallpox was developing instead into a contest of wills between Parliament and the medical establishment on the one hand and the anti-compulsory vaccinationists on the other. The unpopularity of the Vaccination Acts was intensified both by the increased involvement of the Poor Law authorities, especially in areas where the guardians were energetic in carrying out their duties, and by the formulation of the Leicester method which showed that there was an alternative to routine infant vaccination, thus reinforcing the anti-compulsory-vaccinationist case. The growing identification of the anti-compulsory-vaccination movement with the wider nineteenth-century working-class radical movement made the increasingly political nature of the vaccination question inevitable and this trend was strengthened by the introduction of the working-class vote following the passing of the 1867 and 1884 Reform Acts. For Parliament and the medical establishment compulsory infant vaccination continued to be seen as the best means of defeating smallpox and the epidemic of 1870-1872 heightened their determination not to bend to the demands of anti-compulsory vaccinationists. Criticism of the treatment itself continued to be largely ignored in official circles, as was the case for revaccination.

By the end of the nineteenth century consideration of the factor at the root of the controversy had receded with the decline of the disease itself. The argument was now predominantly about the benefits and problems of vaccination, individual liberty and the continued unwillingness of Parliament to acknowledge past mistakes. Firmly caught up in national politics the dispute reached its climax in 1906 when pledges of support for the National Anti-Vaccination League helped secure the working-class vote and an overwhelming general-election victory for the Liberal Party. New legislation quickly followed. While the 1907 Act did not repeal the Acts of 1853-1871, exemption on the grounds of conscientious objection was made so easy that for all practical purposes compulsory vaccination had come to an end. Understandably the 1907 Act was deplored by medical officers and doctors. They knew only too well the terrible potential of epidemic smallpox, which they still perceived as a very real threat, and they were angered that Parliament should have given preference over their professional advice to the demands of the League whose leading members they regarded as ignorant and irresponsible. Moreover the coming into effect of the Act and the eradication of endemic smallpox in Britain was a fortuitous coincidence, one that the Liberal majority in Parliament in honouring its pledge to the League could hardly have foreseen. All further outbreaks of *variola major* were to be introduced from abroad and were successfully contained by the 'English method' of control.

The attention given to defects in the Vaccination Acts has tended to obscure consideration of whether or not the legislation of 1840-1872 succeeded in its underlying objective, the eradication of smallpox. Although subject to increasingly loud and widespread opposition the Acts nevertheless secured protection for a far higher proportion of England's children than would have been achieved by voluntary means and the eradication of endemic smallpox in 1908 could, in the absence of other factors, be said to have justified the actions of Parliament and pro-vaccinationists like John Simon. But any such conclusion would be an over-simplification. There were other factors at work and the same result could possibly have been achieved without compulsion. If the use of compulsion had any justifica-tion it was surely to eliminate the reservoirs of endemic smallpox among the urban poor but it was there that opposition was strongest and one third of London's in-fants in 1898 had not been vaccinated. The means of eradication was more likely to have been a combination of compulsory vaccination, voluntary vaccination by most anti-compulsory vaccinationists when actually faced with an immediate smallpox threat, and the growing use and strict enforcement in London and the large towns of the system of notification, isolation and quarantine developed at Leicester in the late 1870s and reinforced by the 1889 Infectious Diseases (Notification) Act. On the other hand it is difficult to deny that complete observance of the vaccination laws would have diminished greatly the necessity for places like the Metropolitan Asylums Board's floating hospital at Long Reach. It was not the objective that was the problem but rather Parliament's method of achieving it. The situation in south and south-east Essex where doctors and medical officers were exasperated and worried by the public health threat of the Peculiar People, whose literal interpreta-tion of the Bible and unyielding belief in faith healing led many to shun vaccination even when brought face to face with the disease, may have been quite exceptional. While the worst fears of medical officers were never realised it was nevertheless for-tunate that the sect had only a small membership restricted to a well defined geographical area and it would be a mistake to credit it with having had more than local significance in the history of smallpox control.

Although by enabling parents to avoid the vaccination of their infants the 1907 Vaccination Act spelled the end of compulsory infant vaccination in practical terms, it nevertheless remained a legal requirement on parents. Thereafter the Ministry of Health, local authorities and medical officers, by continuing to advocate routine in-fant vaccination, became increasingly out of step with public opinion. When in 1948 routine infant vaccination at last ceased to be compulsory it was widely realis-ed that vaccination was itself far more of a hazard to life than the disease it was in-tended to prevent. Even so the Ministry and county councils embarked on a cam-paign extolling its benefits and highlighting the risks of non-vaccination. The con-tinuation of this campaign into the early 1960s, more than half a century after smallpox had ceased to be endemic in Britain, points to an unwillingness or inabili-ty on the part of the Ministry to modify its recommendations in the light of chang-ing circumstances. The resultant prolonged undermining of public confidence in the advice of medical officers and doctors relative to vaccination against smallpox may perhaps go some way towards explaining the reluctance of many parents in the 1980s to accept their recommendations in relation to rubella immunisation.

The elimination of the smallpox virus in its natural or human-bred form in 1977 was a remarkable achievement of international co-operation under the auspices of the World Health Organisation. In contrast to this triumph of humanitarianism the necessity ten years later in the eyes of at least one of the world's leading military powers to continue routine smallpox vaccination of its armed forces stands as a stark reminder of man's enduring capacity for evil and destruction.

APPENDIX 1

Classification and Pathogenesis of Smallpox

In the 1950s a number of physicians distinguished the existence of as many as eight types of smallpox among the unvaccinated, some of which were common to both *variola major* and *minor* and which ranged in severity from fulminating smallpox with 100 per cent. mortality to abortive and non-eruptive smallpox, both with nil mortality. The classification and descriptions which follow are mainly derived from the typology established by Dr C.W. Dixon in the early 1960s, based on his extensive experience of the disease in Britain and Libya.[1] It must be pointed out, however, that medical opinion, even as late as the 1960s, was by no means unanimous on the subject. The classification was subsequently modified by Dr A.R. Rao in 1967[2] and by two World Health Organisation *Reports* in 1968 and 1972[3] but the world-wide eradication of naturally acquired smallpox in 1977 made further modification and standardisation pointless.[4]

The following descriptions of the clinical effects of the different types of *variola major* are those appertaining to non-immune (i.e. unvaccinated) victims, while the mortality rates are those of the twentieth century. In the seventeenth and eighteenth centuries and, to a lesser extent, the nineteenth century mortality among the unprotected was probably somewhat higher. For each type listed below there was an incubation period of ten to 14 days, but usually 12 days, before the symptoms appeared.

Type 1. Fulminating smallpox was 'sledge-hammer' smallpox with 100 per cent. mortality but was not recognised as smallpox until the later nineteenth century. The patient was suddenly taken ill, complaining of intense prostration accompanied by severe headache and often backache, and with a temperature in the area of 101-102°F. (38.5-39°C.). Thereafter he remained very wide awake until death, which occurred within one to five days. The appearance was very indefinite and clinical diagnosis impossible unless smallpox was thought of and laboratory facilities were available. The patient's condition after three or four days was described in 1903 as being like

> one who has passed through a long and exhausting struggle. His face has lost its expression ... is mask-like ... He speaks with evident effort ... is listless ... though his eyes may be clear and bright ... The patient staggers in his walk and tends to fall if not supported. In the most fulminated case the aspect ... resembles that of one suffering from severe shock and loss of blood. His face is drawn and pallid ... respiration is sighing or even gasping. He tosses himself about continually and cries out at frequent intervals ... and he complains only of agonizing pain, now in his chest, then in his back, his head or abdomen.[5]

If the patient survived more than two days after the incubation period redness of the skin developed, revealing small spots which during the next 24 hours enlarg-

179

ed to form areas of bluish-purple discolouration. During the next two days these became deep haemorrhages. Life was terminated either by massive vomiting of blood, intestinal or uterine haemorrhage or, more peacefully, by blood-poisoning. The absence of any blister eruption increased the difficulty of differentiating fulminating smallpox from other acute haemorrhagic catastrophies. It formed only a small minority of cases in *variola major* and was rarely found as a form of *variola minor*.

Type 2. Malignant confluent smallpox, nicknamed 'black smallpox', had a mortality rate of about 75 per cent. The onset was sudden with a temperature of 101-102°F. (38.5-39°C.). Malaise, intense headache, severe backache, general aching of the muscles, vomiting and acute abdominal pains all commonly occurred. By about the fourth day a dusky redness appeared on the face together with an eruption of red or purple spots on the upper part of the body. The redness on the face changed into a diffuse blistering and during the fifth, sixth and seventh days the rash spread to cover the lower part of the body. From about the seventh or eighth day swallowing and talking became difficult due to blistering on the mucuous membranes. Death could occur from about the tenth day. The rash on the trunk and arms now became blistered, much of it confluent, and because of general dehydration fluid was absorbed from these lesions to leave bluish-white dead sodden epithelium like a scald. Spitting of blood from the lungs, vomiting of blood from the stomach or uterine haemorrhages were common and in pregnant women abortion or premature labour frequently took place. Inflammation of the cornea often occurred from about the eleventh day. A sickly and fetid smell developed, rendering the discharge-sodden bed linen offensive. Relentless deterioration continued with dehydration and great loss of weight. Many patients lived until the fourteenth or fifteenth day when the stripping of the cell tissue of the outer surface of the body became so widespread that life was ended by blood-poisoning or a haemorrhagic catastrophe. The stripped areas were painful and contributed considerably to the patient's frightful appearance and misery. A minority lingered on to the twentieth day in a state of mortification with the appearance of being mummified while still alive. In spite of the ghastly appearance the patient remained rational; the hearing was acute, although vision was likely to be impaired. By this time the virus had probably ceased to have any effect on the tissues but destruction was so severe that recovery was usually impossible. The few who did survive were in a most vulnerable condition, susceptive to secondary bacteriological infection with blindness in one or both eyes commonplace. The classical pitted scar did not occur. Instead there was a fine tissue-paper scar, continuous over large areas, somewhat like that after a scald. Malignant confluent smallpox and malignant semi-confluent smallpox (type 3 below) were confined to a small proportion of *variola major* cases and were very unusual in *variola minor*.

Type 3. Malignant semi-confluent smallpox was, in broad terms, almost identical to malignant confluent smallpox except that the extent of the rash was less and the mortality rate about 25 per cent. If death did not occur between the twelfth and fifteenth days from blood-poisoning or haemorrhage, the lesions dried up at the blistering stage without the formation of pustules and scarring was of the tissue-paper kind. Survivors experienced severe loss of weight, convalescence was commonly protracted and there was a considerable risk of corneal ulceration from about the twelfth day, leading to damaged sight or blindness.

Type 4. Benign confluent smallpox had a mortality rate of about 20 per cent. The onset was sudden with headache, vomiting, backache, general malaise and an initial temperature of about 103-104°F. (39.5-40°C.). By the third day the patient felt much better and the temperature sometimes became almost normal. At the same time a spotty rash began to appear on the face and during the next 24 hours spread to other parts of the body. Pimples quickly developed and by the eighth or ninth day most of the body was covered by pearly blisters. As these enlarged they became confluent and pustular and vision was sometimes impossible. The rash was now frightful and the offensive odour of smallpox was made worse by suppuration. About the twelfth day scabbing began on the face and spread over the rest of the body. By the fourteenth day desquamation had begun and hundreds of scabs could be brushed from the bedding every day until the twentieth day nearly all the lesions had cleared. In this type of smallpox the rash left characteristic pitted scars, those on the face resulting in considerable disfigurement. Benign confluent smallpox and benign semi-confluent smallpox (type 5 below) were the most common variants of the disease, together forming about 85 per cent. of cases of *variola major*.

Type 5. The initial symptoms of benign semi-confluent smallpox were similar to those of benign confluent smallpox but the subsequent rash was of a lesser extent. The mortality rate was about 12 per cent. and death was normally confined to young babies and the aged and debilitated.

Type 6. In discrete smallpox none of the lesions coalesced and the mortality rate was very low, only about two per cent. The initial stage commenced with a sudden fever which declined over the next two to five days. The rash began about the third day with the appearance of spots on the face which in the next 24 hours developed into pimply lesions, blistering by about the sixth day. Some of the lesions tended to dry up in the blistering stage rather than progressing to definite pustules but this varied considerably from patient to patient and in different parts of the body. Once the initial fever had abated the patient felt well with no difficulty in eating or sleeping and the only problem was the inconvenience of waiting for the scabs to fall off. Scarring tended to be fairly severe.

Type 7. Mild smallpox had a mortality rate of less than one per cent. The initial fever could be very high, as much as 105°F. (40.5°C.), accompanied by general and severe malaise, headache and backache. These symptoms usually abated within about two days and thereafter the patient suffered little discomfort. On the third or fourth day a mild eruption of not more than 100 hard, pearly lesions appeared all over the body. Death only occurred in babies and the aged and debilitated. Although the number of lesions was low, definite scarring resulted, particularly on the face.

Type 8. Cluster smallpox (smallpox *corymbosa*) was a very rare type which had a mortality rate of 44 per cent. The lesions appeared in clusters, or perhaps only a single cluster. Normally, however, there were two or three patches about the size of the palm of the hand on different parts of the body, the rest of the body suffering relatively scattered eruption. It did not appear in *variola minor*.

All of these types could also be contracted by vaccinated victims where the immunity was waning. In such cases, mostly people who had not been vaccinated since infancy, the full effects of the disease were modified to a greater or lesser degree according to the level of immunity remaining in the body. There were two further types of modified smallpox which, with rare exceptions, occurred only among the well-vaccinated such as hospital nurses in close contact with smallpox patients. These are listed as types 9 and 10.

Type 9. Abortive smallpox had a nil mortality rate. The pre-eruptive fever, usually accompanied by headache, was sometimes as high as 103°F. (39.5°C.), but declined by the second day. The lesions began to appear between the third and sixth day and numbered between about 15 and 50, most of which did not progress beyond the pimply stage. Scabbing generally began within two days and left no scarring, only a slight discolouration of the skin. The patient suffered no discomfort after the fever had abated.

Type 10. Smallpox without eruption, like type 9, had nil mortality. The initial fever could reach 102°F. (39°C.) with headache and could last from a few hours to two days, after which the patient felt completely normal although sometimes a little weak. No rash of any kind appeared.

APPENDIX 2

Essex Pest Houses 1666-c.1837

N.B. This list should not be regarded as complete, for without doubt careful research would reveal the existence of many more.

Place	Dates	Reference
Ardleigh	1796	F.H. Erith, *Ardleigh in 1796*, 1978, p.12
Ashdon	1804	D/P 18/12/6
Great Bardfield	1773-1808	D/P 67/18/1
Barking	1666	D/P 81/8/1
Great Bentley	1780,1781	D/P 171/8/4
Braintree	1688,1757	D/DU 65/74; *I.J.*, 31 December 1757
Great Braxted	1766	W.A. Gimson, *Great Braxted 1086-1957*, p.38

Chelmsford	*post* 1717-1793	D/P 94/18/42; Q/SBb 248/4
Great Coggeshall	1759-1799	D/DHt T71/71; D/DCm T98
Colne Engaine	1778	D/P 193/8/2
Dedham	1749,1750	*I.J.*, 8 January 1749, 6 January 1750
Great Dunmow	*c.*1790-*c.*1835	D/P 11/12/1; Q/RUm 2/124
Eastwood	1764,1765	D/P 102/1/1
Epping	1760,1837	D/P 302/12/2; G/EZ 6; *V.C.H. Essex*, v, 1966, p.131
Hadstock	1783,1784	D/P 17/12/1
Halstead	1755	D/DCw T2
Harlow	1762	D/DEs T55, 89
Hatfield Broad Oak	1741-*c.*1835	*V.C.H. Essex*, viii, 1983, p.180
Sible Hedingham	1824-1832	D/P 93/1/11
Kelvedon	1772	D/DDw P4
Maldon	1735-*c.*1800	D/B 3/8/2, 3/8/15A
Mistley	1815	D/DHw T120
Newport	1810	D/F 35/3/136, 35/7/280
Prittlewell	1781	D/P 183/12/1
Rochford	1764-1777	Q/SBb 289/27,30; Leslie Thompson, *The Land That Fanns*, 1957, p.44; *V.C.H. Essex*, vii, 1978, pp.180,187
Romford (Collier Row)	1666-?1706	T/A 521/1; T/M 375; *V.C.H. Essex*, vii, p.77
St Osyth	1814-*c.*1835	D/DCr P1; D/CT 305
Terling	18th and early 19th centuries	C.A. Barton, *Historical Notes and Records of ... Terling ...*, 1953, pp.108,109
Great Tey	1799	D/P 37/12/3
Thaxted	1715,1747	D/P 161/12/2; Ethel Simcoe, *A Short History of ... Thaxted*, 1934, p.76
Wethersfield	1730-1792	D/P 119/8/4
Witham	1767-1785	D/P 30/12/1
Woodford	1770,1778,1779	E.J. Erith, *Woodford, Essex, 1600-1836*, 1950, pp.52-54; *V.C.H. Essex*, vi, 1973, p.354

APPENDIX 3

Essex Isolation Hospitals in 1898[1]

R = Rural District, U = Urban District

A *Districts with adequate and satisfactory hospitals*
Chelmsford R, Halstead U, Harwich U, Ilford U, Orsett R, Saffron Walden U, Saffron Walden R, Stansted R, Southend U

B *Districts with hospitals requiring enlargement or improvement*
Barking U, Billericay R, Colchester U, Epping R, Halstead R, Leyton U, Wanstead U and Woodford U (joint hospital)

C *Districts with hospitals too small or of a temporary character*
Chelmsford U, Clacton R, East Ham U, Lexden and Winstree R, Maldon R, Maldon U, Rochford R, Tendring R

D *Districts with hospitals in course of construction*
Braintree U and R (joint), Romford U and R (joint), Walthamstow U

E *Districts without hospitals but with satisfactory sharing arrangements with another district*
Grays Thurrock U (arrangement with Orsett R)

F *Districts without hospitals but with unsatisfactory sharing arrangements with another district*
Buckhurst Hill U, Chingford U, Epping U, Shoeburyness U

G *Districts without a hospital and with no sharing arrangements with another district*
Belchamp R, Brightlingsea U, Bumpstead R, Burnham U, Leigh U, Ongar R, Waltham Holy Cross U, Walton U, Witham U, Wivenhoe U

GLOSSARY OF MEDICAL TERMS

Alastrim	a name sometimes given to *variola minor*
Bacteria	microscopic agents in putrefaction and the cause of many diseases
Benign	of a mild type, as opposed to malignant
Cornea	membrane forming front covering of the eye
Desquamation	scaling off of scabs
Ecchymoses	discolouration of the skin due to extravasation of the blood
Eczema	a skin disease in which part of the skin is red with numerous small papules that develop into vesicles
Emetic	a medicine that induces vomiting
Empiric	an unqualified medical practitioner whose knowledge is got from experience only: a quack
Epithelium	cell tissue of the outer surface of the body and the mucous membranes connected with it, including the closed cavities
Erysipelas	an inflammatory disease, generally in the face, marked by a bright redness of the skin
Erythema	redness of the skin
Extravasation	forcing of blood out of the blood vessels
Fetid	stinking and offensive
Fomes	a substance capable of carrying infection
Fulminating	developing suddenly
Gangrene	the first stage in mortification
Gangrenous	mortified
Haematemesis	vomiting of blood from the stomach
Haemoptysis	spitting of blood from the lungs
Haemorrhages	areas of internal bleeding
Ichor	colourless matter from an ulcer or pustule
Inoculation	the introduction of bacterium or virus into an organism to give a milder form of the disease in order to produce immunity
Keratitis	inflamation of the cornea
Lymph	originally the fluid containing the smallpox virus used for inoculation, later used to describe the fluid containing vaccine
Macular	spotty
Malignant	tending to cause death, or to go from bad to worse
Morbilli	measles
Mortification	the death of part of the body

Oedema	swelling
Pandemic	incident to a whole people, epidemic over a wide area
Papules	pimples
Pathogen	an organism or substance that causes disease
Pathogenesis	mode of production or development of disease
Petechia	small red or purple spots
Prostration	a feeling of helplessness, impotence and exhaustion
Putrefaction	rotting
Rubella	German measles
Sepsis	putrefaction following invasion by pathogenic bacteria
Toxemia	blood poisoning
Urticarial	stinging, irritating, as if stung by a nettle
Uterus	womb
Vaccination	to immunise with vaccine
Vaccine	originally used to denote *vaccinia* or cow-pox lymph, but since 1881 a term for any preparation to confer immunity against disease
Variola	smallpox
Variolae vaccinae	a modified or hybrid virus produced by the bringing together of cowpox and smallpox viruses
Variolation	inoculation with smallpox virus
Vesicle	a small globule, sac or blister
Virus	a pathogenic agent capable of increasing rapidly inside a living cell

Chapter 1   The Cost of Smallpox

1   E.S. de Beer (ed.), *The Diary of John Evelyn*, 1959, pp.794-803.
2   *Ibid.*, pp.819,820.
3   Q/SBb 23/5.
4   D/P 307/28/1.
5   TS 433.
6   T/P 184.
7   See, for example, the evidence for Great Dunmow in the middle of the nineteenth century in T/Z 25/556.
8   T/P 184. Letter from Gerald Tindal-Atkinson to his sister Kitty, 11 October 1952.
9   D/P 179/1/15.
10 Thomas Dimsdale, *Observations on the Introduction to the Plan of the Dispensary for General Inoculation*, 1778, pp.79,80.
11 Cited in Peter Razzell, *The Conquest of Smallpox*, 1977, p.110.
12 D/P 282/1/1.
13 Cited in Razzell, *The Conquest*, p.110.
14 D/P 93/1/12.
15 Quoted in M.C. Buer, *Health, Wealth, and Population in the Early Days of the Industrial Revolution*, 1926, p.183.
16 The disfigurement included the loss of her eyelashes. Lord Wharncliffe (ed.), *The Letters and Works of Lady Mary Wortley Montagu*, i, 1861, p.88.
17 *Ibid.*, ii, pp.446-448.
18 Alison Kelly, *The Story of Wedgwood*, 1975, pp.14,25; Barbara and Hensleigh Wedgwood, *The Wedgewood Circle 1730-1897*, 1980, pp.8,9. I am grateful to Jennifer Butler for drawing my attention to these references.
19 *London Gazette*, 18-22 February 1735, quoted in Derek Barlow, *Dick Turpin and the Gregory Gang*, 1973, p.141.
20 Quoted in G.W. Martin, 'When Diseases Ravaged Essex', *Essex Countryside*, x, no.68, September 1962, p.463.
21 *I.J.*, 29 October 1763.
22 *Ch. Ch.*, 26 January 1770.
23 *Gent. Mag.*, xx, December 1750, p.532.
24 *I.J.*, 19 June 1762.
25 *Ch. Ch.*, 18 February 1780.
26 *Ibid.*, 18 July 1766.
27 *Ibid.*, 1 August 1766.
28 T/B 186/24. Raynbird was appointed parish doctor at Colne Engaine in 1772 and 1774 (D/P 193/8/2).
29 A.F.J. Brown, *Essex at Work, 1700-1815*, 1969, p.141.
30 J. Dunkin, *History of Dartford*, 1844, p.397. Quoted in Razzell, *The Conquest of Smallpox*, p.111.
31 *Gent Mag.*, lxvi, Part 1, February 1796, p.112, giving the years as 1738-1743. But

the disease was clearly still a problem in June 1744 when there were 'twenty-one persons then lying ill of the Small Pox . . .' (notice, 8 June 1744, quoted in *The Essex Notebook and Suffolk Gleaner*, 1884-1885, unpaginated).
32 Q/SBb 55/8.
33 *I.J.*, 6 January 1750.
34 *Ibid.*, 18 September 1756.
35 *Ibid.*, 25 September and 16 October 1756.
36 *Ibid.*, 31 December 1757.
37 See D/P 332/1/6 (Rayleigh parish register 1744-1788) for smallpox deaths registered in April.
38 *Ch. Ch.*, 11 July 1794. In an editorial notice in the issue of 16 May it was stated that 'several persons' were then under inoculation in Chelmsford.
39 *Ibid.*, 11,18 and 25 August 1797.
40 *I.J.*, 7 April 1759.
41 *Ibid.*, 19 February and 2 and 9 April 1763.
42 *Ch. Ch.*, 11 July 1766.
43 *Ibid.*, 26 March 1779.
44 *Ibid.*, 12 September 1783.
45 *Ibid.*, 5 March 1790.
46 *I.J.*, 8 August 1761.
47 *Ch. Ch.*, 26 April 1765.
48 Q/SBb 9/25.
49 Q/SBb 9/25-31.
50 Q/SBb 54/1,38.
51 *Gent. Mag.*, lxvi, Part 1, February 1796, p.112.
52 Q/SBb 246/9.
53 Q/SBb 297/56.
54 D/DBa A21.
55 Q/SBb 56/1.
56 T/B 231/1.
57 *Ch. Ch.*, 7 May 1790.
58 D/P 353/1/2. I am grateful to Miss A.E. Barker for drawing my attention to this reference.
59 E.G. Thomas, 'The Parish Overseer in Essex 1597-1837', unpublished London University M.A. thesis, 1956, p.165, quoting an example from D/P 264/12/3.
60 Q/SR 502.
61 Leslie Thompson, *The Land that Fanns*, 1957, p.44.
62 D/P 141/12/1.
63 D/P 157/12/7.
64 D/P 169/12/1.
65 D/P 16/12/3.
66 D/P 17/1/2; 17/12/1.
67 For biographical details of Stuart (1755-1822), Bishop of Armagh 1800-1822, see *D.N.B.*
68 *Gent. Mag.*, lviii, April 1788, p.284.
69 Thomas Babington Macaulay, *The History*

of England, iv, Everyman's Library reprint, 1965, p.115.

70 Q/SBb 11/9.

71 T/R 209.

72 *Ch. Ch.*, 13 May 1774.

73 *Ibid.*, 5 March 1790.

74 Q/SR 499.

75 See Jack H. Baxter, *Settlement Examinations 1728-1830 Rochford, Essex*, 1985.

76 D/P 129/18/6.

77 Q/SBb 55/8.

78 *Ch. Ch.*, 1 March 1765.

79 Quoted in letter from F.G. Emmison in *Essex Countryside*, vol. 10, no. 65, June 1962, p.362.

80 Q/SBa 2/39.

81 Thomas, 'The Parish Overseer in Essex', p.165.

Chapter 2
Inoculation: the Early Years, 1721-1752

1 For a claim that the cold method was first systematically used by Dr John Crane of Cambridge, d.1652, see *Gent. Mag.*, lx, Part 1, June 1790, pp.509,510.

2 Readers wishing to study the early period of inoculation in greater depth than the outline sketched in this chapter are recommended to consult Genevieve Miller, *The Adoption of Inoculation for Smallpox in England and France*, 1957.

3 Lord Wharncliffe (ed.), *The Letters and Works of Lady Mary Wortley Montagu*, i, 1861, p.67.

4 *Ibid.*, p.225, fn.3.

5 *Ibid.*, pp.308,309.

6 *Ibid.*, pp.352,353.

7 Charles Maitland, *Account of Inoculating the Small Pox*, 1723, pp.7,8.

8 Wharncliffe, *op.cit.*, i, p.90.

9 Maitland, *op.cit.*, p.11.

10 William Wagstaffe, *A Letter to Dr Freind Shewing the Danger and Uncertainty of Inoculating the Smallpox*, 1722, p.25. For biographical notes on Wagstaffe (1685-1725) see *D.N.B.* See also Maitland, *op.cit.*, p.21.

11 Wharncliffe, *op.cit.*, i, p.461. Letter to her sister the Countess of Mar.

12 James Jurin, *An Account of the Success of Inoculating the Small Pox in Great Britain*, 1724, pp.18,19. In fact it is unlikely that his death was due to inoculation. See C.W. Dixon, *Smallpox*, 1962, p.232, where the author states that death was 'most likely to have been from broncho-pneumonia'.

13 Jurin, *op.cit.*, pp.19,20. See also *The Post Boy*, no. 5123, 22-24 May 1722, quoted in Miller, *op.cit.*, p.98, where the date of death is given as 19 May. Dixon considers he pro-

bably contracted natural smallpox from the children shortly before his own inoculation (Dixon, *op.cit.*, p.232).

14 Wagstaffe, *op.cit.*, pp.3,4.

15 Quoted in William Woodville, *The History of the Inoculation of the Small-Pox in Great Britain*, i, 1796, pp.124,125.

16 Wharncliffe, *op.cit.*, i, p.90.

17 *Ibid.*

18 Woodville, *op.cit.*, i, p.98.

19 *Ibid.*, p.170.

20 Royal Society Library, Inoculation Letters, MSS 245, quoted in Dixon, *op.cit.*, p.238. Dr William Beeston was the son of Revd Edmund Beeston, rector of Sproughton, near Ipswich (*ex inf.* Suffolk Record Office). He died 4 December 1732 and was buried in Bentley church, Suffolk, five miles south-west of Ipswich (monumental inscription in church).

21 Wharncliffe, *op.cit.*, i, p.89.

22 James Jurin, *An Account of the Success of Inoculating the Small Pox in Great Britain*, 1724, pp.9-17; Jurin, *An Account . . . for the Year 1724*, 1725, pp.13-15; Jurin, *An Account . . . for the Year 1725*, 1726, pp.56-58; Jurin, *An Account . . . For the Year 1726*, 1727, pp.18-20; John Gasper Scheuchzer, *An Account of the Success of Inoculating the Small-Pox in Great Britain, for the Years 1727 and 1728*, 1729, pp.14-16,40,41,59,60. These works require very careful interpretation. The annual totals given by both Jurin and Scheuchzer are inaccurate because many accounts of inoculations were submitted too late to be included in the relevant year's statistics, and were instead included in those for the next or subsequent years. The most damaging error occurred as a result of the change of compiler following Jurin's retirement from the Secretaryship of the Royal Society in 1727, Scheuchzer failing to notice a postscript on p.26 of Jurin's *Account For 1726* to the effect that

> while these Papers were in the Press, I was favour'd with a letter from . . . Dr. *Thorold*, Physician at *Uxbridge*, containing an Account of above Forty Persons inoculated by his Direction, who have all recover'd. But the Doctor's Letter coming so very late, by reason of an Indisposition . . . and not containing the Names and Ages of the Patients, I could not insert them till my next.

For the purpose of this work I have taken the 'above Forty Persons' to be 42 and have included them under 'In and around London' in Table 1. No further annual accounts appeared after that for 1728 because of Scheuchzer's death in 1729. For biographical notes on Jurin (1684-1750) and Scheuchzer (1702-1729) see *D.N.B.*

23 See explanatory comments in fn.22.

24 Scheuchzer's total of 897 persons inoculated in Great Britain in 1721-1728 (Scheuchzer, *op.cit.*, p.24) is clearly incorrect. Unfortunately this figure and the other statistics compiled by Jurin and Scheuchzer have been copied without correction or interpretation by all subsequent writers on the subject, including William Woodville (1796), Charles Creighton (1894) and C.W. Dixon (1962). Quite inexplicably the 897 inoculations are stated to have been performed in Britain, America and Hanover in Miller, *op.cit.*, p.121, and Razzell, *The Conquest*, p.40.

25 Scheuchzer, *op.cit.*, pp.40,41,59,60.

26 *I.J.*, 25 October 1729, quoted in David Van Zwanenberg, 'The Suttons and the Business of Inoculation', *Medical History*, xx, 1978, p.72.

27 Letter from Hough to Mrs Mary Knightley, wife of John Knightley Esq. of Offchurch, Warwickshire, dated 14 February 1737 [1738], quoted in *Gent. Mag.*, lxxxii, Part 1, January 1812, pp.47,48. For biographical notes on Hough see *D.N.B.*

28 J. Crawford, *The Case of Inoculating the Small-Pox Consider'd, and Its Advantages Asserted; in a Review to Dr. Wagstaffe's Letter*, 1722, p.31, cited in Miller, *op.cit.*, p.166.

29 Miller, *op.cit.*, p.166.

30 *Ibid.*

31 British Library, Sloane MSS., 406B, f.7.

32 *British Medical Journal*, i, 1948, p.79.

33 Evan Davies, 'A Letter . . . Concerning Some Children Inoculated . . . at Haverford-West . . .', *Philosophical Transactions*, xxxviii, no.429, 1733, p.122.

34 David Hartley, *Some Reasons Why the Practice of Inoculation Ought to be Introduced into the Town of Bury At Present*, 1733. For biographical notes on Hartley (1705-1757) see *D.N.B.*

35 Quoted in Woodville, *op.cit.*, i, p.214.

36 *Gent. Mag.*, viii, January 1738, p.55.

37 *Ibid.*, viii, July 1738, p.380.

38 [Isaac Maddox] Bishop of Worcester, *A Sermon Preached before His Grace John Duke of Marlborough, President, the Vice-Presidents and Governors of the Hospital for the Small-Pox, and for Inoculation, at the Parish Church of St. Andrew Holborn, on Thursday, March 5, 1752*, 1752, fn. p.12.

39 Anon., *An Account of the Hospital for the Maintenance and Education of Exposed and Deserted Young Children*, 1749, p.xi, quoted in Miller, *op.cit.*, p.144.

40 *Gent. Mag.*, xiv, April 1744, p.266.

41 *Ibid.*, xiv, 1744, p.663.

42 Charles Perry, *An Essay on the Smallpox*, 1747, p.37. For biographical notes on Perry (1698-1780) see *D.N.B.*

43 Woodville, *op.cit.*, i, p.223. For biographical notes on Mead (1673-1754) see *D.N.B.*

44 For an account of the Hospital see Woodville, *op.cit.*, i, pp.231-236. Maddox had been instrumental in establishing a county infirmary in Worcester in 1745. For biographical notes on Maddox (1697-1759) see *D.N.B.*

45 *Gent. Mag.*, xvii, June 1747, p.271.

46 Miller, *op.cit.*, p.165.

47 *Ibid.*, pp.167,168.

48 Perry, *op.cit.*, p.43.

49 *Ibid.*, p.45.

Chapter 3
The Age of Inoculation, 1752-1798

1 William A. Guy, 'Two Hundred and Fifty Years of Small Pox in London', *Journal of the Royal Statistical Society*, xlv, 1882, pp.431,432, based on *London Bills of Mortality*.

2 *Gent. Mag.*, xxii, February 1752, p.56. From 1751 to 1755 Fothergill submitted monthly notes on epidemic diseases and the weather in London to the *Gent.Mag.* In 1762 he purchased an estate in West Ham and established a large botanical garden regarded by his contemporaries as one of the finest in Europe and which rivalled Kew. His house was later enlarged and became Ham House, the home of Samuel Gurney, and the site of Fothergill's garden is now preserved at West Ham Park. For further details of Fothergill and his connection with West Ham see *Gent. Mag.*, li, April 1781, pp.165-167; John Coakley Lettsom, *The Works of John Fothergill, M.D.*, 1783; R. Hingston Fox, *Dr John Fothergill and his Friends: Chapters in Eighteenth-Century Life*, 1919; *V.C.H. Essex*, v, 1973, p.72; Katharine Fry, *History of the parishes of East and West Ham*, 1888.

3 C. Perry, *Seasonable Thoughts and Advices upon Inoculation*, 1752, p.55, quoted in Miller, *op.cit.*, p.159.

4 *I.J.*, 30 May 1752.

5 *Gent. Mag.*, xxiii, May 1753, p.217. Pugh was more than an ordinary provincial doctor and I am indebted to Hilda Grieve for the following biographical information. He had curved forceps of his own design made c.1736 and in 1754 published *A Treatise on Midwifery*. He was also a pioneer of dieting to reduce weight. Following his marriage in 1738 he moved into a large old house in Chelmsford High Street which formed part

of his marriage settlement. In 1754 he purchased the house from his wife's family, demolished it and built a new house on the site which was completed by the summer of 1755 (now no.26 High Street). Here he lived until retiring to Great Baddow about 1775. For further details see *Essex Review*, lvii, 1948, p.222, and W. Radcliffe, *The Secret Instrument, c.*1948.

6 *Gent. Mag.*, xxiii, May 1753, pp.216,217.

7 Miller, *op.cit.*, p.160. Maddox was first Joint President of the Hospital (with the Duke of Marlborough).

8 Delafaye published his sermon in 1754 under the title *A Vindication of a Sermon entitled Inoculation an Indefensible Practice.* For a contemporary review see *Gent.Mag.*, xxiv, July 1754, pp.342,343.

9 Woodville, *op.cit.*, i, p.267, where the original Latin text is also quoted.

10 Robert Houlton, *Indisputable Facts Relative to the Suttonian Art of Inoculation*, 1768, p.vii.

11 Sutton, *op.cit.*, p.77.

12 Daniel described himself as the second son in Daniel Sutton, *The Inoculator; or, Suttonian System of Inoculation, fully set forth in a plain and familiar Manner*, 1796, p.xv.

13 Nicholas May, *Impartial Remarks on the Suttonian Method of Inoculation*, 1770, p.42.

14 *I.J.*, 21 May 1763. Tumner owned the successful sea-water baths in Bath Street, advertised widely and promoted 'rural and polite entertainments', recommending boating, walking and riding in preference to excessive drinking and late nights. In short he was operating what amounted to an early health centre for wealthy patrons. For further details see Brown, *Essex at Work*, p.125.

15 *Ibid.*, 19 November 1763.

16 *Ch. Ch.*, 9 November 1764.

17 *Ibid.*, 21 December 1764.

18 *I.J.*, 9 March 1765.

19 *Ch. Ch.*, 10 May 1765.

20 *Ibid.*, 28 February 1766.

21 *I.J.*, 31 May 1766.

22 Robert Houlton, *A Sermon preached at Ingatestone, Essex, October 12, 1766, in Defence of Inoculation*, 1767, p.57.

23 *Gent. Mag.*, xx, May 1750, p.206.

24 *Ch. Ch.*, 16 May 1766.

25 *Ibid.*

26 *Ibid.*, 14 June 1766.

27 Quoted in May, *op.cit.*, p.33.

28 William Watson, *An Account of a Series of Experiments Instituted with a View of ascertaining the Most Successful Method of inoculating the Small-Pox*, 1768, p.2.

29 There were of course exceptions to this general rule. See for example John Forbes,

'Some Account of the Small-pox lately prevalent in Chichester and its Vicinity, showing the Degree of Security afforded by Vaccination in that District', *The London Medical Repository, Monthly Journal, and Review*, xviii, July — December 1822, pp.213,219,220 for the case of a Bosham (Sussex) farmer and amateur inoculator called Pearce who in the period November 1821 — spring 1822 inoculated 'upwards of a thousand persons' in his own and neighbouring parishes, and whose father, he boasted, had inoculated 10,000 people, not one of whom died.

30 Q/SBb 342/1.

31 *I.J.*, 29 October 1763.

32 For details of Sutton's and Dimsdale's positions on this problem see below, pp.85,89.

33 *Gent. Mag.*, xlix, April 1779, p.193.

34 For details of the trial and the circumstances surrounding it see pp.77-80.

35 Q/SBb 253/6.

36 James Kirkpatrick, *The Analysis of Inoculation*, 1754, pp.267,268.

37 *Gent. Mag.*, xxiii, February 1753, pp.146, 147.

38 *Gent. Mag.*, xxiii, September 1753, p.414.

39 Letter, 6 April 1753, from Benjamin Pugh of Chelmsford, surgeon, in *Gent. Mag.*, xxiii, May 1753, p.218.

40 *I.J.*, 19 May 1753. The notice was signed by the rector, five churchwardens and overseers, six apothecaries and eight inhabitants. The epidemic did not finally cease until early in July.

41 *Ibid.*, 31 March 1753. This notice was signed by six ministers, two physicians, five surgeons and two apothecaries.

42 *Ibid.*, 15 May 1762.

43 *Ibid.*, 18 June 1763.

44 *Ch. Ch.*, 10 May 1765.

45 E.J. Erith, *Woodford, Essex, 1600-1836*, 1950, p.55.

46 Q/SBb 342/1.

47 *Gent. Mag.*, xxii, November 1752, p.511.

48 *Ibid.*, vii, 1737, pp.561,562.

49 P.E. Razzell, 'Population Change in Eighteenth-Century England. A Reinterpretation', *Economic History Review*, 2nd series, xviii, 1965, p.331.

50 *Ibid.*

51 George Baker, *An Inquiry Into the Merits of a Method of Inoculating the Small-Pox, Which is now practised in several Counties of England*, 1766, p.57. Three of the inoculees died.

52 Razzell, 'Population Change', *loc.cit.*, p.331.

53 I.E. Gray and A.T. Gaydon, *Gloucestershire Quarter Sessions Archives 1660-1889 and Other Official Records*, 1958, p.17. The in-

54 Razzell, 'Population Change', *loc.cit.*, p.331.

55 Letter, 21 June 1766, Dr R. Pulteney of Blandford to Dr George Baker, Physician to the Queen's Household, quoted in Baker, *op.cit.*, p.57. For biographical notes on Sir George Baker (1722-1809) see *D.N.B.*

56 For details of the Maldon inoculations see pp.48,77 and for the Ewell and Maidstone inoculations see pp.79,80.

57 For an account of Dimsdale's career see below, pp.87,90.

58 See below, p.83.

59 William Lipscomb, 'On the Beneficial Effects of Inoculation', Oxford University, *Oxford Prize Poems*, second edition, 1807.

60 See p.46.

61 Houlton, *Indisputable Facts*, pp.16,17.

62 *Ibid.*, p.17. I have calculated the town's population to have been slightly in excess of 1,600 at this date.

63 *Ibid.*, p.17.

64 *Ibid.*

65 *Ch. Ch.*, 13 May 1774.

66 *Gent. Mag.*, xlix, May 1779, p.247.

67 D/B 3/8/2.

68 *Ch. Ch.*, 28 March 1788.

69 T/R 149/8.

70 D/B 3/8/7.

71 D/B 3/8/2, 3/8/7.

72 T/R 149/8.

73 *Ch. Ch.*, 11,18 and 25 August 1797.

74 For details see below, p.114.

75 West Sussex Record Office, PHA K5/7.

76 Brown, *Essex at Work*, p.141.

77 West Sussex Record Office, PHA K5/7 (letter of 1 March 1772). I am grateful to Lord Egremont and the County Archivist of West Sussex for permission to quote from these letters relating to the Newport inoculations.

78 *Ibid.* (letter of 5 March 1772).

79 *Ibid.* (letters of 5 and 15 March 1772).

80 *Ibid.* (letter of 5 March 1772).

81 *Ibid.* (letter of 15 March 1772).

82 *Ibid.* (letter of 29 March 1772).

83 Thomas Dimsdale, *Thoughts on General and Partial Inoculations*, 1776, pp.32,33.

84 *Ibid.*, p.65. For Dimsdale's recommended method, originally prepared for the Empress of Russia in 1768, see *ibid.*, pp.6,7.

85 Thomas Dimsdale, *Observations on the Introduction to the Plan of the Dispensary for General Inoculation*, 1778, pp.58,59.

86 *Gent. Mag.*, xlviii, December 1778, p.575.

87 Day book of John Clifton for 1778, Northamptonshire Record Office ZA 8736. I am grateful to Kathryn Enwright for drawing my attention to this reference.

88 *Ibid.*

89 *Gent. Mag.*, xlix, April 1779, pp.192, 193.

90 D/P 30/12/1.

91 *Gent. Mag.*, xlix, May 1779, p.247.

92 D/P 30/12/1.

93 *Gent. Mag.*, xlix, May 1779, p.247.

94 *Ibid.*

95 D/P 332/13/4. I am grateful to Jack H. Baxter for drawing my attention to this reference.

96 D/P 210/12/2.

97 D/P 195/8/2.

98 John Haygarth, *An Inquiry how to Prevent the Small-Pox*, 1785, p.164. For biographical notes on Haygarth (1740-1827) see *D.N.B.*

99 D/P 40/8/1.

100 T/P 156/1.

101 D/P 219/12/29.

102 D/P 300/12/1. There were six smallpox deaths in the parish in June and early July, including one in the detached part on Canvey Island (D/P 300/1/3).

103 Alfred Stokes, *East Ham From Village to County Borough*, 3rd edition, 1933, p.95.

104 D/P 193/8/2.

105 D/P 111/8/2.

106 D/P 36/12/3.

107 D/P 357/12/1.

108 D/P 219/12/29.

109 D/P 142/12/1.

110 *V.C.H. Essex*, viii, 1983, p.283.

111 *Ibid.*, p.226.

112 D/P 357/12/1.

113 D/DCd Z7.

114 J.E. Oxley, *Barking Vestry Minutes*, 1955, p.254.

115 Charles Creighton, *A History of Epidemics in Britain*, ii, 1894, p.507. For biographical notes on Maty see *D.N.B.* Many doctors disagreed with Maty on the subject of infant inoculation. See, for example, Thomas Percival, 'Arguments against the Inoculation of Children in early Infancy', *Gent. Mag.*, xxxviii, April 1768, pp.161-165, in which it was advocated that 'the fittest season for inoculation seems to be between the age of three and seven, in healthy children, and Four and seven in those who are tender and delicate'. Dimsdale preferred not to inoculate children under the age of two years (Thomas Dimsdale, *The Present Method of Inoculating for the Small-Pox*, 1767, p.9).

116 *Gent. Mag.*, xlv, September 1775, pp.429,430.

117 *Ibid.*, xlix, April 1779, p.193.

118 Haygarth, *An Inquiry*, p.223.

119 James Lucas, 'Remarks on febrile Contagion', *The London Medical Journal*, x, Part 3, 1789, p.261. For a review see *Gent. Mag.*,

lx, August 1790, p.731.

120 *Gent. Mag.*, vii, September 1737, p.560.

121 *Ibid.*, xvii, June 1747, p.270.

122 *Ibid.*, xxii, July 1752, p.313.

123 Angelo Gatti, *New Observations on Inoculation*, 1768, pp.38,39.

124 Buer, *op.cit.*, p.182.

125 *Gent. Mag.*, xlix, April 1779, p.193.

126 James Jurin, *An Account of the Success of Inoculating the Small Pox in Great Britain, for the Year 1724*, 1725, p.12. The Dedham parish register of burials (D/P 26/1/2) is highly defective for 1724 and contains this contemporary memorandum: 'a great Number of Persons who died in this year when ye Small Pox was very fatal, are omitted'.

127 The town's population in 1801 was 1,537.

128 Brown, *Essex at Work*, pp.98,100. The figure of 1,200 is produced by applying a multiplier of 4.45.

129 *Ibid.*, p.126.

130 D/P 227/1/3.

131 It was 1,168 in 1801.

132 D/P 322/1/2.

133 *Gent. Mag.*, xxiii, May 1753, p.218. An unofficial local census in 1738 gave a population of 2,151 and the population in 1766 has been estimated at 2,700 (Brown, *op.cit.*, p.117).

134 D/P 49/1/4. For the population figures see Brown, *op.cit.*, p.104.

135 D/P 332/1/6.

136 *Gent. Mag.*, xlix, May 1779, p.247.

137 With the exception of Hastings, 1731, these examples are derived from Jurin's *Accounts* for 1721-1726 and Scheuchzer's *Accounts* for 1727 and 1728.

138 Razzell, *The Conquest of Smallpox*, p.133.

139 Creighton, *op.cit.*, ii, p.524.

140 *Gent. Mag.*, xxiii, May 1753, p.218. Benjamin Pugh gave these figures on 6 April 1753, claiming the outbreak had started at the beginning of July 1752. It lingered on into the summer of 1753 and it was not until 14 July that notice was given 'to assure the Publick that, this Town is entirely free from the SMALL-POX' (*I.J.*, 5,12 and 19 May and 21 July 1753). The proportion of fatalities for the period 6 April to July 1753 is unknown.

141 Dixon, *op.cit.*, p.197.

142 Creighton, *op.cit.*, ii, p.544.

143 *Gent. Mag.*, xlix, May 1779, p.247.

144 Lucas 'Remarks on febrile Contagion', *loc.cit.*, p.270.

145 Razzell, *The Conquest*, p.133.

146 James Jurin, 'A Letter to the Learned Dr Caleb Cotesworth, F.R.S.', *Philosophical Transactions*, xxxi-ii, 1720-1723, pp.17,18.

147 Perry, *An Essay*, p.38.

148 *Gent. Mag.*, xxii, July 1752, p.313.

149 Sutton, *The Inoculator*, p.156.

150 An outbreak at Wethersfield in the winter of 1702-1703 may have included cases of fulminating smallpox. In the 12-month period 25 March 1702 to 24 March 1703 there were 46 burials, 29 of which took place between 15 December 1702 and 22 March 1703 and the parish register contains the comment 'Hoc anno multi febri perierunt maligna' ('In this year many died of malignant fever'). Transcript of register in E.R.O. Library, Chelmsford.

151 Transcript of register in E.R.O. Library, Chelmsford.

152 D/P 357/1/3. I am grateful to Helen Drew for drawing my attention to this reference.

153 Howlett was also vicar of Haverhill (Suffolk and Essex) from 1774 to 1790. The economist Professor Sir E.C.K. Gonner (1862-1922) considered that 'Howlett's works merit attention on account of his independence of thought and careful investigation of fact' (R.H. Inglis Palgrave, *Dictionary of Political Economy*, reprint (ed. H. Higgs), 1926, p.335). The statistician and economist John Ramsey McCulloch (1789-1864) thought his work to be 'distinguished by ability, correct information and good sense' (quoted in J.L. Cranmer-Byng, 'Poor Relief in Gt. Dunmow During the Napoleonic Wars', *Essex Review*, xlviii, October 1939, p.208). For biographical notes on McCulloch see *D.N.B.*

154 J. Howlett, *An Examination of Dr. Price's Essay on the Population of England and Wales*, 1781, p.94.

155 *Ibid.*, fn. p.83.

156 *Gent. Mag.*, lii, October 1782, p.473.

157 *Ibid.*

158 See p.79.

159 [J. Howlett], *Observations on the Increased Population . . . of Maidstone*, 1782, p.8, quoted in Razzell, *The Conquest of Smallpox*, p.152.

160 *Ibid.*

161 These figures were compiled by Peter Razzell and are cited in Razzell, *The Conquest*, p.143.

162 A. Young (ed.), *Annals of Agriculture*, vii, 1786, p.455, quoted in Razzell, *The Conquest*, p.153.

163 John Heysham, *Observations on the Bills of Mortality in Carlisle, for the Year 1787*, 1788, p.4.

164 Heysham, *Observations . . . for . . . 1782*, p.13 and *Observations . . . for . . . 1787*, p.4.

165 *Gent. Mag.*, lxvi, February 1796, p.112.

166 *Ibid.*, lxxiii, March 1803, p.213.

167 John Haygarth, *A Sketch of a Plan to exterminate the Casual Small-Pox from Great Britain and to introduce General Inoculation*,

168 1793, p.186.

Ibid.

169 W. Turner, *An Address to Parents on Inoculation for the Small-Pox*, 1792, p.10. Newcastle had a population of 28,366 in 1801.

170 Creighton, *op.cit.*, ii, p.520, based on original figures sent to James Jurin and deposited by him with the Royal Society.

171 Creighton, *op.cit.*, ii, p.520.

172 *Ibid.*, p.618. These percentages are derived from a very large sample, almost 15,000 cases.

173 Creighton, *op.cit.*, ii, p.544.

174 *Ibid.*, p.537. See also M.C. Buer, *Health, Wealth and Population in the Early Days of the Industrial Revolution*, 1926 (reissue, 1968), p.182.

175 Creighton, *op.cit.*, ii, p.526.

176 *Ibid.*, pp.553,554.

177 *Ibid.*, p.520.

178 D/P 277/1/3.

179 See above, p.48.

180 See above, p.50.

181 *Northampton Mercury*, 16 February 1778.

182 W.A. Barron, 'Gleanings from Sussex Archives: Brighton and the Smallpox', *The Sussex County Magazine*, xxvi, 1952, pp.605,606.

183 Razzell, *The Conquest*, pp.87,88.

184 *Ibid.*, p.92.

185 West Sussex Record Office, PHA K5/7.

186 Dimsdale, *Observations*, pp.297,298.

187 *Ibid.*, p.126.

188 Razzell, *The Conquest*, p.92.

189 D/P 40/8/1.

190 Vestry House Museum, Walthamstow, L34.41 WP1.

191 Vestry House Museum, Leyton churchwardens' accounts.

192 See above, pp.48-50.

193 See above, p.53.

194 Howlett, *An Examination*, fn. p.83.

195 The actuary Joshua Milne, using figures in John Heysham's *Observations on the Bills of Mortality in Carlisle* in the years 1779-1786, calculated that one half of all children who escaped or survived smallpox would die from other causes. See Joshua Milne, *A Treatise on the Valuation of Annuities and Assurances on Lives and Survivorships*, 1815, pp.418-420.

196 Michael W. Flinn, *The European Demographic System, 1500-1820*, 1981.

197 E.A. Wrigley and R.S. Schofield, *The Population History of England, 1541-1871. A Reconstruction*, 1981. It is interesting to note however that in an essay published in the same year Wrigley asserted that a decline in mortality and an improvement in life expectancy strongly concentrated towards the end of the eighteenth century played 'a major part in explaining the very striking acceleration in population growth rates in the later decades' (E.A. Wrigley, 'Marriage, Fertility and Population Growth in Eighteenth-Century England', R.B. Outhwaite (ed.), *Marriage and Society. Studies in the Social History of Marriage*, 1981, p.172).

198 E.A. Wrigley, 'The Growth of Population in Eighteenth-Century England: A Conundrum Resolved', *Past and Present*, no.98, February 1983, pp.121-150.

199 Razzell, *The Conquest*, p.158.

Chapter 4   The Impact of Daniel Sutton

1 The son of Robert Sutton of Kenton, gentleman, he was baptised in Kenton parish church 12 February 1708 (S.R.O., FB 44/D1/2) and buried 13 April 1788 at Thetford (Norfolk) 'in the 81st year of his age' (*I.J.*, 19 April 1788).

2 P.R.O., IR 1/11 (registered 21 November 1726).

3 S.R.O., FC 129/D1/2. Both were single and of Debenham. They were married in Aldringham church by licence.

4 S.R.O., FB 44/D1/2. For his licence to practice physic and surgery within the diocese of Norwich, 1 July 1735, see Norfolk Record Office SUB/5 Book 19. Robert also had three daughters (Houlton, *Indisputable Facts*, p.14).

5 Houlton, *Indisputable Facts*, p.12. Born about 1739 the author was the son of Revd Robert Houlton of Milton, Clevedon, Somerset. Educated at Magdalen College, Oxford (M.A. 1762), he learnt inoculation from the Sutton family and in 1767 or early 1768 went to Dublin having been appointed to set up partnerships in Ireland. For notes on his career as a dramatist, journalist and inoculator see *D.N.B.*

6 Houlton, *Indisputable Facts*, p.12.

7 *Ibid.*, pp.10-12.

8 *I.J.*, 16 April 1757. Repeated 14 and 21 May.

9 *Ibid.*, 1 October 1757.

10 *Ibid.*, 28 October 1758.

11 *Ibid.*, 24 February 1759.

12 *Ibid.*, 15 September 1759.

13 *Ibid.*, 25 October 1760.

14 *Ibid.*, 25 October 1760, 19 December 1761.

15 *Ibid.*, 1 May 1762.

16 *Ibid.*, 25 September 1762.

17 *Ibid.*

18 Houlton, *Indisputable Facts*, p.14.

19 *Ibid.*, pp.14,15.

20 *Ibid.*, p.15 and *I.J.*, 27 November 1762.

21 *I.J.*, 27 November 1762.

22 *Ibid.*, 28 May 1763.
23 *Ibid.*, 29 October 1763. See above p.44.
24 The numbers of inoculations performed by Robert Sutton senior in each of the years 1758-1767 set out in Woodville, *The History of the Inoculation*, i, p.346, have not been quoted in this work since they appear unreliable.
25 S.R.O., FB 44/D1/2.
26 Sutton, *The Inoculator*, p.iii, fn.
27 *Ibid.*
28 Houlton, *Indisputable Facts*, p.15.
29 Woodville, *op.cit.*, i, p.348.
30 *Ibid.*, p.347.
31 *Ibid.*, p.348.
32 *Ibid.*, pp.348,349.
33 *Ibid.*, p.349.
34 *Ibid.*
35 This was the only public acknowledgement that Daniel ever made to his father.
36 *I.J.*, 5 November 1763.
37 *Ibid.*, 19 and 26 November 1763.
38 James Johnston Abraham, *Lettsom 1744-1815. His Life, Times, Friends and Descendants*, 1933, p.189 and Dixon, *Smallpox*, p.243.
39 *I.J.*, 3 December 1763.
40 *Ibid.*, 19 November 1763.
41 *Ibid.*, 26 November 1763.
42 *Ibid.*, 19 November 1763.
43 *Ibid.*, 26 November and 3 December 1763.
44 Houlton, *Indisputable Facts*, pp.15,16.
45 Woodville, *op.cit.*, i, p.349.
46 *Ch. Ch.*, 26 October 1764. Repeated 2 and 9 November.
47 *Ibid.*, 3 May 1765. Part of the village of Ingatestone lies within the parish of Fryerning.
48 *Ibid.*, 17 May 1765.
49 *Ibid.*, 27 September, 4, 11 and 18 October, 1765.
50 Letter, 26 March 1766, quoted in Abraham, *op.cit.*, p.195, fn.2. Cockfield had married Elizabeth Gurney, daughter of Henry Gurney of Norwich (Fry, *East and West Ham*, pp.240,241).
51 Houlton, *Indisputable Facts*, 1768, p.20.
52 *Ch. Ch.*, 30 May 1766. It has been suggested that the chapel may have been in a house in Ingatestone market-place called Chapel House. See Wilde, *op.cit.*, p.273.
53 For biographical notes on Gascoyne (1725-1791) see *D.N.B.* For details of his political career see Sir Lewis Namier and John Brooke, *The House of Commons, 1754-1790*, ii, 1964, pp.486-491. For an obituary see *Ch. Ch.*, 4 November 1791. Gascoyne was M.P. for Maldon 1761-1763 and Midhurst, Kent, 1765-1768.
54 T/B 251/7; letter to John Strutt, 8 April 1766.

55 *Ibid.*
56 T/M 454/4. See also *V.C.H. Essex*, viii, 1978, pp.36,37.
57 T/B 251/7; letter 8 April 1766.
58 *Ibid.*, letter 29 May 1766.
59 *Ibid.*
60 *Ibid.*, letter 20 May 1766.
61 *Ibid.*, letter 29 May 1766.
62 *Ibid.*
63 *Ibid.*
64 *Ibid.*, letter 6 June 1766.
65 See above p.48.
66 Houlton, *Indisputable Facts*, p.17.
67 *Ch. Ch.*, 20 June 1766 and *I.J.*, 21 June 1766.
68 D/DP M116, p.170. I am grateful to Nancy Briggs for drawing my attention to this and other documentary references relating to Maisonette.
69 For a report issued during the course of the trial see *Ch. Ch.*, 18 July 1766.
70 Houlton, *A Sermon*, pp.55,56.
71 *Ibid.*, pp.56-60.
72 *Ibid.*, p.61.
73 *Ch. Ch.*, 25 July 1766.
74 Houlton, *A Sermon*, pp.44,45.
75 *I.J.*, 11 October 1766.
76 *Gent. Mag.*, xxxvi, September 1766, pp.413,414. The signatories to the report included the vicar, a churchwarden and two overseers.
77 Houlton, *A Sermon*, p.44.
78 *Ibid.*, pp.44,45.
79 *I.J.*, 14 February 1767.
80 *Ibid.*
81 Samuel Tymms, 'Freston Tower', *Proceedings of Suffolk Institute of Archaeology*, ii, 1859, p.271.
82 Wilde, *op.cit.*, pp.265,266. For further notes on Pringle (F.R.C.P., 1763, President of the Royal Society, 1772, Physician to George III, 1774, d.1782), see *D.N.B.*
83 For the full text of the patent see Sutton, *op.cit.*, pp.xv,xvi.
84 Abraham, *op.cit.*, p.194 and Wilde, *op.cit.*, pp.273,274. Rachel, born in St Johns, Antigua, 1746, was the only surviving daughter of Simon and Frances Warlock of Antigua and Millbank, Westminster, and widow of William Westley of Shepton Mallet, Somerset. Their first child, Daniel, was born in 1768 and baptised in the church of St Margaret, Westminster (Wilde, *op.cit.*, p.274).
85 Licence to demise for 21 years, 16 June 1767, in D/DP M116, p.183. In 1775 it was reported in the court of the manor of Ingatestone that Maisonette was 'decayed and out of repair' (D/DP M116, p.243). Ratcliffe was still tenant in 1780 (D/DP M1320, p.16).

NOTES AND REFERENCES

86 D/DMq M27/13; D/DGs M46, pp.49-53.
87 Houlton, *A Sermon*, p.29.
88 *Ibid.*, pp.31,32. The war referred to was the Seven Years War ended by the Peace of Paris in 1763.
89 *Ibid.*, pp.38,39.
90 *Ibid.*, pp.39-41.
91 *Ibid.*, pp.55,56.
92 East Sussex R.O., MSS 2772, quoted in Razzell, *The Conquest of Smallpox*, pp.60,61. The Broyle and Little Horsted are both within a few miles of Glynde. Park House lies on the A26 road, two miles north of Lewes.
93 *Ibid.*
94 *Ibid.*
95 *Gent. Mag.*, xxxviii, February 1768, p.75.
96 *Ibid.*, xxxviii, January 1768, p.23.
97 William Watson, *An Account of a Series of Experiments*, 1768, p.2. For biographical notes on Watson (1715-1787) see *D.N.B.*
98 Houlton, *Indisputable Facts*, pp.21-23.
99 Woodville, *op.cit.*, i, p.350.
100 D/DGs M46, p.49.
101 Quoted in May, *Impartial Remarks*, pp.176-179.
102 *Ibid.*, p.179.
103 *Ibid.*, p.181.
104 *Ibid.*, p.182.
105 *Ibid.*, p.77.
106 *Ibid.*, pp.46,78.
107 *Ibid.*, p.184.
108 *Ch. Ch.*, 26 March 1779.
109 It was known as Pest House. Following Sutton's death in 1819 it passed to his daughter, Mrs Frances Campbell. It stood on the south side of the road from Prittlewell to Rayleigh, now the A127 London-Southend Arterial Road, a short distance east of the junction with the present-day Dulverton Avenue, and remained in the possession of Sutton's descendants until sold in 1897. See D/DGs M126, 134 and Wilde, *op.cit.*, p.275.
110 *Ch. Ch.*, 26 May 1780.
111 *Gent. Mag.*, lxxi, Part 2, July 1801, p.669.
112 *D.N.B.* and Abraham, *op.cit.*, p.194. Thomas' grandfather Robert Dimsdale, surgeon, accompanied William Penn on a visit to America in 1684 taking with him his sons John and William, but returned to Theydon Garnon after a few years (*Gent. Mag.*, lxxi, Part 2, July 1801, p.669). For details of payments by Theydon Garnon overseers to Dr Dimsdale for treating the sick poor, 1721-1742, see D/P 152/18/5.
113 *Gent. Mag.*, lxxi, Part 2, July 1801, p.669.
114 Namier and Brooke, *op.cit.*, ii, p.325. For brief notes on Nathaniel Brassey (?1697-1765) see Namier and Brooke, *op.cit.*, ii, p.114.
115 *Gent. Mag.*, lxxi, Part 2, July 1801, p.669.
116 Dimsdale, *The Present Method of Inoculating*, p.1.
117 *Gent. Mag.*, lxxi, Part 2, July 1801, p.669.
118 Namier and Brooke, *op.cit.*, ii, p.325.
119 *D.N.B.*; Abraham, *op.cit.*, p.195; Dimsdale, *The Present Method*, p.24; Namier and Brooke, *op.cit.*, ii, p.325. Thomas and Anne had ten sons and two daughters of whom seven survived beyond infancy.
120 Namier and Brooke, *op.cit.*, ii, p.325.
121 Dimsdale, *The Present Method*, p.79.
122 *Ibid.*, p.77.
123 *Ibid.*, p.78.
124 Abraham, *op.cit.*, p.195, fn.2.
125 *Gent. Mag.*, lxxi, Part 2, July 1801, p.669.
126 Dimsdale, *The Present Method*, p.82.
127 D/DCm A1. This was not without particular significance for Hanbury was keenly interested in the prevention and treatment of smallpox and had become a governor of the London Smallpox Hospital in 1763.
128 Thomas Dimsdale, *Tracts on Inoculation*, 1781, pp.4-6.
129 *Ibid.*, p.8.
130 *Gent. Mag.*, xxxviii, December 1768, p.586.
131 *Ibid.*, lxxi, Part 1, March 1801, pp.210,211.
132 Dimsdale's own account of his visit to Russia appears in his *Tracts on Inoculation*.
133 Quoted in Abraham, *op.cit.*, p.196.
134 D/DU 649/2.
135 Abraham, *op.cit.*, p.195.
136 *Ibid.*
137 See above, p.74.
138 *D.N.B.* and Abraham, *op.cit.*, p.196.
139 A detailed account of the dispute is to be found in Abraham, *op.cit.*, pp.194-204. See also Dimsdale, *Thoughts on General and Partial Inoculations*, and *Observations on the Introduction to the Plan of the Dispensary for General Inoculation*.
140 Dimsdale, *Thoughts*, p.67.
141 Namier and Brooke, *op.cit.*, ii, p.325.
142 *English Chronicle*, 1781, quoted in Namier and Brooke, *op.cit.*, ii, p.325.
143 *Gent. Mag.*, lxxi, Part 2, July 1801, p.669.
144 Namier and Brooke, *op.cit.*, ii, p.326.
145 D/Z 15/1. His son John was elected Treasurer in 1801.
146 *Gent. Mag.*, lxxi, Part 2, July 1801, p.669.
147 *Ibid.*
148 Fox, *Dr John Fothergill*, p.95 and *D.N.B.*
149 *I.J.*, 19 April 1788.
150 *Ch. Ch.*, 20 January 1792.
151 Sutton, *The Inoculator*, p.xiii.
152 *Ibid.*, p.159.
153 Woodville, *op.cit.*, pp.345, 346, 353.
154 James Moore, *The History of the Small Pox*, 1815, p.267.

195

155 *Ibid.*, p.270.
156 *Gent. Mag.*, lxxxix, March 1819, p.281. Sutton was already at Hart Street by 1811 (D/DGs M47, p.22). The registered copy of his will (made 15 August 1818 and proved 24 March 1819) is in P.R.O. (PROB 11/1614, ff. 356-358).

Chapter 5
Inoculation and Vaccination :
the Transition, 1798-1840

1 See *Gent. Mag.*, lxxiii, Part 1, January 1803, p.69, for the earliest known use of the term 'vaccination'.
2 By the time John Clare's *The Shepherd's Calendar* appeared in 1827 the link between cowpox and smallpox immunity was common knowledge and vaccination a widespread practice, but the traditional appreciation of milkmaids' desirability continued. For example, in January they are 'fresh as autumn roses' and in July 'Ruddy and tand yet sweet to view'.
3 Dixon, *Smallpox*, p.250.
4 E.M. Crookshank, *History and Pathology of Vaccination*, i, 1889, p.104.
5 *Ibid.*, pp.100-103. For an account by his son Thomas of the whereabouts of these papers during the years 1785-1802 see Revd G.C. Jenner, *The Evidence at Large, as Laid Before the Committee of the House of Commons, Respecting Dr. Jenner's Discovery of Vaccine Inoculation*, 1805, pp.140-143, and for extracts from the manuscripts see pp.155,156.
6 Quoted in Crookshank, *op.cit.*, ii, p.271.
7 The full title is *An Inquiry into the Causes and Effects of the Variolae Vaccinae, a disease discovered in some of the western counties of England, particularly Gloucestershire, and known by the name of cowpox*. For a contemporary review see *Gent. Mag.*, lxix, Part 2, October 1799, p.876.
8 *The Medical and Physical Journal*, ii, October 1799, pp.213-225.
9 *Ibid.*, p.225.
10 *Ch. Ch.*, 20 June 1800.
11 *Gent. Mag.*, lxxi, Part 1, April 1801, p.318. For an order from the Duke of York to 'officers in command of regiments, to use their best endeavours to cause the whole of the men, in their respective regiments, on whom there are no marks of their having had one or other of the disorders, to be immediately inoculated with the Vaccine Matter', November 1803, see *Gent. Mag.*, lxxiv, Part 1, May 1804, p.473.
12 *Gent. Mag.*, lxx, Part 1, April 1800, p.303.
13 *Ibid.*, lxx, Part 1, May 1800, p.433.
14 D/DU 251/89.

15 *Gent. Mag.*, lxx, Part 2, December 1800, p.1203.
16 Frank H. Jacob, *A History of the General Hospital near Nottingham*, 1951, pp.101-103.
17 Creighton, *A History of Epidemics in Britain*, ii, p.587, fn.1.
18 D/Z 15/1, p.166.
19 For the Jenner family's evidence to the 1802 parliamentary inquiry on vaccination, see G.C. Jenner, *The evidence at Large, as Laid Before the Committee of the House of Commons, Respecting Dr. Jenner's Discovery of Vaccine Inoculation*, 1805. For a lengthy account of the meeting held on 19 January 1803 in the London Tavern at which it was resolved to establish the Royal Jennerian Society, see *Gent. Mag.*, lxxiii, Part 1, January 1803, pp.69-72.
20 *British Critic*, xiv, 1799, p.432.
21 *Morning Herald*, 31 March 1801.
22 *Ch. Ch.*, 10 April 1801.
23 For Jenner's own account of these problems, see Edward Jenner, *Further Observations on the Variolae Vaccinae*, 1799, pp.28-31.
24 Peter Razzell, *Edward Jenner's Cowpox Vaccine: The History of a Medical Myth*, second edition, 1980, p.14.
25 For biographical notes on Moseley (1742-1819) see *D.N.B.* He was a regular visitor to the seaside resort of Southend where he died (T/P 83/1, p.121).
26 *Gent. Mag.*, lxx, Part 1, April 1800, p.303.
27 *Ibid.*, lxx, Part 1, May 1800, pp.433,434.
28 *Ibid.*, lxx, Part 2, July 1800, p.640.
29 Quoted in Jacob, *op.cit.*, pp.101,103.
30 *Gent. Mag.*, lxx, Part 1, May 1800, p.434.
31 *Ibid.*, lxxi, Part 1, April 1801, p.319.
32 *Ibid.*, lxx, Part 2, July 1800, p.640.
33 *Ibid.*, lxxi, Part 1, April 1801, p.319.
34 *Ibid.*, lxxii, Part 1, March 1802, p.200.
35 *Ibid.*, lxxiii, Part 1, January 1803, p.71.
36 Benjamin Moseley, *A Treatise on the Lues Bovilla; or Cow Pox*, second edition, 1805, p.129. Information about some of the failures was supplied by Daniel Sutton.
37 *Ibid.*, p.94.
38 *Ibid.*, pp.xii,xiii.
39 William Rowley, *Cow-Pox Inoculation no Security Against Small-Pox Infection*, 1805, p.5.
40 *Ibid.*, p.ix.
41 George Lipscomb, *A Dissertation on the Failure and the Mischiefs of the Disease called Cow-Pox*, 1805, pp.104,105.
42 John Birch, *Serious Reasons for Uniformly Objecting to the Practice of Vaccination*, 1806, p.1. For biographical notes on Birch (d.1815) see *D.N.B.*
43 Birch, *op.cit.*, p.28.

44 *Ibid.*, p.54.
45 *Gent. Mag.*, lxxii, Part 2, November 1802, p.1007.
46 *Ibid.*, lxxiii, Part 1, January 1803, p.70.
47 *Ibid.*, lxxiv, Part 1, February 1804, p.128.
48 *Ibid.*, lxxiv, Part 1, January 1804, p.8.
49 Quoted in Creighton, *op.cit.*, ii, p.609.
50 *Plan and Regulations of the London Vaccine Institution*, January 1808 (copy in E.R.O., D/P 263/28/7). See also Royal College of Physicians, MS. 1928 (Royal College of Physicians Vaccination Committee Minute Book, 1807).
51 Quoted in John Baron, *Life of Edward Jenner*, ii, 1838, pp.69,70. The London Smallpox Hospital did not give up inoculation of outpatients until later in 1807 and of in-patients until about 1821 (Creighton, *op.cit.*, ii, p.586).
52 Quoted in Baron, *op.cit.*, ii, p.69. The National Vaccine Establishment was set up on 8 June 1808 at an annual cost of about £5,000 (Creighton, *op. cit.*, ii, p.567).
53 *Plan and Regulations of the London Vaccine Institution*, 1808.
54 Moore, *op.cit.*, p.304 and Creighton, *op.cit.*, ii, pp.609,610.
55 Creighton, *op.cit.*, ii, pp.574,590.
56 *Ibid.*, p.591.
57 John Forbes, 'Some Account of the Smallpox lately prevalent in Chichester and its Vicinity, showing the Degree of Security afforded by Vaccination in that District', *The London Medical Repository, Monthly Journal, and Review*, xviii, July-December 1822, pp.215,216. Although there were about 20 fatalities none occurred in vaccinated patients.
58 *Ibid.*, p.212.
59 *Ibid.*, p.213.
60 *Ibid.*, p.214.
61 *Ibid.*, pp.209,210.
62 H.W. Carter, 'General Report of Medical Diseases treated at the Kent and Canterbury Hospital, from January to the commencement of July 1824, with a particular Account of the more important Cases', *The London Medical Repository, Monthly Journal, and Review*, xxii (New Series ii), 1 October 1824, pp.268,269.
63 *Lincoln, Rutland and Stamford Mercury*, 1 November 1816, quoted in Edward Gillett, *A History of Grimsby*, 1970, p.215.
64 Letter written by Revd R. Marks of Great Missenden, 6 May 1824, in J.J. Cribb, *Smallpox and Cowpox*, 1825, quoted in Creighton, *op.cit.*, ii, p.592, fn.2.
65 John Robertson, *Observations on the Mortality ... of Children*, 1827, p.59, cited in Creighton, *op.cit.*, ii, p.583.
66 Vestry House Museum, Walthamstow, L34.41 WP1.
67 D/P 17/1/3.
68 D/P 124/8/2.
69 D/P 169/12/1. The parish doctor, Mr Foakes, inoculated 53 paupers at 5s. 3d. a head in September 1800. Ten years later, in September 1810, another parish doctor, Mr Vesey, inoculated a family 'with the smallpox' for two guineas.
70 D/P 117/8/7.
71 E.J. Erith, *Woodford, Essex, 1600-1836*, 1950, p.55.
72 D/P 48/8/1.
73 W.A. Gimson, *Great Braxted 1086-1957*, 1958, p.39.
74 D/P 126/18.
75 D/P 181/8/4.
76 *V.C.H. Essex*, viii, 1983, p.13.
77 D/P 157/8/3.
78 *Ibid.*
79 T/A 605, resolution of 21 April 1806.
80 J.E. Oxley, *Barking Vestry Minutes*, 1955, p.144. The 492 inhabitants treated formed about ten per cent. of the population (3,906 in 1801, 5,543 in 1811).
81 D/P 70/12/3,4; D/DU 978.
82 D/P 219/8/3.
83 D/P 300/18/3.
84 D/P 357/8/2.
85 D/P 332/18/9.
86 D/P 36/8/5.
87 D/P 36/11/11.
88 D/P 30/18/1.
89 Erith, *op.cit.*, p.55.
90 D/P 307/18.
91 D/P 67/12/3.
92 T/R 149/10.
93 D/P 36/8/5. See also above, p.113.
94 D/P 70/12/3.
95 D/P 70/12/4; D/DU 978. These Wickford parish vaccinations of 1818 appear to be those cited in Peter Razzell, *The Conquest of Smallpox*, 1977, p.79, but credited by Razzell to a fictitious Berkshire parish called 'Wickforn'.
96 D/P 70/12/4; D/DU 978.
97 D/P 332/18/9.
98 Royal College of Physicians, *Report on Vaccination*, 1807, p.6.
99 T/R 65.
100 D/P 94/8/3.
101 D/P 94/8/4.
102 Creighton, *op.cit.*, ii, pp.604,605.
103 G/BiM 3.
104 D/P 357/8/2.

Chapter 6
The Age of Vaccination, 1840-1907

1 Creighton, *op.cit.*, ii, p.607. For bio-

graphical notes on Wakley (1795-1862) see *D.N.B.*

2 Creighton, *op.cit.*, ii, p.606.

3 3 and 4 Victoria, *cap.* 29.

4 Poor Law Commission, *Seventh Annual Report of the Poor Law Commissioners*, 1841, pp.89,90. Howard's report to the Commissioners was reproduced in Edwin Chadwick, *Report on the Sanitary Condition of the Labouring Population of England*, 1842, pp.294-336. For biographical notes on Howard (1807-1848), Physician to the Ardwick and Ancoats Dispensary, see *D.N.B.*

5 Poor Law Commission, *Seventh Annual Report*, pp.144-153.

6 *Ibid.*, pp.154-157.

7 *Ibid.*, pp.153,154.

8 Poster in E.R.O. Library.

9 Poor Law Commission, *Seventh Annual Report*, p.40.

10 *An Act to amend an Act to extend the Practice of Vaccination*, 4 and 5 Victoria, *cap.* 32.

11 16 and 17 Victoria, *cap.* 100.

12 In the case of children in the care or custody of legal guardians the period was four months.

13 G/RoM 7, p.291.

14 Quoted in W.M. Frazer, *A History of English Public Health 1834-1939*, 1950, p.72.

15 The Public Health Act, 1858, abolished the General Board of Health which had been set up in 1848 and transferred its functions to the new Medical Department of the Privy Council.

16 Anthony S. Wohl, *Endangered Lives : Public Health in Victorian Britain*, 1983, p.132 and Dixon, *Smallpox*, p.279. The National Vaccine Establishment had been set up by Parliament in 1808. See above p.109.

17 24 and 25 Victoria, *cap.* 59.

18 D/DR 025.

19 G/RoM 10, p.198.

20 Stuart M.F. Fraser, 'Leicester and Smallpox: The Leicester Method', *Medical History*, xxiv, 1980, p.328.

21 *The Times*, 11 October 1867, p.7.

22 30 and 31 Victoria, *cap.* 84. It came into effect on 1 January 1868.

23 *Hansard*, Third Series, 188, col. 651, quoted in R.M. MacLeod, 'Law, Medicine and Public Opinion : the Resistance to Compulsory Health Legislation 1870-1907', *Public Law*, 1967, p.116.

24 For a detailed account of the movement against the Vaccination Acts in the national context readers are recommended to consult Roy MacLeod's lengthy article in *Public Law*, 1967, pp.107-128, 189-211. Although his work is marred by a number of inaccuracies (e.g. in the interpretation of the

Acts of 1867 and 1871) it remains an excellent account of the movement during the years 1870-1907).

25 Fraser, *op.cit.*, p.330.

26 G/RoM 10, p.281.

27 *Ibid.*, p.316.

28 G/RoM 11, p.208.

29 MacLeod, 'Law, Medicine and Public Opinion', *loc.cit.*, p.117

30 Fraser, *op.cit.*, p.330.

31 MacLeod, *loc.cit.*, p.117.

32 *Ibid.*

33 For a fuller account of the events leading up to the passing of the 1871 Act see MacLeod, *loc.cit.*, pp.116-119.

34 34 and 35 Victoria, chap. 98. Its short title was The Vaccination Act 1871.

35 G/RoM 11, p.234.

36 Quoted in MacLeod, *loc.cit.*, p.121.

37 MacLeod, *loc.cit*, p.121.

38 G/RoM 11, p.302.

39 *Ibid.*, p.305.

40 *Ibid.*, p.378.

41 Andrew Phillips, *Ten Men and Colchester*, 1985, p.78.

42 G/RoM 11, p.178.

43 Phillips, *op.cit.*, p.77.

44 *Ibid.*, p.78.

45 Revd George Cardew, *Think Before you Vaccinate*, 1873, pp.10,11.

46 Revd Mundeford Allen, *Vaccination and the Vaccination Act*, 1873, p.6.

47 Cardew, *op.cit.*, pp.3,15.

48 Allen, *op.cit.*, p.3.

49 Cardew, *op.cit.*, p.11.

50 *Ibid.*, p.16.

51 37 and 38 Victoria, chap. 75.

52 MacLeod, *loc.cit.*, p.122.

53 Mrs Hume-Rothery, *Women and Doctors or a Medical Despotism in England*, c.1871, pp.2-5, quoted in F.B. Smith, *The People's Health 1830-1910*, 1979, p.166.

54 Barrie Trinder, *Victorian Banbury*, 1982, p.151.

55 *Ibid.*, pp.150-158.

56 *Ibid.*, p.154.

57 F.B. Smith, *op.cit.*, p.167.

58 Fraser, *op.cit.*, p.330.

59 Quoted in MacLeod, *loc.cit.*, p.195.

60 Fraser, *op.cit.*, p.330.

61 *Ibid.*, p.331.

62 MacLeod, *loc.cit.*, p.196.

63 Fraser, *op.cit.*, p.318.

64 *Ibid.* For details of Johnston's career see S.M.F. Fraser, 'Dr William Johnston (1846-1900) of Leicester — an unknown Victorian general practitioner', *Journal of the Royal College of General Practitioners*, vol. 33, 1983, pp.369-371.

65 Other complications included erysipelas (from which deaths 'undoubtedly occurred'), *vaccina gangrenosa* (often fatal), lymphangitis, morbilliform lesions, urticarial lesions, generalised rashes, sepsis, chronic sepsis and tetanus. Some of these, in particular sepsis and erysipelas, were the result of faulty techniques as the lancets were not sterilized between patients but merely washed in warm water. Dixon cites the case of a public vaccinator working in London as late as the 1930s who was known to his students by the nickname Septic Sam. Other complications were benign generalised vaccinia and malignant generalised vaccinia, also known as *eczema vaccinatum*. Mortality from the latter was very high, possibly as much as 80 per cent. in infants. The most common complication of all was *vaccinia encephalitis* which had an infant mortality rate of about 50 per cent. in 1928.

66 Dixon, *Smallpox*, p.285.

67 For a review see *The Lancet*, 4 February 1888, p.228. The reviewer found Creighton's reasoning difficult to follow, the book to contain 'so much that appears fanciful' and thought that Creighton underrated Jenner's labours.

68 *The Lancet*, 24 November 1888, editorial, pp.1027,1028.

69 *Ibid.*, 13 April 1889, p.742.

70 E. Ashworth Underwood, 'Charles Creighton, the man and his work', Charles Creighton, *Epidemics in Britain*, second edition, 1965, introduction, p.91.

71 Dixon, *op.cit.*, p.156. The author deals with post-vaccinal complications at some length in pp.143-159.

72 D/DR C3. Letter from Gladwell to James Round, M.P., 25 June 1894.

73 *Ibid.*

74 *The Lancet*, 13 April 1889, editorial, p.743.

75 *First Report of the Royal Commission on Vaccination*, 1889.

76 *Second and Third Reports of the Royal Commission on Vaccination*, 1890.

77 *Fourth Report of the Royal Commission on Vaccination*, 1890-1891.

78 *Fifth Report of the Royal Commission on Vaccination*, 1892.

79 *The Spectator*, lxxxi, p.673, quoted in MacLeod, *loc.cit.*, p.204.

80 *Hansard*, Fourth Series, vol. 57, 1898, col.789.

81 For information on G.W. Palmer and the Palmer family of Reading, biscuit manufacturers, see Stephen Yeo, *Religion and Voluntary Organisations in Crisis*, 1976, pp.106, 107,206-263.

82 *Hansard*, Fourth Series, vol.62, 1898, cols 369,370.

83 MacLeod, *loc.cit.*, p.206.

84 *Ibid.*, p.207.

85 61 and 62 Victoria, chap.49. It was effective from 1 January 1899 (except section 2 (1.), the 'conscience clause', which came into force immediately) and was to remain in force for a period of five years.

86 Quoted in MacLeod, *loc.cit.*, p.207.

87 Quoted in Mark Sorrell, *The Peculiar People*, 1979, p.157, fn.2. See also John Montgomery, *Abodes of Love*, 1962, p.123.

88 *The Times*, 9 May 1872, quoted in Sorrell, *op.cit.*, p.32.

89 John C. Thresh, *Summary of the Reports of the District Medical Officers of Health in the Administrative County of Essex, For the Year 1894*, 1895, p.112. Dr George Deeping was father of the Southend novelist Warwick Deeping.

90 Thresh, *Summary For 1892*, 1893, p.19.

91 Thresh, *Summary For 1893*, 1894, p.24.

92 Thresh, *Summary For 1895*, 1896, pp.54, 55.

93 A. Clough Waters, *Annual Report Upon the State of Public Health in the Borough of Southend-on-Sea, for the Year 1895*, 1896, p.7.

94 Thresh, *Summary For 1896*, 1897.

95 MacLeod, *loc.cit.*, p.207.

96 Waters, *Annual Report for 1898*, 1899, p.12.

97 Thresh, *Summary For 1898*, 1899, pp.31, 32.

98 *Ibid.*, p.31.

99 MacLeod, *loc.cit.*, p.208.

100 *The Southend-on-Sea Observer and South-East Essex Gazette*, 24 July 1902.

101 Quoted in Thresh, *Summary For 1901*, 1902, pp.29,30.

102 *Ibid.*, p.31.

103 All quoted in Thresh, *Summary For 1902*, 1903, p.33.

104 *Ibid.*

105 *Ibid.*, p.31.

106 *Ibid.*, p.28.

107 J.T.C. Nash, *Annual Report Upon the State of Public Health in the Borough of Southend-on-Sea, for the Year 1902*, 1903, p.26.

108 *Ibid.*, p.28.

109 *Ibid.*, p.29.

110 Thresh, *Summary For 1903*, 1904, pp.39, 40. Dr Savage was Medical Officer for Colchester.

111 Nash, *Annual Report for 1903*, 1904, pp.26-31.

112 House of Commons, *Report of Departmental Committee Appointed to Inquire into the Expenses of Vaccination*, part 1, 1905, sections 91 and 95.

113 Arnold Lupton, 'Vaccination and the State' (paper given to the National Liberal Club Political and Economic Circle in December 1906), *National Liberal Club Transactions*,

v, part xiii, 1914, p.63.

114 7 Edw. VII, chap. 31, *An Act to substitute a Statutory Declaration for the Certificate required under section two of the Vaccination Act, 1898, of conscientious objection, with the short title of the Vaccination Act, 1907.*

115 Arthur Newsholme, *Annual Report of the Medical Officer of the Local Government Board for the Year 1908-09,* 1909, pp.ix,x.

116 Newsholme, *Report for 1910-11,* 1911, p.xxix.

Chapter 7
The Decline of Vaccination, 1908-1971

1 Newsholme, *Report for 1913-14,* 1914, p.-cxii.

2 Newsholme, *Report for 1908-09,* pp. 252-259; *Report for 1913-14,* pp.121-127.

3 Thresh, *Summary for 1911,* 1912, p.29.

4 Arnold Lupton, *Our Armies and Navies and Vaccination-Inoculation* [1916] (pamphlet).

5 William A. Bullough, *Summary of the Reports of the District Medical Officers of Health in the Administrative County of Essex, For the Year 1919,* 1920, p.113.

6 *Ibid.,* pp.113,114.

7 Bullough, *Summary For 1920,* 1921, p.14.

8 *Ibid.*

9 *Ibid.,* p.11.

10 *Ibid.,* pp.9-11.

11 C. Killick Millard, 'Smallpox and Vaccination', *The Lancet,* 1924, p.301.

12 Quoted in Frazer, *History of English Public Health,* p.373.

13 Frazer, *op.cit.,* p.373.

14 Bullough, *Summary For 1928,* 1929, p.25; Frazer, *op.cit.,* p.375.

15 Bullough, *Summary For 1929,* 1930, p.16.

16 Bullough, *Summary For 1928,* p.24; *Summary For 1929,* p.16; *Summary For 1930,* 1931, p.23.

17 Bullough, *Summary For 1930,* p.24.

18 *Ibid.*

19 J. Stevenson Logan, *Annual Report of the Medical Officer of Health for the County Borough of Southend-on-Sea for the year 1946,* 1947, p.46. For source material on the 1946 Essex outbreak as a whole see Logan, *op.cit.,* pp.42-52; Bullough, *Summary For 1946,* 1948, pp.16-21; *Southend Standard,* 4 and 18 April 1946.

20 Ministry of Health, *State of Public Health During Six Years of War,* 1946.

21 Essex County Council, *National Health Service Act, 1946. Arrangements for Decentralisation of Administration of Local Health Functions under Part 111, as approved by the County Council at their Meeting on 18 May, 1948,* revised edition, 1954, p.6.

22 Derrick Baxby, *Jenner's Smallpox Vaccine. The Riddle of Vaccinia Virus and its Origin,* 1981, p.15.

23 George G. Stewart, *Summary of the Reports of the District Medical Officers of Health in the Administrative County of Essex, For the Year 1962,* 1963, pp.71,72.

24 George Dick, 'Routine smallpox vaccination', *British Medical Journal,* 1971, part iii, pp.163-166.

25 Lily Loat, *The Truth About Vaccination and Immunization,* 1951, p.9.

26 Dick, *loc.cit.,* p.163.

27 *Ibid.,* p.166.

28 *Report of the Committee of Inquiry into the Smallpox Outbreak in London in March and April 1973,* 1974, p.10.

29 World Health Organisation, *Smallpox Eradication,* World Health Organisation Technical Report Series No.393, 1968, p.5.

30 For detailed examinations of this complex subject see Baxby, *op.cit.,* and Razzell, - *Edward Jenner's Cowpox Vaccine,* second edition, 1980.

Chapter 8
Pest Houses and Smallpox Hospitals

1 D/P 161/12/2.

2 For the Romford house see T/A 521/1; map, 1706, T/M 375; *V.C.H. Essex,* vii, 1978, p.77. For the Barking house see D/P 81/8/1.

3 D/DU 65/74.

4 D/P 161/12/2. There may have been a pest house at Bardfield End Green as early as 1698 for in that year the overseers paid 1s. 6d. for 'Stuffe which Robert Hickes at Bardfield End Green had in the time of his sickness'.

5 *Ibid.*

6 Ethel Simcoe, *A Short History of the Parish and Ancient Borough of Thaxted,* 1934, p.76.

7 D/B 3/8/15A.

8 *Ibid.;* D/DU 811/4/4.

9 D/B 3/8/2.

10 D/DCw T2.

11 D/DEs T55, 89. It was no longer standing in 1787.

12 D/P 30/12/1.

13 F.H. Erith, *Ardleigh in 1796,* 1978, p.12.

14 D/P 171/8/4.

15 D/P 119/8/4.

16 D/F 35/3/136 and 35/7/280; 1st edition 6-inch O.S. map, Essex sheet VIII. It was sold by the parish in 1852.

17 D/DHt T71/71; D/DCm T98. It is shown on the 1st edition 6-inch O.S. map, Essex sheet XXVI.

18 D/P 193/8/2.

19 D/P 94/18/42; Q/SBb 248/4.

20 E.J. Erith, *Woodford*, pp.52-54; *V.C.H. Essex*, vi, 1973, p.352. The pest house is shown on the parish tithe map, c.1840 (D/CT 408). It stood in the north of the parish and its site was later occupied by Bancroft's School.

21 *V.C.H. Essex*, iv, 1956, p.38. For biographical details of Jenour (1755-1853) see *D.N.B.*

22 D/P 67/18/1.

23 E.J. Erith, *op.cit.*, pp.52-54.

24 D/P 37/12/3.

25 D/P 102/1/1. Ten inhabitants died in the pest house between June 1764 and March 1765.

26 D/P 158/12/2; Leslie Thompson, *The Land That Fanns*, 1957, p.44; *V.C.H. Essex*, vii, pp.180, 187.

27 T/Z 25/556.

28 D/DCr P1; D/CT 305.

29 *V.C.H. Essex*, viii, 1983, p.180.

30 D/P 302/12/2.

31 D/P 119/8/4. For a note of the burial of John Wilsmore 'with the Small pox fr. the Pest House', 30 October 1794, see transcript of parish register in E.R.O. Library, Chelmsford.

32 D/B 3/8/2.

33 D/P 219/12/4.

34 D/P 16/12/3.

35 Q/SBb 27, 30.

36 D/P 18/12/6.

37 C.A. Barton, *Historical Notes and Records of the Parish of Terling Essex*, 1953, p.109.

38 G/EZ 6; *V.C.H. Essex*, v, 1966, p.131.

39 For biographical notes on Beller (1654-1725) see *D.N.B.*

40 They were St Bartholomew's (1123), St Thomas' (1207), Bethlehem (medieval), Westminster (1719), Guy's (1721), St George's (1733), Foundling (1739), London (1740), Middlesex Small-Pox (1746), Lock (1746), British Lying-in (1749), City of London Lying-in (1750), Queen Charlotte's Lying-in (1752), Royal Maternity (1757), New Westminster Lying-in (1767), General Lying-in (1778).

41 For the list of 31 see Buer, *Health, Wealth and Population*, p.257.

42 For further details see Geoffrey Martin, *The Town*, 1961, caption to illustration 91.

43 See F.F. Waddy, *A History of Northampton General Hospital 1743 to 1948*, 1974.

44 See Ernest R. Frizelle and Janet D. Martin, *The Leicester Royal Infirmary 1771-1971*, 1971.

45 See Frank H. Jacob, *History of the General Hospital Near Nottingham*, 1951.

46 Gordon Jackson, *Hull in the Eighteenth Century*, 1972, pp.282,283.

47 Martin, *op.cit.*, p.45.

48 For fuller details see p.38.

49 *Gent. Mag.*, xvii, June 1747, p.270.

50 P. Camper, 'Travel Journals' in B.W. Th. Nuyens (ed.), *Opuscula Selecta Neerlandicorum de Arte Medica*, Amsterdam, 1939, p.95, quoted in Miller, *op.cit.*, pp.146,147.

51 See p.38.

52 Frizelle and Martin, *op.cit.*, p.21.

53 Brian Abel-Smith, *The Hospitals 1800-1948*, 1964, p.13.

54 See also p.55. For fuller details of the Society see Buer, *op.cit.*, pp.185,186 and Razzell, *The Conquest of Smallpox*, pp.145-147.

55 Quoted in Buer, *op.cit.*, p.199.

56 For biographical notes on Percival (1740-1804) and Ferriar (1761-1815) see *D.N.B.* and Buer, *op.cit.*, pp.123,124. For a good account of the Manchester House of Recovery see Buer, *op.cit.*, pp.200-202.

57 The two remaining exceptions were at Northampton, where the nonconformist divine Philip Doddridge had successfully promoted the formation of a county infirmary in 1743 and at Worcester, where Doddridge's friend Isaac Maddox, Bishop of Worcester, was instrumental in establishing an infirmary in 1745. Like Maddox, Doddridge was a keen supporter of inoculation. For biographical notes on Doddridge see *D.N.B.* See also preface by Doddridge in David Some, *The Case of Receiving the Small-Pox by Inoculation, Impartially Considered, and Especially in a Religious View*, 1750.

58 Quoted in Corfield, *The Impact of English Towns*, p.122.

59 Buer, *op.cit.*, pp.206,257.

60 *Ibid.*, p.204.

61 *Ibid.*, pp.198,257.

62 Bristowe and Holmes, *The Hospitals of the United Kingdom*, 1864, p.465.

63 Quoted in Abel-Smith, *op.cit.*, p.38.

64 Bristowe and Holmes, *op.cit.*, pp.639,640.

65 Poor Law Commission, *Fifth Annual Report of the Poor Law Commissioners*, 1839, p.190.

66 *Ibid.*, pp.184-189.

67 For biographical notes on the Twining family see *D.N.B.*

68 Its full title was *Report of the Lancet Sanitary Commission for Investigating the State of the Infirmaries of Workhouses*.

69 For biographical notes on Ernest Hart (1835-1898) editor of *British Medical Journal*, 1886-1898, see *D.N.B.*

70 For biographical notes on Joseph Rogers (1821-1889) see *D.N.B.* An account of his lifelong efforts for better treatment of the sick poor appears in J.E. Thorold Rogers, ed., *Joseph Rogers, M.D.: Reminiscences of a*

Workhouse Medical Officer, 1889.

71 For biographical notes on Dr Edward Smith (d.1874) see *D.N.B.*

72 Abel-Smith, *op.cit.*, p.82. For biographical notes on Gathorne Gathorne-Hardy (1814-1906) first Earl of Cranbrook, see *D.N.B.*

73 For further information about the work of the Metropolitan Asylums Board see Sidney and Beatrice Webb, *English Poor Law History: Part II : the Last Hundred Years*, i, 1929, pp.321-329; J.J. Clarke, *The Local Government of the United Kingdom*, 14th edition, 1948, pp.69,70; Anthony Wohl, *Endangered Lives*, 1983, pp.139,140; Abel-Smith, *op.cit.*, pp.119-133.

74 Abel-Smith, *op.cit.*, p.127.

75 34 and 35 Victoria, *cap.*70.

76 35 and 36 Victoria, *cap.*79.

77 Three were set up in Essex, at Colchester, Harwich and Maldon.

78 M.W. Flinn (ed.), *Report on the Sanitary Condition of the Labouring Population of Gt. Britain by Edwin Chadwick 1842*, 1965, p.407.

79 38 and 39 Victoria, *cap.*55.

80 Wohl, *op.cit.*, p.138; Dixon, *Smallpox*, p.362; Abel-Smith, *op.cit.*, p.127; Frazer, *History of English Public Health*, p.288.

81 Gwendoline M. Ayers, *England's First State Hospitals and the Metropolitan Asylums Board 1867-1930*, 1971, p.74,75; Susan Liveing, *A Nineteenth-Century Teacher*, 1926, p.126. Currie was also promoter of The People's Palace.

82 Letter from Metropolitan Asylums Board to Local Government Board 15 May 1881 quoted in Ayers, *op.cit.*, p.75.

83 George Buchanan, *Annual Report of the Medical Officer of the Local Government Board for the Year 1887*, 1888, p.200.

84 R. Thorne Thorne, *Annual Report of the Medical Officer of the Local Government Board for the Year 1894-5*, 1896, p.197.

85 For details of West Ham Smallpox Hospital see *V.C.H. Essex*, vi, p.110. The others are listed in Sidney and Beatrice Webb, *op.cit.*, p.320.

86 G/CoM 15. See also Andrew Phillips, *Ten Men and Colchester*, 1985, p.76.

87 Frazer, *op.cit.*, p.119.

88 County councils were set up under the provisions of the Local Government Act, 1888.

89 *V.C.H. Essex*, vi, 1973, p.110.

90 Adrian Corder-Birch, *A Centenary History of Halstead Hospital (1884-1984)*, 1984, pp.5,72. It was closed in 1896 when a new infectious diseases hospital in Mount Hill was opened by Halstead Urban District Council.

91 *Ibid.*, p.73.

92 Kelly, *Directory of Essex*, 1882, p.154.

93 Phillips, *op.cit.*, pp.78,79. The hospital still occupies the same site.

94 *V.C.H. Essex*, vi, p.110. In addition to the six hospitals cited in this paragraph there was at Colchester a Government Hospital for Contagious Diseases which had been set up about 1871, but this was only for the use of military personnel (Kelly, *Directories of Essex*, 1870-1886, and information from Paul Coverley and Andrew Phillips), while Poplar Metropolitan Board of Works had built a smallpox hospital at Plaistow, in West Ham, in 1877, despite opposition from West Ham Local Board (*V.C.H. Essex*, vi, p.110).

95 Corder-Birch, *op.cit.*, p.14.

96 John B. Penfold, *The History of the Essex County Hospital, Colchester 1820-1948*, 1984, p.151.

97 *Ibid.*, p.124.

98 See sections 17-19 of the Act.

99 P.R.O., MH 12/3419, 31/34, 81525/90, 91001/90. I am grateful to Ann Morton of the P.R.O. for drawing my attention to these references.

100 Thresh, *Summary For 1892*, p.5.

101 *Ibid.*, pp.5,6.

102 Thresh, *Summary For 1893*, p.6.

103 56 and 57 Victoria, *cap.*68.

104 Thresh had previously been answerable to the Contagious Diseases (Animals) Committee.

105 P.R.O., House of Commons Sessional Papers, 1896, LXXII. 645; [K.C. Newton], *The Essex County Council 1889-1974*, 1974, p.13.

106 Thresh, *Summary For 1895*, p.3.

107 P.R.O., House of Commons Sessional papers, LXXII. 645.

108 Thresh, *Summary For 1892*, p.12.

109 Thresh, *Summary For 1893*, p.5. Linton R.S.A. was chiefly in Suffolk, but included two Essex parishes, Hadstock and Bartlow End.

110 Thresh, *Summary For 1894*, pp.24-28, 49-51.

111 Thresh, *Summary For 1895*, p.46.

112 Thresh, *Summary For 1898*, pp.54-57. See also Appendix 3.

113 Thresh, *Summary For 1899*, 1900, pp.50, 51; *Summary For 1900*, 1901, pp.51-55; *V.C.H. Essex*, v, pp.257,294; viii, p.49.

114 *V.C.H. Essex*, vi, p.111. Although built and maintained by the County Borough, the smallpox hospital in Dagenham served all the places in West Ham Poor Law Union, which included East Ham, Little Ilford, Leyton, Walthamstow and Wanstead.

115 1 Edw. VII, *cap.*8.

116 Thresh, *Summary For 1901*, p.19.

117 Thresh, *Summary For 1902*, p.26. These figures do not include the County Borough of West Ham.

118 The memorandum, dated May 1902, is reproduced in H. Franklin Parsons, *Report on Isolation Hospitals* 1912 (Supplement to Arthur Newsholme, *Annual Report of the Medical Officer of the Local Government Board for the Year 1910-11*, 1912) Appendix A, pp.136-140. For biographical notes on William Henry Power (1842-1916) see *D.N.B.*

119 W.H. Power, *Annual Report of the Medical Officer of the Local Government Board for the Year 1902-03*, 1904, pp.293,294.

120 *V.C.H. Essex*, vi, p.110; Thresh, *Summary For 1894*, pp.25,26.

121 Thresh, *Summary For 1901*, p.20.

122 Thresh, *Summary For 1895*, p.28.

123 Thresh, *Summary For 1901*, p.27.

124 *Ibid.*

125 *Ibid.*, p.28.

126 Power, *op.cit.*, pp.119,120. Dr George Seaton Buchanan became a medical inspector at the Local Government Board in 1895. His eminent father, Sir George Buchanan, was Principal Medical Officer to the Board, 1879-1892.

127 Thresh, *Summary For 1902*, p.28.

128 See p.166.

129 Parsons, *Report on Isolation Hospitals*, p.13.

130 *Ibid.*, p.ii,iii.

131 *Ibid.*, p.15.

132 *Ibid.*

133 *Ibid.*

134 *Ibid.*, p.53.

135 See above, p.165.

136 Thresh, *Summary For 1903*, pp.70,71.

137 Thresh, *Summary For 1910*, 1911, pp.75, 76. The local authorities which had binding agreements with West Ham were the urban districts of Barking, East Ham, Ilford, Romford, Walthamstow, Wanstead and Woodford, and the rural districts of Romford and Ongar.

138 *Ibid.*, p.76.

139 Thresh, *Summary For 1918*, 1919, p.20.

140 *Ibid.*, pp.20,21.

141 In addition to West Ham, East Ham and Southend-on-Sea had also become county boroughs and were no longer under the control of the County Council.

142 Bullough, *Summary For 1919*, p.114.

143 *Ibid.*, p.117.

144 *Ibid.*

145 *Ibid.*, p.116.

146 *Ibid.*, p.114.

147 *Ibid.*, p.116.

148 Bullough, *Summary For 1920*, pp.7-16.

149 Bullough, *Summary For 1930*, p.25.

150 Bullough, *Summary For 1925*, 1926, pp.20-24.

151 Bullough, *Summary For 1928*, p.24.

152 Bullough, *Summary For 1929*, p.17. See also *V.C.H. Essex*, vi, p.285.

153 19 George V, ch. 17 (27 March 1929), which came into force on 1 April 1930.

154 Bullough, *Summary For 1930*, p.23.

155 Bullough, *Summary For 1931*, 1932, p.20; *Summary For 1933*, 1934, p.9.

156 Bullough, *Summary For 1934*, 1935, pp.30-33.

157 Bullough, *Summary For 1935*, 1936, p.36.

Appendix 1

1 C.W. Dixon, *Smallpox*, 1962.

2 For Rao's classification see A.M. Ramsey and R.T.D. Edmond, *Infectious Diseases*, 1967.

3 World Health Organisation Technical Report Series No. 393, *Smallpox Eradication*, 1968; Technical Report Series No. 493, *WHO Expert Committee on Smallpox Eradication Second Report*, 1972.

4 On 8 May 1980 the delegates of the 155 member states of the World Health Organisation unanimously accepted the conclusion of the Global Commission for the Certification of Smallpox Eradication that smallpox eradication had been achieved throughout the world and that there was no evidence that the disease would return as an endemic disease. (WHO, *The Global Eradication of Smallpox*, 1980, foreword, p.3).

5 Quoted in Dixon, *op.cit.*, pp.9-11.

Appendix 3

1 Excluding the County Borough of West Ham.

SELECTIVE BIBLIOGRAPHY

N.B. There are excellent bibliographies in Derrick Baxby, *Jenner's Smallpox Vaccine*, 1981, pp.197-209 and Genevieve Miller, *The Adoption of Inoculation ... in England and France*, 1957, pp.294-339.

(i) Primary sources, arranged chronologically

1722   Isaac Massey, *A Short and Plain Account of Inoculation; with Some Remarks on the Main Arguments Made Use of to Recommend That Practice, by Mr. Maitland and Others* (London)

1722   Legard Sparham, *Reasons against the Practice of Inoculating the Small-Pox, As Also a Brief Account of the Operation of This Poison, Infused after This Manner into a Wound* (London)

1722   William Wagstaffe, *A Letter to Dr Freind Shewing the Danger and Uncertainty of Inoculating the Smallpox* (London)

1722   J. Crawford, *The Case of Inoculating the Small-Pox Consider'd and its Advantages Asserted : in a Review of Dr. Wagstaffe's Letter. Wherein Every Thing That Author Has Advanced against It Is Fully Confuted : and Inoculation Proved a Safe, Beneficial, and Laudable Practice* (London)

1723   Sir Richard Blackmore, *A Treatise upon the Small-Pox, in Two Parts, Containing : I. An Account of the Nature and Several Kinds of That Disease, with the Proper Methods of Cure; II. A Dissertation upon the Modern Practice of Inoculation* (London)

1723   Charles Maitland, *Account of Inoculating the Small Pox* (London)

1723   Thomas Nettleton, 'A Letter from Dr. Nettleton, Physician at Halifax in Yorkshire, to Dr. Whitaker, concerning the Inoculation of the Small Pox', *Philosophical Transactions*, xxxii (January-March), pp.35-48

1723   Thomas Nettleton, 'A Letter from the Same Learned and Ingenious Gentleman concerning his Farther Progress in Inoculating the Small Pox to Dr. Jurin R.S. Secr.', *Philosophical Transactions*, xxxii (January-March), pp.49-52

1724   James Jurin, *An Account of the Success of Inoculating the Small Pox In Great Britain* (London)

1724   Francis Howgrave, *Reasons Against the Inoculation of the Small-Pox. In a Letter to Dr. Jurin* (London)

1725   William Clinch, *An Historical Essay on the Rise and Progress of the Small-Pox. To Which is Added, a Short Appendix, to Prove, That Inoculation Is No Security from the Natural Small-Pox*, second edition (London)

1725   James Jurin, *An Account of the Success of Inoculating the Small Pox in Great Britain, for the Year 1724* (London)

1726   James Jurin, *An Account of the Success of Inoculating the Small Pox in Great Britain, for the Year 1725* (London)

1727   James Jurin, *An Account of the Success of Inoculating the Small Pox in Great Britain, for the Year 1726* (London)

1729   John Gasper Scheuchzer, *An Account of the Success of Inoculating the Small-Pox in Great Britain for the Years 1727 and 1728* (London)

1730-   *Gent Mag., passim*
1820

1733   Evan Davies 'A Letter to Mr. John Eames, F.R.S. Concerning Some Children Inoculated with the Small-Pox, at Haverford-West in Pembrokeshire', *Philosophical Transactions*, xxxviii (July-August), pp.121-126

1733   David Hartley, *Some Reasons Why the Practice of Inoculation Ought to be Introduced into the Town of Bury At Present* (Bury St Edmunds)

1743   James Kirkpatrick, *Essay on Inoculation, Occasioned by the Small-Pox Being Brought into South Carolina in the Year 1738* (London)

1747   Richard Mead, *A Treatise on the Small Pox and Measles: Wherein the Origin, Nature, and the Different Sorts of the Small Pox Are Largely Considered; Together with Those Accidents Which Frequently Occur in That Distemper, and the True Methods of Cure; Also the Case of Inoculation, and the Nature and Cure of the Measles* (London)

1747   Charles Perry, *An Essay on the Smallpox* (London)

1749   Thomas Frewen, *The Practice and Theory of Inoculation. With an Account of its Success. In a Letter to a Friend* (London)

1750   David Some, *The Case of Receiving the Small-Pox by Inoculation, Impartially Considered, and Especially in a Religious View. Written in the Year MDCCXXV ..., and Now Published from the Original Manuscript, by P. Doddridge* (London)

1752   [Isaac Maddox] Bishop of Worcester, *A Sermon Preached before His Grace John Duke of Marlborough, President, the Vice-Presidents and Governors of the Hospital for the Small-Pox, and for Inoculation, at the Parish Church of St. Andrew, Holborn, on Thursday, March 5 1752* (London)

1754   Theodore Delafaye, *A Vindication of a Sermon entitled 'Inoculation an Indefensible Practice'* (London)

SELECTIVE BIBLIOGRAPHY

1754   James Kirkpatrick, *The Analysis of Inoculation; Comprising the History, Theory and Practice of it : With an occasional Consideration of the Most Remarkable Appearances in the Small Pox* (London)

1755   C.M. de la Condamine, *A Discourse on Inoculation* (London)

1759   [W. Heberden], *Plain Instructions for Inoculation in the Small-Pox, by which Any Person May Be Enabled to Perform the Operation and Conduct the Patient through the Distemper* (London)

1760   David d'Escherny, *An Essay on the Small Pox* (London)

1766   George Baker, *An Inquiry Into the Merits of a Method of Inoculating the Small-Pox, Which is now practised in several Counties of England* (London)

1767   Thomas Dimsdale, *The Present Method of Inoculating for the Small-Pox* (London)

1767   Robert Houlton, *A Sermon preached at Ingatestone, Essex, October 12, 1776, in Defence of Inoculation* (Chelmsford)

1768   Angelo Gatti, *New Observations on Inoculation* (London)

1768   Robert Houlton, *Indisputable Facts Relative to the Suttonian Art of Inoculation* (Dublin)

1768   William Watson, *An Account of a Series of Experiments Instituted with a View of ascertaining the Most Successful Method of Inoculating the Small-Pox* (London)

1768   T. Ruston, *An Essay on Inoculation for the Smallpox* (London)

1770   Nicholas May, *Impartial Remarks on the Suttonian Method of Inoculation in a Letter to Dr Glass* (London)

1776   Thomas Dimsdale, *Thoughts on General and Partial Inoculations* (London)

1778   Thomas Dimsdale, *Observations on the Introduction to the Plan of the Dispensary for General Inoculation* (London)

1781   Thomas Dimsdale, *Tracts on Inoculation* (London)

1785   John Haygarth, *An Inquiry how to Prevent the Small-Pox* (Chester)

1788   John Heysham, *Observations on the Bills of Mortality in Carlisle, for the Year 1787* (Carlisle)

1792   W. Turner, *An Address to Parents on Inoculation for the Small-Pox* (Newcastle)

1793   John Haygarth, *A Sketch of a Plan to exterminate the Casual Small-Pox from Great Britain and to introduce General Inoculation* (London)

1795   J. Adams, *Observations on Morbid Poisons* (London)

1796   Daniel Sutton, *The Inoculator; or, Suttonian System of Inoculation, fully set forth in a plain and familiar Manner* (London)

1796   William Woodville, *The History of the Inoculation of the Small-Pox in Great Britain; Comprehending a Review of all the Publications on the Subject: With an Experimental Inquiry into the Relative Advantages of Every Measure Which has been Deemed Necessary in the Process of Inoculation,* i (London)

1798   Edward Jenner, *An Inquiry into the Causes and Effects of the Variolae Vaccinae, a disease discovered in some of the western counties of England, particularly Gloucestershire, and known by the name of cowpox* (London)

1798   George Pearson, *An Inquiry Concerning the History of Cow Pox* (London)

1799   Edward Jenner, *Further Observations on the Variolae Vaccinae* (London)

1799   William Woodville, *Reports of a Series of Inoculations for the Variolae Vaccinae or Cow-Pox* (London)

1800   Benjamin Moseley, *Treatise on Sugar,* second edition (London)

1800   Edward Jenner, *A continuation of Facts and Observations relative to the Variolae Vaccinae or Cowpox* (London)

1800   William Woodville, *Observations on the Cow-Pox* (London)

1801   C.R. Aikin, *A Concise View of all the most Important Facts which have hitherto appeared concerning the Cow-pox* (London)

1801   J. Ring, *A Treatise on the Cowpox* (London)

1802   L. Booker, *A Discourse (Addressed Chiefly to Parents) on the Duty and Advantages of Inoculating Children with the Cow-Pock* (London)

1804   William Goldson, *Cases of Small Pox Subsequent to Vaccination* (Portsea)

1804   John Ring, *An Answer to Mr. Goldson; Proving that Vaccination is a Permanent Security Against Small-Pox* (London)

1805   Rev. G.C. Jenner, *The Evidence at Large, as Laid Before the Committee of the House of Commons, Respecting Dr. Jenner's Discovery of Vaccine Inoculation* (London)

1805   Benjamin Moseley, *A Treatise on the Lues Bovilla or Cow Pox,* second edition (London)

1805   William Rowley, *Cow-Pox Inoculation no Security against Small-Pox Infection* (London)

1805   George Lipscomb, *A Dissertation on the Failure and the Mischiefs of the Disease called the Cow-Pox* (London)

1805 George Lipscomb, *Inoculation for the Small-Pox Vindicated; and its Superior Efficacy and Safety to the Practice of Vaccination Clearly Proved* (London)

1806 John Birch, *Serious Reasons for Uniformly Objecting to the Practice of Vaccination* (London)

1806 John Ring, *An Answer to Mr. Birch, Containing a Defence of Vaccination* (London)

1806 George Lipscomb, *Cow-Pox Exploded; or the Inconsistencies Absurdities, and Falsehoods of Some of its Defenders Exposed* (London)

1806 George Lipscomb, *A Manual of Inoculation for the use of the Faculty and Private Families* (London)

1806 Edward Jenner, *On the Varieties and Modifications of the Vaccine Pustule, occasioned by an Herpetic State of the Skin* (Cheltenham)

1806 R. Willan, *On Vaccine Inoculation* (London)

1807 J. Adams, *A Popular View of the Vaccine Inoculation* (London)

1807 Royal College of Physicians, *Report on Vaccination*

[1810] J. Birch, *Report of the True State of the Cow Pox Experiment, at the Close of the Year 1809* (London)

1817 John Birch, *An Appeal to the Public, on the Hazard and Peril of Vaccination, Otherwise Cow-Pox* (London)

1822 John Forbes, 'Some Account of the Small-pox lately prevalent in Chichester and its Vicinity, showing the Degree of Security afforded by Vaccination in that District', *The London Medical Repository, Monthly Journal, and Review*, xviii, pp.208-220

1824 H.W. Carter, 'General Report of Medical Diseases treated at the Kent and Canterbury Hospital, from January to the commencement of July 1824, with a particular Account of the more important Cases', *The London Medical Repository, Monthly Journal, and Review*, xxii (New Series ii), pp.266-273

1857 J. Simon, *Papers Relating to the History and Practice of Vaccination* (London)

1861 Lord Wharncliffe (ed.), *The Letters and Works of Lady Mary Wortley Montagu* (London)

1873 Revd Mundeford Allen, *Vaccination and the Vaccination Act* (Ipswich)

1873 Revd George Cardew, *Think Before you Vaccinate* [Ipswich]

1885 William White, *The Story of a Great Delusion* (London)

1887 Charles Creighton, *The Natural History of Cow-pox and Vaccinal Syphilis* (London)

1889 Charles Creighton, *Jenner and Vaccination: a Strange Chapter of Medical History* (London)

1889 Royal Commission on Vaccination, *First Report from the Royal Commission on Vaccination* (H.M.S.O., London)

1890 Royal Commission on Vaccination, *Second Report from the Royal Commission on Vaccination* (H.M.S.O., London)

1890 Royal Commission on Vaccination, *Third Report from the Royal Commission on Vaccination* (H.M.S.O., London)

1890-1891 Royal Commission on Vaccination, *Fourth Report from the Royal Commission on Vaccination* (H.M.S.O., London)

1892 Royal Commission on Vaccination, *Fifth Report from the Royal Commission on Vaccination* (H.M.S.O., London)

1894 Charles Creighton, *A History of Epidemics in Britain. 664 A.D. — 1893 A.D.* (Cambridge)

1895 Arthur Wollaston Hutton, *The Vaccination Question* (London)

1896 Royal Commission on Vaccination, *Sixth Report from the Royal Commission on Vaccination* (H.M.S.O., London)

1896-1897 Royal Commission on Vaccination, *Final Report from the Royal Commission on Vaccination* (H.M.S.O., London)

1898 Alfred Russel Wallace, *Vaccination a Delusion its Penal Enforcement a Crime* (London)

1899 W. Scott Tebb, *A Century of Vaccination and What it Teaches* (London)

1914 Arnold Lupton 'Vaccination and the State', *National Liberal Club Transactions*, v, part xiii

1927 Bernhard J. Stern, *Should we be Vaccinated?* (New York and London)

1951 Lily Loat, *The Truth About Vaccination and Immunization* (London)

1971 George Dick, 'Routine smallpox vaccination', *British Medical Journal*, part iii, pp.163-166

(ii) Secondary sources

Abel-Smith, Brian, *The Hospitals 1800-1948*. London, 1964

Abraham, James Johnston, *Lettsom 1744-1815. His Life, Times, Friends and Descendants*. London, 1933

Ayers, Gwendoline M., *England's First State Hospitals and the Metropolitan Asylums Board 1867-1930*. London, 1971

SELECTIVE BIBLIOGRAPHY

Baron, John, *The Life of Edward Jenner*, i. London, 1827

Baron, John, *The Life of Edward Jenner*, ii. London, 1838

Baxby, Derrick, *Jenner's Smallpox Vaccine. The Riddle of Vaccinia Virus and its Origin*. London, 1981

Buer, M.C., *Health, Wealth, and Population in the Early Days of the Industrial Revolution*. London, 1926

Charlton, Christopher, 'The Fight Against Vaccination: the Leicester Demonstration of 1885', *Local Population Studies*, no.30, spring 1983, pp.60-66

Crookshank, E.M., *History and Pathology of Vaccination*. Philadelphia, 1889

Dixon, C.W., *Smallpox*. London, 1962

Drewitt, F.D., *The Life of Edward Jenner*. London, 1931

Edwardes, Edward J., *A Concise History of Small-pox and Vaccination in Europe*. London, 1902

Le Fanu, W., *A Bio-bibliography of Edward Jenner*. London, 1951

Fraser, Stuart M.F., 'Leicester and Smallpox: the Leicester Method', *Medical History*, xxiv, 1980, pp.315-332

Frazer, W.M., *A History of English Public Health 1834-1939*. London, 1950

Greenwood, M., *Epidemics and Crowd-diseases*. London, 1935

Guy, W.A., 'Two hundred and fifty years of smallpox in London', *Journal of the Royal Statistical Society*, xlv, 1882, pp.399-433

Hardy, Anne, 'Smallpox in London: factors in the decline of the disease in the nineteenth century', *Medical History*, xxvii, 1983, pp.111-138

Hartwell, R.M., *The Causes of the Industrial Revolution in England*. London, 1967

Hopkins, Donald R., *Princes and Peasants: smallpox in history*. Chicago, 1983

Luckin, Bill, 'Death and survival in the city: approaches to the history of disease', *Urban History Yearbook*, 1980, pp.53-62

MacLeod, R.M., 'Law, Medicine and Public Opinion: the Resistance to Compulsory Health Legislation 1870-1907', *Public Law*, 1967, pp.107-128,189-211

Miller, Genevieve, *The Adoption of Inoculation for Smallpox in England and France*. Philadelphia, 1957

Moore, James, *The History of the Small Pox*. London, 1815

Razzell, P.E., 'Edward Jenner: the history of a medical myth', *Medical History*, ix, 1965, pp.216-223

Razzell, P.E., 'Population Change in Eighteenth-Century England. A Reinterpretation', *Economic History Review*, second series, xviii, 1965, pp.312-332

Razzell, Peter, *The Conquest of Smallpox*. Firle, 1977

Razzell, Peter, *Edward Jenner's Cowpox Vaccine: The History of a Medical Myth*. Second edition, Firle, 1980

Ricketts, T.F. and Byles, J.B., *The Diagnosis of Smallpox*. London, 1908

Roberts, R.S., 'Epidemics and Social History', *Medical History*, xii, 1968, pp.305-316

Ross, Dale L., 'Leicester and the Anti-Vaccination Movement 1853-1889', *Leicestershire Archaeological and Historical Society Transactions*, xliii, 1967-68, pp.35-44

Saunders, Paul, *Edward Jenner the Cheltenham Years 1795-1823*. Hanover (U.S.A.) and London, 1982

Smith, F.B., *The People's Health 1830-1910*. London, 1979

INDEX

N.B. Except where otherwise noted and with obvious exceptions place-names are in the ancient geographical county of Essex. There may be more than one reference on a page; n. indicates that the reference is in the chapter notes and references.

INDEX

London, Medical Society of: 92, 116
  Officer, 159; smallpox hospitals, advice relating to siting, 161, 168, rôle and utility reappraised, 168
Local Government Board Act, 1871: 14, 159
Logan, Dr J. Stevenson: 146
London: 26, 32, 40, 63, 75, 88, 173; County Council, 14, 159; Deptford Hospital, 160; epidemics, 38, 40, 171; Foundling Hospital, see separate entry; Fulham Hospital, 160; Greenwich, 160; Guys Hospital, 35, 155, 165; Hampstead Hospital, 160; Hatton Garden, 96; Highgate Hospital, 165; Holborn Workhouse, 158; Homerton, 160; Hospital for the Indigent Blind, 19; hospitals, 154-156, 159-161; inoculation, 33, 36, 38, 40, 89, 106, 107, 175; Islington, 38; Kensington Gore, 74, 85, 90; King's College, 164; Lock Hospital, 105; London Fever Hospital, 155; Middlesex County Hospital for the Small-Pox *alias* London Smallpox and Inoculation Hospital, 37, 38, 40, 94, 101, 106, 108, 151, 155, 189 (n.44), 190 (n.7), 195 (n.127), 197 (n.51); Newgate Prison, 33, 133; Poplar Board of Works, 167, 202 (n.94); Rotherhithe Workhouse, 158; Royal Hospital, Chelsea, 96; St Andrew, Holborn, church of, 34, 40; St Bartholmew's Hospital, 33, 106, 156; St George's Hospital, 93; St Giles' Workhouse, 158; St Mary's Hospital, 158; St Marylebone, Infirmary, 106, Poor Law Union, 122; St Thomas' Hospital, 87, 107, 156, 158; Shoreditch Guardians, 157; Stockwell, 160; Strand Workhouse, 157, 158; Sutton House, Kensington, 85; Daniel Sutton's practice, 74, 85, 90, 91; Tower Hamlets, 132; vaccination 93, 95, 96, 106, 107, 119, 122, 177; workhouse infirmaries, 158, 159
London, Epidemiological Society of: 120
London Society for the Abolition of Compulsory Vaccination: 14, 128-131
London Vaccine Institution: 13, 109
London Workhouse Infirmaries, Association for the Improvement of: 158
Long Reach Smallpox Hospital: 161, 167, 177
Lord, John: 27
Loughton Urban District: 170
Lucas, Dr James: 55
Lukely, Mary: 28
Lupton, Arnold: 140, 143
Luton, Bedfordshire: 26
Lynn, Mr: 40, 69

Macaulay, Thomas Babington: 26
Macclesfield, Cheshire: 58
McCulloch, John Ramsey: 192 (n.153)
MacDonald, Dr: 143
Mackey, Mr: 114
MacLeod, R.M.: 132, 198 (n.24)
McVail, Dr J.C.: 144
Maddox, Isaac, Bishop of Worcester: 38, 40, 41, 189 (n.44), 190 (n.7), 201 (n.57)
Maidstone, Kent: 18, 47, 59-61, 79
Maitland, Dr Charles: 32, 33, 35

Malden, Dr Jonas: 42, 46, 48, 49
Maldon: 46, 54, 79, 86, 153, 194 (n.53); All Saints' parish, 49, 114, 150; Borough and Urban District, 165, 170, 171, isolation hospital, 184; Bull inn, 87; epidemics, 23, 48-50, 77; inoculation, 23, 42, 46-50, 53, 65, 66, 114, patients banned from town, 27, 48, by Daniel Sutton, 48, 77; Joint Hospital Board, 169, smallpox hospital at Little Totham, 171; pest house (Pinchgut Hall), 18, 99 (photograph), 150, 183; Poor Law Union, 156; Rural District, 171, isolation hospital, 184; St Mary's parish, 49, 150; St Peter's parish, 49, 50, 150; vaccination failures, 95, 106, 114; White Horse inn, 87; workhouse, 150
Manchester: 95; Board of Health, 155; House of Recovery, 155, 201 (n.56); Institution, 155; vaccination, decline and opposition, 111, 117, 124
Manchester Literary and Philosophical Society: 155
Mannheim: 55
Mansfield, Lord Justice: 77, 78
Markets: closed due to smallpox, 21-23
Marks, Revd R.: 197 (n.64)
Markshall: 24
Marlborough, Duke of: 190 (n.7)
Mary II, Queen of England: death, 13
Massey, Revd Edmund: 34, 40
Maty, Dr Matthew: 54, 55, 191 (n. 115)
May, Dr Nicholas: 190 (n.13)
Mead, Dr Richard: 38, 189 (n.43)
Medical officers: see *sub* Health, medical officers of; Poor Law medical officers
Medical Protection Act, 1855: 158
Medical Research Council: 144
Medical societies: 55, 56, 90, 92, 95, 116, 119, 120, 155, 201 (n.54); see also *sub* individual societies
Menish, Mr: 43
Messing: 75, 113
Metropolitan Asylums Board: 13, 14, 63, 170, 171, 177, 202 (n.73); established, 159; hospitals, at Darenth and Greenwich, 160, at Long Reach, 161, 167, 168
Metropolitan Poor Act, 1867: 157, 159, 160
Middlesbrough, Yorkshire: 128
Middleton Cheney, Northamptonshire: 128
Midhurst, Kent: 194 (n.53)
Mill, John Stuart: 158
Millard, Dr C. Killick: 144
Miller, Genevieve: 38, 40, 188 (n.13), 189 (n.24)
Milne, Joshua: 193 (n.195)
Missenden, Great, Buckinghamshire: 111
Mistley: 50; pest house, 183
Mitchell family: 106
Montagu: Anne Wortley, inoculated 13; Edward Wortley, junior, inoculated, 13, 32; family, 30-34; Lady Mary Wortley, 26, 30-35, 51, disfigured by smallpox, 19
Moor, manservant to Bamber Gascoyne: 75-77
Moore, James; 91
Morgan, Mr: 114
Moseley, Dr Benjamin: 96, 106, 108, 196 (n.24)

213

Mullucks, Henry: 24
Murdoch, C.T.: 132

Nash: Mr, 92; Dr J.T.C., 138, 139; Thomas, 196 (n.5)
National Agricultural Labourers' Union: 125, 128
National Association for the Promotion of Social Science: 158
National Health Service Act, 1946: 14, 147
National Liberal Club: 199 (n.113)
Nelmes, Sarah: 93
Nettleton, Dr Thomas: 34, 36
New England: 35, 37
Newcastle, Northumberland: 62, 128; Infirmary, 155
Newport: 50, 65; pest house, 150, 183, 200 (n.16, Chapter 8)
Newsholme, Dr Arthur: 141
Nightingale, Florence: 158
Norfolk: 22, 69, 70, 110
Northampton: 58, 155, 201 (n.57); General Hospital, 154, 155; vaccination, opposition to, 125, 128
Norton Mandeville: 24
Norwich, Norfolk: 110, 173, 194 (n.50)
Notley, Black: 169
Nottingham: 123; General Hospital, 95, 96, 105, 154
Nurses: in pest houses, 151, 153; paid by parish, 17

Oakley, Great: 21
O'Brien, Percy Wyndham, Earl of Thomond: 50
Offchurch, Warwickshire: 189 (n.27)
Oldham, Lancashire: 128
Omiah, Chief of Tahiti: 89
Ongar: Poor Law Union, 156; Rural District, 170, 184, 203 (n.137)
Ongar, Chipping: 24, 42, 112
Onion family: 26
Onyon, Eleanor: 20
Orsett: 166; Hospital, 143; Joint Hospital Board, 171; Poor Law Union, 156, 167, 168; Rural District, 142, 164, 167, 170, 171, Council, 165, epidemics, 137, 167, 171, isolation hospital 184; Smallpox Hospital, 171, 172
Oundle, Northamptonshire: 51
Oxford: county, 90; St John's College, 59

Page: Daniel, 20; Joseph, 94
Palmer, George William: 132, 199 (n.81)
Palmerston, Viscount: 158
Parliament: 108, 109, 116, 117, 121, 122, 132, 140, 143, 146, 160, 175-177; Acts of, 13, 14, 117-122, 124, 125, 127, 129, 132, 133, 135, 136, 140-142, 144, 147, 154, 156-164, 166, 168, 172, 175-177, 198 (ns 33, 34), 200 (n.114), see also *sub* individual Acts; Commons, House of, 95, 117, 123, 132, Select Committee on Vaccination, 1870, 124; Lords, House of, 117, 124, 157
Parndon, Little: 54
Parsons, Dr H. Franklin: 168, 169

Patterson: family, 17; George, 17
Paxton, Dr Richard: 49
Peale, Mr: 79, 80
Pearce: Dr Charles, 123; Mr, 110, 190 (n.29)
Pearson, Dr George: 93, 96
Pease, Joseph: 125
Peculiar People, The: 133-135, 137, 139, 143, 144, 146, 177
Pembrokeshire: 173
Penn, William: 195 (n.112)
Pera, near Constantinople: 32
Perceval, Spencer: 108
Percival, Dr Thomas: 155, 191 (n.115), 201 (n.56)
Perry: Dr Charles, 38, 39, 59, 189 (n.42); Samuel, 153
Pest houses: 13, 18, 22, 99, 149-154, 175; see also *sub* individual places
Petersfield, Hampshire: 37
Petley: family, 146; Mercy, 146
Philadelphia: 37
Phillips, Andrew: 126
Phipps, James: 93
Physicians: College of, 34, 41, 71; Royal College of, 108, 159
Pine, Mr: 79
Pitman, Henry: 124
Plaistow: see *sub* Ham, West
Plashet House, Sussex: 83
Playfair, Lyon: 125
Pledyard, John: 150
Plymouth, Devon: 58, 86
Pollett, William: 152
Pond, Samuel: 150
Poor Law Amendment Acts: 1834, 13, 154, 156, 157, 175; 1868, 14, 157, 161
Poor Law Board: 14, 157-159, 162
Poor Law Commissioners: 117-120, 156, 157
Poor Law medical officers (workhouse medical officers): 122, 158
Poor Law Medical Officers, Association of: 158
Poor Law unions (Guardians, boards of): 119, 121-129, 135, 154, 156-158, 161, 162, 167, 168, 175, 202 (n.114); see also *sub* individual places
Population increase attributed to inoculation: 59-61, 66
Portsmouth, Hampshire: 37, 162
Potter: Ethel Grace, 125; George, 125; Mr W.A., 124
Powell, Hannah: 114
Power, Dr (later Sir) William Henry: 160, 166, 203 (n.118)
Pringle, Sir John: 80, 194 (n.82)
Prittlewell: 87; pest house, 183; see also *sub* Southend-on-Sea
Privy Council: 14, 157, 159; Medical Department, 13, 121, 198 (n.15)
Provincial Medical and Surgical Association: 116, 119
Prussia: 117, 175
Public Health Acts: 1848, 13, 157; 1854, 157; 1858, 198 (n.15); 1872, 14, 159, 162; 1875, 159, 163, 166
Pugh, Dr Benjamin: 40, 45, 49, 52, 53, 55, 56,

INDEX